MW00893254

THE
DELILAH
ARCHIVES

THE SHADOW AND THE SMILE

R. L. COX

ISBN 978-1-64569-474-8 (paperback)
ISBN 978-1-64569-475-5 (digital)

Copyright © 2019 by R. L. Cox

All rights reserved. No part of this publication may be reproduced, distributed, or transmitted in any form or by any means, including photocopying, recording, or other electronic or mechanical methods without the prior written permission of the publisher. For permission requests, solicit the publisher via the address below.

Christian Faith Publishing, Inc.
832 Park Avenue
Meadville, PA 16335
www.christianfaithpublishing.com

Printed in the United States of America

DEDICATION

Rest in peace, Alejandro "Alex" Valadez.
Born: 1982, End of watch: 2009

The name Xandus means, "Alejandro (Alex) with us."
The name was directly related to an angel no
longer on earth and is now in Heaven.

Psalms 91:11 For He shall give his angels charge
over thee, to keep thee in all thy ways.

CHAPTER 1

RDO

Strategist Delilah removes her iridescent sword from the devil she dispatched. When she does, his black blood squirts from the wound onto her magenta-colored leather armor. She wipes the repulsive blood from her armor smearing the gold accents around her breastplate. She kicks the body away in disgust and anger. She pulls out her chiburi cloth to clean the mess from her armor and weapon. Normally, demon blood slides off her gear, like grease on wax paper. Instead of cleaning the blood, the only effect she produced was to lengthen the foul-smelling streak. The angelic envoy folds her pink wings as she puts her chiburi cloth away.

Master Smith Kromrom crafted the weapon for her thousands of years ago, and named it Prism. Delilah probably couldn't point out the crafter from a lineup if she were to see him now. She pushes down the frustration rising from her scarred memory and returns to the business at hand.

The disfigured demon she defeated was a guard or lookout. She took him out before he could raise an alarm, but there is something about his blood. It might be some organic tag, marking its foe. She can ponder that dilemma later, for she will be long gone before he revives. Lesser demons take longer to regenerate.

The angel rounds the corner of a building when another foe materializes before her—a greater shadow demon. Though his back is to her, she recognizes the bastage. He's unique in his appearance. A skeleton wrapped in a living blanket of darkness. A nonexistent wind whips the shadow about him like a weathered cloak. The shadow is taut around his body and loose farther away from it. This demon goes by the name of Mazck.

Delilah holds her breath and flaps open her wings to halt her momentum. Then one quick beat of her wings to reverse her direction. She plucks a goshenite gem from her studded breastplate and rolls it away from her. Though the gem made no noise, she hopes Mazck won't see her little tool. She hides on the other side of the building—just before the demon twists only his head around. How disturbing.

He's a clever bastage. Exactly who she was looking for. She's been tracking him for over an hour. Apparently, he's *veil* jumping; dashing in and out of the dimension gates that grant access to areas of the human's Natural World and the Spirit Realm.

The Spirit Realm consists of Heaven, Hell, and the Archfiend Zone. In the Archfiend Zone, high-ranking devils dwell in their castles, caves, and constructs. They hold much power in these contested territories. Convicted human souls and incarcerated demons are imprisoned in Hell. Never before had Mazck's metaphysical presence been seen in the Natural World. He seemed content with manipulating Lucifer's forces in the Archfiend Zone. His appearance now brings on more suspicion than usual.

Delilah taps her bracer. Whatever is within the goshenite's range can be viewed on her bracer's display. The greater shadow demon swivels his body around in the direction his head faces—causing him to do an about-face in Delilah's direction. Mazck presses his back against the wall. His shadowy arm stretches forth, gripping the corner. She frowns, switching her glance from her display to his clawed hand. His living shadow absorbs light and darkens the immediate area. The flame-like shadow flickers in the wind. Haunting whispers echo around her. His shadow senses her presence, reaching toward her like strangle weed. It pulses like a heart and reeks of decayed flesh, pungent and foul.

With one hand, she reaches up to her gem-studded breastplate. Her fingers hover over a sun stone, readying her defense. Her current enemy's rank is Class X, which is two grades higher than her own rank A. The difference between the two ranks was like comparing a fox to a rhino. Her heart pounds in her ears. She settles into a defensive position and uses her other hand to ease her sword out of its scabbard. Then the demon blood smeared across her sword, wafts into her nose. She scrunches her nose in disgust—suppressing the urge to gag.

Delilah can hear Mazck sniffing. She allows her sword to ease back into its scabbard—keeping her hand on the hilt. She pulls her sun stone free. She closes her hand over the gem to cover the soft glow it emits. She feeds the sun stone a portion of her vigor and grits her teeth.

A skittering sound attracts her attention. Through her viewer, there is a peculiar eye vermin. The ruffling of Mazck's shadow fades from her location. She peeks around the corner in time to see Mazck following the eye vermin. She remembers to breath and releases her held breath. She collects her goshenite; keeping a safe distance from the interlopers.

Of late, eye vermins trickled into the Natural World. Like angels and demons, these freakish creatures remain unseen by humans. They were the result of some hideous and unsanctioned experiment. A mad scientist discovered a way to attach demon eyes to the bodies of enlarged spiders and millipedes. Most are about the size of a skull. Not important enough to draw her attention as to why, but now the ominous eye stalks were all over the Natural World. The nosy creatures show up wherever bright lights or loud noises are detected. They observe and report their findings to whomever their masters are.

Delilah was first to notify the angelic network of their infiltration to the Natural World. Now the eye vermin show unusual patience, communication, and coordination. They've been spotted at highly sensitive areas. Obvious *charges* like high-ranking officials, community leaders, and activists were watched and followed by these ugly spies.

This creature differs from the normal versions she's encountered. She is close enough to see some of the features of this unique eye vermin, and it worries her. The bulbous eye sitting atop the insectoid's body appeared lumpy. She realizes this eye vermin had the shape of a brain, and instead of veins, it had circuitry. The appearance of this creature and Mazck in the same area can't be a coincidence. She hopes to follow Mazck to his contact.

The vermin could be programmable. She deduces this from the sensors and nodes around its body. If captured, she would attempt to hack its signal and trace the source. Its ability to dive in and out of the *veil* makes its apprehension improbable. The eye vermin may be hack proof. It would take much longer than she had to spare to crack the code, if such was the case.

Mazck must be protecting the construct. The Strategist continues to follow the alpha eye vermin and its shadow demon bodyguard. They take her through alleys and abandoned buildings at a staggering pace.

Delilah feels a sense of relief that humans are unaware of the invisible dangers in their world—just on the other side of the *veil*. Both angels and demons are able to interact or influence humans in the Natural World. Demons also have the ability to incite or even possess humans.

When either spiritual entity drops visage to *physically* interact with humans, such as possession or to frighten or inspire humans with visual sightings of themselves, it diminishes their powers and abilities substantially. This act exposes them to serious risk to their *veiled* foes. The Spirit Realm acts as an overlay with the Natural World; neither exists without the other.

The shadow demon rushes forward and reaches for the eye vermin. Delilah doesn't know his plan, but she'd be a fool to allow Mazck to achieve his goal.

She hisses to herself and surges forward in pursuit. The "head" or eye of the vermin goes into a radical spin. She must do something to try and distract them. "Mazck! No time, long see. You got some 'splaining to do."

Mazck skids to a halt and snaps his head around. Red flaming eyes bore into the angel. "Fool! Do you know what you've done? You ruined everything!" he growls.

Delilah pulls a tiger eye gemstone from her breastplate. Just as she readies her throw, the vermin disperses an electrical charge. An intense flash of light assaults Delilah. She becomes blind and disoriented. Her world moves above her sight line—as she is thrown back from the electrical attack. She fights through the woozy. Her body convulses uncontrollably. She thought she heard a wail from Mazck, but he might use this opportunity to attack her. She crawls back to a wall and pushes herself up to a crouching position. Moments later, her vision returns. Her hands shake, and her legs are barely able to support her weight. Mazck and the alpha eye vermin are gone. "Crap and crud," she mutters.

Suddenly, Delilah's open comm link roars to life with radio activity. She sighs, flapping her wings absently. She rises above the neighborhood, listening to the frantic chatter of chaos on the airwaves.

Human *charges* worldwide are under immediate assault. Delilah has no doubt the whoreson and Fallen Master-Commander, Lucifer, instigated this assault. The Soul Severer wants not only all devils under his banner, but angels and humans as well. As he rose in power and stature, so did his ego and influence. He waited patiently to expand his prestige while he formulated his plans. To put it directly, his primary objective is to kill God and become master of the universe.

In a wave of verbal horror, Delilah listens to angels' request for immediate assistance. *Charges* of varying degrees of importance are injured, and in extreme cases, some humans were killed. Her bracer flashes yellow. Delilah slides her finger across her jawline to switch the channel to the secure link of the squad she belongs to Team Chrysos.

The voice of Aurum, the team's Herald, barks off an order. "Sound off."

"Strategist Delilah reporting."

"Here, Herald," the hoarse voice of Evnore answers.

"I'm assisting an angel in Shanghai. Her *charge* is under assault," Valorian squawks through the comm.

"I'm assisting an angel. His *charge* has been missing for a few hours," the voice of Iulas answers.

"Missing? How can that be possible?" Aurum questions. "Doc the details. I need a full report on your findings ASAP."

"Aye, aye. Will be done in time for our RDO," Iulas responds.

After a few moments of silence, Aurum breaks radio silence. "Anyone have eyes on Xandus?"

No answer. Crap and crud. Just like their Champion not to respond. Sometimes he can be so arrogant and aloof. Two qualities she despises in him, the handsome bastage. "Naomi?"

Naomi sighs through the comm. "He's with me."

Delilah switches back to the still frantic angelic dispatch. Why hasn't Aurum given Chrysos the order to assist? Unless he believes the on-duty angels are sufficient to carry out their protection orders, but she doesn't believe they are. Angels are overwhelmed and outnumbered. Besides, it is extremely more difficult to defend than to attack. Demons have no restraint and have a love to inflict harm and cause death. Misery loves company after all. "Dispatch? Strategist Delilah speaking. Patch me into the all-call."

"Of course," a calm male voice answers. "Strategist Delilah, you have the air."

"Please upload attack locations, demonic perpetrators, and any pertinent data regarding the assault on *charges* ASAP. Any information, no matter how small, may provide valuable insight or in the very least a crime pattern. Send them directly to me. Delilah, out."

Reports already begin to feed into Delilah's bracer. She swipes through the compiling data. Tapping the screen, she opens another menu. A 3-D global image projects above the bracer. Corresponding beacons wink on the globe. Gold dots for successful rescues; purple for unsuccessful rescues.

Delilah clenches her fist in frustration. She needs to be out there. If Aurum would assign Chrysos to help with rescues, officially she could come up with a more efficient plan. The allocation of resources could be streamlined. Lights continue to fill her globe. Swirl icons pop up on the globe here and there. Impressive, some daring angels attempt to input data during their mission. They know how important this is. More purple dots populate her globe. Delilah switches back to the team channel.

"Delilah?" Aurum requests.

"Here, Herald."

"Worry not for the humans. I have two angels covering for Xandus. Finish whatever you're working on within the hour. I need everyone to report to Heaven for a priority-one mission. Valorian and Iulas, your presence is mandatory. Leave your current assignment even if you're not done."

"What happened to our RDO?" Iulas wonders.

"Not with the current crisis going on. Everyone's RDOs been cancelled, and that's an order. Fifty-nine minutes left."

Delilah ascends to Heaven, resting against a great tree. She tucks her feet underneath a rainbow at the tree's base. She uses her remaining time listening to the network and analyzing data. The priority ranks of *charges* are withheld from angels. If the ranks were evident, it would allow angels to make harsh decisions on who should get more attention. Humans should be afforded the same protection no matter who they are and what they'll accomplish.

Reports from all over the world continue to pile in. The protected humans begin to stabilize with the injection of reinforcements. The cancellation of their rest day was the right move, though it should have been done sooner. Never was there such an alliance among the warring factions of demons. Wave after wave of relentless onslaughts. Chrysos, one of the most successful teams in Heaven, held back. It doesn't make sense, or does it?

Very few beings in any realm could pull of such a concerted effort among devils worldwide. Her mentor before the Fall was Chief Strategist of Heaven: Anura. She has the power, notoriety, and intelligence to pull off a sinister plot such as this.

Anura was recruited into the Shadow Domain. A victim of Lucifer's charismatic charms, no doubt. Delilah's mentor was very influential in her development as a Strategist. Now Anura's corrupted existence was as a soul-sucking demon.

While she contemplates her theory, she taps on the display of her bracer. She reviews the footage of the alpha eye vermin in an attempt to discern its true purpose. Was it a decoy all along, or did it send a warning to its owner? She shivers at the thought. The deaths of so many chosen *charges*. The coordination involved was executed precisely.

Switching to a different set of menus, Delilah transfers the gathered data into a new set of parameters. She needs to know the effect the targeted parties will have in the foreseeable future. The program will include circumstances about the *charge* that even angels aren't aware of. If it's pertinent, then that information will be revealed. If the program detects an apocalyptic problem, she can work on a resolution now. If no problem exists, then the demons hadn't executed their end game yet. This could take a while.

Delilah taps her lower lip. Her timer goes off. Time is a wingless bird that floats above the thermals of Heaven. She rises to her feet, switches menus again, and spins the globe on her display. Her eyes bulge. Frantically, she swipes her jawline and reconnects to the network.

"Strategist Delilah here. There are seven major cities that haven't reported any attacks. All remaining units will cover these territories. This could be a diversionary tactic to keep us occupied and away from those cities. I uploaded the data to the TAC bracer's central hub. Any suspicious activity, forward the information to me."

"We have no available units, Strategist," Dispatch informs. "In fact, we had to pull from those regions to keep up with demand."

Delilah shakes her head. Sounds like angels are conforming to whatever plans the demons have. "I need units on standby in those territories. Don't give chase to potential distractors. Fly patrols there to assure demons there is an angelic presence there. Keep me advised. Delilah, out."

***

Delilah pops through the upper clouds of Heaven. She soars over the exotic forest in the Province of Sacred Heart. Enormous sentient trees with upraised branches called sky-seekers take leisurely strides across the grassy ground. Secured within the iron-strong branches are mini-mansions. Remarkably, the structures are held level with the horizon. Delilah can see some souls sipping beverages as they take a relaxing stroll with these gentle giants.

She gasps in awe at the beauty of God's palace. The lines are systematic and linear—wider than the horizon and more beautiful than new life. Honor Guards wave her through after they swing open golden doors. She gazes at the windows on the side of the palace walkway. On one side of the corridor, there are miniature displays of actual star systems. Billions of stars wink at her as she passes.

The star systems are amazing in its own right, but her favorite displays are on the other side of the corridor. The windows capture Moments—actual events in biblical and human history that changed the course of humanity. She passes over the "I Have a Dream" speech, "Creation," man's first flight; David defeating Goliath; and the list goes on. However, she spares a few seconds to gaze at her all-time favorite Moment, "Noah's Ark." For some reason, she can't remember why, but the plight of Noah lifts her tired soul to new heights. The wind whips about her hand when she places it above the ark. The splash of the ocean dampens her fingers. One day, she will remember. One day.

She arrives at the same time as the team's Champion, Xandus. Her heart crashes against her chest, but she keeps her demeanor placid. Their gazes meet, and she hopes she didn't blush. She wouldn't know if Xandus blushed as his skin, wings, and chain-linked armor are all blue. He has a miniaturized lightning bolt, which parts his hair, in stasis. When prompted, he can excite it with vigor and form it into the weapon of his choice. All heavenly Champions have their own personalized emblem. Xandus wears his over his heart—a lightning bolt surrounded by a typhoon that animates when someone gazes or touches it. Her own personalized icon does the same—a knight piece with a maze within it.

The smooth bastage winks at her; she smiles. No time for flirting now—the Honor Guards open the double gold doors and wave them through. He plays a gentleman, allowing her entrance first, but she can feel his eyes on her lady parts. Delilah makes sure she gives him something to look at as she folds her wings and struts down the pathway. As the pair round the corner, she meets up with her other *kameraads*.

The eagle-angel, Valorian, is first. She nods at him, but the aggressive angel doesn't acknowledge her. He glares at Xandus with huge orbs that could count the number of facets a bee's eye had. Gold feathers are speckled throughout his other brown feathers.

Naomi and Evnore are next. Fallen angels call Naomi the Eye-blotter. Though the lowest-ranked angel on the team, she also retains the highest renown and notoriety. Her wings and leather armor are both camouflaged patched—allowing her to blend with most surroundings. The current colors allow her to blend with the sky and starlight.

Evnore, in her true form, is a lioness humanoid with reddish fur. Her wingless feline features are exotic and beautiful. She hides her features with an intricately detailed lion's face mask. Her mohawk is decorated with large feather plumes.

The never-serious Iulas is an ethereal angel. He is probably the most unique and fascinating angel to gaze upon. Other than pin-pricks of light for his eyes, his facial features are almost totally hidden. Instead, his transparent body show tree leaves floating through his body and small clouds that are pushed around by his bio current. He can absorb his surroundings to clone himself with the actual particles he touches.

Bringing up the rear is their team Herald, Aurum, also known as the Resplendent One. The metallic angel is gold and has a red lion's head as the center of a sun as his personal logo. In Delilah's opinion, he is the most confident angel in Heaven. Team Chrysos's members all wear his team coat of arms—a cockatrice on either side of the crest as supporters holding a shield. The team's motto is stamped above and beneath it: "A corroded past accrues a polished future."

Everyone steps aside to allow Aurum to enter first, and Delilah falls in right after. The squad approaches God's throne. Like the horizon, the boundaries of the room are limitless. Whenever she visits the Lord here, the throne room has a different appearance. This time, an aurora light show illuminates the room as it changes colors above the roofless structure.

God stands tall before His golden throne awaiting the most successful angelic squad in Heaven. He waits with the patience of a growing tree, counting the stars on a cluster around his fingers. He wears white robes with the word "love" embroidered in every language along its fringes. His hair flows behind Him as if He's underwater, and a lightning storm forms His beard. All in attendance drop to a kneel with their palms up.

Aurum announces, "How may we serve you, Lord?"

"Greetings, Chrysos. I regret I have to cancel your day off," God informs.

About time. Now we can step into the fray with the assault on humanity.

"We are but the king's pawns, Master," Aurum responds. "What is thy gambit?"

"An infestation," God answers.

The squad members look at one another in confusion. Valorian squawks his disapproval. Delilah notices Naomi frown at Xandus. When they were together earlier, something must have happened. Come to think of it when she updated her feeds, Xandus's queue showed his workload was incomplete—including his most important assignment, the heavenly anomaly he was supposed to investigate. "Here? In Heaven?" she asks. She drills Xandus with a sideways glance.

Screens materialize around the squad and show an overhead view of Heaven. The screens zoom in to a dark corner of Heaven. As the image approaches, an inky substance spreads over a large area.

"The anomaly lies within the Province of Whispering Winds," answers God.

No angel had ever seen the length or width of Heaven; it metaphysically extends to the edge of the universe. Aurum and Delilah quickly check their TAC bracers—which are essential tools for the Virtuous Culture. They house *aether* chains and cuffs, can display and issue warrants, and show the points of reference to mark locations by the stars.

"I can get us there," Evnore replies.

Delilah smiles at her *kameraad*. Of course, she can. With Evnore's expansive knowledge of charts, they can arrive in their location in the shortest amount of time.

"What form is the anomaly taking?" questions Delilah.

"A soul well has spawned," God answers. "Each time one is erected, it creates an anomaly. It can occur anywhere in Heaven, the Archfiend Zone and Natural World and Spirit Realm. This one is in Heaven."

"Must we descend into the Archfiend and destroy it?" Xandus wonders.

"Soul wells are indestructible," Valorian replies, folding his arms.

"Demons are fighting over the territory the soul well formed in. To the victor goes the spoils. Defeated demons are absorbed into the soul well until the sector is claimed and secured," God clarifies.

"So the anomaly infestation is actually expelled demonic residue that's ejected from the soul well," Delilah theorizes.

The squad stares at Delilah in amazement.

"Yes, Strategist," God replies.

"So we have three problems," Aurum begins. "First, until we plug or close the soul well on our end, it will continue to spew residue. Second, the residue will assimilate characteristics of any host it comes in contact with. It could consume or absorb heavenly creatures here. And last, we don't know how much mass the soul well can take. It could very well expand—allowing greater mass to pass through."

"We don't want demon folk to run rampart!" says Valorian.

"It's possible the soul well could become unstable and explode as well," Delilah replies while she taps and swipes on her TAC bracer.

"Aurum will give you the rest of the details. Make haste," God orders.

The squad bows in unison and rushes out of Heaven's doors.

CHAPTER 2

THE SOUL WELL

Delilah decides to question Xandus at a later time. Right now, her anger simmers just under drilling a diamond through his forehead. He was given this mission hours ago. His orders were to scout the heavenly anomaly and, if able, handle it. Otherwise, the team could contain the event while it was less of a threat. Instead, he figured he would "assist" Naomi because he thought her mission was more of a challenge. Now the squad must be called away from assisting the Host with the protection of humans. Xandus should be ashamed of himself.

Team Chrysos follows Evnore, their resident expert on cartography, as they hurry to the nearest *veil* gate. The female guard stationed there gives the team a crisp salute. Chrysos responds in kind, though Delilah's surprised Heaven can spare her with the shortage of manpower. The guard pulls open the *veil,* and the squadron flies through.

She realizes why there was a guard stationed here. When the group enters the gate, they see hundreds of windows that feature a glimpse of the locales that lie on the other side of the *veil.* This major junction features electric nodes that lead to each window and down the narrow corridor. Delilah could enter their destination through her TAC bracer, and the nodes would have directed them to the correct exit. She hated to disappoint Evnore and not take advantage of her expertise, so she just allowed her to lead on. Obviously, Aurum felt the same way too.

The Lioness glances as each of the internal *veils* have thumbnail glimpses of where it leads to on the other side. Once Evnore finds the correct exit, she darts through without a word. Her *kameraads* follow, and the squad is greeted by a winter wonderland.

Some of the Ascended enjoy the beauty that is ice and snow. Frosted mountains display its innards in all its glory. The mountains are real-life lava lamps as the harmless flows change colors. Frozen igloo mansions and crystal castles decorate the landscape off into the distance as the squad continues toward their destination. The temperature does not sting the squad's exposed skin. The immortal angels are nigh invulnerable to extreme heat and cold.

"We're not doing enough," Valorian accuses.

"What else can we do?" Xandus answers. "We work tirelessly. This is our off day, remember?"

"Not all of us," Naomi mutters.

"We need to do more! It takes ten million condemned souls to create a soul well. If we were so successful, then how did another one form?" Valorian squawks heatedly.

As the squad's expert on fiend factions, his knowledge of demonology and their origins and history is priceless. *If it is known, I know it*, he would say.

"So many?" Naomi wonders.

The eagle-headed angel squawks as he nods his head.

"It was—what—two centuries from the last time we had a soul well anomaly?" Delilah says.

"True, but before that, it was five centuries. Each was erected faster than the last," Valorian explains. "At this rate, we'll have another next week!"

Frozen clouds block the sun as it tries to peek through the obstructions. Delilah notes Xandus as he looks off in the distance and furrows his brow suspiciously.

"Once we get to the soul well, I'll do an analysis to weigh our options. What else do we need to know about this mission, Herald?" Delilah questions.

"We can't let any of the demonic residue escape. If we miss even a worm-sized creature, it could be years before we're aware of the corruption," Aurum replies.

Valorian squawks, "That—and it won't be the size of a worm the next time we see it."

Aurum nods. "Discovering the source element of the soul well is an optional objective."

"Source matter?" Iulas ponders.

"Each soul well erected is made up of a source material. Some are derived from emotions, such as fear or wrath. Others use the corruption of nature, like decay or petrification," Aurum answers.

"What can we do with this information?" Evnore wonders.

"Lucifer chooses the source matter of the soul well. Knowing the element gives us some insight on why he chose it. Does he want to increase the power of a particular demon's region? Is he levelling the playing field? Does he want to attract certain types of demons for a strategic advantage?" Aurum explains.

"Lucifer?" Delilah says under her breath.

The last time she saw the blood-skinned bastage, it was before the Fall of Angels, the rebellion that was led by Lucifer himself in an attempt to usurp God from His throne. He was the Lord's chief angel—the greatest, brightest, and God's most trusted ally—nothing but a glorified traitor. Angels that sided with Lucifer as a part of his rebellion were cast down from Heaven like meteors. Delilah tried to shake off her hatred of Lucifer, but she can't. His sacrilege was inexcusable, not to mention what the Soul Severer did to her. How can anyone follow such a despicable being? How she wishes to be there to witness his next Fall.

The wind intensifies. The silence of the lazy landscape of fresh snow is disrupted by the fleeing of wildlife. Moose, bears, and snow leopards run in the opposite direction that the angels are heading. Not a good sign when apex predators don't protect their territory. It must be worse than they thought.

"Almost there!" Evnore notifies the squad.

A cool film glazes over the sun. It struggles to burn through the large gathering of clouds. Once the sun quits, the clouds blot out the star completely—casting a shadow over the land.

Aurum raises his fist; the squad finds a landing zone on top of a crystallized precipice overlooking the region. The landscape changes before their very eyes. Rocky terrain juts out sharply from the smooth rolling hills at extreme angles. In some places, the ground breaks away—forming dangerous floes that dip and rise precariously. A snowstorm whips around the squad. All but Valorian must shelter their eyes from the stinging wind. The nictitating membrane over his eyes, protects his sharp vision.

Then the squad's attention falls upon the actual threat. A pillar of power expels silvery energy into the sky. Smoke billows out from the pillar, thickening the clouds and stretching across the sky.

"That must be the demonic residue," Naomi informs.

"Ya think?" Iulas says.

"Quiet, fool," Naomi warns.

The demonic residue ejects from the pillar dozens of meters away, and then flop around like fish out of water. Then the residue figures lumber around like zombies.

Delilah stares at the pillar. She rubs two of her fingers and a thumb together. The effect creates a matrix overlay over the tips. Naomi catches her eyes and bites her lower lip. She shakes her head slightly, rubbing her fingers again. The overlay disappears.

Aurum chins to his second-in-command. "Your assessment, Strategist?"

Xandus gently grabs her arm. She snatches away, reflexively covering her scaled skin. She apologizes with a gentle smile.

He smiles back, then points to the sky. "Before you answer, add those to your assessment. I don't think that's a natural cloud formation."

"You can't know for sure. We can't waste angelic power on a hunch," Delilah responds.

"Nope, not a hunch. If we don't address it now, we'll have to later. We're already pressed for time. That pillar is spewing residue into the sky. Not all of it falls to the ground. A whole new creature is forming," he answers.

Looking to the sunless sky, Delilah studies the expanding cloud. She prides herself on covering every conceivable angle. She hates when she misses a threat. Xandus, however, was right. She initially believed the water vapor cooled and condensed into large clouds. Aurum nods in agreement.

Delilah scrolls through the menus on her TAC bracer and analyzes the pillar and the surrounding area. As the data displays, she performs some calculations, running scenarios in her mind. "He was right; it's not just a storm cloud. I have a plan, Herald." She faces Xandus. "We'll need to split up the team to contain and address all the problems simultaneously. Xandus, you and Evnore take on that cloud entity. What?"

Xandus interrupts Delilah by shaking his head. He wags his fingers, points to the sky, shakes his fist, and nods his head.

"Okay, guess you're going solo," she revises while rolling her eyes.

"You'll still have less renown than I have, Xandus!" Naomi shouts.

He ignores her response. "What is it?"

"You wanted to fight that alone, so you'll have to figure it out," Delilah answers.

"Aw, come on."

"Unidentified. The properties of the residue don't permit the most accurate analysis," she replies.

Xandus nods as Delilah continues, "Naomi is on rescues."

Naomi balls up her fists and scoffs. "Sad to know that I have more notoriety with demons, than I have prestige with my own squad. I am not the weakest link!"

"No one said that," Delilah replies.

Naomi raises her chin and leans forward. "Didn't have to be said!" she growls.

"Naomi, do it noow!" Aurum shouts as he points off into the distance.

Everyone looks in the direction that Aurum points to. The residue mass merges with an alligator-demon that crashed through the ice, chasing a group of escaping wildlife. A snow bunny is tossed into the air from the breaking ice. The alligator-demon opens its mouth wide to gobble the helpless creature. The angels look on in shock.

Suddenly, a snow wolf darts in, diving into the alligator-demon's mouth, grabs the bunny by the scruff of its neck, and leaps away before the demon crunches on both creatures.

Naomi is gone in the blink of a wink.

"Iulas, Valorian, and I will close this pillar. We'll also try to determine what it's made of," Delilah continues.

Valorian and Iulas nod in agreement. As Delilah begins to speak again, an enormously, grotesque fly gets tossed from the pillar. The force of the fly's transparent wings, push the snow into drifts as it flies off keeping low to the ground.

"Recca!" Valorian caws. "Or used to be!"

"How do you know?" Delilah asks.

"I can see her brand using my ultraviolet vision. Before the Fall, our former team had a coat of arms brand. Recca's was on her back. She was number six. I should be the one to take her out of her misery."

"I was her Herald…I'll do it," Aurum responds.

"She's disgusting!" Evnore says.

"Evnore, you just volunteered. You're with me!" Aurum yells. "Do it noow!"

The rest of the angels split up into their smaller teams, determined to finish as quickly as possible to assist anyone else that needs aid. Delilah points to Iulas, then to the ground he stands upon. He expunges the airy cloudscape he had within his body; then he internalizes the crystalline properties of his landing. Facets form around his muscle grouping. Once he finishes, her faction takes off toward the pillar.

"I have an idea on how to close the pillar!" she yells.

Iulas taps his ear and shakes his head. The unnatural wind drowns out all other sound. She faces her team and brushes her finger alongside her jaw. Her subordinates do the same.

"Computer, link me with Valorian and Iulas."

"Connected," a computerized voice acknowledges.

Four orange LED lights wink onto each of the angels' jawline. Now that her faction was linked, she can talk at regular decibels and be heard. "I have an idea. I've calculated the pillar's frequency. If

Iulas can magnify Valor's screech to match the anomaly's correct frequency, we should be able to collapse it."

"Should, huh? Sounds easy enough. Bring my blankey?" Iulas says sarcastically.

"Not now, Iulas!" Delilah grunts through gritted teeth. "There exists no purer form of crystal than from the heavenly realm. That should help loads!"

Valorian squawks, "I won't be able to reach any decibel high enough to disrupt a wormhole."

Delilah softens her gaze in response. "You can do it, Valor. I know you can."

"Yeah, Valor," Iulas chides.

The eagle angel points at Iulas. "You don't call me that."

Valorian turns to Delilah and nods in response. She scrolls through the menus on her TAC bracer. The team moves closer together. She hopes to get a better analysis of the pillar. If she can find its weakest point, then they can collapse this anomaly.

***

Naomi's anger simmers right under exploding. She forces herself to calm down, no need to get sensitive now. These minor devils needed to be dealt with, but why always her? She had to work hard to obtain a higher rating than Xandus. Everyone underestimates her power and ability—delegated to demonic filth. She sighs and reminds herself to focus on the mission.

She decides against using camouflage. She wants to draw the attention of the residue demon mass, not surprise them. She weaves through the ever-changing landscape, like it was an obstacle course. The very land trembles as if under siege. The terrain seems to be attacking her too. Each time she dodges, the next object seems to calculate her next move. Does this anomaly exert control over the very land? The pillar is making the whole sector volatile, causing unnatural and radical mutations to the tundra. Giant sections of ice collapse into the deep waters of the Seas of Jonah.

She must reach the fleeing wildlife, but also must contain these zombie demons as well. What would Delilah do? Maybe a corkscrew strategy. She'll move through these creatures, rescue the animals, then attack the mobs in a wide circle, working her way in. Once they see her, they'll more than likely give chase. Then she can use her sat-in-sword technique. They'll never know what hit them.

Demonic residue and black blood will desecrate the purity of the sea. She'll remind Aurum to send out a purging squad to cleanse the area. If it were up to Delilah, Naomi would be part of said detail. She sighs again and focuses on the mission. Rising high in the sky, she gathers the attention of the residual demons. Once they clump together into a giant mass, she can draw them away from wildlife. However, the higher up she flies, the less interest it seems to have with her. The mass separates into smaller chunks, going in different directions.

Naomi dives to the ground—in a tuck-and-roll maneuver—as she draws out her vigor-imbued, silver-steel swords. She slashes into a group of demons. Her silver-steel dissolves the shade, like acid to onion skin.

Keeping her momentum from her dive, she slides toward the next grouping. Flapping her wings speeds her movement as she crashes into more residual demons. Through her spinning slashes, she locates the wolf and rabbit. The wolf flees blazingly fast. The alligator-demon breaks the ice with its heavy body and gains ground. With a snap of her wings, silver-steel razors protrude along the edges. She spins in a tight spiral—eradicating the group.

Increasing her foot speed, Naomi angles toward the animals. Under her feet, a thunderous rumble vibrates the tundra. The ripples increase. She calculates her next move; at the point of where the ice breaks through the ground, she launches herself into the air. She surveys the region with the two or few seconds she has before the fighting commences.

Above her, she sees Xandus charging into the ominous sky. From this vantage point, she can see eyes aglow within the billowing mass. What dwells within? She had better wrap this up so that she can assist, if necessary. She can't help but respect him. Unknown danger and all alone at that. Any anomaly is terrifying, too many unknown factors to consider. One in the heavenly realm is frightening indeed.

About two hundred meters away, she discovers the rancid fly trying to escape. What if there are nasty eggs on its body or something worst? Aurum and Evnore chase after the fly demon. Hopefully, they will be enough. Their squad is being tested today.

Afar off, Delilah and her team fly toward the pillar. Delilah seemingly has the most impossible task, but hopefully the squad can reallocate their resources to help her if needed. The squad deals with demons on a daily basis. A rift in Heaven has never happened before. If it weren't for the demonic assault on humans, a phalanx would assist them.

Naomi flips and stretches her lean body out into another dive. She missiles toward the alligator-demon. It hisses at the wolf and rabbit. Now the ground melts into slush causing her steps to become heavier. The underbelly of the lizard glows red hot as it drags itself across the terrain. The wolf sinks and must lunge forward to keep ahead of the lizard demon and its allies. Naomi takes flight again. She hasn't failed a rescue before and won't start now.

Landing on the alligator-demon's back, she drags deep trenches with her swords behind her and along the back of the demon. It growls and goes into a death roll.

The nimble-footed angel runs along the demon's body as if it were a rolling log. She continues slicing around its torso, then opening up its molten-core belly. She leaps away as it explodes. Black goo splatters the area. Naomi uses her wings to shield her and the animals.

The goo rolls off her wings like slick off a frog. Acidic steam rises from the demonic body. Moments later, the body turns into ashes. The bunny leaps into Naomi's arms, and the wolf wags her tail. Naomi hugs the rabbit. "You're okay," she assures. "You're safe for now."

She puts the rabbit on top of the wolf and points in a safe direction. "Go now. Go with the other animals."

The wolf shakes her head. She growls at the still-gathering demons. The bunny wrinkles its nose. They'll just get in her way. "Go, I'll be fine."

She turns to walk away, but the wolf pads behind her. No time to get her to safety. The demons are spreading out. She'll have to widen her corkscrew if she doesn't hurry. "Okay, stay close."

The wolf yelps. Naomi begins running again. Without the alligator-demon melting the ground beneath the wolf, she is able to stay with Naomi. The rest of the demon residue gives chase while she tries to encircle the zombie creatures. The barking draws the demonic residue to her. Maybe the wolf is useful after all. She might have to give her a name.

The demonic residue has been rounded up. Though instead of many smaller demons, it fuses together into a giant mass of teeth and body parts. The grotesque horror towers over her as it pulls itself closer and closer. The wolf stays near, baring her teeth at the monstrosity. Without turning back, Naomi gives her the signal to stay. She loosens her shoulder as she approaches the mass of demons, twirling her blades.

Omnikrom crafted her weapons. The best there is in Heaven, though these aren't his greatest creations. She just loves the weight and balance of them, and the weapons are quick as if made from shards of wind.

"We are Legion, for we are many," Legion shouts in an echo of deep voices. "Your insignificant weapon holds no power over us!"

She takes one last step toward Legion as it shifts into different forms. Some formless, others of mythical creatures like multiheaded ogres. She bows her head in a quick prayer. Her silver-steel swords glow menacingly.

"You'd be surprised. I remember the last time you bragged about being Legion. That didn't work out for you either, did it?"

The demons merge to make a giant maw. It spews a stream of flame as wide as a car. She enhances her strength and speed with vigor and crosses the blades before her, blocking the attack. The fire splits in half, but the sheer force and heat of the flames push her back. Her hands and face are singed. Keep this up and her skin will melt. The ice beneath her begins to melt as well. The mouths, not spitting fire, laugh at her. This thing thinks she's a joke – it dares underestimate her. This bastage insists on provoking her. First and last mistake.

She loses ground and won't have much to lift off of soon. She crouches then lunges forth toward the monster's maw. She redirects the flame back into Legion's mouth, then flips into a overhead slash. She yells and floods her weapons with vigor, cleaving the atrocity in half—riding the separation all the way down until her swords hit ice. White flames spread throughout the monstrosity, disintegrating it. The dissolving Legion melts the ground beneath Naomi. Part of the ground breaks away.

Naomi drops to a knee. She holds herself up with one of her swords, breathing hard. She winces in pain. Her body—especially her hands and breastplate—smolders. The skin begins to regenerate over the partially exposed tendons.

The wolf and bunny leap off ice blocks to reach her. The she wolf whimpers with concern and tucks her head under her armpit. She leans heavily on the wolf. The bunny hops onto her shoulder and sniffs her ear. She almost has the strength to giggle. She nods a silent thanks to the animals as she catches her breath. Soon, the ice solidifies under the frigid temperature. The wind dissipates the smoke that was left behind from Legion.

After she heals and catches her breath, she smiles at her new animal companions. "I think I'm gonna have to give you guys a name." Imitating Delilah, she taps her chin. "Now let me think. How about Yelp and Snowball?"

The animals sneeze at the names.

"No?" she says, tapping her chin again. "Well, how about Ice and Fuzzy?"

The creatures hack their response. She taps her chin again, but then the she wolf barks at the sky. Naomi turns around and gasps. Xandus, the Champion of Chrysos, streaks to the icy ground below in a lifeless heap, leaving a trail of smoke and fire.

***

Delilah's remnant floats at a safe distance from the pillar. The strong wind pushes their wings behind them while the drifts climb up the nearby cliffs. She surveys the area and analyzes the stream from the pillar again. "We must hurry. The pillar is growing. It could become unstable."

Iulas nods, and Valorian squawks in agreement. Iulas lowers his head and presses his way through the wind, taking up most of the drag. The others push on each side of the ethereal angel's shoulder toward their goal as she directs Iulas by applying pressure on his arm.

She taps Iulas on the shoulder. The smaller crystalline properties of ice he absorbed earlier are used to reform into larger panes. Ultimately, his torso forms into one large crystal. He stretches his arms out, palms up to increase intensity. She looks through him, trying to look for any visible imperfections. Dirt, cracks, or discoloration could hinder the pure sound and magnification they will need.

Thumbs up.

Delilah points to the spot on Iulas's back where she wants Valorian to focus his power on. He positions himself and takes deep breaths. She gives the eagle angel a reassuring smile. He takes one more long, deep breath and holds it. His crest puffs up like a rooster about to crow.

The high-pitched sound he emits is unbearable. As the sound waves pass through Iulas, the screech becomes a concentrated beam that crashes into the pillar. Unfortunately, there's no sign of the pillar collapsing. The current beam is insufficient. They must make the beam purer before Valorian collapses from exhaustion.

Slowly, the honorable angel's crest deflates. Once it does, he's done. Delilah thumbs up to Valorian multiple times. The eagle angel increases his pitch. The sound knocks her back. She can feel blood trickle out of her ear. His chest deflates faster now that he hits a higher note. She pulls a diamond from her breastplate and positions it in front of the skinnier beam. Vigor meshes with pure sound through the diamond and into the pillar, but it's still not enough. His crest deflates, as his stomach nearly touches his spine. He is still trying, and even more impressive, the note continues to rise. Cracks form through Iulas's torso. He reconstructs himself on the fly to keep the imperfections away and to keep a clear line of sight for Valorian.

Even with their Heaven tech communication devices, they are unable to hear one another. She gets Iulas's attention and uses her free hand and shapes it into a soft fist, then a tighter fist. Instantly, he concentrates all the crystal into a tight cylinder where Valorian's screech is passing through. In a microinstant, she contemplates on calling on the entity—Time. Negotiating with him is more of a hassle than the benefits right now. He's such a bastage.

She must restock her supply of diamonds. Instead she snatches a quartz off her breastplate, floods it with vigor, and places the gem in front of the diamond. Her hair whips around her wildly as she resists the knock back from Valorian's screech. The last notes passes through the diamond and quartz. The beam is now a laser. It punches through the pillar of energy. The pillar rumbles and shakes. Vigor-infused light and sound cracks the pillar, then collapses it.

The explosion knocks the angels back. They flail to the ground. The cacophony of demonic screams reaches a crescendo, then dies. The unearthly stream fades away. Valorian fell from the sky as soon as his strongest and highest note left his beak.

She hits the ground hard, banging her head on the ice. Her busted eardrum caused her to lose her equilibrium. She begins to panic as she loses consciousness. No, not again. Her vision darkens and crowds in on her. The shadows chase the center of her eyes as her eyelids begin to close.

She squints as she tries to adjust her fuzzy vision above. Her teammates scream, but the sound is muted. It must be the vibrations of their yells. She's useless to the squad—again. Chaos all about her—and she is unable to control any of it.

Meteorites streak toward the ground. She can pick out one of the meteorites that is actually of Xandus. Her Champion falls from the sky; his wings and body engulfed in smoke and flame. At this height, he could break through the frozen tundra to the watery deep beneath. It could do serious harm because angels can't regenerate water-filled lungs. If his rescue is delayed, recovering him could prove impossible in the unfathomable depths of the sea.

An angel streaks to their Champion's rescue. With darkness encroaching her vision, Delilah can't tell who. She reaches out her hand. The visual effect appears as if she catches the listless Champion—only to see him pass behind her hand. She tries to rise to her feet, but dizziness overwhelms her. She collapses to the frozen ground. She rolls onto her back and touches her ear. She pulls back red fingers. So much blood.

Please no. Not the darkness. Unfortunately, Delilah succumbs – and where her consciousness ends, her nightmares begin.

CHAPTER 3

A VICTIM OF CIRCUMSTANCE

Xandus's concern over Delilah's well-being had him stressed out and angry. Seeing her so helpless after the pillar collapsed upset him to no end. Blood from her ear and a lump on her head was her reward for a job well done. In time, her physical injuries will heal, but her mind was the problem. Whatever happened to Delilah right before the Fall of Angels affected her memory and caused major psyche damage. Somehow, parts of her mind were stolen in the form of what spiritual entities call *enodes*.

For thousands of years, the trauma causes her to be susceptible to memory loss and head injuries. Though Delilah is fiercely independent, Aurum prefers for her to have a partner in case she lapses into unconsciousness. Her weakness is the only thing that jeopardizes the success of the mission. This was one of those instances. She will recover, she always does, but to see her in such a vulnerable state reminds him of how humans watch their loved ones deteriorate as they become older.

Everyone was worried about Delilah. The team was no good if she was out of commission. They were given time off until further notice. It has been over an hour since her injury and Xandus is going out of his mind with worry. He wishes to be by her side, but the female angels refused. What did they think he would do? Attach puppet strings on her limbs and make her dance? For now, he stares at the stars above the Province of Hallowmore. He rests atop a cloud chewing his shard of lightning. He is lost in thought until Iulas lands near him.

Before he could say a word, Xandus rushes to infirmary. His *kameraad*'s appearance means either Delilah took a turn for the worst or was starting to feel better. In either case, even the burnt bast-age Lucifer wouldn't be able to stop him from seeing her. Traveling through the resting area of God's palace, he flies in and around the halls where he and Iulas arrive at Delilah's room. Aurum stands in front of the door that has a life-sized portrait of Delilah displayed on the door. He gestures for Xandus to stop, but the Champion doesn't slow down. He and the rest of the squad brush their way past Evnore and into Delilah's room.

"How are you, Strategist?" Xandus inquires.

She's already dressed and ready to go. "We have to debrief."

"Already taken care of," Aurum replies.

"You must accompany us. We are rewarded with another RDO," Valorian adds.

"Affirmative. Time to decompress," Aurum agrees.

Xandus smiles with relief. Delilah's well-being is of the utmost importance to him. Now, he can relax his tight jaws. Valorian assists Delilah to her feet and holds his arm out. She smiles and hooks her arm around his. She sneaks a flirtatious gaze at Xandus.

The squad members all stream to a banquet hall. Finally, they have an official mission accomplished award. Once seated, manna is presented to the team.

"Nom-noms!" Iulas says with glee.

Xandus rubs his hands together in anticipation. Angels can go forever without food but love the taste of it just the same. As they think it, so shall it be. The manna on his plate forms into steaming hot, seasoned pheasant, roasted potatoes, and rolls. "When was the last time we had a banquet? A year? Two?"

"When did we last eat? A year? Two?" Naomi says.

"You guys ate?" Iulas teases.

Xandus snaps his fingers twice at a floating platter containing butter. "Butter is my favorite fruit."

"Save some for the rest of us," Naomi demands. Her plate is full of prime rib with extra gravy and mashed potatoes so creamy it could be sour cream. She snatches some of the falling butter off the serving dish before it was consumed.

The team members laugh and enjoy the variety of food that is set before them. Sliced fruits and all types of desserts appear on their plates. Cakes with the perfect amount of frosting drizzled over it. Strawberry tarts larger than Valorian's eagle eyes. They share and pass around their favorite dishes to their *kameraads*. Each lavishing the aroma of everyone else's favorite just as much as their own.

Naomi yelps and starts rubbing her eyes. "I got hot sauce in my eyes."

"You're supposed to eat with your mouth, not your eyes." Iulas jests as he mocks Naomi by putting a mouthful of food into his eye. His transparent body reveals the trek the food traverses. It slides down where his throat would be and into his stomach.

The team grunts with disgust. Naomi throws a fork at him, which he catches between his two fingers.

"The assault on humans. What were our losses?" Delilah asks.

The team members all lower their eyes.

"Herald, what happened?"

"Reports are still coming in. The situation is stabilized. Not as many fatalities to the humans," Aurum answers.

Delilah's eyes bulge with shock. "What are we doing here then? We should be out there helping!"

"Sister, calm down. The seven of us won't make that much of a difference. We just cleansed Heaven. Don't we deserve a respite?" Naomi challenges.

"No, we don't!"

"We don't tire easily, but we are fatigued. All of us. This may be part of a demonic plan to keep us that way. Have you thought of that? You and Xandus were just downed. Our Strategist and our Champion. Evnore almost succumbed to the depths. Did you know that? We can't afford to lose any of you for any length of time. We have to allow everyone to recover."

"Xandus, this is your fault! If not for your negligence—"
Delilah sighs. "Disregard. I'm fine." As to emphasize Aurum's point, she steadies herself placing her hand on the table.

Aurum speaks slowly, "All of us could suffer from combat fatigue. We can't afford errors, inattention to duty, slow reaction—"

"Irritability," Iulas chimes in.

"I'm not irritated-able," Delilah answers, pushing irritation away.

"You sound defensive," Iulas says.

Delilah takes a deep breath. "Think about it. Seven. There are seven major cities with countless *charges* that are not under assault. Isn't that suspicious?"

"Or fortunate," Xandus adds.

Delilah shakes her head. "Not only do I think that someone in one of these cities will come under attack"—she pauses looking into each of the team member's eyes—"I think one of us is under attack as well. If each of us were to cover a city, we could be targeted. Does the enemy have a way of knowing which of us would cover which city?"

Team Chrysos's members trade uncertain looks with one another.

Aurum quiets Iulas's unspoken sarcastic remark with a glance. "We're Earth's last defense, and we will always be ready. Stand down, Strategist. That's an order."

"I just want the best for humanity."

"We all do, Delilah," Aurum replies.

Delilah shakes her head. "Sorry. Maybe you're right, Aurum. I'm sounding paranoid." She curtsies. "Mother, may I?"

The Herald sighs and nods with a weak smile.

Delilah gathers her sword and makes her way toward the exit.

"Killjoy," Iulas mumbles.

"You need to eat something," Evnore says.

Delilah snatches a drumstick from Evnore's plate and raises it in triumph as she heads out the door.

***

Delilah uses small tools to manipulate miniscule mechanisms in the device within her hands. The device is translucent and weightless. She admires her work in the sunlight and continues her labor. After a few more final adjustments, she puts the device away and boots up her bracer and cycles into the network, or tries to. Access denied. Then she tries to check her data feed. Access denied. On her bracer, a timer swirls into view, counting down an hour. She sighs. Aurum forced her to take time off. How can she not worry about her angelic kin, especially when she and Chrysos could make a difference? She can't even pull up her eye vermin footage. She rested long enough while she was unconscious. Time to get to work now.

She has another option of passing the time. Instead of heeding Aurum's advice for R & R, she decides to get some training in. Her war room in Heaven is mammoth. The marshmallow clouds in front of the entrance follow her into her assigned room. She used to conduct her planning, practice, and informational activities here. She remembered when she was first granted the resource. It was one of the proudest moments of her young promotion.

The Son walked with her as she made her exit from God's throne. His smile was warm and reassuring. A galaxy was draped around His neck like a strand of beads. Strapped across His back was a great sword completely composed of the word "truth" in every language. She followed Him until they arrived at this war room. He pointed above the door. Her insignia—the knight's chess piece with a maze within—was above it. Her name was over the insignia. She smiled so, with pride and gratitude. Her very own office. She didn't use the room much now, but with only a little time to spare, she might as well sharpen her skills for whatever trial there is to come.

Giant portraits of God during creation are fixated along the ceiling. To be more accurate, the portraits were actual Moments of Him separating day and night. The images move magnificently along with his other works during His Six Days. More portraits line up alongside the war room, numbering in the hundreds of thousands. Each depiction is of the most powerful devils in Hell and in the Archfiend. Some she had the honor of taking down herself.

She passes up Krolox the Annihilist—One of the first to join up with Lucifer in his quest to usurp God and His throne. Now he resides in the Archfiend Zone with dominion over magma. Ukla the Sneak. Troc the Rampager.

She passes over all the most feared Fallen angels until she arrives at Abbadon's portrait. Time passes like a diving osprey. She stares at the corrupted angel with dread. Thoughts of her former Herald pop into the unscathed regions of her mind. Maybe blowing off some steam will help. She paces back and forth looking at those eyes. Despite being a portrait, the eyes follow her. She taps one of her three Words of Power: Fearless. She stands straighter and raises her chin in defiance.

Abbadon was the first occupant in Hell. The very first to curse God's name to His face. He'll forever pay for his sacrilege as king of Hell. Abbadon the Demigod, Abbadon the Defiler, Abbadon the Betrayer, Abbadon the Bastage. His place in Hell doesn't give Delilah sweet dreams. Not only did he betray God, but betrayed her trust as well. Someone she trusted to her core. He is every ugly word she can think of—and she can think of plenty. She stares at the portrait with contempt. God tried to warn her, but she didn't take heed.

She swipes the life-sized portrait of Abbadon toward the center of the room. His digital self electronically comes alive. His black eyes track Delilah and smiles. Even now, the bastage had a smile that could make a roach blush. He roars in laughter, never taking his piercing gaze off her. He folds his reptilian wings behind him as he cracks his knuckles. Rings adorn his fingers. Her eyes wander to the circle of gold she gave him when he was promoted to squad leader. It was given to him as a brooch, but he made it into a ring. The bastage still wears it, even as a blasted digital clone.

Abbadon picks up on everything. He taps his finger. "I have mine. You have yours?"

"Difficulty?" an electronic simulator queries.

"Maximum," Delilah responds.

"May I suggest a lower difficulty, Strategist."

"You did. I won't."

Abbadon paces back and forth like a leashed dragon, flexing his bulging biceps. Charred skin and curved horns replace his former comeliness. Reptilian wings beat subconsciously. He stabs his enormous lava sword into the ground, where the flames flicker coolly off the red metal. There was a time when he was gorgeous to behold. More honorable than a twenty-one-gun salute.

"My love! When were you last here? Months? You're still beautiful to behold. Time hasn't changed that. So beautiful I could eat your face!"

In the war room, all portraits and any TAC bracer simulacrums are imbued with true-to-life responses, actions, thoughts, and personality.

"Shut up," she responds in barely contained anger.

His eyes glance at Delilah's sword. The iridescent colors solidify into a blood red. "You learn how to use that yet? Not the sword, your temper. Use your ire to defeat me. Let your stronger emotions fuel your strength! Or I can show you myself. How many spars have you lost to me, Delilah? A thousand? Ten thousand?" The electronic Abbadon roars in laughter.

"Simulator, cut off his tongue."

"That will lower his difficulty to 83 percent, Strategist. Proceed?"

She sighs. "Negative."

"Delilah," Abbadon says as he clicks his tongue, "we used to talk all the time. Now you wish to silence me? We would talk for hours."

Yes, they would talk for hours. They dabbled in discussions about the future of humanity and Heaven. However, they frequently spoke of her favorite subject; strategy. They discussed how they could best complement each other's attacks, how to avoid a focused based strike, and which hand signals were the best, as well as countless other subjects. Delilah was under the impression that he enjoyed the talks. Maybe he saw how excited she was and just played along. He was a perfect gentleman back then. Delilah boots up her TAC bracer and swipes into existence electronic versions of Naomi and Evnore. They settle into battle positions, flanking her.

"Now it's a party!" the demon yells.

Delilah orders her *kameraads*, "Evnore, piercing strike!"

Before anyone is able to initiate the battle plan, Abbadon takes one giant step toward Evnore and cleaves her in half with his sword. A horrible yelp escapes her maw as she collapses and her body erupts in flame. In the same smooth motion, he follows through in a tight spin and throws his sword at Naomi. She crosses her swords in front of her to block the attack, but her swords shatter. His sword does not as it impales Naomi just under her clavicle, pinning her to the wall. Fortunately, once he threw the sword, the flames were extinguished. He grabs Delilah by the neck with his final move. He beats his wings once, sending them both to the wall's edge, and he slams her against the wall next to Naomi.

"NO!"

"All your preparation is in vain!" the image of Abbadon taunts.

"No!" Delilah yells in frustration. How was Abbadon able to discern her plans? Every strategy she comes up with, he uses a pre-emptive strike against it. The simulations will never reveal their intent or how the demons that they emulate come up with their strategies. They are always one hundred percent accurate, so it isn't as if these results couldn't happen—especially on maximum difficulty.

The simulator breaks in, "Terminate?"

Delilah ignores the computer as she punches and kicks Abbadon. She tries to wrench his thumb back to force open his hand, but she hasn't the strength. Oxygen cuts off its trek to her brain. She begins to lose consciousness.

The real Naomi and Evnore walk into the war room and see that Delilah's in serious trouble. Evnore roars with protective anger. She shifts into a red lion the size of a bear and the speed of a cheetah. She leaps toward the devil's throat. However, the Demigod twirls to face his new threat. He steps forward and head butts Evnore. A sickly crunch is heard throughout the room as she crumples to the ground with a loud yelp. Right behind Evnore is Naomi. She uses her twin swords in a furry of attacks. Delilah snatches a pearl from her armor. She juices it with vigor, crushes the gem, and flings it at Abbadon's head. A dense cloud springs up from the pearl fragments and surrounds him. The cloud drops a deluge of acid rain on his head. His skin begins to smolder. He inhales deeply and snorts, dispersing the acidic cloud. Delilah gasps for air as she collapses to the ground.

Abbadon snakes his hand in between Naomi's attack and grabs her wrist. He torques his body and twists her wrist to fling her to the ground. With a powerful beat of his wings, he lifts himself into the air and crash-lands on Naomi's ribs, cracking her cage.

"Terminate simulation!" Naomi screams, then faints.

Abbadon backs away and into a duck squat, wearing that winning smile. "I was sure you could land a blow on me that time," he brags. "One more time. Keep the doppelgangers too. I'll wear a blindfold!" he suggests, laughing maniacally.

The angels gaze at the looming figure. He lifts their wrists and allows them to drop to gauge their willpower to proceed. Once Delilah catches her breath, she gazes at his electronic form sullenly and deletes him. She wipes her eyes. The pain of defeat feels almost as bad as the physical pain she heals from.

It takes several minutes for Naomi to fully heal. She wheezes as she tries to fill her deflated lungs with air. She lies down on the ground and feels around her ribs, pressing them occasionally. Her pain must be immense, yet she refuses to moan. After Naomi fully recovers, she pushes Delilah against the wall. "This is stupid! We're wasting valuable time!"

"I need to form a strategy for defeating him."

"I apologize! I didn't know hitting his fist with your face was a strategy!" Naomi mocks. She knocks on Delilah's head. "Start using your brain for more than zombie munch! Oh, wait…last I checked, the Demigod was still in Hell. Did his status change?"

Delilah lowers her head. "I was on my own time, remember?"

Then they both notice Evnore slumped against the wall, staring at their defeated counterparts. She winces in pain as she feels her skull mend. She is visibly dizzy as the swelling recedes and her balance is compromised. She touches the soft parts of her skull, waiting for it to harden. They both sit on either side of Evnore.

Delilah taps on her bracer and deletes the images. "We won't submit. We will subdue and conquer," she responds with more confidence in her voice than she had in her heart.

"You can't continue to behave so rashly. Your decisions affect us all," Evnore replies as she struggles to her feet and staggers away.

Evnore is right; she's always right. Delilah sighs as she turns her attention back to Naomi. "What was it you wanted with me?"

"Aurum summoned us. New assignment." She glances at her timer flashing zeros. She has no idea for how long.

"What is it this time? More news of the assault?" Delilah questions.

Naomi lowers her eyes. "We are on our way to assist Xandus. A *charge* died under his protection...Benjamin."

Delilah's eyes widen with shock. "Benjamin? Impossible!"

Naomi lowers her head in response.

CHAPTER 4

DEATH OF A *CHARGE*

Delilah, Aurum, and the rest of her *kameraads* touch down on the street near the deceased. Valorian is verbally bashing Xandus with a tirade of disappointments and accusations. She searches the immediate area for a potential ambush, but nothing stands out. The great City of Chicago. Reports claim that death rates are lower now than it was in twenty years. Aggravated battery continues to rise, but technology can keep victims of violent crimes alive longer, but not today. Typically, Xandus needs no assistance or relief from duty. The typical response from devils who know Xandus either flee from the sight of him or avoid his sector altogether. Now he was challenged and wonders if he will be challenged more often.

Chrysos investigates the sad scene, though Delilah can't pull her eyes away from the torture and anguish Benjamin endured in his last living moments. Herein lies the former scientist extraordinaire. The top of his skull is cracked open with blood streaming down his face. He is slumped against a car, where police process the scene for evidence and crowd control.

Xandus's radiant silvery blue skin appears dull now, almost as if he was malnourished. Valorian continues to berate him. She can only imagine how they both feel. Poor Xandus. A Champion of Heaven and guardian angel was somehow outmaneuvered and outmatched. How did this happen? He was perfect for eons protecting his *charges*.

He was also very successful at protecting the "unassigned." Something went terribly wrong.

Her eyes drop to his exposed waist, and she gasps. She discovers his faulds in a puddle and recovers the armor. She takes the piece of armor and cleans and hands it over to Aurum. The team leader rubs his thumb over the word "protect." Then he gives it back to its rightful owner.

He accepts the faulds in his shaking hands. He gives Delilah a sideways glance, but her stern glare reinforces Aurum's gesture. He girds himself in armor once more.

Delilah assists Xandus to his feet. Her eyes harden with intensity; her mouth widens with shock. She grabs his chin and tilts his head into the light to get a better look at his eyes. "Blood! You have blood in your eyes! What did you do?" she demands. "If you took away Benjamin's Death Affliction, you could be 'marked' by Death!"

Xandus shrugs.

"Ben is in Heaven! Tempt Death, and you'll be sent straight to Hell!" Delilah adds.

Valorian squawks, "His choice. I don't care. What is important is that you lost a *charge*! Chrysos holds the greatest percentage of success! How did you allow this to happen?"

He bats away Delilah's hold of his chin. Valorian reaches for him, but she halts him with a gentle touch to his arm. The eagle-headed angel turns his head to look at her, then steps back.

"Give him a chance, Valor," she demands. "Tell us what happened."

He continues to stare at the ground, refusing to make eye contact. "I got separated from Benjamin. A stupid demon distracted me."

Faster than adrenaline, Valorian lunges for Xandus and head butts him. The force of the blow knocks him to the ground. Before Xandus can grunt in pain, Valorian lifts him back up by the neck. He tilts his large eye at the Champion. "So the man you're responsible for guarding is rewarded an untimely death while you go demon gazing? Incredible!" he squawks. "Maybe you were right to discard your faulds! You don't deserve it!"

Valorian pushes him away in disgust. Medical examiners take Benjamin's physical body away. A couple of squad cars stay to guard the scene to assist two detectives when they arrive. One begins a discussion with the guard officers, and the other wades into the crowd of onlookers. When she starts asking them questions, the crowd turns and walks away.

"I apologize. I brought shame to our team and to your command, Aurum. That was never my intention," he responds sadly.

Delilah rubs her fingers across Xandus's jawline. Four lights wink into life just above his skin. His bracer rapidly blinks red, then a slow black light. Soon the lights stop altogether. His bracer flashes green with "link established—Chrysos Squadron."

"If your bracer was online, you would have had enough time to save Benjamin—even if distracted. Obviously, you allowed his soul-shield to expire," Delilah admonishes. "How long were you engaged with the demon? Minutes?"

Valorian points his finger to Aurum. "You're too easy on him."

"Enough!" Aurum shouts. "This is getting us nowhere. Xandus, take me to where this demon was. Valorian, see what you can find here."

Valorian squawks as he folds his arms behind his back and under his wings. He walks a circuit around the crime scene. Sharp eyes scour the area for physical clues an officer may miss. If he finds physical evidence the humans missed, Valorian can interact with the clue, causing it to shimmer or make a sound to attract attention. He will also seek out metaphysical clues called *enodes* that no human can photograph or dust for prints.

The rest of the team search other areas for anything out of the ordinary. Their only source of natural light comes from street lamps and some indoor lighting. Nosy humans become bored of the excitement Benjamin's death caused and leave the view from their apartment windows. More of the pesky eye vermin keep their distance—possibly to report any findings the angels discover. Mischievous imps laugh and snicker in amusement.

The team arrives at the mouth of an alley, where Xandus shakes his head in denial. Naomi wanders off peering through the darkness, away from the rest of the squad. Everyone checks the area for anything that could shed light on this mystery, except Xandus.

Aurum's firm voice shakes him back to the task at hand. "Here?" He nods.

Delilah's ire starts to boil. Even though she's unaware of what exactly transpired, this could have been avoided. He takes his duties and his rank too lightly. Even a hundred years ago, he wouldn't neglect his responsibilities to a *charge*. If what he says is true, it is obvious to her the demon he interacted with was there to stall him. She stomps over to Xandus, whispering in a harsh voice, "I'm shocked that you fell for a diversionary strategy that is on page two of your *Stratics Handbook*."

Aurum overhears. "Concentrate on the task at hand. What happened here?"

Pointing into the alley, he replies, "Lizard-demon was over there."

"No, his faction? Are you sure he was alone? What weapons did he wield? Anything you can remember?" Delilah adds.

The Champion shrugs. "I didn't think it important to acknowledge him."

"Evnore, can you pick up any scents?" Delilah queries.

The lioness looks embarrassed. She shakes her head slightly. "I've been trying since we arrived here. Somehow, demonic scents in this whole sector were...erased."

Delilah taps her chin in thought. "You should have said something sooner. That's pertinent information, Evnore."

"If demons went so far as to mask or erase their scent, it means they definitely targeted Benjamin and our squad," Aurum informs.

He is most certainly right. If they knew Xandus would be here and they knew the assassination was going to be successful, then demons also knew one of the best trackers in Heaven would contribute toward the investigation. Not only can Evnore track scents like the feline species she resembles but with great ability and vigor and can track an entity by their soul scent. "The question is how were they able to neutralize their scent though? It's not like they used soap and water."

Naomi's voice cracks the silence of the squad's contemplation. "I got an *enode* here."

Everyone turns toward Naomi and rushes down the alley. She stoops over a purple-spotted worm creature with a claw at the end of it. Upon closer inspection, it's a demon's finger—and it moves.

"His finger," Xandus recognizes. "We didn't clash though, so I don't know why it's here. No, wait." He takes a closer look at the finger. "The edges aren't serrated. It looks almost as though it were pulled off."

"Not pulled, sliced off," Naomi corrects.

"You said you didn't fight him," Delilah reminds him.

"He severed his finger in his rush to close the *veil* gate behind him," Xandus explains.

"Which hardly ever happens... But a *veil*? Here?" Delilah asks.

"Yes, a mobile *veil*. He sealed it behind him," Xandus responds.

"A lot of effort to make a one-time-use gate. And he still could have come back for his finger," Delilah adds.

"So it was planted after all," Aurum surmises.

"Why?" Naomi questions as she scoops up the gross finger.

"The thief comes only to steal, kill, or destroy," Xandus recites.

"In other words—it's a trap," Delilah informs.

Aurum seemed deep in thought, flexing his metallic wing. He accepts the offered finger from Naomi and tucks it away into a belt pouch. "Valorian's familiarity with demon factions can prove useful. His knowledge of Shadow Domain is second to none. You both can follow this through."

"I don't need him riding me on this," Xandus replies with a deep frown. "I can do it alone."

"I'll go with him," Delilah offers. "He feels bad enough already."

Aurum shakes his head. "You are not going alone. Those are your orders." He points to Delilah. "I want you, Naomi, and Evnore to finish up here. Doc any findings, pursue any leads you discover, and stay out of trouble."

"Not gonna happen," Naomi responds with ire. "Our squad is mocked, and a *charge* died. I'm in a trouble-seeking mood tonight."

When the ladies arrive back at the scene of the crime, the police, paramedics, and any onlookers are gone.

"Are you going to use seek mode?" Naomi asks.

"Yes, since I wasn't actually here when the assassination happened, I won't be able to go back in time too far. The generosity of our patron is suspect."

Naomi nods. Both she and Evnore place a hand on Delilah's shoulders. She acquired a unique ability or, more correctly, a tentative partnership. The supreme being said their meeting was coincidental, but Delilah always had her doubts.

Time. He's such a bastage.

It was after the Fall, and Delilah was deep in thought. It was hard for her to think of anything else other than the betrayal of Abbadon, Lucifer, and the rest of the Fallen. It was easy to sink into despair, anger, and depression. She flew absently with no destination when a stitch in Time materialized before her. The sliver in space was undetectable until she flew into it and was swallowed. The abrupt change of scenery and the eerie feeling of a sheet of ice that enveloped her skin put Delilah on high alert.

She halted, trying to discern her surroundings. Strands of gold in a complex pattern similar to a spider's web was all around her. All the strands led to a single source. Beautiful timepieces, each ageless in its design, hovered around the immense chamber. Two large golden clocks make up Time's eyes.

The web extended in every direction from him into infinity. She realized that these weren't strands of gold but sand. The entity Time appeared to be sleeping. When she flew to his side, she noticed his "eyes" were indeed open and very interested in her.

"Welcome, Delilah," Time whispered.

"You know who I am?"

"Of course. You are no stranger to Time. I've seen your moments."

Time leaned forward, but the open sky captured her attention. She stared long enough and would swear she could see that the distant stars moved.

"You act as if this is your first time viewing the sky," Time stated.

"I've never seen them move so quickly. Is it because space and time flows differently here?"

Time nods. "I am the Master of Moments; the Treasurer of Ticks; the Sentinel of Seconds, my dear Delilah. I control the ebb and flow of time."

"I never thought how important the management of time could be."

Time leaned back against his web, shutting his eyes. He yawned rudely. "Alas, the mundane mainframe of minutes is monotonous."

"You should get out more," Delilah responded with a smile.

Time chuckled. "Unfortunately, I'm not omniscient. I cannot foretell the future." Time grabs a handful of sand and demonstrated how it slipped through his fingers. "The future is like sand—formless and impossible to hold. It spreads beyond its borders—it slips within grasped hands. Decisions are innumerable, even in an instant. Even a constant can change, such as the sun. It rises every day, but when it rises varies. Therefore, I only see what was done, not what will be done. I can't partake nor interfere."

"Once an exciting moment has occurred, why not review it?" she asked.

Time shakes his head, shaking loose sand from his body. "How exciting is it to see the result of what is known? Once an outcome is decided, the how is but a boring highlight. It becomes a firm fact. The present, the future, the unknown is what excites the mind. A possibility. Hope! Most would not dash into danger if they were certain death or defeat were the outcome, no? Be you a pathfinder or a trailblazer? Time is unable to anticipate action; therefore, I am loathed to document days."

She nodded as she looked to the sky again. The stars moved significantly from where she last viewed them. She turned back to the penetrating gaze of Time. Her gaze no less intense than his. "How long have I been here?"

He chuckles menacingly. "What is the length of time? What is three days, eighteen hours, thirty-two minutes, and eight seconds?"

Delilah's eyes bulged in horror. "What? I must leave! My squad will worry!" She abruptly turned from Time and dashed to the stitch she encountered, but strands of Time blocked her route.

She turned back toward Time. "What are you doing? You can't keep me here!"

"Can't I? You've been one of my most entertaining guests. Correction, my only guest. Time gets lonely. Can you not spare a second?"

"Release me!"

"Never! You are a prisoner of Time!"

Naomi clears her throat, bringing Delilah's attention back to the task at hand. "Ready when you are, boss lady."

"Of course." A matrix overlay glows over two of her fingers and thumb. She hesitates for a fraction of a second, meeting Naomi's wary eyes.

The Eye-blotter bites her lower lip. "Poor Benjamin. I relieved Xandus of protection details many times. He was a good man. For him to die in this manner is inexcusable. I still can't believe he was stupid enough for this to happen."

"Ease up on Xandus," Delilah requests.

Naomi displays a startled look at Delilah. She bites her pinky and smiles deviously. "Sorry, boss. Didn't know you had the likes for him."

"Quiet, you," she orders. She taps her glowing digits and calls out, "Time!"

Gold clocks appear faintly in the background. The Sands of Time swirl. Color becomes a wispy black and white as Time slows. The gold clocks are the eyes of Time. They spin around the angels in recognition. "Strategist. How can I help you?"

"No time, long see great being of antiquity. I need access to the time stream."

Time puffs up his sand. The angels squint and cover their eyes with their hands and use their wings as a protective barrier.

When Time speaks, his voice rumbles the ground. "Oh, now you wish to summon Time? I missed the heavenly anomaly event. A very compelling crisis. Time should have been summoned then! We had an agreement, and you reneged!" he responds.

"That wasn't part of our agreement! Battles are what I'm honor bound to call you for. Not ordinary missions."

"Ordinary? A heavenly anomaly? Ordinary?"

"She will swallow her tongue before dishonoring your name again. Please. Time is of the essence," Naomi breaks in.

"Time is of the essence…but aren't I always?" He laughs. "Maybe I should have chosen you, Naomi. Because you found your manners, I will grant you twenty seconds. Use it wisely, Strategist."

"Twenty seconds? What will I do with that? That's not enough time to remove dirt from my fingernails! I have to go back further! This is ridic—"

"Sixteen seconds."

"What?"

"Perfect, Master Time!" Naomi compliments as she covers Delilah's mouth.

Time is whisked away into the time stream. The clocks that make up his eyes dismantle. The sands picks up in intensity as it spins around them, then swirls out to encompass the area of effect. All time within the barrier reverses in an instant.

Heaviness engulfs Delilah. She is angry about Naomi's interference and Time's arrogant display and control of his power. Then she remembers it's not about her. They must resolve this crisis and bring closure to Benjamin's death. Once the feed begins, she understands that it will be the last time she will see him alive. Even as a recording, the weight of his death will press down on her. Bad enough when a chosen must die. So much worse when a man who was not Fated dies. She can only imagine how Xandus must feel. The guilt must be overwhelming.

The ladies follow Benjamin with their eyes as he hobbles around a corner. Suddenly, Benjamin collapses. The top of his head splits open. Freeze. She taps her fingers together, pausing the recording. Dread and horror joins heaviness as Benjamin's death unfolds. No human should suffer the pain and torment he endured.

"What happened?" Delilah says.

"There's a blur. Slow it down," Naomi instructs.

She nods. It makes her sick in the stomach. Rising rage replaces the sorrow. Benjamin's death was barbaric and merciless, even for a demon. A push of adrenaline gushes through her veins. She wants to engage with her enemy. Not now, but right now. However, this is not the time to be irrational. She pushes down the anger, steadies her breathing, and works on the task at hand.

Now she manipulates the time stream within this time frame. Using the matrix overlay on her fingers and thumb, she backs time back. With the precision of a surgeon, the angels view Benjamin's death frame by horrifying frame. The anticipation and unraveling of this death scene is agonizing. Knowing that within the next few frames, a person will be murdered. Then she gets to the killing blow.

A female demon with large compound eyes like a fly wielded a set of silver curved blades. She wore a gothic robe in shades of purple. There's a slit up the thigh to allow freedom of movement. There is a gaudy fly fetish nestled between her breasts. She appeared in front of Benjamin. Her blades made a silvery streak, and in a single overhead strike to the head, the scientist crumpled to the ground. The demon waved a hand over his body and appeared visibly upset. Then she slapped a strip of paper over his ear. Within the blink of a wink, she vanished. The whole incident took about a second.

Naomi's eyes widened in recognition. "Sinxin! I'd know those eyes anywhere! Those blades are exquisite, custom. They're carved from single shards of soul stones. The ingots are used to create what is called a Kcorelass blade."

"Kcorelass blades?" Delilah repeats.

Naomi nods. "They combine the essence of human souls with moonlight. Soul stones are harvested from leased souls like gold. Once the essence is extracted from a soul slave, it's chilled in Hellfrost."

"Moonlight," Delilah responds thoughtfully.

"What about moonlight?" Evnore asks.

"That's the same energy that the soul well was made of," Delilah answers.

"Coincidence?"

"Probably, but I think not."

As the paper dissolved on Benjamin's ear, the angels hear a voice. Sinxin's voice. "Crackle Blade just got played!"

"Crackle Blade? That's what they call Xandus!" Naomi points out.

"Which means Benjamin was targeted," Delilah adds.

"And Xandus. I guess you were right," Evnore admits.

"I hate when you're right," Naomi says.

"That doesn't help us now," Delilah responds. Then to Naomi, she says, "Refresh my memory on her profile."

"Your *enodes* will be returned to you, sister. Fret not," Evnore says assuredly.

Delilah shrugs nonchalantly. Feeling like the weak link irks her tremendously. She rubs at her temple, revealing a scar. Another battle wound that will never completely heal. Ever since her *enodes* were stolen from her, she suffers from bouts of memory lapses, fainting spells, and identity loss.

"Sinxin? Her notoriety precedes her. Valorian probably knows more about her. She didn't display her power, but typically she doesn't need to. I had no idea that she was so fast. She dropped her visage so fast it seemed like a blur," Naomi says.

The demon dropped visage to interact physically with Benjamin. Doing so made her vulnerable to angelic attack. When spiritual beings drop visage, their power is diminished tenfold. She needlessly exposed herself to risk when attacking a sixty-year-old human. Had Xandus arrived on the scene on time, he would have had the advantage.

"Rewind it again," Naomi orders.

Delilah does. Naomi squints in thought as she examines the footage. Then she points at Sinxin. "Did anyone notice the silence in her movements? It was an elderly human she was attacking, but she didn't disregard him. She was efficient, professional, fluid, and deadly. She's a trained warrior."

"An assassin," Evnore adds.

"A murderer," Delilah finishes. "What else do you know about the blades?"

"Those blades are the work of a master blacksmith. I'm not sure if our own Omnikrom could make those."

"My question is who was truly targeted? Was this done to avenge some affront that Xandus caused, or was Benjamin's death imperative to some insidious plot?"

"Or both?" Evnore infers.

"Or both," Delilah agrees as she replays the footage again, then stops it. Her mouth wide open. She takes a step toward Sinxin and reaches for her. A soft foreboding chuckle can be heard in the fabric of Time.

Evnore yanks her back, screaming at Delilah, "Stop! What are you doing? We can't move! We'll be siphoned into the time stream!"

Delilah tries to speak, but it comes out as gibberish, pointing at Sinxin. Now it is Naomi's turn to gasp. This enemy, this demon with the compound eyes. The one who outsmarted their Champion is the keeper of one of Delilah's *enodes*.

Her *enode*—which resembles a topaz—was trapped within Sinxin's gaudy fly-inspired fetish. She moans in distress. A part of her that was lost is now found, but is literally outside her reach. Her eyes narrow. She grinds her teeth. Maybe both she and Xandus are the intended targets? Why would the demon possess it? How can anyone get so many moving pieces to fit so accurately? Lucifer and Anura, the black-blood bastages.

She was elated at the discovery of her *enode*, but now she must discover the demon's whereabouts. Eons passed with no clues to its whereabouts until now. Never has Delilah's goal and mission converged until now.

Goody.

CHAPTER 5

QUICKENING THE PLOT

A hideous figure catches the attention of the viewer. An ugly female demon with large compound eyes who had the likeness of a fly. Sinxin the Atrocious stops to stare at the reflection—hers. Most of the Fallen lost their charisma and comeliness when they were evicted out of Heaven. Most suffered from scarred, wrinkled, or decayed flesh to replace their smooth and radiant skin. Others had undergone transformations that gave them animalistic or undead features, but her fate was worse than all other demons combined. She leans in close enough to see her refracted image within those eyes a thousand times. She places a hand on the mirror, applies pressure, and shatters the mirrored surface.

She braces herself against the wall, wondering how she was going explain the misinformation she received about the human she murdered. Though not her fault, it will always be her fault. Her disfigured features make it easy for her superiors to place blame on her failures. No excuse justified her ineptness, and they made sure to add a derogatory comment or two on top of any reprimands she received. Sinxin was ensured that the fleshling was the *turnkey*. Correction, she was told it was a high probability her target would be the key to the Gates of Hell. As long as she was able to avoid direct confrontation with the Class X, it was a simple matter to kill the fleshling. She still should have been prepared to follow up on the next of kin if the target was a false positive. Decades of planning were wasted on falsified information. Anura will stick her head on a dull stake in the ground. Sinxin updated the results, mentioned her next objective, and severed communications. She doesn't want to get distracted from her current conquest. She can ill afford two failures in one day.

Through a broken mirror shard, she gazes at her fetish. Then she cups it within her hands as if it were a baby mouse. All fetishes are compatible and interchangeable with each other. Her focal fetish, called the "Dregs," is a large bejeweled fly. It can accommodate five jewels nestled between her breasts. The more fetishes a demon controls, the greater their power and influence—and she holds four. Dregs enhances her natural abilities and gives her the ability to shape flame, but at a price. She is forever disfigured, even if she were to lose the fetish. Having the quickness, reflexes, and three-hundred-sixty-degree sight of a fly gives her a distinct advantage. In particular, she is nigh impossible to sneak up on and ferocious in battle.

She despises her grotesque physical traits; it's her blessing and curse. Without the artifact's power, she wouldn't wield the influence of an imp. With it, she commands her own phalanx. Without the artifact fetish, her existence would fare less than a shadow scraper in Hell. Even an imp wouldn't fear nor respect her—shadow kin would only be repulsed by her.

Sinxin believed Lucifer to be the most beautiful angel of all. Gorgeous, masculine, strong, and intelligent. Even after the Fall, his comeliness was still there. No longer did jewels embed his skin. They fell from his body like summer leaves in a winter wind. He didn't let the loss of his glorious ornamental skin dissuade him, however. Instead, he imbued his seemingly unlimited jewels with vast amounts of vigor to create the fetishes. Unlike the selfish God, Lucifer shared these vigor-enriched relics with his faithful followers—sort of. He didn't just hand them out to demons as if they were welfare recipients. He placed them throughout the Archfiend Zone and Natural World to be discovered like hidden treasure. Demon folk would use all available resources to search for clues and at times even work together to extract the epics. The strongest and most cunning demons fared well. Holding one fetish was a prize in and of itself.

Why must she rehearse this in her mind at all times? God's curse was a vivid reminder of the Fallen's defeat at their believed peak of power. Unbeknown to God, demons have never been more powerful than now. Lucifer is a rewarder of those who diligently seek him and his "Fetishes of Dominion," of course.

"Her are lates," a demon questions as he approaches Sinxin. "Traffic?"

Sinxin ignores the mercenary as he interrupts her forced thoughts. He goes by the name and title Nil the Blue Demon. He is a mountain of gristle dipped in dread. He wears a three-eyed set of goggles, arranged in a triangle. His blue-skinned bare-chested torso is adorned with tribal tattoos and piercings.

Now that her attention is back on the task at hand, she surveys the area. Castle Bloodroot is akin to a nefarious cathedral. Grand in its design yet dark and foreboding. Sinxin likes it much better than the tiny mansion she previously schemed in.

Her forces were in the process of mopping up the lesser devils from the acquired castle. When Sinxin was selected from all the qualified lieutenants to lead this offensive, she was honored and ecstatic. Her habitation in this castle hinged upon her ability to actually take and hold it from its previous owner. There was a time when she believed Lucifer forgot about her oath of allegiance to him. She was told after the great exodus of Heaven that the Separatists will be rewarded. She's accumulated power and her army over the eons in an effort to be ready for the call to serve. That time was finally here. Many are called, and even more respond. She organized her disciplined henchmen quickly, once she was forewarned of the soul well's existence and location. Her rivals call her henchmen the "Hideons."

Her organized forces contrast with the chaotic frenzy of devils who were systematically hewn down. Once the opposition was defeated, their listless bodies became absorbed into the soul well. The devils that still fight are less bold and more cautious. The smart ones asked to join and swore a blood oath to join her army of woe. "We need a secure hold on Bloodroot. They're running out of time," she answers. "Where is the other guardian?"

Nil shrugs.

"Maybe he'll want his old job back."

A splendid victory, Hostess! A voice within Sinxin's head compliments.

It is a splendid victory. With a new soul well came a new conquest and thirst for power. Demons from every territory came to claim. Bloodroot had the closest proximity to the soul well—where the hottest fighting occurred. Sinxin can almost claim her victory. With her disciplined army, she was able to cut a path through her enemies like a mower does weeds. *Blast! I'm becoming too used to Prexel's presence!*

Silence, fool! Sinxin says within herself.

The mental fortitude she must maintain to keep her sanity is exhausting. The utterings of the madman within her mind inhibited her strategic thought process. Prexel has the inclination of giving perfectly good advice. Advice she can never follow—he could be advising her into a trap. She touches one of the fetish jewels absently, the "Intellect Devourer." True to its name, it houses the mind of her former partner turned rival, Prexel. Eons ago, the jackal-headed devil betrayed her partnership and took the fetish he was now imprisoned in. He was superior in strength, but his feeble mind was unable to wield the Devourer. He could not control the fetish, so it controlled him. It's what the betrayer deserved. Together, they both would have done well with adjoining territories and held much influence. *He's literally an afterthought,* she chuckles to herself. Now she wields its power, but the hold on her own mind becomes less so while Prexel's becomes more powerful. She rarely uses this particular fetish for fear that it will host her mind as well.

Prexel ignores her command. *With our position in the Shadow Elite, we will etch out our own corner of the Archfiend Zone!*

There is no we! Stifle yourself!

Surely, you must heed my advice here. Stay at Bloodroot and siphon the power of the soul well. Then you can stretch your borders.

He's always trying to trip her up. He infiltrates her mind even more than usual with the proximity to the soul well. She must discover a way to purge his annoying voice without discarding the Intellect Devourer, of course. "The time is now! I can't wait a decade to absorb that much power!" Sinxin yells.

"Yeah, the time are now," Nil agrees.

That was out loud, she curses to herself. With great will, Sinxin pushes Prexel into the rear of her mind. Her verbal outbursts are getting worse. His hyena laugh is his response to the banishment of his presence. His voice becomes silent now, but his presence lingers, lurking like a lion waiting to spring from the reeds.

She stares back at the blue devil who awaits her next command. His mirrored goggles are yet another reminder of her obnoxious image. She was lovely once—now she's an adult maggot. "After the battlefield is secure, come see me inside."

Sinxin walks a circuit of her new domain. Long corridors, lined chandeliers, and tall columns continue its theme of the cathedral. Despite her grotesque features, she appreciates the advantage her fly eyes gives her. Her head cocks to the side as she pauses. Above her is an intricately worked interior balcony. Skulls riveted into the iron appear very realistic; that was where she saw movement. She leaps the eight meters toward the balcony. Her insectoid forewings catch the hot breeze as she floats to the landing. She lands without a sound and drops into a defensive crouch. She cocks her head to one side, then the other in search of danger. Her arms cross her body, and her fingers interlock the hilts of her blades as she moves toward the inner room.

In this vast chamber, black drapes are hung from the tall ceiling to floor. Sewn on them are eyes. *I suppose he likes an audience*, Sinxin jests, or was that Prexel's voice speaking? There are times when she's unsure. The eyes stare at her from all around – each eye following her movement, but her compound eyes can track them all.

This room opens up to one of the bedrooms, but drapes are all within this space. They billow to and from as the hot breeze pushes and yields. The farther in she enters, the greater the breeze. A drape separates itself from the rest—eyes and all—creeping along silently behind her. In one instant, Sinxin faces one direction. In the next, she slices in the opposite direction and severs the drape in half with a horizontal slash.

The "drape" tears as the lower half flutters backward. The upper half lands on her outstretched sword, flips off, and reattaches to the lower. A malicious grin scrawls across the striking vampyre-demon, Nameer—the ousted lord of Castle Bloodroot. "Greetings, hideous one. Nothing gets past those appalling eyes, do they?"

Sinxin grinds her needle-sharp teeth together, ignoring the insult. She sheaths her kcorelass swords and opens her palm. A purple light forms above it and hovers between the two. She cocks her head to the side at the demon. He is in all black, and his batlike wings fold into a cape that glistens with a metallic sheen that shimmers across its surface. Eyes roll around the exterior of his wings. Two large eyes, each settle on his deltoids. Very handsome for a demon. Beautifuls are a rarity in the Archfiend Zone, and charismatic fetishes are priceless. Her rage rises to the surface. This arrogant bastard belittles her with his first comment. It is of no surprise. Most Beautifuls do.

"I thought you fled, Nameer."

He rubs his chin and closes his eyes in thought. "I felt a fight wasn't worth the effort."

"Or," Sinxin responds, "your undisciplined force disbanded when they saw my banner, because that's exactly what happened."

The vampyre-demon's eyes flicker in the purple light she summoned. He wraps his winged cloak around him. He lowers his glance to Sinxin's feet. "You didn't take your shoes off when you entered." Nameer shakes his head. "Manners, manners."

With one of her kcorelass blades, Sinxin knocks off a thick layer of mud on the plush carpet with a smile.

Nameer laughs. "It's your carpet now. Yours to clean up."

"It could be yours still—if you choose to join the Shadow Elite."

"The Shadow Elite broke the alliance. We followed your plans and helped cause chaos against the angelic folk and humans, only to be besieged while away. I'm an Independent and will stay that way. All Lucifer's grand goals and promises, did he fulfill them? Will he be able to?" He dismisses Sinxin with a wave of his hand. "You go follow Lucifer's commands like a whipped dog. I'll be sure to let the other Independents know what to expect, or maybe I should use my influence and join Beelzebub."

"We can accomplish more under one standard, fool."

"Then tell Lucifer to join Beelzebub. If he does, I surely will. And I'll use my significant influence to make sure others do as well. I've already sent those loyal to me to strengthen my allies. The next fort you come upon with swords raised will not fall." He stretches his arms wide to encompass his former home. "It is likely that you won't feel at home here yourself, ugly one."

A humorless laugh bellows from Nameer as he bursts into a cloud of bats. They fly directly toward her. Sinxin stands her ground as each of the bats are inherently tracked with her compound eyes. The rodents bypass her and exit through the wall behind her. She must look into the other hidden passages and map them.

She makes her way back into the main reception area. The previous fool had soul slaves as his servants. That's more freedom than they would get from her. One such servant slithers to her now. The dark green slug is unable to rise its hunched back higher than its waist. It stops at a respectful distance—he better not get any of his filthy ooze on her. She leaps into the air and hammer smashes the slug on top its head. He crashes to the ground—slime sloshing on her.

She yells in anger at the mess he made. Puss and mucus coats her tailored armor dress. "I will slice your soul into pieces! What do you want, foul creature?" she commands.

The slug gathers itself and cowers before its powerful new queen. "Mistress, the guardian Vahzkil resides in his den."

"He had three guardians? I'm impressed Nameer was able to conceal that information. What is Vahzkil doing?"

"Resting, mistress. Guardian Vahzkil polishes and sharpens his scales and spikes at this time. Shall I lead you?"

"I know the way. Did you think I happened across this castle on accident before I stormed it? Leave me." She snaps with her fingers.

The slave soul slithers aside—making way for Sinxin to pass. Might as well start with the guardian before it leaves. The ribbons on her purple dress flap in the breeze. She struts down a spiral stairway with no handrails. The ribbons on her purple dress flap even more as she descends into the depths of her castle. She walks with her hands behind her back as she observes the smooth hallways turn into earthen rock. The corridors widen into a massive cavern. Multiple passages converge into this area. In its midst dwells the wyvern-demon, Vahzkil. She hears his loud snores until she steps one foot into his den. Once she does, one of his large eyes pop open. She strolls up to him and analyzes the great wyvern-demon.

Corded muscles are attached to his wings and trunk-sized legs. His outer armor is spiked and looks to be as hard as the kcorelass steel blades she wields. Most of his armored back is golden—with the center black with silver spikes. His long whiskers coordinate with the spikes.

"Greetings, Vahzkil. Do you know who I am?"

The wyvern-demon closes his eye lazily and partially opens it again. He readjusts his head in the nook of his arm while his tail pounds the stony earth absently. "The new master, I 'spect," he says through a rude yawn.

Sinxin fans the air before her. The bastard just breathed on her. She steps closer to his eye. His cold stare was insufferable and defiant.

"It is fortunate that you didn't assist Nameer."

Vahzkil scoffs at Sinxin, spraying saliva on her. "Fortunate for you," he responds.

He slowly closes his eye again, but Sinxin grabs the eyelid and pulls it away before it shuts. Now his other eye opens. An angry stare bores into Sinxin, but only his eyes move. His body remains still as the dank air in his den.

"I see we have a failure to communicate. Allow me to introduce myself."

Faster than a murderous rage, Sinxin whips out her kcorelass blade and plunges it into Vahzkil's eye. The wyvern throws his serpentine neck back, thrashing about. His pain-filled roar shakes the foundation. He cups his eye to staunch the flow of black blood.

Sinxin flies back, staying out of striking range. His black blood pools under his head. She waits until he recovers. Once he does, he pulls his teeth back into a snarl, stretching his neck toward Sinxin.

She stares at his good eye. "I am Mistress Sinxin to you. Repeat it."

Vahzkil removes his claw from his wound, keeping his eye closed. The wyvern-demon glances at her fetish. Through clenched teeth, he repeats her words. "You are Mistress Sinxin," he repeats in barely contained anger.

"Very good," she praises. She leans over and pats the guardian in the middle of his forehead, like he was a puppy. She displays her own sharp teeth in a sinister smile. "I have big plans for you, Guardian," she informs in a cheerful voice. Then with mock concern, she adds, "Your eye will heal up in no time. Don't you worry. Great talk...I said, great talk!"

The stream of black blood is staunched. "Fare thee well, Mistress Sinxin."

She turns about-face and back up the lower tunnels. Candelabra light the blood-colored carpet until it reaches the throne. The throne is wide enough to fit two of her size. Dragon skulls top the edges while velvet lines the interior of the chair itself. Precious stones are embedded into its frame.

She sits on the throne, trying it out for size. A sneaky smile of triumph spreads across her face. Three "eye vermin" race toward her. They have one large bulbous eye atop six insect legs. A squiggly line for a mouth—sharp like broken glass. Sinxin can't help but smile at her pets. She stoops down and allows them to crawl up her arm. They start chittering.

"What? So soon?" she asks.

"What her know?" Nil asks.

"My eye vermin just reported that two angels are already on their way to the Swamplands of Orr. The fool Blusis won't follow orders through my vermin. I have another assignment for you."

The devil folds his arms. He snorts smoke from his nostrils. He grunts, then turns, and storms off. "She not the boss of I. Me not doing nothings," he replies. "Done with soldier crap."

"Wait."

Nil stops, keeping his back to his former employer. She doesn't have time for any delays. Too much at stake, her reputation was on the line, and the time constraints are tight. She sighs. "I'll give you what you want."

A sinister grin etches across his face. He mocks her with a perfect about-face, marches to her, and stands at attention. Sinxin stretches her hand out to the devil.

"Uh-uh. A eye for a eye," Nil says.

With her hand still outstretched, Sinxin manipulates her fingers so deftly that the jeweled eye that is now in her palm seemed to magically appear. Clear as glass with a floating pentagram inside.

Sharp canines glisten as the devil opens his wide mouth in a smile. "The Eye of Mystneed!" he exclaims in awe. He snatches the fetish and lifts his goggles.

Sinxin thought she was ugly. Under his googles, Nil has three eye sockets. His left eye socket is empty, but his right and center eye are both...occupied. He puts the Eye of Mystneed in his left eye socket. The pentagram glows a bloody red as it spins. He clenches his fist in triumph. "What needs crackin'?"

"My turn," Sinxin says as she snaps her fingers.

Nil removes a different eye. Once detached, spider legs poke out of the eyeball and crawl down his face, shoulder, and ultimately to his hand. She snatches the eye, scrutinizing it in the dim light. Nodding to herself in approval, she tucks it into the hissing mouth of her snake belt.

"Her better remembers. Me gots him's eye on she. Me gonna need that back. Her not lose it, or I are kill her!" Nil threatens.

Sinxin snickers. "Anytime you think you can"—she cracks her knuckles—"come at me."

***

Sinxin arrives at a network of caves within an expansive forest. The labyrinth gives demons the aura of protection, security, and anonymity. The shops are hard to find and harder to get to, at least for angels. None of the Virtuous Culture dares to intrude in the Swamplands of Orr, much less tread deeper into the network, until now. A pair of vexed angels seeking justice – one a Class X angel. She begins to feel apprehensive dealing with "Sizzle Stick" and "Fish Hooks." She welcomes the challenge, but under her terms.

She traverses throughout the network until she arrives at the center of the network. "Murkwood Tavern" is a bar that has horrible customer service. Demons of varying levels of notoriety are seated at the rickety tables. Imps flitter about helping their partners cheat. Souls smashed into large test tubes that yield frothy tankards of sin on tap. From the combination of needles and compression of the unwilling souls yield an alcoholic extract from concentrate. She would partake if she didn't have so much planning ahead of her. Lust demons dance on top of tables. Patrons whooping and throwing silver pieces at their feet.

Sinxin strides into the bar with confidence. She quickly scans the patrons, where she locates Blusis at the rear of the establishment. He is a purple-spotted lizard-demon who wears armored pieces over his forearms, torso, and legs. He slams his mug of sin hard on the table, which looks like he's drinking pride. Its contents running down the sides of his maw.

"I would have words with you," Sinxin orders.

Blusis is hugged up with half-naked lust demons, who are laughing and drinking his coins up. His tongue slides between his fangs as he hisses. He motions for Sinxin to join him. "Ah, how about a drink?"

"Fool! Clear this table!"

The lust demons see themselves in Sinxin's compound eyes and leave.

"You're a killjoy," Blusis responds in disappointment.

"Sizzle Stick and Fish Hooks are on their way here now! They are already in the Swamp of Orrs!" she explains.

Blusis's eyes widen in fear. He cuts his reptilian eyes to the sides as if the angels were there now. He calms himself after seeing nearby demons watching his reaction. He lowers his eyes and voice. "What isss your plan, mistress?"

Without looking back, she raises her hand for silence. In seconds, she has every demon's attention. Drinks cease to be served, the music stops, and the dancers climb down from tables. She turns around peering around the room, meeting their eyes. Not many are able to look directly at her for fear of an assault. She pops Nil's eye ost for Nil the Vanquisher?”

out of the snake's mouth and holds it up for all to see. “I need a volunteer. Who will be the honored host for Nil the Vanquisher?”

The room falls quiet as moonlight. Each demon glances at one another; then all at once, a shout erupts. Each and every imp, demon, and devil clamor at Sinxin. Every demon offers one of their eyes in return for the honor.

CHAPTER 6

CASTLE BLOODROOT

Delilah struggles against the electronic image of Sinxin. The fly-eyed devil pins her down with one foot while she floods the angel with purple Hellfire from her palms. The Strategist crosses her arms in front of her, using her bracer to block the flames. Sinxin laughs hysterically until Naomi and Evnore approach.

Naomi waves her hand to stop the training exercise. The electronic figure backs away, keeping her eyes on the new arrivals. Sinxin points to their defeated images, then paces around the real angels with contempt.

"My first go at you three. No match, though I shouldn't be surprised," Digital Sinxin cackles loudly. "Oh, right. Want to check on your heroine? She appears injured."

The *kameraads* rush to Delilah and assist her to her feet. Naomi flashes a frown at Delilah. The Strategist yanks off an aquamarine from her armor and crushes it. This gemstone was harvested at the base of a rainbow ending in the pristine waters of the Creeks of Tranquility. The fragments turn into a deluge of water. Her *kameraads* watch as Delilah's body heals once the hellfire is snuffed out. Even after her body regenerates, the Strategist retains the scaly blemishes around her cheeks, neck, and arms.

"One more round?" Sinxin challenges.

Naomi deletes the training image, but not before the demon's laughter echoes throughout the war room. Naomi grabs her by the ear. "Let's go, baby! We were looking all over for you!"

Delilah swats her hand away. "Not funny, Naomi," she responds weakly.

"You're right! It's not funny. We're supposed to be working on Benjamin's murder. Why are you here?"

She lowers her head. "Every strategy results in our defeat by Abbadon. Now I'm having the same problem with Sinxin. I must find a way."

"Abbadon is in Hell right now!" Naomi yells. "Why are you even thinking about him? You know who isn't in Hell? Sinxin! It's up to us to put her there!"

"She's right, Delilah," Evnore agrees. "Fret not. You will think of something. You always do, right?" she continues.

"Yeah," she says unconvincingly. She starts to walk away.

"Are you the rain or the lightning?" Evnore asks.

"Rain or lightning? What do you mean?"

"Lightning is a flash of light. It is fast, violent, and powerful, though not the best way to carve a canyon. Rain is subtle and gentle. It can become a flood unsuspectingly and can cut rock over time," Evnore explains.

"What are you talking about?" Naomi questions.

"I wish I knew," Delilah agrees.

Naomi disregards Evnore's comment with a frown. "Well, we must attend to new business. I suggest we do it chop-chop."

"New business?"

"We must head to Castle Bloodroot in the Archfiend Zone," Naomi responds.

"Bloodroot?"

"I believe the craftsman of those kcorelass blades that Sinxin wields dwells on its grounds," Naomi explains. "Now let's get a move on. Stay focused!"

***

Naomi grabs her boss by the arm and hauls her out. She snatches her arm back, subconsciously rubbing a blemish there.

Delilah rarely frequents the Archfiend Zone. She admonishes herself for not memorizing the maps of the area and what factions of sin" are represented there. Instinctively, she surveys the area. Seen from the sky are great castles. Acidic smoke and fumes cough into the burnt sky. As the angels approach the sector where Castle Bloodroot is located, she notices its towers and keeps are strategically placed to repel a demonic attack from rivals or an angelic onslaught. The towers were forged with dark-red bricks in the shape of twisting tridents. She can see the shimmer of a force field that defends the fortress from most aerial invasions. Lookouts are placed from the towers and have long-range attacks for sure. She isn't sure how many guardians this castle hired, but most forts of this size require at least one.

Signs of a recent battle are evident. Crude weapons, shields, black blood, and broken armor are sprawled all around the gate. The prevalent signs of said battle must have been short indeed. For one reason, a siege would take a much bigger force and sustain greater casualties. The siege engines were scarcely used and show no wear. Come to think of it, the gates weren't bashed in either—as if the defenders just allowed the attackers access. She wonders if a coup d'état happened here. Then Delilah gasps. "Is that what I think it is?"

Naomi and Evnore follow her pointed finger and gasp as well. Off into the distance is a soul well. In the Archfiend Zone, it looks like a solid line of silver energy in a glass tube. The angels gape in astonishment. A beautiful representation of Lucifer's immense power. Delilah immediately starts to evaluate the surroundings.

"What do you see, Delilah?" Evnore wonders.

"This is the first time I've seen a soul well. Did you catch how it seems to feed this province? The street lamps—and Bloodroot itself."

"You're right. They're pulsing in unison. I wonder why," Naomi queries.

"Where was I? When were you here last?"

Evnore glances at Naomi, but the Eye-blotter folds her arms and raises her chin.

Delilah frowns. "Information is needed and must be shared. You can't keep your whereabouts from me. You can't go off on your own like that. It's too dangerous."

Naomi squints her eyes and stares at her Strategist. She walks right past her, brushing against her shoulder. "We were doing recon. We can take care of ourselves. Somebody's gotta do it."

Delilah decides to drop the subject. No dissension in the ranks, not now when they need one another the most. The squad members seem to be at one another's throats, especially Valorian and Xandus. With everyone bickering among themselves, it plays into the plans of their enemies. The fact remains, Naomi doesn't fully trust her. Then a dark thought wafts to her consciousness. What if Naomi is doing something illegal or something Delilah wouldn't approve of? Is Naomi keeping her out of the loop to give her plausible deniability? She prays Naomi isn't involved in any unscrupulous behavior. "Do you think we can find the soul smith of Sinxin's weapons here?"

Naomi nods. "The greatest soul smith in either of the realms has his shoppe here."

"Kromrom," Delilah says.

Naomi ignores the response, pointing down to the ground. They all land far enough from prying eyes. Evnore is drawn into her lion's mask. It hovers for an instant before Naomi snatches it out of the air and places it over her face.

"I feel my talents are best served to empower Naomi," Evnore suggests.

"Yes, we may need the element of surprise," Delilah agrees.

"Back here, I know a way in," whispers Naomi.

"Yop, through the front door," Delilah boldly responds.

Naomi frowns as they hop-fly to the oversized portcullis. She doesn't have a visual on the guards, though signs of activity are heard within.

With a mighty voice, Delilah speaks, "We are angels of the Lord. We are conducting a murder investigation of a protected *charge*. We have authority here to investigate any and all grounds within this territory! It would behoove you to open this gate before I approach it!"

She stalks toward the gate. The demonic lookouts get a good look at the angels. Once they recognize one of them is the Eye-blotter, the armored demons spin wheels and mechanisms to allow them entrance.

"Not wise, Delilah. Better to not alert our presence so soon. Whatever leads that are here could be covered up. Ambushes planned and traps devised," Naomi advises.

"We'll cook this egg with fire, not a microwave," Delilah retorts.

Within the fortified walls of Bloodroot Province are shops of all types. The wares are angelic body parts, human organs, blood, and all types of other forbidden items. One of the largest black markets in the Archfiend.

Another thing the shops have in common are soul slaves. Shopkeepers use condemned souls like a dwarf uses mithril. Demons and other hellions can lease souls for short periods of time—usually up to five millennia. Other shopkeepers lease out the souls for playthings. Delilah crinkles her nose in disgust. The sights, smells, and sounds of tortured souls overwhelm her. Shop owners and their patrons both hide their illegal wares when they catch sight of the angels. They have no time to deal with this problem.

"Where do we start?" Delilah questions.

"Follow me," Naomi responds.

"How do you know?"

Naomi ignores the question and leads Delilah through the twisting streets. The streets glow in a variety of ominous colors. Blacks, purples, and reds are most dominant. Scratching the storm clouds is Castle Bloodroot proper. The placement of the soul well is right behind the fortress and within Bloodroot grounds.

The angels stop as they raise their eyes at a monstrosity off into the distance, in the neighboring sector. Farther in the distance climbing atop a high precipice is a creature that looks like a land-crawling squid. Its multiple eyes scan the castle grounds. Its translucent head houses souls, all congealed together. Is it a food source, or power source?

"Who the what the?" Delilah questions.

Naomi shakes her head. "You don't remember that either?"

"When Lucifer took my memory, the synapses were severed. They are unconnected or crisscrossed," Delilah explains.

"Yeah, you mentioned to me a hundred times," Naomi continues. "Its name is Rahab the Befouler. It was one of Wrath Reign Courtyard's guardian."

No matter how infamous a demon is, its identity and location remains hidden and safe. Kromrom the Shaper won't set up shop on the doorsteps of the black market. Naomi leads them away to an informant. Against Delilah's better judgment, the angels slip into a nearby alley and take the winding back ways to a shack of a shop. The sign above reads "Crawlers in the Squalor."

The angels enter the rickety shop. Customers hear the door open and turn. When they see the angelic police, they excuse themselves abruptly and leave even faster. Jars of essence, jewels, giant germs, insects, and animal parts are all preserved here.

The shopkeeper, Torix, resembles a dark praying mantis in draping robes. He pops up from behind his counter happily. Then whimpers at the sight of the pair. He rubs his claws together, and his large mandibles click, with a healthy dose of obvious fear. "How may I be of service, Deducers? And everything," the insectoid offers.

"Why the rush, Torix?" Naomi replies as she takes a long look around the shop. Probably for things to break.

"I'd hate to waste your time. Surely, you have more important things to do," Torix responds. "And everything."

"All I ever wanted was to come to your shop, and here I am," she responds with sarcasm. "But since you'd rather get right to it, let's then. We're looking for Kromrom the Shaper."

"Kr-kr-Kromrom? The name doesn't ring a bell. And everything."

"The quicker you tell us, the quicker you can get back to your customers," Naomi responds with rising impatience.

Delilah thumbs behind her at the demons gathering at his door. Eager shoppers wanting entrance, but afraid.

"Look, see? All my—most of—some of my permits are valid… and everything," Torix pleads.

"Eye-blotter, this is the cleanest place in this dump. I think we should set up camp here. We can start with this shop. The valid per-

mits should reflect only the items on display. If not, we'll confiscate those items and revoke all licenses and permits. Understood?"
Delilah advises.

"We'll have to be very thorough. This could take decades,"
Naomi adds.

Torix chitters to himself nervously, dry washing his claws. He
closes the shades and beckons them away from prying eyes. They
oblige him.

"Don't tell anyone—"

"Yeah, I know, and everything," Naomi breaks in.

"Kromrom is a recluse. He chooses to work in Bloodroot Sub-
terra. And everything."

"This information better be accurate. I can hold a grudge longer than a fish can swim." Then Naomi steps in close to Torix. "And
when I'm begrudged, I take an eye for an eye," she threatens, satu-
rated with menace. Even Delilah feels a shiver down her spine. "Stay
here."

Torix shakes noticeably while the angels confer in the rear of
the shop.

"Delilah, stay here. I'll be back. Evnore will stay with you,"
Naomi whispers.

"Wherever you're going, we're all going," Delilah corrects.

"We can't trust this guy. I need to confirm this intel."

Delilah becomes angry. "Of course, we can't trust a demon! Why
did we even come here? And who are you confirming this with?"

"If we leave him unguarded, he could warn others of what we're
doing here, where we are, or set a trap. You're safe here. Just make
sure he doesn't do anything stupid."

"Did you forget? Demons already saw us here. They could arrive
any minute," Delilah reminds the Eye-blotter.

Naomi shakes her head. "They won't. They need this shop.
If anything happens to us here, the store will be shut down for a
multitude of license violations. Demons don't want that. What I'm
worried about is an attack once we leave here. I never question your
commands because I trust you. No matter how insane the command
sounds. You've earned my trust. Have I not earned yours?"

Delilah sighs and waves her away. "I'll be fine. Take Evnore with you."

Naomi backs away and hoods herself. A fluorescent light shines in the eyeholes of the lion's mask. The Eye-blotter's armor and wings meld with her surroundings. Black darker than a shade's shadow.

"Don't lose yourself, Delilah," Naomi cautions.

The shadows don't stop there. The darkness encroaches Delilah like a noose. Whispers in the dark become louder. Her heart thumps faster. Her pupils widen in an attempt to absorb every iota of light left.

CHAPTER 7

BLOOD SPAWN

A man enters his apartment, keeping the lights off. The fading light of day peeks through the blinds and windows, trying its best to stave off the impending darkness. He grabs a couple of cold ones from the six-pack he brought with him and takes a seat. No rugs or paintings, just a simple table and a couple of chairs decorate his humble abode. Loud music shakes the thin walls. The wail of sirens passes by his block. The man pulls the tab and takes a swig.

Suddenly, the chair on the other side of the table swivels around. "Welcome home, Cyrus," the invader announces.

The man drops his beer as he jumps up to brandish his blue steel nine millimeter. "Who are you?" he yells.

"Me are friend," the shadowed man replies in a deep voice.

"I have no friends!"

"Me are called Nil. Me and him will be bestest of friends," the shadowed man states. He lights a cigar with his thumb, sitting in a blue-and-gray camo tank top, pants, and combat boots. His face is hidden except for the three-eyed googles he wears as he keeps his thumb lit. Blue reptilian scales are barely visible in the ambient light. He increases the fire to wash the home owner with its glow.

Cyrus is powerfully built, with reddish brown hair. His eyes are so bright they almost seem golden. His teeth are so white they are almost blinding. He wears a dragon T-shirt and jeans. "What do you want? How did you get in? Who sent you?"

Seemingly oblivious to the blue-skinned appearance of Nil, he stomps up to his seated guest and sticks his gun a foot away from the intruder's face.

Nil appears unimpressed. "Me had to track he," he said, laughing at his own joke. "Think about it, if me wanted he dead, he would've been dead…real dead."

Cyrus growls and sticks his gun into Nil's mouth, but the intruder opens wide, then chomps down on the weapon, devouring the gun. He snatches his hand back in time for him to keep his fingers. He falls back, his mouth hinges open in fear and amazement.

Nil licks his claws and burps loudly. "Mmm, blue steel are me's favorite. Iron good for I's blood," he cackles.

"Who are you?" Cyrus demands, trying to keep fear from squeaking into his voice.

"Just think of Nil as him mentor. Nil are here so that him can be all are is. Have a seat."

"I'll stand."

"Me wasn't requesting he."

Cyrus eases into a chair with extreme caution as if he expects the chair to devour him like the intruder did his gun. He pops open a new can of beer and needs to use both hands to keep himself from shaking. Nil chews on a cigar and stares at the can shaking in his hand.

"What is this about? Drugs? Money?" Cyrus guesses.

Nil laughs. "Power, but not earthly power. Them chaos on streets am children play. Like am tarantula catching am gnat. Nothing. No, what me speak of am control over the universe."

"The universe? Who has that kind of power?" Cyrus wonders with curiosity winning over his fear.

"Cyrus does."

A slow smile spreads across his face. He pulls the tab on another beer and takes a swig. He needs to get drunk for any of this to make sense, and more importantly, for his liquid courage to kick in. Too bad he's not even close enough to be even tipsy yet. This guy must be high. Whatever the intruder is on must have affected his brain. Nothing has ever gone his way. He has no family he knows of, and bad luck always follows him. "I hate to ask this, but how do you know I'm the right person?"

He is so enthralled with his visitor that he fails to notice a thick blanket of mist forming beneath him. Cyrus gasps as 3-D images swirl into life above them. Stars, the earth, clouds, all in vivid detail before them. "How did you do that?"

"Me have dominion over are Mist."

"What is the mist?"

"Capital M in Mist, sucker," Nil corrects. "Him not know how to talk?"

Images swirl to show a female demon wielding the Mist to make her arms a meter longer. The female demon has compound eyes like a fly. The Mist wraps around her arms, allowing her to move them as an extension of her own arms.

He pushes himself back into his seat, gripping the arms of the chair in shock and curling his toes in his shoes. "Who is that?" he whispers to Nil.

"Her am Sinxin. Her hire I to find and protect he," Nil answers.

"The Mist is a tool, one could say. However, if we exhaust too much of our allotted pool of vigor, we will be one with the Mist," Sinxin explains.

"What would be wrong with that?"

"If we become one with the Mist, we would have no consciousness, no form, no plans. No demon wants to exist only in the Mist. Almost as bad as being confined to Hell. Not an option. The imprisoned souls that are in Hell are the main source of our power. It fuels our vigor, which enables us to fuel weapons and abilities. Thus, we have the ability to siphon the souls that are condemned to Hell. The more souls that become condemned, the higher our power threshold becomes."

Nil shakes his head in sarcastic sorrow as Sinxin continues, "Unfortunately, drawing from the ultimate soul forge that is Hell causes souls great pain. Like slicing the back off a live pig to make bacon."

The images change to show a multitude of glorious jewels. They are all different sizes, shapes, and colors. Some are jewels within jewels while others have unique glyphs, icons, and symbols within them. From what Cyrus can tell, no two jewels are alike.

"Fetishes allow us to enhance our own innate abilities or give us new powers and abilities altogether. The more fetishes we obtain, the greater our own power and status."

Cyrus's eyes bulge at this female demon's generous cleavage. Then they widen again at her large flylike "locket" with jewels in them. She must be powerful if she wears something so big with that many jewels in them. He thinks back to what she just said. With the realization of Sinxin's words, his pulse quickens as he looks around him. "Demons? Is that what you are?"

"What am him think my was?" Nil takes another pull off his cigar. "A chewawa, a chiwama, a dog?"

He sinks back into his chair in deep thought. "What am I? What does that make me? Human? A demon?"

"Before you can know the present, you must know your past," Sinxin sneers.

Beads of sweat run down Cyrus's face. Fear turns to wonder as the image swirls. He sees what appears to be himself in the images, but with stunning angelic wings. The image stares back as if it senses his presence. He reaches out, and the demon mimics the action. "Who? Is that me?"

"Technically, that is Abbadon. You and he are they," Sinxin explains.

The images reform into a group of angelic beings. The tallest had wonderful gems for skin, and glorious wings. He was having a conversation with three angels. The angel that resembled Cyrus, was the size of NFL defensive end, wearing reddish armor. The next angel was finer than Marilyn Monroe. Her sleepy eyes could hypnotize a striking cobra. The last was a silver-haired angel that exudes confidence. He reminds Cyrus of warrior elf who could smite his foes with either sword or sorcery.

"Master-Commander Lucifer planned to usurp God. Abbadon was his right hand, equivalent to a five-star general. The others are other brilliant commanders under Lucifer's command," Sinxin explains.

"Lucifer? You mean Satan?"

"Now him are catching on."

"Yes," Sinxin agrees with great awe. "Lucifer is the Soul Severer; the Father of Lies; the Great Dragon; the Prince of Darkness—"

"Stifle herself! Her getting excited!"

"Yes, yes. Now where was..." Sinxin checks the images in the Mist. "Ah, the Brain Trust needed more than just itself to be successful."

The collection of angels opened hi-tech scrolls and moved 3-D images around, laying out formations and units.

"This was all prewar consul," she continues. "During the planning, Anura mentioned that to tilt the odds more into Separatists' favor, they would need the help of an extraordinary Strategist. Her name is Delilah."

Delilah's image replaces the Brain Trust. Nil pinches and zooms to enlarge it.

"Delilah? What's so special about her?"

"She was recruited by and trained under Anura who was Chief Strategist in all of Heaven. What do you think would happen when the greatest trains a subordinate equally brilliant with all of Anura's knowledge, power, and love?"

Cyrus speculates, "Ah, I see. They are bound to be at least as successful as their trainer. Optimally, they will be greater."

Sinxin smiles proudly. A glean races across her razor-sharp teeth. "Exactly. Anura saw Delilah's power and potential. Would you rather have one nuclear bomb? Or two? However, when Lucifer and Abbadon approached Delilah, she openly refused. Refused!"

The images darken and tremble. Not just the images but the whole building. Cyrus could hear car alarms blaring off in the distance. Cracks form along his walls. Dogs bark in warning. Did her angry outburst cause the commotion?

Nil pans the scene, showing the expanse of Hell. "This are what am at stake. Hell."

Hell is for real? All manners of torment and torture are here. Tidal waves of hellfire crash on burning souls. Worms burrow and grow within the souls. Fiery pit fiends whip and flay the imprisoned souls like great overlords. In the midst of it all is Cyrus. No, that's not him. It's Abbadon, king of Hell. He remains in chains, though they don't constrict him. The chains hook into his flesh as he drags weighted spiked balls behind him.

He paces his immense domain. Hell heat is razor-sharp flaming wind. It pummels into him with a ferocious appetite for flesh. As the Hell heat washes over the great king, it rips the forever-healing flesh and feathers off his wings. In other word, the pain is never numbed, from the Hell heat and the hooks in his flesh, black blood streams from his body and falls. Here, Nil freezes the image. Thousands of leeches are under his feet, but one albino leech is attached to Abbadon's brow.

"See that?" Sinxin informs the pupil.

"A leech?"

"Licheen. Genetically altered and enhanced leeches from the Archfiend Zone, compliments of Anura," Sinxin explains.

Nil pinches and zooms at the licheen under the drop of blood and hits the playback. The critter absorbs the blood. Nil zooms in on the licheen again and speeds the image. The insect takes an eternal journey through Hell until it enters an undetectable burrow. It squeezes through with just enough room for it not to burst. Once out of the hole, a burgundy-colored crow scoops it in its beak and takes flight.

The crow flies high into the scorched sky. Violet winds push the avian along until it reaches its destination. It enters a vast mountain shrouded in heavy mist. The crow flies through a maze of turns until it enters a small room. The nondescript room of dirt contains a priceless sarcophagus in its center. Ancient engravings adorn the box, which is gem studded around the edges. Two funnels lead through the sarcophagus where the eyes would be.

The licheen crawls out of the crow's beak, entering the funnel. The creature excretes its bloody contents. This particular time, the sarcophagus explodes. The last image viewed is of a man that resembles Abbadon, screaming and flying at full speed through the mountainside...*flying!*

Cyrus gapes at the frozen image of what looks exactly like him. He reaches for the image, shaking. After a few moments, he slumps back into his chair, utterly confused. There is no memory of his youth or his adulthood. He thinks back on what his earliest memory of, and it is of him waking up in an alley. He has always thought he was hit on the head and robbed. Blood was all over his body. He assumed it was blood, but it couldn't be because it was black, nor did he have any wounds. He assumed he suffered from some form of amnesia and figured he would never know his past. So he found himself in a shelter, but he got robbed there and has been on his own ever since. Ironic that he knows more about his past now than his present.

"As you can see, Master Lucifer has a vested interest in your development," Sinxin continues.

"What the hell am I?"

"Exactly!" Sinxin yells. "You are a blood spawn. This was all Anura's plan, the Archfiend's overlord Strategist. It took six millennia to siphon enough of Abbadon's blood to become the skin that is draped over your bones right now, and that was the easy part. Your memory, the use of your vigor, and powers are the hardest. You are still incomplete yet formidable. The process was aborted once you became Aware, and now that you are, it pushed our timeline up considerably. We had to manipulate millions of demons to distract angels. We couldn't afford to have them discover you."

Cyrus rubs his temples, trying to ward off his throbbing headache. Too much to process. Then he raises his eyes and sits up with a new intensity. "I am a god, and you are my subordinates," he states with vehemence.

A sneaky smile spreads over Nil's face as he wags his finger. Both the blue demon and the fly-eyed demon laugh—dissolving any power he thought he had.

"Having a knife doesn't make you an assassin. You won't convince anyone that you are Abbadon incarnate if Nil can't unleash your power," Sinxin's explains.

"So why take over Heaven? What's the point?" Cyrus questions.

"The point was to give angels, humans, and civilization freedom."

"Freedom? This is America. We're already free."

Sinxin scoffs. "God's commandments restrict freedom. Thou shall not…Why not? It's a way for him to exercise control, not protect mankind. True power is given to the death wielder," she explains. "To those who control the instruments of fear. To take a man's life and control his destiny or to end it. To watch a being's soul bleed is intoxicating. To feel an angel's blood pulse as it is defeated is exhilarating. Absolute power is given to the one who can control a man through fear and death. When Nil swirled around in this chair and ate your gun, you feared and respected him. Nearly every action movie and book depicts this. Everyone wants notoriety and power. What is one willing to do to obtain it? Make friends? Hardly. Any true system can only have fear and death at its core. Even God says, 'The fear of God is the beginning of knowledge.' Why didn't he choose love?"

Nil takes another pull and chews on his cigar, allowing the smoke to escape through his nose and mouth. Cyrus rubs his hands through his hair. As incredulous as this story seems, it resonates a core truth. As the truth presents itself, he visualizes it. His soul confirms every word said. The truth is as tangible as the can of beer in his hand. "I mean, how can this work? The police are everywhere. They caught me a few times. Aren't you all losing?"

Sinxin and Nil both laugh again at the spawn. He switches his gaze back and forth between them, confused. Then he shrugs his shoulders.

"Him think polices are winning? Ha! They're not even the problem! Angels am the nuiz, nuassance. Angels are the problem!"

"Think about this: there is division among countries, cities, races, even family. Humans can't accomplish anything. Angels and humans can't organize anything with a house divided, but on the other hand we have sex, drugs, money, and power. Those are all directives that Satan wanted executed. Which do you think is more successful? Would you rather have a pocket full of money or a sack full of faith?"

"So the freedom you speak of is true freedom! Freedom from persecution, freedom to do what you will. Freedom to control a man's destiny!" Cyrus says with understanding.

"Yes, yes! As Lord Lucifer demands, 'Indulge thyself!' God puts all these rules and regulations on angel kind. In turn, it shifted to mankind."

"So what went wrong?"

The images show Lucifer rising above the throne of God, pointing his finger. Most every angel is in attendance. Most are angry themselves—fired up from Lucifer's boosting of their morale. A roaring shout is heard from the mutineers. They shout their anger and displeasure—snarling and cussing. They point and yell. God wears plate mail armor, watching the angelic uprising with anger.

Then a mighty yell is heard. Abbadon shoves through his fellow insurrectionists and breaks rank. Like a flash of lightning, he charges God with a monstrous two-handed sword. He flies before any can react or assist. Most importantly, he initiated an unauthorized offense before Anura's plan could be implemented. "Damn you, God! God, damn you!" he bellows.

"No, Abbadon!" Lucifer yells.

It is too late. Hearing the curse from Abbadon's mouth, God roars his anger back. "Do not use My name in vain!"

Lucifer fails to signal for the attack to begin before Abbadon is in God's face. With a surging overhead strike, he cleaves the very air in half. Everyone in attendance is sure he will succeed, but a hair on God's head shatters the sword, and Abbadon is frozen by His glare.

Abbadon, the leader of Alpha Strike squad; Abbadon the Angry; Abbadon the Demigod, now Abbadon, the first occupant of Hell. Ebon chains punch through the firmament and envelope him like a mummy's wrappings. The chains hook, then sear into his flesh like a brand. The chains crush his bones – then he crashes from Heaven and through the earth. Mountains collapse in on him, like a mega earthquake. Trees topple over; the ground is cracked asunder. He continues to crash through layers of bedrock and magma into a fiery abyss. He lands into a lake of fire. His flesh melts, his eyes burst, and his bones fuse together. His body floats to the top of the fiery lake, then sinks.

God reaches high into a neighboring galaxy and scoops a handful of stars. "You are cursed, Abbadon! You are condemned to the Abyss."

He tosses the stars into the angelic mutineers. All angels who are spitting and pointing at God cover their faces in shock and shame. Some even beg for mercy, but it is too late. The stars crash into the main Host. Those who side with God are spared, and the stars pass harmlessly through them. Those that are loyal to Lucifer, however, are attracted to the stars like magnets. They are gathered helplessly to the stars as they speed toward the earth—falling like meteors. The heavenly shower bombards earth, breaking up the Pangea into continents. Others crash into the vast oceans. Here, Nil freezes the scene.

"The first complication was that Abbadon lost his composure," Sinxin explains. "His anger cost us our initiative, our coordinated attack."

Sinxin exits the image and stretches directly into Cyrus's face. He shrinks back into his chair, turning his head.

"The rebellion did not get a chance to execute our battle plans," she continues. "Delilah was the second problem. She would not convert. We Separatists believe if we can either persuade or capture Delilah, then we can usurp God."

"You're trying again?"

"Yes, and you will join us! Our other primary goal is to free Abbadon and the rest of the demonic hordes. But you must learn quickly."

"Won't God just stop it again?"

A knowing smile creeps across Sinxin's face. Cyrus shudders at her confidence, lowering his eyes.

"We haven't revealed our full plan to you, Spawn. Let us worry about the particulars."

Cyrus raises his eyes. "What do I do?"

Nil smiles a crooked grin. His eyes aglow as he drums his fingers together. "To lead, him must follow."

CHAPTER 8

A WORTHY FOE

Naomi stands before a staircase that crisscrosses underneath another set of stairs. Each time she comes to the Matrix of Madness, it conforms to a different "template." In the Archfiend Zone, the laws of physics takes a seat where even the bizarre seems reasonable. Within the Matrix of Madness, insanity converges with the preposterous. Twirling blades dart in at every angle. The walls drip some slick ooze, or is that demon's blood? Whispers echo unnaturally as ghostly apparitions moan in her ear.

The master…they must hurry and find the master. She squints to peer through the darkness. With the assistance of Evnore and her mask, her vision is enhanced…there.

Below, a black figure can be seen in the pit. Blacker than the shadow that envelopes this realm of lunacy. A path lights before her as she treks toward him. In fact, the path seems to emanate from the landlord himself. The path pulsates as if connected to his life-blood. More than likely, he's using his vigor. The Matrix of Madness is Mazck's dwelling ground—his piece of property in the Archfiend. The greater shadow demon waits in the depths of his keep. She and Mazck spiral toward each other down a crumbling stairway.

Each step she takes extinguishes the path behind her. Ghastly hands grab at her ankles. Naomi feels Evnore's vigor-enhanced courage surge throughout her. She'll need it here. Phantoms whiz past her in an attempt to knock her off the steps. Naomi deftly sidesteps the monstrosities as they dart and dash and peel their skin back to reveal their hideous skulls. Ear-piercing screams emit from them. They scratch and tear out their eyes, trying to ease some unknown pain that won't relent. Disembodied heads float around the angels. The mouths whisper obscenities and scream atrocities.

The creatures that are attempting to scare her are prisoners themselves. Demons that tried to conquer Mazck's realm or perhaps angels that tried to apprehend him in his domain. Once they lose their minds, they become pawns and guardians of the matrix. To show fear here would trap her in the matrix for all of eternity. She refuses to be his eternal puppet—his concubine. With only a slight gesture from him, he could call forth a thousand of his imprisoned souls to do his bidding. They stop five meters away from one another.

"How may I be of service?" Mazck's raspy voice asks. "Seems like yesterday. Actually, it was."

"I will never understand why you dwell in this madness."

"Home is where the heart abides," the demon says. As if in answer, tendrils of darkness stream away from his body. The shadow about his skull pulls away revealing his once-beautiful teeth—now yellow and crooked. The inside of his mouth glows the same red light as his eyes. "So should I continue to help you? Should I report you to my master? Will you ever love me?"

"I can answer that last question," Naomi responds.

"You deny it now. It wasn't always so."

"We all made our mistakes. I repented; you didn't."

"Well, Naomi. You were…very persuasive."

Thinking back, she was very persuasive. He gave in way too fast. She believed Mazck was the most honorable angel in Heaven. Even looking at him reminds her of the handsome features that once belonged to him. He didn't have eyes like most angels. He had actual nebulae the colors of deep purple, blue, and pink that swirled as his orbs. He was both courageous and wise. She once adored the being that stands before her.

She reflects on so many instances where he showed mercy to the undeserving humans. Always worked overtime to help the unassigned souls and keep them safe. Anything in his power to help humanity, he was there. The most important being he was unable to save was himself. His Fall was complete. How did he come to be this blotch of absurdity? Mazck just said it; she was persuasive.

The structure shifts as walls of brick reform to other parts of the keep, creating a new construct. The stairs that spiral in the center of the tower are now along the wall.

"Gjestice—"

Mazck billows himself with air, expanding his chest like a puffer fish. "Never call me that name! This is your last warning!" he roars.

Her eyes soften for a fraction of a second. How the mighty Fall. "You never say it. Why won't you say it?"

Mazck shushes her, touching his finger to where his lips would be. Only black gums and yellow teeth are visible. Large floating eyes—red with anger—fall into an orbit around Naomi. With a casual wave of the greater shadow demon's hand, the floating eyes roam to another corner of the matrix.

"Then I'll say it. You still had a choice, Mazck. You didn't have to join the usurpers. I won't continue to carry that guilt with me."

"I never asked you to," Mazck agrees. "You're right. Back then, you weren't always the Eye-blotter. You cared much for other's opinions. Is this why you neglected to call out to me and stand firm against the rebellion? It was my choice—and I will live and die with it."

"How…how did you know?" Naomi replies in surprise. It was she who approached Mazck—then known as Gjestice. Fortunately, the couple could date because they belonged to separate squadrons. However, he put duty before desire. Their relationship took on an extremely slow arc.

When Naomi was approached by Lucifer's representative all those eons ago she couldn't wait to share the news with her love. She caught up with him and hugged him tight, bubbling with excitement. "I'm telling you, we should do it! We should join Lucifer! He promises us everything. Enough with our boring existence. Our lives should have meaning, excitement! Not a future of babysitting."

The anticipation from Gjestice's gaze dropped as his eyes narrowed. A shocked gasp escaped his mouth. "Resistance? Against

God?" he whispered. "I can't believe you're even considering this! You know I would follow you to Andromeda and back, but this? This is a battle we can't win!"

"We can win, but only if everyone is on board! We must act now! Lucifer has promised us our own territories. We can be royalty. Conquerors!"

He grabbed Naomi by the arm and pulled her away.

She yanked her arm free, speaking with boldness. "What about us? When will it be our time? Even though we're from different squads, there are still regs that must be adhered to for us to date. Mandatory counseling, our squads are unable to have joint exercises or missions. We must submit a letter of intent! How absurd! Shouldn't it be our choice? God took the natural out of our relationship. We need a change in leadership and direction!"

"We'll do as we're told! God wants the best for us. Our intentions must be pure. To condemn us from having joint missions, prevents us from losing our composure if one of us is under attack! We can't do this!"

"It's idiotic for him to forbid us from having joint missions! Much less all the other stipulations!"

"Watch your tongue!" Then Gjestice took a deep breath. He relaxed, trying to keep anger away from his voice. "Naomi, I understand why we can't have joint missions. If I were there and anything happened to you, I'd forego the mission and seek destruction and vengeance! I don't know what would become of me if anyone injured you."

Naomi's eyes softened. She reached around his waist and kissed his neck. "Nothing would ever happen if you were there to assist me," she countered.

Gjestice kissed her on the forehead. "You do bring up a good point. I still have my doubts, but what's the worst that could happen?"

She raised her eyes to meet his. "Then let's get started! I'll make the proper notifications."

Her first recruit. She was so relieved. It would be much easier to get others to join if the "Valiant Knight," as most angels called him, was on board. She stared at his sad swirling eyes as they followed Naomi through the clouds. He'll get over it. Success cures all doubt.

On the night of the raid, all angels were in attendance—filled with curiosity and suspense. However, she thought back on what Gjestice said. Maybe, maybe he was right. The more she pondered about treason, the more doubt flooded her mind. The mutineers surged toward God's throne while she fell back. Guilt washed over her. Just ahead of her, she could see Gjestice and her other recruits as they followed the mob. Curses, battle chants, and shouts drowned out all other sound.

Naomi was afraid and embarrassed. She dared not utter his name for fear of attack from the mutineers. She would be labeled a traitor to Lucifer even before the rebellion truly began.

She allowed the swarm to pass around her. She grabbed her chest—filled with sorrow, fear, and absolute terror. She sweated profusely; her hands shook with a nervousness she had never felt before. Despite her panic attack and the bobbing of heads the Host made as they surrounded God, she was able to keep track of Gjestice. Why didn't he look for her? Was he so caught up in rage that he forgot about her?

Just then, he indeed turned around. He searched frantically for Naomi. Ultimately, when his swirling orbs met hers, she was full of shame and doubt. A questioning look appeared on his face. She opened her mouth to yell for him to come back to her, and damn, everyone else. If they were captured by the rebels, then at least they'd be together. Just as she shouted out to the Valiant Knight, the sky cracked, and Heaven was ablaze. She saw it all as his flesh was ripped from his skeleton. He was burnt by the blaze of falling stars. Black flames erupted from his bones. She shut her eyes from the horror. She shouted his name and wept for his condemned soul. He was gone now—forever and always. The love of her eternal existence crashed through the clouds as he and millions of others bombarded the earth like a meteor shower.

Her thoughts of her former lover fade as she gazes at the greater shadow demon walking the steps before her. In retrospect, she realizes that those black flames cool against Mazck's body. They form the pliable shadows that he control now. She is certain those shadow flames burn his flesh for all eternity. The blistering heat will never subside nor extinguish to give him relief. She is thankful for Evnore's lion mask as it hides her guilt-ridden tears.

"I idolized you. You instilled both honor and duty in the Virtuous Culture. I wanted you to talk me out of the rebellion. I needed you to. You were the one to give me a reason to choose the right side…to tell me we can make it together. To be honest, the whole time…I was confused."

Mazck's mouth contorts with confusion and pain. He grabs the sides of his head in anguish, then tears at the shadowy skin that is about his face. His head stretches as it spins around his neck. Wild shadow tentacles flail about his body—grabbing and crushing anything that gets within its grasp. He grits his teeth until a loud crack is heard. Heavy breathing inflates and deflates his skeletal chest. Finally, a guttural roar emits from his mouth. A section of his keep explodes, only to reform in mere moments. "No. No! NO!"

The trapped ghosts spiral away from Mazck in fear. His scowl washes over Naomi in pure rage. She slides one foot back and leans forward. She crosses her arms in front of her to grab the hilts of her silver-steel swords at her waist. He enlarges his fists and bangs them on the ground, causing tremors in his keep. Evnore's helm glows—pumping Naomi with courage and calm.

"Why do you tell me this now? My entire existence is because of your indecision? Because you wanted me to coax you like some child?" He flings away bits of his shadow skin. "This form I abide in is because you wanted to be pampered? Leave me!"

"Be brave, Oather. I am with you," Evnore's comforting voice says.

"I won't feel sorry for you, demon. I risked humiliation from Nameer and persecution from the Virtuous Culture to capture his fetish and free you from his bondage. I risk everything to be here. I'll not leave until I get what I came for," Naomi retorts.

The demon wraps his arms around himself. Steam releases from his shadow form. The red pinpricks of light that are his eyes bore into Naomi. Focusing on her seems to calm him. Long moments pass before he speaks. "What do you need?"

They pinwheel closer.

"Why didn't you tell me about the assassination? For you not to give me important intelligence like that must mean you are working for a higher authority. Who?" Naomi demands.

"I still cannot reveal my master to you," Mazck states calmly.

"Cannot, or will not?"

"The true objective of the distraction was only told to a very select few! I won't be much help to you if I'm branded a traitor and demoted, or worst, imprisoned!"

"Name them!"

"I cannot," he answers. He reaches out an arm to hold her hand.

She snatches back and holds her hand against her breast.

He frowns in fury. "Naomi, how long will you make me wait? The only reason I share information with you is because of my love for you."

"That's an oxymoron. A demon in love…just shut up. You are in the right place because that is madness. If anyone saw me with you, it could be reported as treason. This you know. Because we were *kameraads* before the Fall—"

"You are in love with me?" Mazck finishes.

They stop in front of each other. His blanket of shadow reaches out toward her but is repelled.

"I pity you," she corrects.

Mazck gathers his darkness and fills himself with shadow, enlarging his mass. Chaos forms within this pocket of reality. Steps begin to crumble about. The wind charges in anger. The clouds flash. Dark shapes are seen within that loom and lean toward Naomi. She receives more assistance from Evnore in the form of vigor.

"Pity me? Pity me not! It is I who belong here! You belong with me! Leave now, or you won't be able to!" he bellows.

"Thanks for the talk. If you are of no use to me, then this will be our last," she threatens.

Mazck calms as he watches Naomi back away from him. The darkness diminishes. His skinless face is seen again. Phantoms back away, and Mazck's keep stabilizes. "Wait. I do have that other information that you requested."

He gestures to a brighter corner of his madness and offers her a seat. A spotless space in the center of the former lovers appears. Probably the cleanest area in the Archfiend. A simple rose is the centerpiece and two chairs facing each other. A table for two.

CHAPTER 9

ANURA THE CONNIVER

Anura the Beautiful, known as one of the fairest of all angels—who no longer art in Heaven—now takes the form of a toad demon. Seated on her throne covered with ivy, lily pads, and moss, she croaks to the sky. Her large pupils are star shaped. Her lavender hues and orange patterns cover her skin. Her toothless mouth crumples into a frown, like a sock puppet. Straps and buckles along the sides of her armor hold her bulbous shape together. Different types of gadgets and technological devices on her straps and bandolier are placed within reach of her sticky digits.

She maintains her own domain in the Archfiend Zone. Most castles in the Archfiend construct their dwellings to emulate death, skulls, and other aspects of fear. Anura's vision differs. She bestowed her fortress as the Nexlore Nodule—which conveys her idea of modern beauty. A futuristic fortress with a unique blend of freaks of nature and wild science.

Many of her accomplishments from genetic experiments are forever frozen in her inner sanctum. Most notable are the goblinoids she created from splicing chimpanzees with imps. A chimp's ability to use tools along with their high intelligence and dexterity blended well with imps. The result yielded far more obedient hatchlings, who were less mischievous and less aggressive. She needed not give an order a dozen times, nor was she needed to supervise every aspect of an experiment. The goblinoids were a complete success. They were capable of overseeing the mass production of eye vermin and skull spiders. After all, she must supply the demonic demands.

Her towers resemble shards of jagged glass and mirrors. These towers are maneuverable to capture the dance of lightning and the blood-red moon. Oh, how she loves to watch the lightning. The bolt pulses with life, power, and destruction; it scratches the sky and scorches the ground in hot rage. How the lightning reminds her of her lost love.

Greenery has a place in the Archfiend Zone too, she would argue. Not sunflowers or roses, but ghost plants, doll eyes, and thorns. Red-colored peat moss cushions her courtyards. Living vines slither and sway around her throne room. It is costly to smuggle nature into the Archfiend Zone, but worth every piece of silver to Anura. The Nexlore resides on the highest piece of flat land in the Archfiend Zone—with a clear vantage point of the scorched sky.

Suddenly, a large flame erupts onto her forearm. She covers the conflagration with her four-digit hand. She resists the urge to show pain or weakness in front of her subordinates. "Hellfrost!" she yells.

One of her goblinoids scrambles away to obey her command. Her vision melts as her mind drifts to her fall all those millennia ago. She starts from the exact moment when everything went wrong. When Lucifer and Ikrlez came to see her. Lucifer called his talks of persuasion "enlightenment."

The elegant and stately Lucifer was the most beautiful being ever created. Ever. Stars for eyes and jewels for skin. Silk for hair and pearls for teeth. His voice was as pure as chimes through a soft breeze, wrapped in thunder. He had the respect and adoration of every angel. Male angels wanted to be him; female angels wanted more. When he and the silver-haired angel, Ikrlez, approached her, she was sore afraid.

Anura was in the midst of a deep forest. A crescent moon shone through the copse of trees. Night critters crept about in near silence. In the cover of night, she experimented with runes that she created in a small clearing. She etched a rune into the air and empowered it with a portion of her vigor. It hung there as if pinned to an air mole-cule. She filled it with negative energy and threw it.

The rune sought the closest life-form and found a human hunter and slammed into him with the force of a hammer. He crumpled and writhed on the ground. The hunter's skin decayed as he shrieked. No it was his soul that shrieked, for death came to his body far too quickly and unexpected. A death wail—agony and suffering were in that rune. His blood dried up until nothing was left except his skeleton. The skeleton aged and yellowed. Anura smiled, for she just learned control over life. Her experiment was a success.

She etched another symbol of power into the air—filled to the brim with vigor. Much experimentation went into this rune, which took decades to perfect. She tossed the rune at the hunter's skeleton. The rune burst into green flames that floated above the corpse, then suddenly drilled into the bones. Everywhere the flames embedded itself into the bones, and glowed with an ominous light. Anura waited anxiously for long moments believing her experiment had failed. Seconds turned into more seconds before his bones creaked. The hunter-skeleton arched his back and lurched to his feet. The howl his physical body was unable to expel, finally caught up to the undead being that stood before her. His eyes glowed with a green light. He gasped and moaned in excruciating pain. He approached her as if heavy and weary, but the skeletal hunter stood before its master. Anura yelped with glee. She learned power over death. Now the recently deceased can live on. They could become protectors of a forest, or an ever-present vigil for a town. It would make the job of an angel easier.

Now for another. She wrote another rune that was fused with elements of fire. Each part of this glowing rune represented her only living embodiment of oxygen, heat, and fuel. She had searched the vast Heavens for a minuscule sample of each of the living beings in its purest form. She expanded its power and condensed its size. Now the being was a concentrated form of a living inferno. The longer the blaze "lived," the more apparent its humanoid features were—taking muscular definition from the male species. When she combined its elements, she asked him what he was called. He responded Ifreet.

She pushed the inferno glyph toward a tree, and he caught fire. The fire shot up fast, as Ifreet spread to the tree's branches and limbs.

He engulfed its leaves and danced to trees and other greenery mischievously. She couldn't help but smile at her "child." Soon, the whole forest was engulfed in flames. After reviewing the results of her experiment, there are better ways to protect the people of this land. This forest can be a barrier. If the inhabitants believed that the forest was haunted, it would create a natural boundary for warring factions. Humans would leave their neighbors to live in peace. It would relieve angels from duty, and allow them to concentrate their efforts elsewhere. She can protect the wildlife as well. If humans believed the forest was haunted, their superstitions would make them believe the animals were sacred or cursed. Creatures would be free to roam without fear of trespassing humans. As the fire spread and the smoke rose, she felt a powerful presence approach her—and clapping.

"Beautiful. Beautiful! So this is what you've been up to," Lucifer said.

"Master-Commander, I didn't know I had been summoned! I saw the great fire from afar and thought to contain—"

"Spare the lies, Anura. We've been watching you for a while," Ikrlez replied.

Ikrlez was the *kameraad* of her beloved Xandus and her subordinate. Though one couldn't tell that from his demeanor. Hidden in his slender frame, he was strong and confident. His grin—permanently etched upon his face. Ikrlez's blazing orange eyes squinted as he gazed upon Anura. Because of those striking orbs for eyes, many who feared and respected the powerful angel called him Noviris. He didn't just gaze; he analyzed her.

Lucifer held out a hand—silencing the sun-eyed angel. The forest flames of Ifreet flickered and danced as a reflection in his eyes. Though he inhaled deeply, his chest barely expanded. The consuming forest fire was stripped off the trees, limbs, leaves, and even the floating ash. It all streamed right toward them. The flames joined together to create one enormous inferno. The conflagration roared like a suffering dragon. Anura dropped to the ground as did Ikrlez. Lucifer slurped the fire like spaghetti. The full blaze streamed into his mouth, every ember.

Once the last char entered his mouth, he snapped his mouth shut. The fire wasn't extinguished, no. Ifreet lived and thrived in his mouth, without scorching his skin or innards. Anura didn't realize that she was trembling. Her knees knocked, and her body sweated. Not from the heat, but of fear. Both subordinates stayed on their knees.

Each word he spoke thereafter had the power of the inferno behind it. "I've watched you, Chief Strategist," Lucifer's bass-enhanced voice began. Flames backlit his intense gaze. "I know the desires of your heart. I know the aims of your goals. You wish to be free. Free to choose and destroy. To experiment, to toy. The world could be your plaything. Decimate whole civilizations if you wish! Have them worship you, if you so please. No sneaking about like a petty thief!"

Flames stretched out of his mouth as if trying to escape. Ifreet was a prisoner of his orifice. He clinched his jaws biting into the conflagration like so much jerky—causing the blaze to withdraw back into his mouth as it looped around his tongue. "You hold a high position now. With me, your place would be higher. I can grant you power beyond your imagination. Fulfill dreams that only your brilliant mind can conjure and achieve."

The power of Ifreet sat behind his irises. Her child. She dared to lift her head a half a centimeter to peek. Ikrlez stayed crouched as well.

Anura, still on her knees, felt his eyes burn through her mind. Anura grabbed a fistful of dirt in an attempt to quell her nerves. "I cannot, Master. God would hold me tragically responsible just for the thought," she answered with caution.

"If that were so, you would already be punished! Where is thy God? You are in danger of judgment now, Anura. Could you not use His assistance now? He'd be here now if that were so! He cares not for what you do! If this were true, He would have come to the aid of the fleshling you just destroyed! You killed him because you possessed the power to. You destroyed life with no regard to the circumstances. I have no problem with your choice. It's your prerogative, but I know your thoughts as I know the oxygen in this flame's lungs," Lucifer declared.

Smoke escaped from his nostrils as he stalked toward Anura. He brushed his finger along her cheeks. Her skin cracked into pieces like baked clay. He opened his mouth—giving the blaze freedom. The flame roared as he reached for Anura's silken skin. He screamed like a ghost chasing a child. Her creation betrayed her without a second thought—as if he could resist. Ifreet screeched like a harpy for the kill.

Lucifer held his palm open to Anura—freezing the flame once again. "It is, of course, your choice. I would never want to be accused of persuasive tactics to coerce you to our side, dear Anura. For now, I will take your first answer. Therefore, as Master-Commander of Heaven and its Sovereign Host, I must use my authority to punish the death of life. For unauthorized and abhorrent experimentation, and for vandalizing this peaceful forest; I furthermore confiscate this elemental being named Ifreet as my subordinate! Anura, guilty or innocent?" he asked.

"I'm innocent! You don't understand!" she begged. "Please!"

The flames were freed again washing over her face. Her eyes popped. She was unable to scream as her larynx melted—then her entire body. The blaze washed over her and ripped away flesh like a skinning blade. Her blood boiled and her veins melted. Her organs burst and her tongue shriveled. The flames broke through her bones, singed her marrow, and fused her to the ground. Anura's voiceless scream echoed in her mind a million times. It mingled with the echoes of Lucifer's laughter. Or was it the fire? Both.

"I beg thee. Please give me your final answer now. Speak now, for death and life is in the power of the tongue!" Lucifer yelled through the laughter.

Her thoughts snap back to the present while her mental anguish turns into an audible and agonizing croak. Her minions crowd around her throne, cowering in fear. Mock concern on their faces. She fans them away with a wave of her hand, breathing heavily. Sweat pours down her face. She can still feel Ifreet sometimes, like now. It was the first time she actually experienced pain—pain that doesn't spring from the heart, that is.

The memory of her "coercion" depresses her. Her decision was both advantageous and unfortunate. She slumps into her chair thinking of Xandus. Where was he when she needed him most? Lounging on a stupid cloud form more than likely. Despite his failure or concern over Anura's well-being, her heart belongs to him still, though she is still irate at his unwillingness to join the Separatists. She will never understand why he didn't sacrifice all to be with her, like she did for him. Her thoughts haunt her, pondering if things would be like this, even had he joined them. Did he not feel the same way?

The goblinoid runs full speed to its mistress. The large container it carries freezes rapidly. Out of breath, it bends low and offers Anura a shard of Hellfrost. She gazes at the goblinoid while its knee remains bent and head low. Anura could take the shard before it freezes into one of her many statues on eternal display, but misery does love company.

The frozen flame etches up the sides of its container to the intricate handle. The poor critter murmurs with panic. Then its fingers are frozen through. It screams silently but continues to hold the container. When the frozen flame reaches halfway up its arm, Anura takes the container—its frozen appendages along with it. It bows humbly. Shards of its digits and bone break off from the goblin and the container to litter the ground.

"Clean it up!" she yells.

A mass of goblinoids rush to keep her floor spotless. She gazes at the beautiful shard. The cold flame within it moves like a seductive dancer. She rubs the shard along her face and arms. It feels so good to cool the fire. It seems as if it is the only thing that yields relief from Ifreet's torture. Why won't it speak to her anymore? She will need more Hellfrost soon.

After rubbing the fragment on her skin, she again stares at it. The flame within it becomes a thunder cloud surrounding a lightning bolt. Anura tilts her head to the side in confusion. She shakes the shard and looks again. Was she imagining things? She was, but how could she forget the ever powerful natural phenomenon of lightning? Yes, she remembers. Thanks to the vile and vindictive God, she'll always remember the last conversation she had with Xandus.

He reclined underneath a fluffy cloud, watching the sun in the distance. He chewed his lightning blade like it was a toothpick. She loved how the sparks tickled her face. He sensed her presence and popped through the top of the cloud. He stretched his hand to her—assisting her landing.

"I thought you'd be here, my spark," Anura said.

"You know me all too well."

"Have you given Lucifer's offer much thought?"

"Of course! It's idiotic!"

Anura's face was full of hot anger. She tossed Xandus a scowl that would make a bear sit and stay. "What? You're not joining the rebellion?"

"You are? Anura, not you too? You're Chief Strategist!"

"That's why this will work!" Anura yelled back. She dropped his hands and turned her back to him. She took a deep breath and calmed herself. She turned back to him, grabbed his hands, and kissed them.

Xandus's anger melted like the spring thaw. She rubbed her fingers along his cheeks, then his neck. A breeze passed by, pushing one of her wavy bangs into her face. He moved the lock behind her ear. Reluctantly, she pulled away, ready to take flight.

His pained face made her heart simmer. His eyes had a tear screaming to rush down his face. "Don't go, my blossom," he pleaded.

"Why not?" she asked. "This is exactly what I mean, my spark. *Kameraads* are forbidden to date within the same squad, but aren't we stronger together? Our teamwork got us this far. It got me this promotion! Why would God not want us to mate? It's cruel and unusual punishment! What could stop us? What can separate us? It's ridiculous that we have to hide our relationship…our feelings."

Anura stepped closer to Xandus. They both regarded the constellation of stars that was close enough for him to hit with a stick. He twirled a long lock of her hair with his fingers.

She hugged him tight and kissed him gently on the neck. "Our love. You are the reason why I joined the rebellion. You are why this must work. I will love you forever. Our relationship means that much to me. Does it not to you?"

The toad demon forces her thoughts to her current concerns. Though a thousand times, her last question to Xandus echoed in her mind. He never did answer her. With a wave of her hand, multiple displays wink into existence. With her froglike digits, she searches many provinces and landscapes. She learned to fine-tune her monitors to search the sky for high concentrations of electrons. Her scrying only works when he is in the Archfiend or in the Natural World of earth.

Therein lies Xandus. She enlarges his image to stretch across all the monitors. He made it to the Swamp of Orrs. Just thinking of him makes her blush. She doesn't recall standing. She steadies herself before taking a seat on a throne of gold, glass, and grass. However, this isn't her throne room. Anura looks around in confusion. Now she dwells within her personal quarters. How long had she been in here?

Hands cover Anura's eyes. She croaks in shock and surprise.

"Guess who?" the voice of Xandus asks.

Anura removes the hands from her eyes and turns around. "My spark! It's been over ten thousand years since we've seen each other! What are you doing here?" she croaks.

"To see you, of course," Xandus explains. "Why haven't you come back to me? Are you still angry? I will do anything you ask as long as we're together."

"Join me, my love," Anura begs. She steps closer, wrapping her arms around him.

"I cannot, my heart. I am duty-bound. I can do anything but that. I can't leave my *charge*," Xandus explains as he turns to leave.

"NO! Don't go! Your *charge* can't be more important than our love!" Anura yells.

"Ugly thing, I found someone else to love. It was never you," Xandus says as he disappears from view.

"Ugly? I-I'm not!" she yells in confusion. Why did he say she was ugly? She's the fairest of them all. Anura rushes to one of the many mirrors she owns in her castle. Yes, still beautiful. Then her eyes widen. She cranes her neck to get a closer look in the mirror. She pulls the skin down from her cheekbones for a better look. Spots? Anura only sees minor imperfections. "NO!" she screams. "Moles!"

She bashes the mirror multiple times, then stares at the ground in sorrow. The mirror mends itself as she steps away. Even minor imperfections are unacceptable. She whirls back to the mirror and rubs an area of her face hard. After moments with no success, she grabs her sides and drops to her knees. Xandus won't accept her like this. Everything was more important to him than her. His stupid *charge*. If he didn't have any fleshlings to protect, then he would come to her. She will eradicate them all. He must know she'll do anything to have him back. Then he would know that she won't let anything stand in their way. He would join them, and they could rule the Archfiend Zone together.

What did he say? His heart no longer beats for her? How could a low-class strumpet take her place? She was the greatest of angels and the mightiest of demons. Surely, he must acknowledge her beauty and power. Yet he said, "It was never you." Of course. Delilah, the filthy whore. Anura paces back and forth in her laboratory. She doesn't remember walking to her lab. Time keeps slipping by her.

There are four things that dominate her mind: Delilah's treachery, Xandus's love, Delilah's *enode*, and Xandus's love. She will never forgive Delilah for betraying her. She gave her budding pupil recommendations for promotions and mentored her. Anura will never trust another again. She will strip the knowledge she has from her mind like Lucifer once did. Yes. Anura starts to fling tables and her experiments against the wall and ceiling. Her vocal sac enlarges; then she emits a great croak. She hops in an uncontrollable rage.

Then something, someone, grabs Anura's attention. Her eye moves the full circuit of her bulbous head. She watches as a figure emerges from the deepest shadows of her lab. The figure's face, shadowed by a hooded cloak. A reflection catches her eye. The clasp that closes a thick cloak. An insignia of a fanged silkworm coiled through the eyelets of a skull.

The mercenary goes by the name of sSylk. He swaggers to a nearby table and leans. Many of her experiments are destroyed. Though she stopped before destroying the table that contains

Delilah's *enode*. No experiment takes as much time as this *enode*. Anura takes deep croaks. She was honored when Lucifer gave her this crystalized piece of Delilah's mind and consciousness. She hoped to extract information from it. The frag isn't just a rock – it's alive and intelligent – a part of Delilah's brain dwells within, as much a prisoner as it is protected by the facets.

Anura knew it all along. Xandus and Delilah loved each other. Sure, he tells Anura that duty is the reason that they can't be together, but she's no fool. She was once Chief Strategist. She had noticed the sideway glances that they gave each other. Though Delilah has become strong. A scientist, Strategist, fighter, philosopher, dreamer. Everything Anura was. Maybe she should be honored that Delilah tries hard to emulate her. She would if that didn't include Xandus.

Emulate her.

She must figure a way to infiltrate Delilah's body. She must implant her consciousness into her *enode*; then she could puppeteer her. She would harvest the intel in her inferior brain and feed the rest to her spider skulls.

With renewed energy and focus, Anura starts experimenting on the *enode*. She tries the vigor of Ikrlez, murk from the Shadowlands. She exercises patience. She will figure out a way; she always does. sSylk, however, is not so patient. He clears his throat.

Anura almost forgot he was here. "What is it, sSylk?"

"I have a report for you."

"Yes?" she responds with tired impatience.

"I've discovered that Crackle Blade has a female *charge*," he informs.

A loud croak escapes Anura's throat. Her vocal sac inflates and deflates with anger. She knew it, she just knew it. What a fool. God is as dumb as ever, making the same mistakes again – not if she were in charge.

"That's stupid! Male angels only guard male humans!" she screams. "When male angels protected females in the Dark Ages, they created the Nephilim! Now, they could fall in love with each other! I will not allow that to happen! No! Do what you must, sSylk. Kill her, seduce her, separate her, anything to get her away from Xandus. I will double your reward! Triple it!" she demands.

"Interestingly enough, his new *charge* is the daughter of Benjamin—his previous *charge*."

Her star-shaped pupils bulge. Her vocal sac deflates. She taps her large head in thought. Ikrlez and Lucifer both blame her for Sinxin's insolence. The Hale bloodline are few, but she discovered from her sources that Xandus's primary *charge* was the fleshling, Benjamin. The probability was high that he was the *turnkey*. In retrospect, she should have ordered a simultaneous strike against all the fleshlings he guarded. It would have been much harder to coordinate with their soulshields. It was a stroke of luck that Xandus neglected to restore Benjamin's soulshield. He will be much less likely to do so in the future. The Shadow Elite will never have him off guard as they did this time. He will be sure to overlap the refresh rates on the fleshling's soulshield from here on out. A horrible predicament Anura finds herself in, though nothing she can't overcome. So his new primary *charge* is the female. "Now that is suspicious."

sSylk shrugs at his employer and smiles. "Isn't it?"

CHAPTER 10

A VISIT FROM THE ALMIGHTY

D elilah peers through a hole in the wall of the "Crawler in the Squalor." Why Naomi left her with this untrustworthy mantis demon, she has no idea. He reminds her of a roach when she looks around in his filthy storeroom. Would it kill him to hire someone to spruce up the joint? She must constantly check on him to make certain Torix doesn't betray her while anxiously waiting for Naomi's return. The mantis demon seems content to stay behind the counter.

In the Archfiend Zone, an angel's eyes don't adjust to darkness like a human's would at night. Darkness here in the Archfiend is thicker, more substantial. Even "tangible" could explain the terrifying substance. Moments after her *kameraads* left her, she removed an opal from her breastplate. Lost in thought, Delilah simply stares at the stone. The precious gem brightens when rubbed and provides her with soothing light and warmth. She pours more of her vigor to expand its range. Now the gem becomes a fairly sized light and heat source, extending its range to about four meters.

She brings up the recorded footage of Benjamin's death on her bracer. She forces herself to check the grisly scene again. Hopefully, she can pick up more details that she may have missed during the original viewing. The dread she must endure as she views poor Benjamin die in such a horrific way. She can't, for the life of her, figure out what the bug-eyed demon was searching for. Whatever her purpose, surely the item wasn't something material or physical. She left his money and briefcase there. As a matter of fact, she didn't even search the briefcase. If the item or object was spiritual or metaphysical, how did she know in a fraction of a second that her objective was unmet?

Then she debates whether she should share this with Xandus? He'd definitely want to learn of his demise no matter how brutal the scene was. He's way too close to this, and he could become distracted. As his guardian, it is his right to know. She opens a connection to Aurum.

He answers right away. "Delilah, where are you? Is everything okay?"

"Of course. I just wanted to get your approval to send the footage of Benjamin's death to Xandus."

"Footage? How?"

Delilah has kept her uneasy alliance with Time from everyone except Naomi and Evnore. A sliver of guilt shimmies up her spine, not sharing intel this important from her *kameraads*. She can't reveal this information to anyone else. Not now anyway. "Not important. So, no?"

"Of course. Forward it to me."

"Sure, I'll send you and Xandus a copy."

"Just me. Xandus is already distraught and distracted. He doesn't need this to cloud his judgment."

"Let him decide? I mean he's a mature angel, right?"

On her bracer, Aurum rubs his beardless chin in thought. To keep Xandus ignorant of the details is cruel and unusual punishment. He should realize her suggestion is insistence. He might as well agree with her. Besides, once their Champion understands the mistakes he made, he will be more cognizant of his behavior in the future.

"Maybe you're right, Delilah. I was wrong when I didn't listen to you about the demonic invasion on humans. He has to deal with Benjamin's loss sooner or later."

"I'm so glad you saw my point of view, Herald."

"Not that you gave me much of a choice. Now where—"

She severs the connection and disables the locater in her bracer. She also disables Evnore and Naomi's locator. With a heavy heart, she taps her bracer and forwards the footage along with her introduction to Aurum and Xandus.

This storage room appears larger than Delilah thought. She examines the area turning in a slow circle. A sparkle catches her attention. It appears to move out the corner of her eye ever so slightly. A dim glow flickers where the eyes would be. Placing a hand on her hilt, Delilah creeps up to where the glint was. A weathered cloth made of velvet covers some man-shaped statue. It seems to be holding a sword, hilt up.

A couple more steps to discover what lies beneath. She reaches slowly for the cloth. Then snatches it off and draws her sword. She breathes a sigh of relief. Only a suit of tarnished armor. She smiles to herself. She's nervous like a child with a monster in the closet. She views her reflection on the breastplate. The metal must have caught the light of her opal. As she turns to walk away, she catches the reflection of her gems in the suit of armor. She withdraws a diamond from her breastplate and stares at the precious jewel. She recalls a blurred but precious memory of her and Xandus.

She's grateful for the few memories that were placed between the severed regions of her brain. Short-term memories seem to stay longer. Somehow, her brain can store them in safer regions. Not very long ago, maybe about four centuries ago, Xandus hovered over Delilah's favorite rainbow. She wiggled her toes under the warmth of the rainbow. She wrapped her arms around her legs, pretending she was unaware of his presence.

Xandus cleared his throat. "May I approach?"

She turned and smiled. She nodded her permission for him to join her.

He landed next to her and knelt down. They stared at each other uncomfortably for a few moments. He moved her hair behind her shoulder—exposing the multicolored gems on her breastplate. "Which of those gems are your favorite?"

She removed a handful off her armor, and with great agility, she rolled four gems around her fingers. "You have to ask? You know what they say."

"A diamond is a girl's best friend," she answered.

"Pearls are for the girls," Xandus said at the same time.

"No one says that!" The angels both reply simultaneously.

"What power does the diamond have in your hands?"

"I thought you knew."

"You usually sic me on the bad guys first like a trained dog," Xandus said with a smile.

"Sit Bo-Bo!"

Xandus flopped unceremoniously to the ground. Both laughed at their silliness.

"Because we're so aggressive, it only makes sense for me to concentrate on support and defense."

"Ironic that you say we are aggressive when actually, you're the most aggressive member of the squad," he responded.

She shrugged. "'Success of the group is more rewarding than the prestige of the individual,'" she quoted.

Xandus lowered his head. "'It is the best way to share victory.' Yeah, Anura used to say that."

"Of course she did, she got it from me," Delilah replied with a dab of venom. "I'm sorry. She was my friend too. I miss her, do you?" Delilah asked.

Xandus shook his head and looked away. Absently, he looped his finger in rainbow's color spectrum. The colors yielded before resetting in its appropriate color source. He swallowed hard before resting his chin in his hand. "I should have stopped them. I could have tried harder."

Hey, don't beat yourself up about it, sport. I mean, what really do you think you could have done?"

"Everything," Xandus said. "Would you let Naomi or Evnore do something that they'd regret for eternity? I did. I couldn't stop them. My best friends. Did I try hard enough, knowing they would be damned if they do?"

"I know you and Anura were more than friends, Xandus."

A barely audible gasp escaped from his lips. He furrowed his brow as he stared at Delilah. He opened his mouth to talk then sighed deeply. He nodded his head. Delilah slid closer. She took his hand, rubbing her thumb along his.

"We loved each other," he began. "Her and Ikrlez both tried to persuade me to join the Defectors. She joined because she wanted to…she wanted us to be together openly. Not banned because we belonged to the same squad," he explained.

Her eyes widened; her heart raced. She squeezed her eyes shut for a moment. "Look at me," she said. He did. "You can't blame yourself. They made their own choice. They have to live with that. Beating yourself up about it? What does that solve?"

"Do you truly believe that?"

"I do," she answered.

"Why the anger toward Abbadon? I mean, if he made his own choices, why do you hate him so much? More than that, he's in Hell. Whatever he did to you, he's paying the price for eternity."

Delilah dropped Xandus's hand and stood to her feet. She turned her back and folded her arms, looking to the sky. Constellations winked at her. She closed her eyes as a cool breeze brushed across her face. "That's different. He took—something from me. Never mind," she said.

"Delilah, your scars are safe with me."

"If only that were true."

Now Xandus rose to his feet. He grabbed Delilah by the shoulders and rubbed them. She grabbed his hands reflexively, resisting his affection. She applied slight pressure near his thumbs. She had to force herself to relax. Xandus wasn't Abbadon. She relaxed her grip and leaned her head against his strong chest.

"I'm sorry. I shouldn't press," he said. "So show me what you can do with diamonds."

Delilah forced a smile as she turned to face him. She imbued the diamond with her vigor and crushed it between her fingers. She shaped the fragments around them into a hovering barricade. It sparkled and was transparent. Xandus smiled. He had such a beautiful smile. For a few precious moments, they did nothing but gaze into each other's eyes.

"You always protect us. It is we that should protect you," he offered.

"I'm no clay pot. Besides, it's my job to keep everyone safe," she stated.

"It shouldn't be. Such an honor should be mine. I mean…how do you crack gemstones so easily? Is there a trick to it?"

Delilah smiled and nodded her head. "Mm-hm. Finger ups." She placed the gems that orbited around her fingers back on her armor. Then she dismantled the diamond structure with the touch of her hand, scooping up the fragments. She squeezed while layering a net of vigor around the frags. She tightened the fragments, producing extreme pressure until they reformed into a diamond.

"How can you reform the gem?"

"All in the wrist," she said while flexing her muscles.

"I'm impressed! I knew you were strong mentally, but physically too?"

She frowned. "For a girl, right?"

"No…no! I didn't mean it like that," he said, stammering.

"Mm-hm. Since you're so strong, let me see you do it," she challenged as she tossed the diamond to Xandus.

He had enough time to stretch his fingers before he snatched the diamond out of the air. Delilah giggled. He looked the diamond over and squeezed. Delilah looked on in mock amazement. Nothing. He used both hands, gritting his teeth. Nothing.

"I'm surprised! I thought you would be much stronger. You know, for a boy," she teased.

Xandus laughed with embarrassment. "How do you do it?"

"See, I press here and here." Delilah took his hands into hers, showing him the gem's pressure points. He placed his fingers over hers and squeezed. The diamond cracked like a peanut. The angels grinned as the diamond dust was caught up by the wind. The beautiful sparkles reflected in the sunlight. They looked at the sight, still holding hands.

Xandus raised Delilah's chin and turned her face toward his. Her blemishes. She was certain he stared at her blemishes.

"What are you doing?"

"Something I've been wanting to do for three millennia," he replied.

Xandus reached for her. She leaned in to meet him. Centimeters away from kissing him, her vision became distorted. She shook her head in confusion. She is—where? He was just here? Did something happen to him? "Where am I? Evnore? Xandus! I don't have a visual! Rally to my coordinates!"

She places a hand over her forehead feeling light-headed. She stumbles backward, knocking over the suit of armor. The sword just misses her head. Glass preserve bottles filled with body parts and unholy creatures roll around her. Eyes glare at her through murky glass containers. When she moves to orient herself, the eyes follow. The Mist rises all about her, almost to her knees. It grabs at her—wrapping its tendrils of fear about her arms, legs, and neck. She detects a powerful presence behind her. As Delilah whirls around, she gasps. The Mist withdraws. She kneels.

God stands before her, brandishing the Rod of Virtue. He signals for Delilah to rise. He places His hand over her forehead. The stress of this mission, her frustration, and fatigue vanishes immediately as she relaxes.

"Let your mind be at peace, Strategist," God says.

Delilah regains her balance, and takes a deep breath.

"Thy rod and thy staff, they comfort me."

God smiles. He uses both hands to spin one end of the rod on the ground to wrap the Mist around the shaft. In moments, the area is clear. He snaps the rod, flinging the Mist to the ground in a large ball-like mass. Tendrils stretch forth and tries to separate itself. God smacks the Mist with the rod, and with an electrical spark, it dissipates.

Delilah can't remember the last time God came to visit her during a mission. Maybe during when she was assigned to protect Job? Normally, He dwells not on unhallowed ground. However, if His presence is any indication of the severity of their investigation, this can't be a good sign. God continues to smile. He transforms the rod into a meteor shower, which was swallowed up into a black hole that hovers just above His other hand.

"How may I serve thee?" she asks as she curtsies.

She and God circle each other in this room. He points to her bracer. She activates it and swipes through the menus, looking for new information. "Unfit for Duty" report submitted by Naomi.

The report located in the squadron's queue must be read and commented on. If Aurum agrees, the report will get pushed through to Master-Commander Michael the Archangel. She could be suspended, reassigned, or demoted at his discretion. She keeps her composure but the tendrils of betrayal sadden her. Naomi submitted the report without even consulting her about it. Evnore didn't mention it either, though that's not surprising. She's loyal to a fault; she won't betray anyone's trust. This will bring shame to Chrysos Squad in general and Aurum's command specifically.

"I will address this report later. More importantly, this was not a simple assassination on Benjamin. It is a full-on act of war! Find out Lucifer's plan and who he has enlisted. We will need the intelligence you and your squadron gather to quell their plans. I have given Xandus the word that his mission, all your missions, must succeed. The Shadow Domain believed Benjamin was the *turnkey*."

So it's not a myth. For eons, a key to the gates of Hell was rumored to exist. For reasons unknown, the Virtuous Culture were unaware of its accuracy. To her knowledge, the host was unaware of who or where the main component of the key was. If the rumors were true, it would help protect the angel's identity, in case an angel was captured and tortured for information. A *turnkey* means a metaphysical part of the key to Hell was hidden within a human. It must be a safeguard in case the other half was taken. If demons were incorrect about Benjamin, then it must mean—"Katherine is the *turnkey*!"

"Per your Herald, Xandus and Iulas are her guardians. If Chrysos fails, then the End of Days will begin."

Delilah gasps in shock, mouth wide open. "The apocalypse?" she responds in shock.

"Will you and Chrysos be able to prevent it? I leave it all up to you. The persistence of demons and the disobedience of humans will merge. Both of the worst possible outcomes will cause the fall of humanity and the rise of demons. You, my love, are instrumental in preventing the Second Fall from happening. Now that we have that out of the way, what else did you wish to discuss?"

She blushes and lowers her head. "Why weren't you there? Why did you let them attack me? Why didn't you answer my prayer?"

"Precious Delilah, fearless Delilah. I always answer prayers. All things work together for good. Patience and temperance will help you with your inner rage," God replies.

"I know, but I saw the words…I…"

God frowns – not at Delilah but to the ground. "Trust when I say, Abbadon in Hell continues to pay for his crimes against you."

"I thought you sent him to Hell because he cursed your name?"

God clenches his fist. An implosion occurs when He crushes the black hole within it. "Who's imprisoned, Delilah? Him…or you?" God taps His temple. "Remember my love, it's what you keep alive that can restrain you or free you. Do you trust me still?"

"Of course. Without question," she answers.

"No matter what the circumstance, no matter how bleak a moment is, I will never leave you nor forsake you. Your enemies will fall before you like a collapsed star. I will make them your footstool. I love you and have since before I orchestrated the foundations of the earth, and I always will."

Delilah's mouth hangs open. She drops to her knees, only now realizing the ground is cleaner than the Caribbean waters. Her thoughts are all over the place. She feels honored and important. God came to the pit of the Archfiend Zone just to spend a few moments with her. Abbadon's treachery recedes into the recesses of her mind. His torture and betrayal a distant memory—for now. She rises to her feet, straights her back, and unfurls her wings. She clenches her fist and locks gazes with God. "Thank you, Lord. Your faith in our squad humbles me."

"Repeat my epitaph," God commands.

"God wants to see what He knows that I think I can do," Delilah recites.

God nods grimly. "Be certain that you do not give into wrath. Control yourself or lose yourself."

God produces a small box. Delilah's eyes enlarge with awe. She cups the box with both hands, rubbing the engraved workmanship with admiration. It is made of marble and inlaid with silver and gold. She inspects the box for a mechanism to open it. There is none. It is made from a solid piece of marble. The box was made *around* whatever lies within. Then she understands. The box, no matter how beautiful it is, was made to be destroyed to retrieve what is inside. With a sad sigh, she grabs both sides, applies pressure, and cracks open the exquisite box. Within it, a violet gem hovers. Delilah's smiles, like she's seeing the magnificent sun for the first time. Small lights float within the gem. There is no string attached, but as God takes the gem and reaches around Delilah's neck, a silken thread materializes.

"Beautiful! I've never seen this gem before. What is it?"

"I thought of you when I created it. I call it angelite. Like you, there is only one. The only honorable death for a honey bee is when she defends her hive. To sting an annoyance, away from the hive, jeopardizes the queen unnecessarily. Control yourself or lose yourself," God explains.

"What do I do with it?"

God glances past Delilah for a fraction of a moment, in the direction of the peephole leading to Torix's front counter.

Then he withdraws and dissipates, like smoke in a breeze. His voice but a soft whisper in Delilah's ear.

"Crumble wounds that stem from rash decisions. Soothe words that inflame with crystals of life," He riddles.

She bows her head in reverence, though her brow furrows in confusion.

CHAPTER 11

FLIGHT OR FAIL

Cyrus follows Nil to a dilapidated alley. Garbage cans line the sides and cardboard boxes with vacancies aplenty. He looks around, scratching his head. A fog lifts, and memories stir. He remembers this location as where he woke up covered in black ichor, having a severe case of amnesia. The acidic smell of urine fills the air.

The blue demon waves a claw across his goggles. His fluorescent eyes flash devilishly through his goggles as his goggles switch from tint to mirrored. Nil pulls the air to the side, like a curtain. Cyrus's eyes pop wide in amazement.

"This am the *veil*. Demons and angels travel far to Archfiend Zone am to the Natural World." Nil pushes his finger into Cyrus's chest. "Him has this power to use its too. Later for that." He gives Cyrus a sarcastic bow and cocks his head toward the *veil*. "After he."

Cyrus peers through the opening. As soon as he sticks his head through, he gasps. An inherent HUD pops over his field of vision. He reflexively wipes his eyes and squints, but the HUD remains. His eyes adjust, allowing him to get used to it. He is able to filter through different menus, with but a thought. Maps, the locations of nearby friendlies and enemies as bleeps, updates, and other information on this new world scroll past his eyes. He learns that he can mentally speed or slow the flow of data. He can change the font or lighten the overlay.

The Mist is all around. With little effort, he can zoom his vision through the obscurities with no apparent setbacks. In the distance, the two super powers lock in battle, perhaps for eternity. The darkness is deep and penetrating, though his range of vision drills through the different powers, principalities, and dominions. His eyes widen in awe. Castles, mountains, caves, caverns; all these landmarks seem hauntingly familiar to Cyrus. The HUD allows him to view the landscape with a map legend overlay of the region. He can see the invisible borders of each territory. The factions they represent from the Greater Sins. Territorial battles ensue to claim more of the vast uncontested lands in the Archfiend.

To the south is the Denizens of Death. He can pull up general bio and stats for this principality. Venrath, the queen of this particular castle, was worshipped as the goddess of death in the Dark Ages. She has a large sphere of influence and has priority over leased souls of the damned. Cyrus smiles to himself. Not a fan of history before, but this new realm fascinates him. So diverse and powerful. How weren't they able to defeat God? Maybe that's what Sinxin meant. Imagine what they all can do under one standard. It worked for warlords, Nazis, Alexander the Great, and the list goes on. This network of contacts could all be under his authority. He fully buys into Lucifer's philosophy. He tries to drink it all in as he looks all about him.

When he looks up, he realizes that demons are in the sky too. One never thinks of demons that dwell in the upper atmosphere. Rows of dark clouds against a darker sky expands the length of the horizon. He must arc his neck way up to see the tips of the black towers. Lightning threads within the clouds. Could that be some sort of defense? Before his newfound knowledge can pull up the bio for the castle, Nil growls with impatience. Cyrus can sightsee later. For now, enter. There are no steps or walkways before him. Are they invisible? Can he breathe in there? He cautiously places a foot into the Spirit Realm. No solid footing.

"No fear! This basic! If him fail here, me wasting I time! Do not scream! Do not show weakness nor fear! Fly!" he yells.

Cyrus puts his whole self in and falls. He nearly bites his tongue off to refrain from screaming. He whizzes past a pair of imps that flitter about. They get spun around; then they start pointing and laughing at him. Even still, they chase him down, mocking and swiping at his exposed back. That is until Nil belches a stream of fire that singes their scaled hides. He continues to fall in this encompassing darkness. Why can't he fly? He is unable to orient himself as he falls faster. Nothing on his HUD to give him instructions. He can't stop. He can't fly. He can only fall. He finally gets his body prone.

Then a pair of dreadful eyes appear on the whole horizon. They pierce his soul, and he is sorely afraid. Cyrus can't look away. Something familiar about those eyes. He doesn't need his HUD to inform him of this most powerful being's identity.

"Lucifer? Master Lucifer!" he yells in recognition.

The eyes seem to accept the address. "Welcome to the Archfiend Zone, Spawn. You have much to learn and little time to acquire it. Your mentor has explained what must be done, yet even an imp can fly," Lucifer states.

Cyrus can't stop spinning.

"It's all in your blood. Your fear. Fear is real. It is your weapon, if you wield it. If you can control it, fear can be your strength, your reputation, and your power! If you let fear consume you now, you'll die here. Conquer fear and rise. You are made from one of the most powerful being ever created. I need you to become my sword. Flight or fall, Spawn," Lucifer commands.

Cyrus's blood boils from rage and surges with adrenaline. His HUD corrects his thought process. Not only adrenaline that courses through his veins. So his power source is called "vigor." His HUD notifies him that he uses a trickle of vigor to power his HUD. His greatest desire right now is to make his master proud. He will not disappoint his creator, after it took thousands of years to construct him. For the first time in his relatively short existence, he belongs somewhere. He'll be a leader. He won't make the same mistakes as his predecessor made. The copy will follow orders and become stronger than the original. He dreams to sit at the right hand of the all-knowing to change destiny and wrap eternity around the crown of his head. All he has to do is figure out how to fly. Is his problem physical, because he doesn't actually have wings, or psychological?

Nil obviously can fly, but he has no wings, so it must be a mental problem.

If those stupid imps can do it, surely it can't be so hard. He was mocked by those baby bat imp creatures. He always hated to be embarrassed, for as short as he can remember anyway. He hated to be made a fool of and picked on. Time to be the aggressor. Time to be the bully.

Negative emotions thrive here in the Archfiend. They assault his senses and overwhelms him with dread. He is going about this the wrong way. He stretches his arms out and inhales deeply. He will assimilate the abundance of energy around him and become one with it. He absorbs the hate and fear around him and fuels his strength with it. He is mighty. Rage causes his muscles to bulge, fear darkens his aura. A loud hum pulses from within his belly, causing the air to shimmer. Veins protrude from his skin, as a surge of black blood courses through them. Virtual wings sprout out, beating powerfully. He halts his descent and hovers—moving the Mist like a hurricane moves clouds. He quickly gains control of his movement. He can dip and ascend and perform a barrel roll at will. How natural they feel. Electronic nodes are within them. Pulses of neurons filled with vigor travel up the length of them. Cyrus flexes his wings all the way behind him, then one more strong beat. In the distance, he topples over ruins with monsoon force winds.

Power incarnate dwells within him. His skin tingling as if miniature stars are expanding. His tendons bulge with knotted muscles. He can move his primary and secondary virtual feathers as if they were his fingers.

"Yes, my son. Yes! Caress the power. Embrace your true self. Power and might are within you. Use it. Flaunt it! Roar like a lion! Stalk like a panther. Crush like a rhino. Kill like a dragon!" Lucifer yells.

Cyrus howls proudly, like a werewolf baying at a full moon. Angels and demons break off their battles. The trainee wears a smile that would make a tiger turn tail. He spots a small angelic unit and dashes toward them. The angels hurry to get into a formation, but are too late. He surges into the midst of them, blocking their feeble attacks with his iron-enforced forearms. He cackles madly as the angels swing their blades and gasp in shock when they realize their weapons have no effect against him. In fact, there is an electrical discharge when their blades connect. This causes an intense surge of electricity to knock their blades back and, in some cases, out of their grasp. "You are no match, fools! I will break you! Fear me!"

The angelic squad leader signals for a retreat, and the unit backs away. Vigor-lined laser blades spring forth from Cyrus's forearms to impale one of the angels. Demons from all around the region gather to join him and wrap the wounded angel in chains, tormenting him all the way. It must be an impossible decision the squad leader must make—to leave the one to save the rest. Cyrus raises his arms in the air, in triumph, pointing to the sky.

Satan's eyes see it all. He is well pleased.

CHAPTER 12

THE CASHING OF INFORMATION CURRENCY

Delilah lets the information she received from God saturate her soul. If Chrysos fails in this most important assignment, the End of Days will begin. Hell on earth will usher forth atrocities to torment humanity as demons will overrun and enslave the populace. Souls and Fallen angels sentenced to Hell will be released to vex humans forever. She thought angels were on an eternal backlog now, she can only imagine their workload if the apocalypse happens. She can't allow this to happen.

Delilah stifles a growl when Naomi enters the storage area. They need to come to terms. Not now, but right now. *Kameraads* shouldn't keep animosity, but right now she can think of a hundred ways she could pluck her wings featherless. She knew Naomi was not to be trusted. She shared more secrets with her female angels than she did with anyone else. Delilah does a mental "downward dog." She pushes out her anger, her feelings of betrayal, isolation, and resentment. Benjamin's death affects them in more ways than she believed. Aurum was right about combat fatigue. It wasn't long after God gave her mental relief, but her frustration erased His calming presence. Everything was connected somehow, but she can't make the pieces fit. She takes a deep breath and speaks. "Naomi, I know about your report."

Naomi shrugs. "It's in plain view waiting to be commented on. Of late, the decisions you've made hindered our investigation. I made note."

"You were right. I was preoccupied with my own vendetta. We'll address those issues later. I just want justice."

"Vengeance," Naomi corrects.

"You weren't there! How could you ever understand?"

She turns her back to Naomi. Struggling to contain her emotions. No matter how much she tries to exorcise her demons with pure thoughts, Abbadon always shoves them away. She can still smell his putrid scent all over her. No matter how much she scrubs or covers it with scented oils, the smell of his death and desecration sticks in her nostrils for eternity. Every day for thousands of years. Her inability to exact revenge on the one person she despised the most. Even his sentence in Hell isn't comfort enough. It's probably for the best. She can't even defeat a clone of him. Each day, the clones, and all other demons for that matter, become stronger as the "Threshold of the Damned" raises their power.

Naomi sighs heavily. "My dear Delilah…you were the second."

Delilah braces herself against a cruddy shelf as she almost loses her balance. Her mouth hinges open as she's struck with this revelation. There were others. How can Naomi be so calm? How could she keep this from her all these thousands of years? She rushes over to comfort her. Naomi looks away but accepts the hug, keeping her arms folded.

"Naomi! I am so sorry! Why didn't you tell me? Was it Abbadon?"

Naomi continues to avert her eyes, shrugging Delilah off. "It was…it is. Mentally, he torments me still."

"Evnore, were you aware?"

"I'm shocked you think I would invade someone else's privacy. Is that why you never wear my mask? Though I share a link with whomever I am bonded with, it is not my place to tell. She freely shared the traumatic experience with me. Her pain is my pain. I believe my bearing such pain helped her to deal with the shame," Evnore explains.

"True, my sister," Naomi says with sincerity. "I don't wish to talk of it now. The mission is all that matters."

Delilah sadly lets the subject drop. She had so many questions, but Naomi refuses to be debriefed. "Have it your way. So we discussed what is in your report. Let us discuss what is not."

Naomi cocks her head to the side like a curious puppy. Gem frags gather in Delilah's hand from off Naomi's body. She then clinches her fist tightly, reforming a goshenite gem.

"Why did you meet with Mazck?" Delilah demands.

Naomi gasps and speaks in a harsh whisper, "You spied on me! Who have you told?"

"No one...yet. Tell me why it should stay that way. Don't tell me he's your confidential informant."

Naomi nods. "He's given me vital intel on some of the major demonic raids we've had in centuries."

"But not the assassination," Delilah finishes. "Our Heaven tech is far more reliable than a demonic informant. I understand he was your...friend, but that's no reason to maintain a relationship with him or to keep it from me. We're *kameraads*! I trust you with my soul!"

"So much so that you put a tracker on me," Naomi says.

"Don't turn this around! I need answers! Not now, but right now!"

Naomi rolls her eyes, but a sigh of resignation seeps out of her lips. "It took this long for me to obtain information from Mazck that I've been demanding from him for ages. I didn't want to get your hopes up if the leads turned out to be dead ends. I can tell you something our Heaven tech cannot. I can tell you which demons possess your stolen *enodes*."

The Strategist stops in midstep, but Naomi continues on, silencing Delilah with a subtle shake of her head. Delilah follows Naomi to the front of the shop.

Torix paces back and forth, biting his claws. He glares at the partners as they emerge. "I cooperated with you. Now leave! And everything!"

"We have new business," Delilah states. She points to an intricately decorated box. Though the shop is draped in cobwebs, this corner is kept clear of them.

"Let me lookit," Naomi says.

"No! I have an exclusive rights agreement! And everything!"

"I suggest you tell us what we want to know, before someone finds out," Naomi suggests.

Delilah walks over to the blinds and holds it taut. Torix chitters nervously, dry washing his claws.

"I'd do it fast. More of your patrons are lining up outside. If it were me, I'd be pretty suspicious: cooperating with angels," Delilah adds.

His tall insectoid frame stretches to the upper shelf and gently brings the box down. Naomi reaches for the box, but Torix nearly slices her fingers off with his claws. In an instant, both angels ready their weapons centimeters away from each of the bug demon's eyes.

"No, no! A trap is on the box! And everything!" he explains.

He presses an intricate pattern on the glyphs. The angels sheath their weapons after they're sure Torix isn't setting a trap. Afterward, he carefully removes the top. The angels peer inside.

"Counterfeit money?" Naomi asks.

"No, you fool! Err, I mean, no, Lady Eye-blotter. And everything."

"Ghostwriting parchment," Delilah says in realization.

"What's that?"

"Paper that can be empowered with vigor made from the flayed skins of condemned souls. Spells, traps, elements, even sound can be captured on this," she explains.

Naomi gasps, but Delilah quiets her with a subtle shake of her head. So this is what Sinxin used when she slapped that parchment over Benjamin's ear. Ghostwriting parchment was mostly used to set traps, like the box that the parchment was in. There are a variety of uses, but most devils prefer to use brute force. What was the point though?

Xandus is passionate in his protection details. He developed such an intimidating persona so most foes will leave humans under his protection alone. It forced demons to harass weaker opponents. Even still, why taunt him? So he wouldn't see the shadow from the shade? Maybe. "I'm only going to ask you this once. Who has the power to make this? Especially in mass?"

"Anura the Contriver."

***

Hooded figures creep down an alley. A demonic guard blocks the gate, sipping on sin. One of the hooded figures slaps the bottle of sin out of his hand. The demonic guard grumbles something unintelligible.

"Admission for two," Naomi demands.

"Two silver."

Naomi bounces something at the drunk. He scrambles after them. When he picks them up, he gasps. Demon eyes. He drops them in fear, then hurries to the heavy chain attached to a grate. He pulls with all his might. The grate flips open with a loud clang. The angels drop into the darkness. Once they are through the tunnels, they come across a clearing.

Delilah stops Naomi. "Now that we're clear from prying ears, I need that information."

"There are four demons who have your *enodes*. We know about Sinxin. Anura, your former trainer, maintains one. Another demon who goes by Teratech carries another, and Lucifer hoards the last four," Naomi reveals.

Delilah paces back and forth. She wanted this information for ages. She values her intellect more than anything. Without her mind healed, she feels like an eagle without wings. To acquire this information, Naomi must have performed treasonable acts. Just meeting Mazck could cause her to be court-martialed. There's no way to do the wrong thing for the right reason, but this was different. Naomi did this for her. This could help her be complete. Despite everything Naomi says about the mission before desire, her *kameraad* would do anything for her.

Delilah thinks back. She theorized her memory was never destroyed. The destruction of the *enode* encasement would return her

122

memory. If her memory is corrupted, she would suffer from unbearable cranial spasms. Her superiors would suspect her of being puppeteered. She has no desire to be quarantined and subjected to an *aegis* analysis. The tests are mandatory if the subject is under suspicion of demonic influence.

She tries to connect the names with the memories. Anura was a dear friend at one time in the youth of her existence. She loved and honored her most. Everything Delilah is, she owes to Anura. She encouraged her to become a Strategist in the first place. She was only a messenger before Anura showed her to study and to decipher clues and discern her opponents' intention. Her *enodes* in Anura's hands could be lethal.

Then there's Lucifer. Delilah's not surprised that he keeps her memory. What will he do with them though? He's not one to experiment with them like Anura. She recalls how Lucifer actually took seven sections of her memory. He placed some of her *enodes* onto his body immediately.

Naomi snaps her fingers twice to get Delilah's attention. "Hey, you in there? Did you hear me?" Once Naomi grabs Delilah's attention, she continues, "Fret not. You've gone this long without them. You'll continue to do so."

"Did I just hear you correctly? Do you think they can stand in my way? Am I to roll on my back and play dead? I will recover them alone if I must. I will retrieve what was stolen!" she says with determination.

Naomi's smile turns into a sinister grin. "Your pain is my torment. If you're going to slit Lucifer's throat, I'll grab him by the hair and give you the razor. You won't be alone, *kameraad*. I am with you!"

"As am I," Evnore chimes in audibly.

The Mist gathers; the angels leave. They rush through the tunnels, doing their best to avoid detection. The Tunnels of Bloodroot are bleak sewers. The stench is thicker than an elephant's torso—thick with fear, madness, and despair. She reaches out to the cave wall to keep her balance. Naomi steadies Delilah with a firm hand.

"I don't like mucking around in these tunnels like a slithering snake," Delilah says.

"We don't have the luxury of time. Confrontations will slow us down. This is the only way," Evnore replies.

"There is no doubt in my mind that the assassination and the whereabouts of my *enodes* are connected," Delilah reasons.

Naomi stops suddenly. "What do you mean?"

"This is no coincidence. We are being distracted – pulled in different directions and split up. We are one of the most powerful squadrons in Heaven when we are together, like how we dismantled that pillar in Heaven. After eons, now the location of my memory is revealed? I wouldn't be surprised if Mazck told you this to set us up for a trap," she explains.

"Bastage! That demonic bastage!"

"You were right. As long as my memory and any leads are directly linked to Benjamin's death, we'll follow it."

Naomi nods in agreement. They continue down the tunnels until it branches into many passage.

"We don't have time to blaze through each trail. We dare not split up. We only get one chance to take the right path. Let's make it count," Delilah says.

"I'll take care of that," Evnore says.

"What do you suggest?"

Long moments pass before the eyelets of her mask glow with the syncing of an idea. "A master smith of Kromrom's prestige would not clunk ore like a goblin. No. His sound would be unique, like wind chimes in a gentle breeze. I will empower Naomi's senses to filter for that sound," Evnore explains.

"May I?" Delilah asks.

Naomi removes the mask and gives it to Delilah.

Are you sure, Delilah? I'll understand if you don't trust me.

I trust you with my very soul, Oather.

Once Delilah dons the mask, she filters through the influx of Evnore's vigor. Her hearing is on sensory overload. Sounds of all types bombard her. A pounding headache pulses against her cranium. Her brain works to decipher the many different sounds. Delilah must master their symbiotic union fast.

Breath. I'll slow the flow. Introduce sounds intermittently. Maybe this isn't the time to do this. Naomi has the experience.

I need to understand how your abilities work. I have done so for everyone else except you. I apologize for not doing so eons ago. Guide me through the connection between you and your mask. If I lower my mental shields, would that expedite my...training?

Of course. Your barrier halts the flow of all information we share, like a firewall or a peephole. We can try later if you'd like. I know you hesitate to lower your barrier.

Delilah drops her shields in an instant. She can feel Evnore smile. Now the Strategist can see sound. Deeper sounds dwell in the lower color range. Higher pitched sounds in the higher color spectrum. She filters the sounds easier now. Anything darker than yellow, she swipes it away. Evnore continues to introduce more complicated sounds. Combinations of deep sounds. Shrieks that start out high then drop. Sounds that move across different terrain or bounce off different walls. In seconds, she learns to siphon out these extraneous noises. She needs to find a pure sound. *Faster, Evnore.*

Evnore opens the floodgates, and Delilah is the dam. She moves sound like a tai chi master. Her physical self moves farther down the tunnel to hear deeper as she hears clanging and banging. She walks a few steps and circles around. Evnore amazes her. The most unselfish angel she knows. One of the wisest and strongest in their squadron, though not a Class X like Xandus.

Unlike most angels, Evnore has no desire for renown. Angels with such a high reputation are respected by demons. If they have respect, then information comes freely. Naomi's company and her reputation as the Eye-blotter gets them tips fast.

Delilah watches as eye vermin gather nearby. They are always on the lookout. No matter what direction the angels are going or direction the vermin are running in, their hideous eyes are always on them. She hates the creepy sight of them. She was on the lookout for the brainiac eye vermin ever since her day off. No results.

There—deep within. The ringing she hears are like crystals in the wind. A sound so pure it is almost blinding. Such clarity. What a waste of craftsmanship to use such a talent forging demon blades.

Delilah beckons for Naomi to follow. The trail descends sharply. They are close to the soul forges that all shadow smiths use. Eye vermin continue to keep tabs on their movements. Once they gather enough intel to be useful to their masters, they will scurry off to inform them. Then they are replaced by more. The clanging gets louder. Finally, they are at an overlook. Beneath them, a sprawling community. "This must be…"

"Demon Craft," Evnore finishes audibly.

CHAPTER 13

SUNEATER STRONGHOLD

T he intimidating edifices shrink below Cyrus and his mentor as they fly high above the Archfiend Zone. The boundaries merge into a few massive landmasses as they continue to rise higher. Rivers of lava appear as ribbons from this vantage point. The fiery tributaries act as rivers to create natural borders between the territories.

He has so much power coursing through his veins. He can hardly wait to test his talents again. He already forgot how he made the circuitry etch its way across his body. The virtual blades that sprung forth from his forearms were gone as well. It must be driven by instinct or adrenaline. He must find out what his limits and strengths are. Does he have a weakness? He doubts that. His reflexes are faster than thought. His strength is that of a titan. There is no limit to what he can do.

He follows Nil to a long stretch of dark clouds, black enough to be indiscernible from the night sky. A massive fortress is located at the highest layer of space in the Archfiend Zone. From his HUD, he can determine where each storm cloud begins and ends. Upon their arrival, the clouds part to reveal the main entrance to Suneater Stronghold. It stretches across the horizon with its massive structure. If he were on the other side of the world, he would still see Suneater.

Now, the red joins the black sky, highlighting the dark and foreboding castle. Roaring flames of minor suns blast through multiple points of the castle. If it were not for his eyes automatically filtering the intensity of the flames for him, he'd be blinded. Surprisingly, the suns don't emit heat, or is he invulnerable to temperature extremities? He will have to experiment with that. Lightning races throughout the cloud nexus. Thunder roars its displeasure continuously as if it is trapped in the airy firmament, maybe it is.

The cloud gate he steps through is erected from blackened bones arranged in an arc. His HUD names the arc Shatter Spine. He touches a fossilized bone. He is startled as the spine shifts and resets itself—rattling like a snake. Nil looks back and laughs at his pupil.

A massive dragon is imprisoned just under the storm clouds. Hooks and chains are anchored into its flesh, keeping it motionless. Fresh black blood oozes out of the deep wounds. They must pass over on the dragon's back to reach the door. It growls its agitation as they step on its snout. The head as wide as the length of a truck. Most of the dragon's features are obscured by the clouds, but not its glowing eyes, for they are as red as fresh human blood. They reach the halfway point, and the dragon stirs, trying to free itself or knock them off its back. He can't imagine how intimidating an unleashed dragon would be. The creature must have failed an important objective to be humiliated in such a fashion. An eternal example of crossing the most powerful god in the universe.

As they get closer to the castle proper, thousands of eyes stare at him. Monstrosities as far as the eye can see. Thunder roars louder near the entrance. Rumbles vibrate the firmament under his feet. Cyrus realizes it isn't thunder he hears; it is the roars, screeches, yells, and bellows from the nightmarish demons that take up residence.

This fortress houses behemoths, aerial leviathans, enormous multiheaded snakes, giant devils, and all other unimaginable nightmares he can think of. Some gnaw on souls like they were a dog's chew toy. They are desperate to open the enslaved spirits to get at its precious contents. Others argue among themselves, bragging of their might or power or followers. They argue until Cyrus walks through the cloud gate. All stare at him with anger and envy. Many charge and lunge at him. If not for Nil's presence, he'd be shredded to pieces. The blue devil must be highly respected. When he turns his head, the monsters cease their advancement. Nil has the notoriety he can't wait to possess. The ability to stare down a demon and make him huddle in a corner.

The demons darken the skies like an eclipse. They crowd the path like a thicket of unclipped hedges. They all gnash and chomp their maws at him as they near the castle proper. Cyrus slows to a stop. He can't help but be intimidated at these atrocities. These beings would tear him apart with but a thought. There goes his confidence. He was a fool to think he was the strongest or that demons would just accept him. Nil growls with impatience.

"What are we doing here? What does the master want with me?" he wonders.

"Him is wanting to meet he. Don't him want to meet he's maker?" Nil questions.

Giant ogre demons open the five-story high doors to allow them entrance. Their muscles strain as they lean back to pull open the heavy entryway. The Hall of Champions leading up to Lucifer's throne is enormous. Majestic murals of their most infamous demons are lined up on either side. Cyrus feels pride from the flattering depictions of Velous the Ogre and Mvdorn the Massive. In fact, they were both outside of Suneater's mocking him as he entered. Angry clouds are underneath the roof, yelling at one another and competing for dominance. The Mist layers the ground like carpet. Tentacles creep from under the dark as if lifting the bottom of a bedsheet.

Even Cyrus's sharp vision can't penetrate the dark corners. Innumerable mirrors and polished skulls spin in different shapes to reflect the atrocities and brilliance that both reside here. Some of the skulls' teeth chatter as if it were freezing while others shout obscenities. Monsters honored with dwelling inside Suneater Stronghold are much calmer. Most seem content admiring their own power or semblance of beauty in those polished skulls.

Yet the castle can never retain Lucifer's colossal ego. Cyrus's heart races to bursting. His fear rising—racing up his throat, yelling to be free. He can barely breathe. He sweats nervously. His mouth is dry as baked dirt, and his eyes dart to the sides for an emergency exit. The closer he gets to the throne, the more apprehensive he becomes. The beings outside the fortress are ants compared to the supreme master. The Prince of the Air.

Satan.

Lucifer lounges on his massive throne, with his leg over one side. When Cyrus approaches, he sits up with his hands clasped. Lucifer, without a doubt, the most powerful being in the universe. He stands up—taller than a storm giant, stronger than Atlas's back. Shards of obsidian protrude from his brass-colored skin. Black veins bulge from his arms. Large ox horns are atop his head. Storm clouds make up his colossal wings. The dark clouds rumble within, like trapped lions. Lightning dances angrily across the width of his wings, like a malfunctioning transformer. Magma pronounces his muscle grouping. Tattoos and piercings are all along his chest. Cyrus wonders what could mark his flesh? He answers his own question: his own finger.

Nil and Cyrus both avert their eyes and bow. Beads of sweat run down his forehead. His heart tightens up as if he's going into cardiac arrest. Deep breaths, calm down. Lucifer's royal seat is comprised of millions of skulls, and each one lives, or can this be a human's afterlife? Each moans in extreme fear and anguish. With a wave of Lucifer's hand, their mouths continue to move, but the heads are silenced. He must enjoy the cacophony of torture. Cyrus wonders if it is a sound he will come to appreciate. Lucifer steps off his throne. He moves as if all power and time is in his hands.

He can scarcely look up, but he tries. Some force seems to press down on his body. Lucifer reaches out of one of the high windows of his castle. Arms that reach past the ceiling, past the roof and into the sky. Arms that reach without stretching. Far off in another galaxy he plucks an itsy-bitsy star from the sky. Cyrus peeks from under his quivering eyelids as Lucifer pulls the star from its seated position. He neither strains nor grimaces as he reels in the star to his Archfiend Zone.

Suneater shakes and vibrates. The ground quakes, and the ceiling moans. He can hear the frightened screams of the occupants of the Archfiend. Lucifer the Deceiver brings the star inside his castle.

He closes his fist around the star to compress it. Light and flames attempt to escape his mighty grasp, but no. They are as much his slave as a tiger on a leash. Lucifer squeezes the star until it can fit into the palm of his hand.

All gathered begin to melt and fry. Their regenerative powers can't keep up with the destructive force of a star. They yell for mercy from their master as Lucifer brings the star to his mouth—and eats it. Cyrus's screams are drowned out by the rumbling of Suneater Stronghold. He face plants to the ground, quivering like a frightened mouse. Dust falls from the ceiling in an avalanche of crumbling debris. Lucifer chews the star as if he were sampling caviar—relishing the mega explosions that erupt in his mouth. He swallows hard as a black hole collapses down his throat. Solar flares escape out of his nostrils and mouth. He roars in wild laughter. The cloud quakes fade, the rumblings cease. The regular occupants lift their heads.

"I like my stars sunny-side up!" Lucifer bellows.

Every creature on Lucifer's storm cloud join him in laughter. Then all of a sudden—silence. Cyrus remains stuck on the ground. He peeks out and sees Lucifer's eye, the size of a shield, glaring at him. Every demon now on bended knee. Cyrus realizes that Lucifer wants total fear, adoration, and respect. However, he also wants his subjects to be fearless, intimidating, and ruthless. How can he attain that balance?

Nil steps on Cyrus's hand. "Get up."

Cyrus scurries to his knees. "Your will is my way, Master!"

"Let this be the beginning of your knowledge," he responds. Black clouds caress Lucifer's burnt skin as he walks a circuit around his throne room. He ignores the lightning strikes that assault his body as if they were gnats. His black cloud wings gather to stretch into infinity and beyond. He elongates and shrinks at will to achieve whatever effect he so chooses. He expands to intimidate and contracts to coerce. He molds darkness like clay and wields sin as if it were a machete. "You have much to do and much more to learn. We need knowledge and experience. Had you not become Aware, the true Abbadon would have what we need. You were a last-resort contingency plan at worst and a bonus legionnaire at best. As his placeholder, you must embody all that he was. What do you know of strategy, Spawn?" as he addresses his son.

"Point-and-shoot, Master."

Lucifer shakes his head. "First of all, we have a weapon that angels don't have access too."

"Fear," Nil says.

"Fear," Lucifer agrees. "It is the ultimate weapon. It can speed your attacks and slow your opponent's to a halt. Fear debases the soul—creating a foothold for impressions by my forces. A fearful soul becomes indecisive and vulnerable. Ultimately, it will become susceptible to complete degradation. You have learned of the 'Threshold of the Damned,' no? For every turned soul, it empowers the Shadow Domain. Yes, fear is the ultimate weapon. It can surge your power and freeze them where they stand. For instance: lesson one." He snaps his fingers.

A dragon drops from the dark clouds underneath the ceiling. His dark reptilian hide absorbs light. He lands meters away from Cyrus. His powerful roar slams into him, knocking him back.

Cyrus's HUD flashes across his eyes, giving him a quick bio of this dragon demon. Ikrlez, former anchor of angelic Team Shadowscorn—currently known as Chrysos Squad. Now he's second-in-command to Lucifer the Deceiver. Cyrus's fear makes him unable to move. His mouth hangs open in shock. A jewel-adorned crown sits atop Ikrlez as he grins, displaying razor-sharp teeth. Not teeth, swords. He uses great swords as fangs, and they recede to daggers near the rear of his mouth. He has shadowy tentacles that make up his left arm, and swords make up his fingernails on his left hand. Another power demon.

Cyrus flops over on his hands and knees and tries to crawl away. Sinister laughter echoes in the massive great room. The laughter becomes closer. He's being chased. Is this a real attack? The tentacles of Ikrlez wrap around him and squeeze. His breath is forced out of his lungs as he gasps for air. Ikrlez doesn't relent. The acidic smoke burns his nostrils. His skin flakes away like so much ash. The tentacles bulge in waves back toward its owner. Not only can he not breath but his strength leaves him. The tentacles siphon his health.

His life force ebb away. He becomes weaker as he begins to age. His hair begins to gray. Fine wrinkles form on his face. Eyes: dim, vision: blurry. His bones stiffen, creak, then crack.

Ikrlez displays his sword nails and severs his arm. He's too weak to yell. He drifts into a barely conscious daze. He feels himself dying. Black blood pools beneath him. Laughter is heard throughout the keep. Is this how it ends? His severed arm flopping like a headless snake. Muscle tendons from the severed limb creep across the floor to make up the distance to Cyrus and attach to his stump. Ikrlez releases his shadowy grip, then lies on the Mist-filled ground, drumming his sword nails in a complicated rhythm.

Once the tentacles release Cyrus, his youth and power return. He looks over his body. Everything appears back to normal. Not even blood on the ground. No scars or pain. His HUD explains why. The tentacles only affected him psychologically. Other than the tentacles squeezing him, Iklrez caused no physical harm.

Lucifer looks at his newest pledge and grins. "Now that you know who Ikrlez is, tell me. What is his rank?"

The spawn looks upon the mammoth serpent with caution, giving him deference and respect. "May I gauge your prowess, Mighty One?"

In answer, Ikrlez partially closes his eyes and yawns. Sword teeth glint with a sinister glow. Cyrus's eyes filter to his HUD. His eyes update his previous fight—or should he say attack—with power levels ranging from strength to abilities, to wit, and even size, but the power that is factored in most is fear. He is just learning these power ranks, but it doesn't take a genius to realize that this powerful wyrm has a high-power level. All these attributes and powers form an analysis almost as soon as the question is out of Satan's mouth.

"Class S, Master."

"What is your rank, Spawn?"

He hadn't thought of evaluating himself, not that he had the time to. Taking in this new world has been overwhelming in itself. He looks at his hands. His inherent HUD display analyzes his own powers. They take in his powers though he isn't aware of what they are or how to use them all. So his potential then. His HUD tells him the answer. He's is class D. He's not much better than an imp. No, it is rising. His untapped potential is realized in numbers and data.

"Class S, Master!" he realizes in shock. He is just as powerful as this dragon demon. Impossible. It took him out in seconds, and he was just toying with him, taunting him. There's no way. Without realizing it, he uses his HUD to look at his master. The master opens his arms in a broad welcoming gesture and smiles.

Three question marks are displayed. Lucifer's rank is unchartable.

"Fear is my weapon, Spawn. I need not employ any other power if you gaze upon me in fear," Ikrlez says in a deep resounding voice.

"In the simplest terms: fear will decrease or increase your rank. Do you understand, Spawn?" Lucifer questions.

"Yes, Master."

"Lesson two."

The polished skulls that float around Lucifer's castle open their mouths. A "screen" displays moving images within their mouths. Each displays an angel at her best. The HUD reveals her name: Delilah. Outwitting, outsourcing, or outmaneuvering all her opponents. She never seems to use the same strategy twice using minimal effort, maximum effect. Each skull screen shows her highlight. In fact, her very existence is a highlight.

Cyrus stares at the screens in awe. He pinches and zooms the screen. His inherent knowledge of the Shadow Domain encompasses knowledge of high-ranking foes. In one image, she's partnered with an eagle-headed angel named Valorian. Aggressive and vicious with his talons. Only class D though. A wimp.

They move together as one. She flashes her iridescent sword between his attacks. She twirls and dips as he lunges and leaps. Nothing can get through their attack, and no one can get behind them. They move too fast to expose a weakness in their defense. Impressive.

Scanning the other screens, he discovers no matter who she works with, each teammate is an extension of her will. She compliments every attack and is decisive in her actions. He never thought a woman was even capable of such intelligence and ability.

"She was nearly Chief Strategist of Heaven. She could be in line again. A subtraction from Heaven is an addition to Hell. I need you to learn her ways. Mimic her actions. You must anticipate her thoughts," Lucifer instructs.

"I will master the powers you have granted me, Master. I will move faster than her thought," he brags.

"Not good enough. Anticipation is faster than speed," Ikrlez explains.

Cyrus ponders on those words. When she gave a command, she knew exactly the attacker's vulnerabilities. She covered the exposed areas with a complimenting defense. Incredible. How much time would he be given to learn her ways?

"But, Master, how can I?"

Lucifer displays a gorgeous blue gem that spins and reflects ambient light. Inside, a prick of light moves and crashes off the encasement, like a prisoner bouncing off bars.

His eyes filter to his HUD setting for a definition. "An *enode*?" Cyrus asks.

"A gift."

Lucifer presents his present. Cyrus cups his hands to accept it. The gem starts to turn red. The light within begins to turn black.

"Ah, ah, ah! Careful. Your very thought can cause this to decay or lead her to you. Let this be your weapon, not hers," he explains.

"This belongs to Delilah? How, Master?"

Lucifer opens his mind. He allows Cyrus to view a memory. It was the twilight of God's reign as far as he was concerned. A last-ditch effort to get Delilah onboard with Anura's plan to usurp the arrogant God. If she's in, their success rate rises exponentially. She can follow plans and adjust on the fly, if needed, but today is the day. Abbadon will initiate the sale, and Lucifer will close the deal just like they've done with the other essential prospects.

It isn't going as good as he'd wished. Abbadon is raising his voice. Lucifer's very presence should give credence to the squad leader's proposition. Lucifer rises from underneath the rainbow the two are standing on, rubbing his hairless chin in thought. The red of the rainbow grips Lucifer, like a wet cloak. He arrogantly flaps huge golden wings—like an eagle readying himself for flight. His eyes can bore holes into iron. His very body reflects starlight from the uncountable gemstones embedded on his body. As he passes through, the red of the bow slowly snaps back to its source. He approaches from behind Delilah. She spins away from him in surprise. Lucifer splashes a mocking smile. She is trapped.

"Did I frighten you, Strategist?" he says with bass-booming gravity. Delilah probably thinks to report Abbadon to Lucifer. Now she knows the truth; they are all in this together.

"I fear nothing that does not fear God," she responds bravely.

"You're correct, Strategist," Lucifer agrees. "I do not fear God. Why should anyone? He just sits on his throne unconcerned about humanity or angel kind alike."

Delilah becomes angry. "Of course, you don't fear God. You're too stupid to be scared."

"You are so confident in God?" Lucifer challenges. "Call Him! See if He raises a finger to save you!"

Lucifer pierces through her mind. He can see her mental plea for God's help. Lucifer encases her mind and words into a barrier with his *aegis*. He points to her words as they leave her mind. The letters drop visibly through the rainbow, crumbling like so much rust. Lucifer and Abbadon laugh, pointing at her. Mocking her and her pitiful God.

Delilah raises her voice, "Though He slay me, yet will I trust Him!"

Abbadon tries to plead with Delilah, "Our cause is just!"

"I will believe your 'truthful' tongue over my lying eyes," she retorts with heavy sarcasm.

"Our plight is honorable and righteous!"

"Your righteousness is nothing but dried dung, unfit to even be used as fertilizer, uncircumcised Philistines!" she swears.

Lucifer steps in. "I never took you to be disobedient."

"I'm sure God could say the same of you. How does it feel?"

Abbadon starts toward her angrily. Delilah stands her ground. Lucifer grabs his shoulder. No mistake, he is as hot-tempered as Abbadon, but is better at controlling his outbursts. Anger fills his mind with thousands of tortures. Millions of ideas to force her to his will. Flaying her skin with his flaming sword flashes into his mind, but he has a better idea. If she won't join him, he will cripple the Loyalists. Suddenly, Delilah is frozen. His gaze is like that of a basilisk. "Your fear finally sieged you. You are cornered and helpless. God can't hear you. You're all alone. I will take what you value most, Strategist."

Lucifer knows she values her mind above all things. Therefore, he will ravage it like a pirate. His *aegis* breaks through her mind's eye like a hawk diving through clouds. While the female is frozen, his brilliant mind can bore through her dismal defenses like a wrecking ball. Instead, he scouts her mind like a ranger, allowing her to realize he is there. Lucifer can almost see her gasp in realization when he stops masking his presence.

"No weapon formed against me shall prosper!" Delilah yells.

"Let's see!"

She throws up walls desperately. He laughs at the makeshift labyrinth she constructs. He is wrong about her. She is unnecessary for the assault on Heaven, if this is the best she can do. She is of no conquest—only a frightened little girl. Lucifer is under tremendous time constraints, but he wants his influence to be felt permanently.

He mentally snaps his fingers. He will take pieces of her mind and crystallize them into *enodes*. He steps to her first barrier. She erects walls thick enough to stop a charging elephant. He chooses not to fly over and rip open the roof of her mind. Instead, he feels along the mortar with both hands. This is not a design made from a standard template. To throw up such an impressive barrier, she *must* incorporate a flaw in its design. Doing so discounts the vigor used and allows rapid construction of defenses. Interesting, she had the forethought to generate her own template. He discovers a slight impression and presses it. The result is typical to Lucifer—the barrier shatters. With a domino effect, the walls crumble in both directions in a heap of dust. The labyrinth appears to be made of thorns and brambles, but it is an illusion.

"Too easy, Strategist. All too easy," Lucifer taunts.

With one step, he approaches the maze. Not a bad construct after all. He admits that she has some potential. Though her *aegis* is raised in desperation, it is solid with many winding paths and pitfalls no doubt.

137

Places where she can mount up an offensive. Lucifer shakes his head. He heads for the first crossroad. "Which way, Strategist? The high road? Or the low road?" Then he continues, "Ah, the middle road!"

He forms his hand into the shape of a dragon's claw and slashes against the labyrinth. Interesting, she expected that. The wall is actually gray tape. Stepping forth with his attack is where she placed her first trap, activating her first counter. The tape wraps around him in quick circles. He tries to raise his arms, but the tape forces them to his side. He is cocooned within, and the tape around his legs pulls from under him—causing him to fall. Stiff as a mummy.

Multicolored vapors rise from the taped mold. The cocoon deflates like an airless balloon. The vapors rise, and the intertwined colors drift on a nonexistent breeze. All the way to the temple door. Once at its destination, the colors separate and take its proper placement along Lucifer's body. The colors solidify into the dazzling gemstones that make up his flesh. Then the gold colors stiffen into his wings. Then finally, his face. "Playtime is over, Delilah!"

He rears back his fist, and it blasts her temple door. It shatters inside from his aggressive onslaught. Each step he takes toward the center causes the floor tiles to crack. The walls fall away, and debris from the ceiling collapse around him. Each angry step he takes toward the center is filled with hate and malice. He reaches the center and inhales. The falling debris, the cracked tiles, and the walls come toward him into a funnel. Then he exhales. A hurricane of rubbish blows apart her temple *aegis*.

To her credit, the girl isn't blown away with it. She stands defiant against him, deep cuts and gashes along her face and arms. Tears stream down her delicate face as she holds her arms to her side. Lucifer steps right into her personal space. Shards of light poke through her mental picture. "Defiant to the end," he says.

She doesn't answer. She can't. Her last defense is to show no fear. He grasps her head roughly. She tries to grab his thumbs and pull away his hands. Lucifer laughs. "Fool! You can't defeat me. I am the chill that streaks down your spine! I am the haunt that invades the graveyard! I am he that controls your nightmares! I will scramble your brain! Terrorize your soul!"

She continues to resist as he stretches toward her. He slices a deep gash along her temple with his fingernail. A tear falls from the somewhat pretty angel as Lucifer pulls at the contents of her precious brain. He will rip parts of her mind away, like it is cotton candy. It sparkles with information and concentrated data. She moans in protest. She tries to fall back, but the Master-Commander holds her up.

Her mind is organized, easy to find what is important. He finds parts of her mind that are brighter than others. Her dreams, he will take; her aspirations, he will take. Her desires and goals, he will take them all.

"No!"

Must be some last-ditch defense. Her mind starts to turn into blue smoke, attempting to escape her head. He grabs at it, but his hands go through. Impressive. Not all of her brain transforms yet. He assimilates his *aegis* to grasp some of the smoke, but he expends far more energy and effort in order to do so. He snatches what he can – seven juicy *enodes*. This would have to do. Her mind shatters—and she is extremely aware of it.

Lucifer tells her mind, *You are nothing. Dust. A mite. You are insignificant. A distraction. Everything you are,* he snaps his fingers and gestures to the blue vapor, *just went up in smoke.*

"Master, what happened?" Abbadon wonders.

Lucifer explains, "Since it is obvious that she will not willingly help us, I will confiscate her memories, knowledge, and parts of her mind. It will be a great resource for our affiliates. Impressive! I've never seen this much capacity! Especially from a female!"

He wraps some of the smoke around his finger and licks it. It melts in his mouth, like sugar. His eyes widen. His pupils dilate. The smoke crystallizes into topazes in his hand. He then embeds them on his skin along with his other gems.

Her wound begins to mend. The rest of the blue smoke reflexively retracts roughly into her head.

"Your brain will try its best to restructure your mind. Your neurotransmitters and nerve terminals will try to reconnect to receptors, but many will become crisscrossed. Your sharp memory will be dulled like a rusty knife, forever. Your most precious asset will now be ineffective. Your loss, your fault." With his index finger, he plucks her on her forehead, barely even touching her. He practically caves her skull, causing blood to pool in her eyes, her nose spouts blood, and her ear drums rupture. He gazes into her mind again and watches as she tries to stay conscious. Her receptors winking out. Darkness entraps her.

"By the time she comes to, the battle will be over. I'll have eternity to punish her. Let us meet with Anura to finalize our plans."

Delilah, the Strategist of Alpha Squad, is utterly defeated. Mind, body, and soon her soul. Tainted and tarnished forever. He knows she realizes it too. Body language speaks volumes over her brave and defiant words. Her body slumps, and her head droops to her breasts. Tears mingle with drool from the corner of her mouth.

If only Lucifer had the time to pay each loyalist a visit as such. Or he can show them what was done to one of God's most important soldiers and how He refused to aid her. How she was brutally dealt with. That should limit the number of loyalists dramatically. "I would love to stay and watch," Lucifer says with feigned sadness.

Abbadon wears a malicious grin. "Do I have time for something else?"

"You know what I always say. Indulge thyself!" Lucifer smiles and fades from view.

Lucifer removes the spawn from his memory. "That is an actual part of her brain and consciousness," he further explains to Cyrus. "I have kept it uncorrupted so that you can use it. Learn from it, but use it wisely. It will be the only one you'll receive. Now isn't your father kind?"

CHAPTER 14

THE MONARCH OF WHISPERS

From this distance, Iulas can see his fellow angels enter and exit the *veil* gates to expedite travel between realms. The dark matter that exists in the upper atmosphere is thick with substance. With outstretched arms, he uses vigor to absorb the dark aeriform into his body. The actual atmosphere that he dwells in now dwells within him. Wispy smoke with sprinkles of astral dust imitate the distant starlight.

He ponders the moonlight dilemma, going over what he knows. Xandus used his power of "blood murmur" to gather more information. Only the primary guardian angel assigned to the human can use this ability to speak with the deceased if the blood was expelled from a violent attack.

What Xandus discovered was that the assassin used moonlight to power its attack. No coincidence the newly erected pillar uses a lunar source or how the demon possessed said source to kill Benjamin. For Lucifer to choose lunar for his pillar must mean that there is an abundance of moonstones available, or a way to store or channel it. Moonlight is a powerful source. There are limited resources demons can use in nature. Even the glow from the moon is too weak to farm consistently. There are more reliable sources of destructive elements and its subcategories such as fire and lava. Moonlight is unreliable as it drains quickly, like a short fuse. It is easier to wield, carry, and share however.

Now, Iulas guards this *veil* entrance. Artifacts of power or items of significance should have an angelic guard on duty. They protect the item, the gate, or both. With so much activity going on in all the realms, it has left many high-profile targets unguarded. Delilah was right; she's always right. Someone is pulling big strings somewhere. Sure, demonic activity has been on a constant rise since the continents were merged, but this? Ridiculous. He is in the precarious position to either stay and guard one museum or run a circuit of the museums. He chooses to run a circuit of those targets.

Before he heads to the museum, he taps on his TAC bracer, where three small discs electronically materialize. With them, he sets up proximity alarms that create an invisible barrier. If a red target enters the area, he will be notified. He travels to the Museum of Modern Art to patrol the sector as he anticipates a theft here.

He has a hunch. The most consistent way to replenish moonlight is through artwork. The very best artisans unknowingly have the ability to embody their art with emotions, actual natural effects, or the essence of beauty. He paces the vast museum taking in the wonderful works of art. At times, he metaphysically brushes his fingers across the oils to feel the fusion of sunlight or rose petals. He stops to view the famous painting, *Starry Night Over Rhone*. He appreciates the beautiful colors that seem to hypnotize him. His mind drifts as the soft waves seem to move slowly. The stars at the top of the painting twinkle, and even the bridge to nowhere has a destination.

Iulas loves the art world. Impressions of some of the art pieces bloom within his body. Ethereal flowers spin and slowly expand. Rainbows twist and bend luxuriously in on itself. The flowers push back a small part of his aeriform to make room. Iulas prefers to collect a variety of backgrounds and landscapes for his camouflage. He never knows which will come in handy.

A proximity sensor bleeps on his TAC bracer. What the—? Already? He snaps to attention and swipes across the *Starry Night Over Rhone* painting, snatching a fistful of stars. He inserts them within his torso. He can always put them back, but over time the painting will regenerate. The flowers recede into the founts of his body.

He flies through the ceiling and roof of the museum like an apparition, high into the night sky. The lights along the shoreline become more distant and faint, and the skyscrapers shrink from his view. He makes sure to hide the florals and any other background within the dark of the aeriform, pushing out astral dust to sit on top. In moments, he is back to the *veil* gate. It isn't long before he sees the new arrival. He assumes a battle stance while camouflaged. Not hard to identify the enemy. Delilah issued a flash message of the bug-eyed demon. Just his luck that she arrives at his checkpoint.

Sinxin stops just outside of the gate. She folds her arms, tapping her finger on her elbow impatiently. "Step aside, Deducer," she warns.

Crap juice. How can she see him? No sense in concealing himself. Iulas specializes in hit-and-run tactics and espionage, not direct combat. He can hold his own, but guerilla warfare tends to be more his style. With no surprise attack, there's half of his power gone. He normalizes his opacity. Might as well conserve his vigor. "Not gonna happen."

The demon with the compound eyes looks around and grins. "Aren't you going to request assistance?" she taunts.

"I bet you have a hard time fitting glasses for those eyes."

Sinxin scoffs at Iulas. She shoots purple energy from her eyes. They miss him horribly. The beams take different angles. He realizes that was to cut off his escape. The lenses surround, then converge on him. Just before the lasers intersect, he quickly pulls up the plates of ice he used from the Province of Whispering Winds. The ice transforms his body to a reflective mirror surface.

The energy reflects off his skin and back to its source. She catches the energy in her hands while it pulses like a dying heart. It's absorbed into her left eye, and her right eye shoots out a stream of purple flame. "Reflect that!" she yells.

The flames spread apart and engulf him. His body is encased in fire—melting the ice as Iulas starts to burn. He can absorb the flames, but her corrupted energy will cause any artifact within him to rapidly decay or worst. The demon floats near the gate, giving him time to extinguish her attack. Is she toying with him? "All right!" Iulas yells. "Where's my fly swatter?"

He takes a deep breath and exudes the depths of space he absorbed earlier. The aeriform of dark matter and astral dust hiss out of his body, freezing the hellish flames. In moments, the wild fire crystallizes. Once it does, he flexes, cracking the outer shell. For those moments, he was vulnerable to attack. She could be anywhere now. He looks about frantically. Why didn't she take advantage? He hears her whistle. He looks up and sees Sinxin wave at him.

Iulas smacks himself on the head. He realizes he's too far from the *veil* to protect it. He looks back toward his opponent. That girl gone. This could be a diversionary tactic. He races back toward the museum.

CHAPTER **15**

DEMON CRAFT

Delilah frowns while she analyzes the rocky landscape. Crags give the terrain its spiked appearance. Smoke stacks stick out from the underbelly of the crusty formations. Demons call the area Satan's Spine. She prefers to name it "Coward's Backbone."

It's of no surprise the terrain is full of places to set up an ambush. The interlocking spines provide great cover. The angels could be followed without the assailants ever needing to hide. Traps can be set here as well. The sand could easily cover foxholes, trenches, pits, or glyphs. Even the atmospheric smoke gives any potential aerial threats cover. Demons from above could scatter them with fireballs and pick them off.

A stream of living lava divides Satan's Spine. Powerful demons can manipulate lava like lesser demons can with the Mist. Flight is ill-advised. They would be seen for hundreds of meters and easy targets from long-range attacks with no cover. Also, the smoke above them could actually be a mass of Mist. A dominant devil could use the Mist to gain a huge advantage without exerting much of their own power.

While Delilah continues to survey the land for threats, she misses the obvious. Naomi motions at enemies that approach them from their flank. She hates missing any danger and mentally thrashes herself.

From their insignias, they represent the emissaries of greed, pride, and wrath. They stride toward the angels, snarling and growling. Contempt on their face and their spiked weapons unsheathed, as they try to entice a battle. Naomi is eager to oblige them. She drops into a duck squat, then places a knuckle to the ground.

Delilah halts Naomi with a raised fist. "We have authority here. We are conducting an investigation. If you persist in blocking our progress, you will be taken down with extreme prejudice. We have probable cause to arrest and detain throughout our investigation. Do you understand?"

After hearing her proclamation, their demeanor softens – all except the emissary of greed. He stares at her gemmed armor and gathers courage. "Hand over the armor and I'll let you pass." The greedy demon stomps up to Delilah and grabs her arm.

"We don't negotiate with demons, fool," Naomi responds and inhales deeply. In one smooth motion, the greedy demon's eye is pulled toward Naomi. Lightning quick, she severs his optic nerve and balances the eye on her blade. The eye rolls back and into a velvet pouch that she opens. She sheathes her sword and closes the pouch. "I bet you didn't see that coming," she mocks.

Shock and fear make his mouth open in awe. Black blood pulses out of his socket. The greedy demon realizes he is missing an eye and screams.

"The Eye-blotter!" the demons yell.

Naomi places her finger over her mouth. "Restrain thyself, or I'll snip ye tongue next."

All three demons dive to the ground in front of Naomi. Competing to lower themselves closer to the ground than the other. Their faces hug the dirt. The greedy demon wins by piling dirt around his face in fear.

"As long as your eye is intact, it won't regenerate," Delilah explains. "I suggest you listen to her."

"Forgive me, Eye-blotter. You are more dangerous than your reputation."

Naomi scoffs as she leads the way. She steps on the greedy demon's back and heads toward the city entrance. The gate blends so well with the terrain that Delilah missed it in her initial survey. More demons begin to gather. They see their comrades and appear unsure on whether or not they should intervene.

"Is that Death?" Delilah questions in a loud voice.

Demons scatters. No one wants to be around when Death arrives. Naomi's presence and the thought of Death on the scene makes demons turn tail. Naomi's wings and armor blend with the reds and tans of the fiery sandstone. The angels take this opportunity to sprint to the portcullis.

Evnore makes her voice audible for both angels to hear. "Why didn't you command the greed demon to tell you where Kromrom was? It would have expedited our search."

Delilah shakes her head. "I don't want them to give Kromrom a heads-up. We'd have to bring them along or subdue them. Hopefully, Torix didn't already alert him."

"He won't," Naomi answers with confidence.

Naomi takes the lead as the search for Kromrom continues. Now Delilah can hear the rings of clarity without Evnore's empowerment. She returns the mask to Naomi. Already, she misses the lioness's calm presence and power augmentation but mostly her companionship. In all this time, she refused to don her mask, but now she almost feels an addiction to it. She can accomplish so much more using the mask, and they make the ultimate team if they were to work together. Evnore is also very wise. Her patience, kindness, and protection was physically felt when she wore the mask. She is most honored having her as a *kameraad*.

The chimes are music to their ears. The sound reminds her of a church bell ringing in the noon day. They follow the winding street of Venom Guard. She wonders who could design something this confusing and chaotic. She slows down as she tries to take in every detail involving this city. Can they cordon off areas to set up barricades? Are the roads hilly, and do the curves provide adequate cover? Where would snipers set up?

Naomi nudges Delilah. "Come on, we can't stay in one place too long. They can smell us like a starving dog would a raw steak."

Delilah nods. The angels avoid any military training exercises. They continue following the crystal sounds of a master craft smith.

The narrow street becomes even tighter. They have to step on or over drunken imps to continue on.

Working demons make innumerable crude blades. Imps stack them on racks and roll them away. They are gearing up for war. She must doc their numbers, factions, and generals in charge. This data and intel she must enter into her bracer.

Naomi taps Delilah on her shoulder. Her fingers tap her temple then points forward. Delilah nods with a sigh. Stay focused. She must leave the demons to their work.

They continue to follow the sound of music until they arrive at a building. Fire and smoke are seen. A bulky demon hammers sweet music on some hardening black metal on an anvil. He turns and folds the hot ore upon the angels approach. It is the crafting of a masterpiece; unlike the crude weapons that smash about with the other black smiths. He embodies precision with care and even love? He takes his time as the onlookers are fascinated with his work.

Though all angels as well as Fallen angels were created at the same time, this demon looks past prime. A thick layer of soot covers his ashen gray skin. His rotten teeth chomp together with each strike as he works tirelessly. An external vein connects to the demon blade from Kromrom's heart, or where his heart would be. It appears to be a moonstone constructed with a heron within the hilt. It pulses and throbs with ominous light, moonlight.

Delilah inspects the demon and his workshop. "Talk about pouring your heart into your work."

No visible fetishes on him. She is certain he uses them to empower his weapon making. His only apparent source to imbue his crafting is a huge soul forge. The massive blight takes up most of Kromrom's smithy.

"This soul forge is an extension of demon's power," Naomi explains. "He had direct access to his personal forge, for the purpose of crafting high-quality blades, no doubt."

Dark souls swirl slowly within the forge. One soul tries to prevent itself from being sucked into the large tube connected to the master crafter. The more it resists, the brighter the glow. Delilah opens her mouth to speak, but this demon seems familiar. How does she know him? It couldn't be recognition. She's certain he didn't have this same appearance as an angel.

"We would have words," Naomi threatens.

Delilah remembers more than just his name now. She and Kromrom grouped together at one time. What else can she remember? The demon continues to hammer and ignore their presence.

"I'm going to need you to stop," Naomi continues.

The Shaper continues to hammer and ignore Naomi. She stalks toward the demon and grabs his throat. His eyes grow large as he tries to continue his work. The Eye-blotter slaps his tools out of his claws and flips him to the ground. The tube that is connected to his back disconnects. The souls trapped within the forge stream toward the exit, but the forge's fail-safe prevents them from escaping.

"No! I can't stop! Let me up!"

"I'll let you up as soon as you tell me where we can find your client, Sinxin!" Naomi demands.

Kromrom clamps his jaws tighter than slimeproof boots. Harder than the ore he melted, his rotten teeth hidden behind a crude smile. His external vein disconnects from the weapon he was forging. Knee in chest, Naomi throttles him in anger.

"It would behoove you to allow me to continue my work," he demands. "The only sound of any importance here is my crafting. The residents here will start to wonder why it stopped. Trust me, you don't want the legionnaires to come around, and they will if I don't get back to work."

If the legion gets involved, they could be in trouble. Delilah's remnant can defeat hundreds of lesser demons and scores of minor demons, but major and greater demons are a big difference.

"He's not lying, this time," Naomi agrees.

Delilah checks her surroundings—shadows flicker across campfires outside of Kromrom's building. Reluctantly, Naomi loosens her grip.

The shaper pushes her hands away roughly and dusts his leather apron off as if she soiled him. He lumbers to his feet and crosses his huge arms across his chest. "Maybe I should take a break. I haven't had one in four ages."

Naomi pushes him against the wall and pulls out her sword. It is centimeters away from his unblinking eye. His stare could stop water from rippling. She doesn't recall him having as much resolve as he does now. He is tougher than shade-skin rope. Kromrom isn't afraid, and Naomi doesn't bluff.

Delilah steps in. "Let him go."

"Do you know who I am, demon?" asks Naomi.

"Yeah, Eye-blotter. I know exactly who you are."

"Stop," Delilah commands.

"You're as beautiful as ever. I guess you're the good angel, eh, Delilah?"

"I'll give you a hint!" Naomi yells. She plunges her sword toward his eye.

The demon doesn't blink. Delilah uses her own sword to knock away her *kameraad*'s weapon. Then she steps forth to block any further attack. Kromrom laughs as Naomi scowls.

"He can talk with one eye!" yells Naomi.

"Or it would make him clam up. He's not intimidated," Delilah explains.

Outside, the sound of training ceases. The squeaking of moving carts stop. The demons notice the musical sound of sword art is no longer being forged.

"We don't have time to break him," Delilah adds.

"Then I'll put in for his death warrant. I have justification. He's interfering with a legal inquisition on a murder investigation. You want that, demon?" Naomi threatens.

Kromrom shrugs. "Check my hand. I'm holding a royal flush. Don't believe me?"

"Where can we find Sinxin?" repeats Delilah.

"I'll cooperate with you, Delilah, but I need something from you first."

"We don't negotiate with demons!" Naomi yells.

"Well, aren't you just a bag full of rainbows? You do still love rainbows, don't you, Delilah?"

Something is happening. Her mind swirls, and she is woozy. She hears Naomi yelling at her like she's underwater. Then the musical clanging restarts. Her vision is full of various colors, rainbows. What does she remember about rainbows?

Her memory goes back to a time before the Fall when Kromrom was her teammate. She was sitting atop the rainbow. She sensed someone approach her from behind.

"You always know where to find me, Kromrom."

"Rainbows are my favorite spot too. You always beat me to it."

"This one isn't the only rainbow."

Kromrom was thick necked and barrel-chested. He was already pouring himself into craftsmanship. He was chosen from among all angels to become the head weapon smith and gadgeteer. He created many of the angel's basic gear pieces. "You don't mind my being here, do you?"

"Yes," she responded.

He took a seat anyway. They both watched the universe swirl with life. Celestial bodies enlarged in front of their eyes. The lights of billions of suns glowed with infinite energy. The rumbles of creation creaked and moaned—and they enjoyed every nanosecond of it.

Then the male angel revealed a blade he hid behind his back and twirled it in his hands. A work of art in its own right. Testing its balance, he then sharpened it with a diamond.

Delilah's attention was drawn toward it. "Beautiful," she said in awe.

"Just a li'l something I've been working on. I call it Prism. You like it?" "I've finally created my first masterwork, and it's yours," he said with pride.

"Why?" she says, glaring at him with suspicion.

"Maybe it will give you an advantage in the upcoming War Games... I sure would like to be on someone's team..."

Delilah gasped with glee. He presented the blade, and she accepted it with both hands. She looked at the weapon closely. The colors of the rainbow reflected on its surface. She touched the multicolored surface, and her fingers went through. It reacted with a liquid-like ripple.

"I had to use a bag full of rainbows to create that surface," Kromrom said with a laugh.

She grasped the hilt of the sword, and basic sword data was transferred to her tactical bracer. She glanced over the sword's digitalized instruction manual. The main function of Prism gives the user the ability to "weave" with the characteristics of precious metals and gems. Weaving allowed power and damage from gem fragments to merge with other properties. However, it used massive amounts of vigor. "That's incredible!" she exclaimed.

She continued to admire the craftsmanship, then frowned. "Why would you use a symbol of peace to forge a weapon of destruction?" she asked.

The vision fades as she squints her eyes to try and focus. Her eyes open, but can only see blurry shapes. She moans in pain, grabbing her head. This is the worst headache she's ever had. Maybe Aurum was right. Maybe she overexerted herself by pressuring her and the team to their limits, or at least to her limit, Evnore and Naomi appear to be fine.

Naomi sets Delilah down. Her senses return to her as well as her vision. Her *kameraads* assist her to a sitting position. She scans the area to update their status for danger. She grasps the hilt of Prism.

"Oh no! Not again," Naomi yells as she dashes forward and stops Delilah from unsheathing her sword. "Calm down, boss lady. We're safe…for now."

Delilah sees no immediate threat and releases the hilt. "What happened?"

"Before or after you gave the Shaper your word?"

"I did what?"

Naomi shakes her head in disappointment, folding her arms. "Something happened to you. It was like you were in a trance. I steadied you before you fell, but you spoke as if you were conscious. You told the Shaper that you would get the source he needs in exchange for Sinxin's location."

"What? No."

"I tried to stop you, but you gave your word."

This must stop. Delilah can't continue to hinder the squad. Once again, she's put her *kameraads* in a horrible position. Wasting time and vigor because her subconscious self made a vow to a disgusting demon. Inexcusable. "And an angel without her honor or her word is a demon. So what's the source?" she asks.

"The beak of Rahub the Befouler."

The angels arrive at the meticulously maintained Wraith Reign Courtyard, the current home of Rahub the Befouler. Delilah uses her sharp eyes to discern potential hazards. There are horrors here, such as the planted souls that are entrenched into the ground called yisks. Each one is a tree made from condemned souls. The more souls used, the greater the size it will become.

Hundreds of the abominations comprise the entrance. The lord of this castle displays his power with the blatant overindulgence of souls. The yisks have bark that absorbs the properties of the ground. Faces are molded into the trunks in frozen agony. Wyrmworms emerge from the soil and burrow themselves into the souls. Mausoleums line the pathway to the castle door.

Delilah wonders if the stone tombs could be used as access points to move troops behind the enemy in case of an attack. Hundreds of blood crows caw at the angels in defiance as they hop from branch to branch. They are not much of a threat, but they could provide interference, or they could grab loose items like a gem from off her armor or a dropped weapon.

The demon guardian Rahub approaches the angels. His three large eyes are disturbing. She shutters to think if any of the souls within its transparent head belong to defeated angels. The number of angels defeated in battle saddens her. Not just in the massive raid recently, but over the millennia. With everything that happened since the death of Benjamin, she hasn't had the time to check in or factor in other crime patterns for the angelic host. Not even a spare moment to further decipher the constantly updated intel. She can only hope Master-Commander Michael contained the situation.

Michael was promoted to Lucifer's former rank after the Fall. For now, his rank incorporates the Chief Strategist position as well. That was over ten millennia ago. Delilah hopes she still has a chance for such a prestigious advancement. If and when she attains Chief Strategist, she will form an elite tactical unit whose sole purpose would be to assist squads who are in danger of being defeated. They will also be the first to breach strongholds for fallen angels, especially those who are held in the "Crypt of the Conquered." Extracting fallen angels must be a priority. Right behind finding the hidden location of their captured kin. The unknown location of angels that have fallen in battle are tortured until they curse God.

No such unit exists now as Michael spread all squadrons under his control stretched too thin. If Delilah were in charge, she would have to sacrifice a lot of patrols and concentrate on the greatest demonic activity and quash them at the source. If demons are busy defending, they will have less resources and units to attack.

Naomi breaks Delilah's thoughts. "Hey! What's the plan?"

Once a few steps into the courtyard, Rahub climbs down. His long tentacles grapple and swing from the crooked yisks. Soon, he lands in front of them. Upon closer inspection, each of Rahub's eyes are different. A reptilian eye, an eye with protruding veins, and a bloodshot eye. Each attaches itself to a soul within his bulbous head. Razor hooks are underneath the eyes as they suck in a soul and hook into its neck. The souls' muffled screams die off.

"Guess we have an audience," Delilah adds.

Naomi nods.

Delilah touches her fingers and thumb together to produce the matrix. Only she can hear the chuckles of Time. The bored bastage's laughter echoes within her cranium. His laughter is almost as bad as Abbadon's pristine smile. Who is she kidding? Not even close.

All those eons ago, Time was unfair and ruthless. Her encounter and potential imprisonment with the powerful entity spurred her to action. She had to figure out a way to escape Time. Anger clouded her judgment. Delilah grabbed a fistful of gems from her breastplate, earning maniacal laughter from Time.

"Who can defeat Time?" he taunted.

The Strategist took a deep breath. She searched for another way out, though she realized all too soon that there was none. It appeared that Time was right. Unless she could think of another option, she'll be his prisoner for eternity. Delilah tapped her chin in thought. "Is there anything I can do to change your mind?"

"Entertain me," Time responded.

A flash of renewed anger filled the angel. "I'm no prancing poodle!" Then she sucked in air, and released it slowly. The fruits of an idea came to mind. "I have a way that I can entertain you." Time leaned forward.

"But only if you release me."

Time shook his head. "No. You won't keep your oath."

"I'm an angel. Of course, I'll keep my word."

Naomi hisses, bringing Delilah's attention back to the present. "Operation: Event Horizon. We better get this right the first time," she commands.

"I thought you were out of black star sapphires?" Naomi asks.

"I am."

Black star sapphires are one of the rarest gems she owns and one of the most powerful. To create such a rare phenomenon, it takes rainbows centuries to create. Plus, there is no guarantee a black star sapphire would be created just because the proper time had elapsed. No risk, high reward, massive patience.

Naomi bites her lower lip. Delilah takes two gems from her breastplate; a red star sapphire and a black opal. She crushes a gem in each hand, then places all the frags in one hand. She shakes the frags like they were a set of dice, then clamps her left hand over her right.

"Hurry up, Delilah," Evnore warns audibly as Rahub swings closer.

Delilah pours a heavy dose of vigor into her hands. She gnashes her teeth as she applies extreme pressure to the frags. Her muscles strain. She rolls the frags smooth, mixes them, and applies enough pressure for the frags to bind. Something she's never done before, not with two separate gems anyway. Her options are few with the composition of Rahub's body. The souls within make this demon nigh invulnerable. If he uses the souls as shields, the team will never defeat him.

When Delilah opens her hands, she yells in anger. The gems are deformed and unusable. She wasted too much vigor trying this experiment too. She discards the lump in frustration. Rahub shakes the ground as he strides toward the angels, bringing Delilah back to the problem at hand. Two tentacles sweep across in an attempt to grab them. The angels scatter and buzz around like hummingbirds. They dodge and weave with great agility. Within the Mist, just on the outskirts of the battleground, demons and imps gather and bang on their shields.

"Buy me some time!" Delilah yells.

When Naomi turns her head to acknowledge Delilah, she gets struck. As the tentacle slaps her, she rolls to the ground. She snatches off Evnore's lion's mask in anger and drops it, emitting a fierce battle cry.

Delilah tries again with her last opal. She keeps to the rear of Rahub to avoid his attention. Though he literally has eyes in the back of his spear-shaped head, Naomi does an excellent job of keeping his focus. Obviously, even high-ranking guardians have heard of her. Despite her low rank, very few demons take her fighting skills for granted.

The gems are ground into a coarse frags. Delilah winces as Naomi takes another slap to the head. She crashes into a mausoleum. Her head smacks hard against the stone blocks.

"Naomi!" Delilah takes two steps before she realizes that the best way to assist her is to make her black star sapphire. Again, she combines the frags into one hand, shakes it, and places hand over hand.

Two tentacles streak toward Naomi. A loud crash thunders across the courtyard. Delilah gasps. Unable to determine if Rahub crushed her along with the mausoleum. The dust settles, but she doesn't see her *kameraad*. She must be under the debris. Delilah is frantic and yells out, "Naomi!"

The demon turns to Delilah. Perfect. She got Rahub's attention. It raises up on its tentacles and stalks toward the Strategist.

"Crap and crud," she mumbles. She fills her palms with vigor as the demon closes the distance. Instead of flashing her hands with vigor, she threads it throughout the frags. Weaving it in and out. She makes a mesh netting around the coarse frags, rushing the process as much as possible. She dares not move. The process is more complicated than she hoped. The demon growls his displeasure. Delilah roars her hostility right back at him.

She tightens the net, adding more vigor strands throughout so that the frags won't slip out of position. Her upper chest, arms, and hands strain with the pressure she applies.

Tentacles race toward Delilah while she continues to apply pressure and tighten the net. If Rahub knocks her off her square, she can forget this plan. The frags will scatter and maybe her brain too. She winces in anticipation of the blow.

Suddenly, a shimmer flashes in front of her. The shock wave of the blow should have shattered her bones. The screeches of the demon in pain echoes throughout the courtyard. The ground cracks before her in the shape of two footprints in a wide stance. Raising her eyes, she realizes that Naomi is using her camouflage technique. After the impact, the camouflage drops, revealing Naomi with her swords raised up, impaling Rahub's tentacles. It snatches his tentacles back, wailing.

Naomi turns back and gives Delilah a wink. She appreciates Naomi's attempt to ease her concern. However, the numerous cuts and bruises haven't started to regenerate. Her red blood streaks down the sides of her head and arms. A crud load of dust and debris matted with her blood. Naomi looks seriously injured, but she can still fight.

Delilah refocuses on the gem combo. She ties off the net and uses pressure and friction to rub it smooth. She closes one eye and peeks. Success. Though she won't benefit from the full characteristics of a true gem, it will have to do. One black kinda-sorta star sapphire. On the opposite side of Rahub, Delilah cracks the vigor-rich gem and drops the fragments to the ground. With a snap of her fingers, it creates a vortex.

Rahub focuses on Naomi as she takes flight. The three eye monsters with the attached souls, fly out of the guardian and chase Naomi. She now has to avoid the tentacles and these eye creatures.

"Behind you, Naomi!" Delilah screams.

The vein creature spews a web from its iris at Naomi. He tries to encase her, but she twirls her swords in a whirling dervish and slices through the web.

The lion's mask begins to rise. The ghostly shape of Evnore in her great lioness form appears. Two meters high with razor claws and sabretooth fangs. The reptilian eye emits an energy blast at her. The attack goes through the intangible Evnore. Delilah stays behind the black hole, which increases in size. Naomi continues to dodge while Evnore positions herself in front Rahub, keeping him in the middle.

"Get ready!" Delilah yells.

Delilah snaps her fingers, and the black hole creates a gravitational pull. Everyone can feel its tug. The larger, heavier Rahub is dragged toward the hole faster. He curls himself into a ball. He creates enough escape velocity as he rotates away from the black hole.

"Crap and crud!"

The diluted version of the gem needs more fuel to increase its power. She floods the miniature black hole with vigor, and increases the gravitational pull. He screams. Tentacles lash out and grab the trunks of nearby yisks. Naomi hacks at the anchoring tentacles. Rahub is partly inside the black hole now.

Delilah snaps again, and the black hole begins to collapse. "Now!"

Evnore solidifies and charges Rahub full on. She rams him, pushing him into the consuming vortex with her full three-ton weight. The guardian continues to scream and flail. The eye creatures rush to aid its master, trying to pull him out of the vortex.

This will take perfect timing. Delilah leads the charge toward Rahub, with Naomi close behind. The black hole is almost closed. Evnore still on top of him jumping up and down. The monstrosity grapples the lioness with his tentacles, preventing escape and pulling her down with him.

With a two-handed grip on her sword, Delilah swings Prism at Rahub's still-exposed beak. The radiant colors ghost behind her swing, like a sharp-edged rainbow. The beak flies upward—severed from its owner. Evnore uses her hind legs to push Rahub down and lift herself up. To escape Rahub's tentacles, she recedes back into her helm. The helm and the beak both fall toward the collapsing black hole.

Delilah turns her head. Her eyes bulge in shock as she realizes the beak and the mask are too far apart for Naomi to grab both. She can only choose one and grabs the beak and rolls to the ground.

"Evnore!" Delilah screams.

The helm falls toward the collapsing black hole. Delilah arcs her back as she cracks a vigor-juiced jade between her fingers. A branch extends from the shards and catches the mask through the eyeholes moments before the black hole completely closes. The angels drop to their knees in relief.

Naomi smiles at Delilah. "Nice catch," she says as she reaches for the mask.

Evnore materializes and slaps her hand away from her. A snarl forms across the angry lioness's face. She spreads her claws, ready to slash her partner's face.

"Evnore, you know the mission is more important! We can't complete the mission without the beak!" Naomi explains.

"Trust that is broken is a bond best forgotten," Evnore says. Then the lioness turns abruptly, leaving the angels. The Mist thickens behind her.

CHAPTER 16

THE SYMPOSIUM

Ikrlez approaches Master Lucifer with the audacity of a pride of lions. In Suneater's Stronghold, two of the Shadow Elite's Brain Trust gather. His tail snakes behind him back and forth in the massive room. This room could accommodate a thousand dragons. Tormented souls trapped in transparent columns weep and wail. Each column holds tortured souls, but each is unique. One columns contains Hellfrost as a torturing method while another contains Hellfire. Yet another contains wyrmworms that slither inside and out of the helpless souls, and the list goes on. A wonderful sight in the eyes of Ikrlez. After thousands of years of protecting the ungrateful fleshlings, it was the fate they deserved. He wished his master had thought of the rebellion eons earlier. It would save him from babysitting cretins for most of his angelic existence.

The dragon demon remains Lucifer's second-in-command, for now. He proudly takes the place of the imprisoned Abbadon. He could very well lose his status upon Abbadon's return, but there will be plenty of territory to preside over once the Shadow Elite cast God down.

Ikrlez enjoys the role of being provocateur. For ages, he ruthlessly accumulated power and territory. For the longest, he avoided the angelic folk—or utterly defeated them—keeping his name in anonymity. He wields his power differently than most demons.

Satan's infamy scrawls throughout all realms. His notoriety has its place. Ikrlez prefers to overwhelm his opponent with fear, like an unsuspecting tsunami after a seaquake. He prefers to keep his foes guessing, the most excruciating way of defeating an enemy. Even among his fellow demons, the less they know about him, the less intel they will confess in an interrogation.

Sinxin's inability to capture Nameer enrages him like a dragon with no gold. The bug-eyed demon was nothing but an amateur. The vampyre demon is strong and is invaluable to Lucifer. As liaison with other demonic Independents, he can sway their allegiance to him. Once a keep lord loses his territory, they pledge their services to another lord. What greater lord to pledge to than Lucifer?

Ikrlez loves Lucifer as his master. Of course, every demon wants to be in charge, but he can think of no stronger entity, no deity, to defer to. The Soul Severer generously shared his power with him after the Fall. He is one of the few dragon demons in the Archfiend zone—few, meaning hundreds. His master gave Ikrlez the dragon form instead of keeping it for himself. This allowed him to conquer large territories quickly in Lucifer's name, now known as the Core.

The toad demon, Anura, approaches—completing the current and original Brain Trust. What a despicable sight. She was once regarded as the most beautiful angel, having the most brilliant mind in Heaven. Her influence through strategy and gadgetry were second to none. He was guilty of honoring her as well. Now she's as welcome to him as a dull dagger in the throat. His version of Anura's plan was much better. It definitely didn't include Abbadon on the front lines. Abbadon the Demigod was as reliable as a paper sword. Ikrlez knew he couldn't be counted on to keep his temper, but whether it was from Lucifer's insistence or Anura's fear, her version of the plan had Abbadon where the hottest battle would be. It was a mistake that cost the Separatists certain victory.

"The soul well was perfectly placed, Anura. You've done well," Lucifer praises.

Ikrlez's maw stretches back into a sneer.

"Thank you, Master. The anomaly spawned in Heaven. It caused quite a disturbance," she says through a croak. "It contributed to the defeats of many other angels and the death of protected *charges*."

Pitiful frog. She's trying to showcase her most recent victories so their master won't disintegrate her where she stands. Lucifer nods with approval. Embers of hate for God clearly visible in his master's cold eyes.

It was but one mistake that caused their failure to overthrow God. Lucifer's favorite, Abbadon. He can't completely blame him. Abbadon hated God like the rest of the Fallen, but his rash actions dismantled their carefully laid plans. His temper urged him to leave the safety of the group—of Lucifer—and attacked God. Pitiful idiot.

"Master, Sinxin reported that Nameer dispersed his army and left his castle with minimal resistance. He refused to join your allegiance," Ikrlez reported.

A flare of anger flashes on Lucifer's chiseled jaw. The storm clouds that make up his wings, thunder his rage. He turns his back to his generals as he paces to his throne. "Nameer holds much more sway over the Independents than I'd like. We'll correct that soon."

"I've been working on a plan for Nameer to come into direct conflict with Crackle Blade, Master," Anura discloses.

"Not Crackle Blade, Xandus!" Ikrlez shouts. He understands how an angel's reputation is synonymous with their name, but he refuses to acknowledge his former team member's rising notoriety. The fool never even beat him in a spar. How could a Class X even obtain an intimidating rep if he could never defeat any of his *kameraads*? He hates Xandus like the night hates sunlight. The fool outright refused to ally with him, even after Ikrlez carried him on all those missions. It was he who made Xandus and the team to achieve such a high rate of success. Ikrlez was instrumental in Xandus receiving his Class X ranking. Twenty thousand years and he never achieved any further promotions.

That was why Ikrlez left in the first place. God doesn't realize how important ranks and recognition to His troops are. Stale advancements decrease morale. Something God certainly knows nothing about, the fool. Meanwhile, Ikrlez increased in power by two ranks more than his former partner.

Xandus believed they were best friends, though the blue-skinned angel was never his rival. He defines a rival as someone who is equal in power, with similar aspirations, though they may go about attaining them differently. Xandus never was, nor will he ever be better than he.

As an angel, many of his *kameraads* called Ikrlez "Noviris." Combining the words "nova" and "iris" because of his blazing flame-like eyes. Demons in the know now call him the "Sword Devourer." His sword fangs and sword nails have everything to do with the name change. Xandus sits on his stupid cloud, chewing the weapon that should be Ikrlez's canine right now. Instead, he'd rather chase around idiotic fleshlings. Xandus will come to find that his ability to protect humans goes as far as him allowing the fleshlings to live.

Ikrlez is most proud of his collection of swords. Achievements from foolhardy angels and puffed-up demons that he relinquished their weapons from. He ran out of places to attach his trophies on his body, though he could affix more along his spine. The five swords that make up his claw are his most prized. They were the first to fall to him. Except his own master-forged blade Contra. The weapons he carries on him are some of the most powerful, yet, he has no need of them. His only use is to instill fear and remind his foes of his absolute power, of course.

When Ikrlez approached Xandus, he outright refused. It was he who pushed the blue-skinned bastard to greater goals. How can he be content with having the same irrelevant rank that he was before the Fall?

Ikrlez vainly admires his reflection against the hundreds of mirrored skulls that float around. He is lovely to behold. There is no greater entity than the form of a dragon. Fleshlings honored them for thousands of years. They worship and fear them, and with good reason. He is the object of both humans' and demons' desires alike. Power. Oh, the power. Just pushing his black blood through his veins at an accelerated rate surges his body with mountain-crushing strength. The ability to freeze an ocean with his gaze is all his. He allowed soul servants to polish his scales to a gleam, before arriving at Suneater's. Soul smiths keep his "sword nails" sharpened like a tiger's tooth.

A particularly large skull slowly circles his enormous form. His eyes fall upon his fetish; the "Crown of Vanity." The multi-jeweled reddish gold crown that sits atop his head was bestowed to him. Ikrlez raises his serpentine neck and puffs his chest out as he glares at his crown. That is how a leader attracts followers. Lucifer knows how to treat his generals. He could have been like God and kept all the power to himself, but no. He generously gives and shares his vigor, relics, powers, and territory. Even in his defeat, he still shared.

Shortsighted Xandus couldn't handle this power anyway. Lucifer's throne room is no place for weak minds. Ikrlez thinks of torturing the angel almost as much as he gazes his majestic and powerful form. He will cherish the day the angelic Champion begs him not to rip his jelly spine from the base of his skull. Maybe he should start with the new fleshlings he'll be assigned to protect. Yes.

Anura hops to a command table which consists of the last-known whereabouts of different units. He recalls when Anura was one of the most beautiful angels in Heaven. Too headstrong for his tastes, but he respected her—for a female. She was one of the few of the Fallen that was cursed directly by God—she and Lucifer.

For Anura to be unaware of her toad appearance continues to surprise him. She still believes herself as the beautiful creature before the Fall. He supposes that even a strong mind like Anura's can snap. He was unaware of her and Xandus's relationship when they were all angels, but it was obvious over the millennia that she loved him. She was increasingly jealous over the last few centuries. She may want to kill Xandus as much as he wants to. He can barely restrain himself now for wanting to flay his blue skin from his cowardly bones.

"What of the location of Chalice? Are you any closer to delving his whereabouts?" Lucifer asks.

Everything hinges on the location of the angelic gatekeeper, Chalice. His whereabouts are unknown, but he must be found to obtain his half of the key to open the gates of Hell.

"We have intel on the angel, Aurum, who is part of Chalice's honor guard," she croaks. "It isn't easy getting surveillance on a restricted area of Heaven, Master."

"My patience with your insignificant reports wears thin, toad!" Ikrlez rumbles.

Star pupils bulge. Her vocal sac enlarges and deflates rapidly, and her wide mouth crumples in anger. Her digits tighten into a fist. Ikrlez must swallow back a laugh.

"Stop calling me that! Why do you say such things? Who do you think you're talking to?"

Ikrlez turns his head in surprise. "What did you say?"

"Shut up, Ikrlez!" she screams. "Your arrogance is a distraction, and your disrespect is intolerable!"

His serpentine neck draws nearer to Anura. His reptilian eyes glare hatred. "Interesting, tadpole! You've either grown a spine or you finally realize what you are. In either case, it shall cost you your pitiful existence!"

"You forget, Ikrlez!" Anura yells. "You forget what I'm capable of! You couldn't figure your way out of a labyrinth! What have you contributed to Lucifer's designs? Nothing! You are the expendable one! Just like Ann was!"

"Wha-what did you say?" Does the toad whore know what she's unleashed? She knows not to even utter Ann's name. His mind boils with wrath as he remembers the past. Remembers the destiny of a soul. A past where he was still a guardian angel. An angel unable to protect his Fated *charge*. A red-colored, rage-filled film settles over his eyes as he is tormented again with a human that died in his embrace. Millions of times, he recalled Ann as she grabbed her throat, falling to the ground. The killer fled without a backward glance. Delilah. It was she that stopped Ikrlez from protecting his *charge*. It was the first time an angel was sent to stop an angel from protecting a human.

Ikrlez dropped his sword and visage and rushed to Ann, catching her before her long hair brushed the ground. She fell into his arms like a sleeping princess. She looked drowsily into his eyes, unable to widen them with fear. Her last breath was denied a peaceful end. She simply stared—and gurgled…and died.

Unbridled rage fills Ikrlez, but he knows not who he should aim it toward. Anura, Xandus, or the gem whore Delilah who prevented him from saving Ann. He can't wait to engage the angels, but Anura is right here, right now. He roars, shaking the Suneater's Stronghold with his rage.

Lucifer cracks open his mouth a sliver. The inferno, Ifreet, escapes Lucifer's mouth to separate the potential combatants. Ikrlez lowers his head and squints. The wicked flame has eyes. Those eyes seek to extinguish life. A maw that wishes to gnaw flesh, held at bay by Lucifer. The two back away from the blaze wisely. A wry smile etches across Anura's bulbous head.

"Kill yourselves on your own time. Right after all my objectives have been met. Not a second sooner!" Lucifer commands. He swats away the polished skulls and motions to the command table. Smoke escapes from his nostrils. His Brain Trust bows before him as angry lightning strikes the ground around him.

Lucifer expands himself into monstrous proportions. Black veins sprout around his black eyes. He cracks clouds with his scowl. All in and around Suneater's Stronghold quiver like baby chicks.

"Let all be forewarned! Disrespect me in my house once more and I will cast down all from my presence! I will swallow your souls and ingest your bones! Not in my house!"

As quick as his anger was ignited, it recedes. All in attendance rise from their prone position. He chins for Anura to continue her report. She dries her palms on her soiled tunic as she points to Ikrlez's shadow. Lucifer and his general turn their gaze to see what she points to. A shadow peels away from Ikrlez and stands before the Brain Trust. The shadow demon, Mazck, increases his size as he folds his arms.

"Excellent," Lucifer approves.

***

Anura is back at work in her lab, as she leans forward against a table. It is clean now since her last tantrum. New tables and test tubes replace the broken glass and upturned lab equipment from earlier. She won't have long to conduct any experiments as she is on a tight schedule. She has to keep bombarding Lucifer with successful intel, objectives, and completed missions. She must fend off Ikrlez's attempts to lessen her worth, the dragon-headed bastard. His envy and attempts to thwart her status grow tiresome. However, it will only be a matter of time before Lucifer ultimately agrees with him. The Master-Commander is closer than ever to usurp God, and he won't tolerate any setbacks.

Delilah's *enode* floats in front of her. She continues to watch as the *enode* of light bounces off the sides to break free of its encasement. She's tried all types of combinations, proportions, and formulas. Demon blood, strands of madness, water from the Deep, Lucifer's light. None is able to penetrate the living gem.

She must be careful. It will try to escape if the prison is cracked or broken. Easy to trap when it is inside of a skull. Nowhere for it to go. Ironic that the prison prevents the *enode* from escaping, but protects it from seduction too. Maybe that is why Lucifer rarely used this power. As far as Anura knows, he lost the ability after the Fall.

Once again, sSylk peels away from the darkness. He struts up to Anura and smiles. His face, horribly burnt and deformed. The skin is taut like a new drum. However, the right side is pulled down to his neck. The effect makes that side converge. His eye, nose, and mouth angle down sharply.

"You always know where to find me," Anura says.

"It's not hard to figure."

"You look wretched," she says, giggling. "What happened beautiful one? I've seen prettier slices of bacon?"

"I could ask you the same," he answers defensively.

"It's a mole," she croaks with anger.

He grins. Only the left side lifts. "I fear the the Monarch of Whispers does more than speak softly."

Anura croaks in laughter. "No peeking."

"I wouldn't dare."

She reaches inside of her soiled brassier and tosses a pouch to her guest. He rubs a handful of the contents on his face and gives her a sarcastic salute. In mere moments, the concoction causes his face to become smooth and handsome once again.

"I liked you better before."

"Pity this doesn't work for you."

"Why would I need it?" Anura asks in confusion. "Now what of your assignment? What of the human girl?"

"I have other employers, Anura. I have many demands I must meet." sSylk holds up the pouch Anura gave him. "Your request will be given priority now."

Anura snorts her response. She conjures a globe of light and pushes it toward sSylk's face to see her handiwork. He instinctively shades his face from the brightness.

"A shadow prefers the company of darkness."

Anura's star-shaped pupils spin in realization and excitement. A smile etched on her mouth connects to her ear holes.

"sSylk! I could kiss you! That's it!" Anura exclaims.

CHAPTER 17

CONVERGENCE

Delilah, once again, wears Evnore's mask. The angels storm back into Kromrom's forge. Clinched fists and angry scowls dominate their demeanor. The Shaper isn't distracted by their entrance. He finishes spinning a glowing thread into a weapon mold. Without looking up, he holds his hand out.

"We need the information first, Shaper," Naomi replies.

Kromrom withdraws his hand and continues crafting. Souls spin around in the soul forge, unable to prevent themselves from the suction of the transparent cauldron. Their moans are barely audible from the dense container they are trapped within.

The Mist is thicker than usual here—almost waist high. It creeps up the lower extremities of her body, like a stretching shadow, and is tangible. It makes her skin itchy and slimy. She folds her arms. "We'll just take Rahub's beak elsewhere. Maybe someone else could use this as a relic in exchange for information."

"So you'll go back on your oath because I don't bend immediately to your will? Go ahead. I have a couple of those types in there too," he replies as he thumbs behind him at the forge. He holds his hand out again.

Delilah slaps the beak into his calloused hand. It is burnt and scaly from crafting with unholy flames, no doubt. He must be very resistant to pain. He tosses Rahub's beak to the side and continues his work; twisting, folding, and layering black steel and shade into a wicked blade mold. A weapon God would be ashamed of and Lucifer would be proud of. A couple of eye vermin fight over the discarded body part. The angels' eyes bulge in surprise.

"Kromrom!" Delilah yells. "I gave you the beak! If you didn't need it, why'd you make us get it for you? Where's Sinxin?"

The Shaper wipes sweat from his brow, clearing the black smudges. Then he continues hammering on—unconcerned about the angels' anger. "So which question did you want answered?"

"All of them! Why did you have us get that beak?" Naomi screams.

Delilah looks at Naomi, then Kromrom. "We vanquished someone's guardian. Obviously, a rival to whichever side he's on."

A frown etches on Naomi's face. "Bastage! You demonic bastage!"

She starts toward the demon blacksmith, but Delilah raises her hand. Naomi looks at her in anger and balls up her fists.

"I told you—the inhabitants here must hear my hammering on time."

"Continue hammering; finish talking," Naomi threatens.

"Fine. Now where were we?" Kromrom asks as he continues to work.

"Quit stalling, demon!" Naomi shouts. "Or I'll lop off your limbs and leave you rolling on your back like an overturned turtle! I don't care who comes looking for you! Where is Sinxin?"

Kromrom cools the blade in a vat of Hellfrost, moonlight, and shadow. He pulls the weapon dramatically out of the vat. Black ooze slides off the edge. Hellfrost etches a channel for the moonlight to settle—down the center of the blade. He raises the blade to the sky, admiring its beauty. The weapon absorbs light just as much as it reflects light. "Oh, you wanted to know where Sinxin was. Why, she is—"

"Right here!" Sinxin finishes.

Most of the Mist transforms into the bug-eyed demoness, Sinxin. Kromrom flips the blade over his shoulder, end over end. Sinxin catches the blade by the hilt. Delilah's mouth hinges open in shock. She was too slow to react to the weapon exchange. The

Mist was much too thick than it was when they were previously in Kromrom's forge. She admonishes herself for not anticipating the trap. Stupid.

Sinxin checks the blade. Runes cover the blade, and the edge is luminescent with the silvery glow of moonlight. She performs a quick weapon kata, testing the weapon's balance and speed. She settles comfortably into a defensive stance. "What do you call it, Master Shaper?"

"I call it Izum'vlema. In old demonic tongue, it means—"

"The Soul of Moonlight and Shadow," she finishes. "An appropriate name for a magnificent sword, Shaper. You made a legendary sword, and I will give it notoriety."

Delilah meets Kromrom's eyes with an angry glare.

"Oh, did you expect us to pick up where we left off, Delilah?" he replies with a laugh. "I did tell you where she was after all. Though betraying a client is a terrible business model."

Delilah analyzes their opponent. Setting up this trap without even Evnore being aware means she's intelligent and able to mask her scent. Though with all the other competing smells here and the Mist, detecting her scent would have been nigh impossible anyway. Her compound eyes will give her almost three hundred sixty degrees of vision around her. An attack to her rear may pose no real advantage. She is proficient with melee weapons. From the image of Sinxin that Delilah fought in her war room, the bug-eyed demon emits negative energy, so she is likely a wielder of sorcery. She hails from the devil class of a melee mage, highly proficient with close combat and magical ranged assault.

"Delilah, she has something of yours," Naomi says in a deep growl.

She chins to her *enode*. "Yes, you do have something that belongs to me, Fly Eye."

Sinxin takes a few dangerous steps toward the Strategist, twirling her blade and displaying needle-sharp teeth in a wicked smile.

***

Sinxin checks her surroundings as she approaches the angels. So this is Delilah. Her masters warned her about the gem-wielding angel. How can she be dangerous if she's unnamed? The real threat must be the Eye-blotter. Not dismissing Delilah as much as she acknowledges Naomi's prowess. The feisty angel's notoriety is known all around the Archfiend Zone. She estimates her rank to be class C—much lower than her own X rank. However, she didn't underestimate a weak fleshling when she assassinated him, and she won't underestimate this foe either.

Naomi was credited with many Class X captures. Even if she wasn't alone, it was the Eye-blotter who initiates, presses, and finishes the attack. She is aggressive, ruthless, and relentless. Sinxin wonders if the she possesses an extensive knowledge of weapon lore. Of course, she does—it must be how the angels were able to track her so fast. Naomi's knowledge of lore led them to Kromrom. Her weapon lore hastened their investigation—very impressive. She begins to respect her opponent all the more. She will need to focus her attacks on this angel. She will attain even more notoriety for defeating her. Though other than her weapon dances and lore knowledge, she doesn't really know much about this cutesy angel. Once the angel is subdued, she'll rip off her pretty face and tape it over her own.

Sinxin realizes she made a mistake when she materialized into the midst of them. However, she has to show the angels that she is unafraid. She can take both of them on easily, and she wants all to see her do it. Now she must secure the ground she gained and make the angels fall back on defense. She takes a deep breath and fills the area in front of her with vigor-rich fire. The flames bind and bulge, creating an enormous fireball. Then the demon launches it at the Eye-blotter.

The angels scatter as the miniature comet crackles toward them. Sinxin follows closely behind the fireball as it explodes upon contact with the earthen wall behind them. She had hoped the fiery splash would impair them, but the angels were too quick. She follows up with her weapon, slashing low and high.

Naomi dodges and blocks the attacks with her swords and bracers. Then she counters. Sinxin is as fast as a fly. She almost disarms

Naomi, sneaking between her twin blades. With her three-hundred-sixty-degree vision, she catches Delilah raising her sword to attack her flank. A sharp-edged rainbow approaches her at a perfect forty-five-degree angle. Sinxin spins to block the attack, then concentrates on Naomi again. Delilah reverses her blade and at thirty degrees, then ten degrees, her attacks hitting its mark.

The combatants back away and reassess each other. She looks at her silver-cream skin, angry at the sparks of vigor that escapes through the cracks. Sinxin backs away and spits a smaller, faster fireball at Delilah. "Unnamed! You cracked my silver skin."

She brushes away the flakes of silver skin casually, but she is impressed. Her timing was perfect, and her form was textbook. The unnamed must be the reason the Eye-blotter was so successful at taking down Class Xs. Since fear accounts for a great percentage of a demon's reputation and power, it is always beneficial to be "named." Angels benefit from their prestige, though this unnamed has an advantage as well. Sinxin has no idea what weapon the angel wields or her powers. What strategy she leans on or if she specializes in ranged attacks, melee, or support. She made a mistake when she neglected to research her tertiary targets. She could have at least had her eye vermin to run recon on Delilah. She's in for a long fight if the unnamed is fulfilling a support role. If so, the unnamed must be defeated first.

She uses her vigor to draw the Mist to her. She wields the Mist with her free hand. While blocking Naomi's renewed attacks, she grapples Delilah from behind with her Mist-empowered hand. She loops the Mist around her foe, encasing Delilah like a mummy. The angel struggles to break free. Sinxin squeezes her hand, and the Mist-fist responds in turn.

Delilah screams, and a sickly crunch is heard. Naomi backs away in shock as the unnamed is crushed. Sinxin cackles wildly as the remaining angel shouts in anguish. Ah, the power. A surge of adrenaline course through her. She expended much vigor for her grand display, but it is worth it. The look on the Eye-blotter's face right now is glorious. She crouches menacingly over the Eye-blotter. Her sharpened teeth highlights a sinister smile. "Your friend was becoming a nuisance. Now what should I do with you?"

Then Naomi laughs. Sinxin frowns in confusion and looks to where her vanquished enemy had fell. What she initially thought to be blood is actually crushed gem fragments. She wasted a lot of the available Mist on that attack. Wait, if that's not the unnamed, where—? A myriad of colors come at Sinxin from above in an overhead slash. She raises Izum'Rahub just in time to see Delilah emerge. Naomi slices fast and low—breaking away more of Sinxin's silver skin.

"Cute trick, but that won't work twice!"

"We couldn't make you talk before. Now you won't shut up!" Naomi yells.

***

Delilah detects Kromrom reach for a large hammer. It appears as if he won't stay out of the fray. She tosses the lion mask toward the soul smith. "Evnore, my light work!" she commands.

Evnore leaps into existence from her lion's mask and pounces on top of Kromrom. She presses down on his chest with her enlarged paw, holding him down. He slams heavy punches into her side, but she doesn't seem to notice. Sinxin steps up her attack on Naomi.

Delilah catches movement from the corner of her eye and analyzes the newest threat. A figure darkens the doorway. Abbadon. His tall frame stoops down to look inside while resting his forearm on the door frame. She nearly drops her sword in shock. His appearance freezes her where she stands. How is he here? How did he break out? What does he want?

Her mind reels as it swims back in time to when she last saw her former Herald before the Fall of angels.

"Strategist Delilah, I have a proposition," Abbadon said with authority.

"Sir."

Abbadon circled around her, adoring her every curve. He lightly curled her hair letting the strands slip through his fingers. She tilted her head away so that he wouldn't touch her skin. His pinky moved down her arm, giving her goose sores. She crossed her arms over her breasts, but that didn't stop him from staring. She felt completely embarrassed, but her shame only seemed to entice the squad leader even more.

"First, I want to express my love for you. You are the most beautiful creature in Heaven."

"What?"

Abbadon opened his hand revealing a miniaturized version of a planetary disk, not unlike the Phoebe ring around Saturn. He grabbed her hand and attempted to place the disk around her finger, but she snatched it back.

Abbadon's mood darkened. He crushed the circlet within his fist. "You deny me?"

"I'm sorry. I can't do this. I was unaware you felt this way about me." She backed away. "It's all so sudden. I need time to think. I don't know what to say."

"Say yes! What is there to think about! You desire me as I desire you!" He took an angry step closer. So much so that it caused cracks to form in the rainbow they both stood upon. The colors bled into a soft mist. Abbadon was mad. And when he's mad, he's unpredictable—becoming the most dangerous angel in Heaven.

"But we can't. God forbids inter-squadron relationships."

He circled Delilah again. He touched her waist, just above her hips. She resisted the urge to remove his hand and fly away. "Which brings me to the second reason why we're here. I've talked to Lucifer. He's given me a splendid idea. An idea that would allow us to be together forever. We can make our own rules. Govern our own kingdom. Would you like to know how?"

Delilah nodded. Abbadon clenched his fists, drilling her with his eyes.

"Very well, Strategist." He grabbed her by the chin. "Pay attention and look at me! Let us talk business! This is what we came up with. Your Master-Commander, Lucifer, needs you. As my right hand, I need you to help formulate a plan to usurp God."

Delilah tried to talk, but couldn't. Before she realized it, Abbadon grabbed her by the throat, cutting off her air supply. She tapped his hand. The realization that he was hurting her came to Abbadon like a splash of cold water to the face. He released her. She dropped to her knees, coughing and gasping for air. Nothing seemed to be broken.

Arrogant fool. Delilah lost complete respect for her squad leader. The chain of command was gone in her eyes. He never put a hand on her in anger before. "As your Strategist, I can't advise you of this course of action!"

"Watch your tongue, Strategist," he threatened. "I suggest you reconsider. We need you! Your mentor, Anura, recommends that you join us to maximize our probability of success!"

"Anura? I can't believe that she's a part of this too!"

Delilah started to feel trapped. A shiver went down her spine. As she turned, she saw Lucifer as he rose from underneath the rainbow. He arrogantly flapped huge golden wings. Abbadon's face became darker. She spun away from him in surprise. Now she was truly trapped.

Lucifer smiled his mocking grin. "Did I frighten you, Strategist?" he taunted.

"Delilah!" Naomi screams.

Her *kameraad's* yell snaps Delilah back to the present. She was unaware that Naomi was in front of her, blocking Sinxin's attacks. Something different about this demon standing in the doorway. Almost like he is preserved in fresh flesh and unscarred by Hell. This can't be. This version of Abbadon with the virtual wings, rolls a blue gem between his fingers. A tiny spark bounces off the encasement as if trying to escape. Her *enode*.

She charges the new threat. Thoughts and emotions rush through her mind all at once. Betrayal and pain are most prevalent. She rushes toward him in an uncontrollable rage. All thought and reason now elude her. She abandons her strength, her wit and intelligence shelved. She discredits her mind telling her to stay with her *kameraads*. Only rage remains. Rage and wrath.

***

Naomi tries to disengage Sinxin to follow Delilah, but is cut off. The demoness flings a wall of fire to the stony ground casually—like she was tossing flower petals in a pond. Sinxin wags her finger in disappointment.

"Evnore, go with her!" Naomi commands.

Obvious indecision on who she should assist, as her eyes shift between both endangered angels. Evnore must understand their leader is the priority and must be protected. Though the size of a great lion, her *kameraad* pumps her limbs with vigor to give her the speed of a cheetah. She becomes intangible and obediently pursues Delilah.

***

Delilah abhors Abbadon's beautiful smile. He flies backward effortlessly. He weaves through the town as if this were his only home, smiling broadly. Taunting her with those white teeth. That was the last thing she saw before he... Revenge is all that she can think of. Red is all she can see. His beautiful teeth are all she can focus in on. That and her *enode*.

Abbadon spins and flies away from her, drawing her farther away. A flame erupts from Delilah's sword, and it starts to envelope her. Her movements are swifter, but inaccurate.

"There's no need to fight," he says.

Her strikes are closer to her accursed target. She's all instinct. He uses his forearms to block her sword. She presses the attack as he continues to fly backward and spin around to get separation. Delilah slashes an X across his chest.

He hardly acknowledges the hit. Seconds later, the scar heals. "Feels good to let go, doesn't it? You know what they say. Fight fire with fire!" With one great beat of his virtual wings, he maximizes his distance from her. He inhales and spews black flames out of his mouth.

She can't avoid the attack, and there's hardly enough time to get her arms up. Her body instinctively braces for impact.

Evnore appears out of nowhere and phases through Delilah. With her enhanced speed, she passes through Delilah; then she solidifies her body. The red lioness absorbs the full brunt of the fiery blow.

The concussive force knocks her to the ground. The black flames seem alive as they inhale oxygen and become brighter, or is it darker? The lioness whimpers in extreme pain. The blaze stretches itself around her and burns hotter.

"No!" Delilah screams.

She drops to her knees next to Evnore's smoldering body. Abbadon backs up to a safe distance and watches the angels, laughing. Forever, he laughs at her. Evnore's pitiful eyes look back at her. Delilah's rage fades, and the Strategist emerges. She reclaims the wit she shelved from wrath. Evnore cringes when she touches her scorched fur while she keeps alert of the danger that stands before them.

***

Naomi crosses her swords in a defensive stance and backs up to a wall to protect her back. Show no fear. She must bide her time until her *kameraads* come back.

Sinxin closes the gap while laughing at her. "Oh, this is not even a challenge now. The unnamed was the true strength, not you, Eye-blotter," she taunts, shaking her head.

She stands ready to deflect any attack—courageous in the face of defeat. "Beach please! I'm no easy win," she promises with a cocky grin. "Don't make me mad, angry, or upset!"

Demons from the surrounding area converge on her location. They laugh and snarl at Naomi. Kromrom pounds his hammer in his palm. The wall is so dark it feels oily and alive. Shadowy arms suddenly wrap around Naomi. The Mist? No. "Mazck! Let me go!"

"You know this demon, Eye-blotter?" Then to Mazck, Sinxin queries suspiciously, "Is this your girlfriend?"

Without hesitation, Mazck answers, "If she were, would I do this?" He hardens the shadow at the fingertips into claws and plunges it into her back. Naomi screams in agony, nearly fainting. She turns to look at him with utter betrayal. Dead coals gaze back at her blankly. He withdraws his claws, allowing her red blood to drip to the ground. Naomi begins to heal, but she is still bound by Mazck's other arm and weak after his attack.

"I suppose you wouldn't," Sinxin responds.

Naomi's reflection is refracted on her eyes a thousand times as Sinxin's neck lengthens. The demon's head closes in on the injured angel.

CHAPTER 18

A THREEFOLD CORD

Red dust stirs across the hard ground as the wind begins to intensify. As Delilah's rage fades, her perception becomes sharper. While squatting over Evnore, she checks behind and above. Behind her to see how far she came and above her to check her points of reference by the stars—the few that are visible through the scorched sky. She chooses an aquamarine off her armor and crushes it over Evnore's smoldering form. She sits up when the frags turn into a deluge of water to extinguish the flames and refresh her.

She observes no other visible threats. The area is wide open, so no real threat of ambush. She wipes her forehead with the back of her hand. She feels dizzy. Possibly from exerting so much negative emotions and energy when she wielded her weapon. She expended a nice chunk of her vigor pool as well.

That smile. That beautiful, hateful smile. She can't help but think back on his betrayal. One of the strongest angels ever created—nothing but a treasonous bastage. Their Master-Commander, Lucifer was the ultimate deceiver. She shouldn't be shocked though. In retrospect, Satan walked the line of every major sin. He got as close to disobeying God's direct orders as possible. He did his best to subtly keep the royal host loyal to him and hint at his displeasure of the way God went about mandates. Anytime there was a questionable order God issued, Lucifer pointed out the discrepancy.

She worked hard to earn the respect of her peers. Gender racism, not as prevalent in Heaven as with humans, but it still existed. God did much to ensure women held high positions of authority. Yet just having the title didn't always yield the respect it deserved. Not like it would with males.

Delilah always believed respect was earned through hard work. After all, you can't shape a diamond with a rose petal. She acquired much prestige when she requested the most difficult assignments. She finally attained the upper echelon when Abbadon insisted they team up for the heavenly war games.

She needed to recruit another member for her squad. She aspired to team up with Ikrlez, but he was already drafted. Her rival was not an option. Delilah wanted to beat the best, at her best. Her hardest challenge was Anura. A victory against her would cement her battle prowess to the Virtuous Culture.

She was absolutely honored that Abbadon wanted her on his squad. Angelic folk called him the Demigod. A dream come true. She already designed her icon for winning. She even went so far as to gather a few words for her speech. She knew she would win now.

Kromrom was an average warrior, at best. However, he gave them a distinct advantage—master craft weapons. He had already given her Prism. When Delilah told Kromrom that she and Abbadon were going to be squad mates, he wanted to join. How could Abbadon refuse to include the craftsman when he promised him his own custom-worked weapon?

The competition was fierce. Though there were no restrictions to winning, not all angels played honorably. All's fair in war and winning after all. When matches were set up, some would try every advantage to win. The title meant that much. Abbadon insisted that they follow suit, but Delilah refused to comply. She wouldn't use her *aegis* to gain advantage, for more than one reason.

Though mental warfare wasn't banned, she would have a great advantage against others. There was nothing wrong with that, but *aegis* attacks had lasting effects. If a mental assault intensified, she could cause irreparable damage to the mind of a friendly, and she couldn't live with that.

Second, she didn't want anyone to delve a pattern or develop a familiarity to her *aegis*. She wanted to remain as much of an enigma as possible.

Third, mental warfare exhausted much vigor. Her power wouldn't replenish fast enough to make it to the finals. She must conserve her power to last throughout the prolonged competition. It was good she established a reputation of winning. Very few would challenge her at her strength.

Despite being unfamiliar with one another's attacks and abilities, the team worked together well. To no one's surprise, they worked their way up the rankings. Abbadon was a beast at point. He always took down their opponent's strongest gladiator, and she always had an edge over the other Strategists. Their weapons always gave them an advantage over inferior weaponry. Kromrom created a magma-infused two-handed sword for the Demigod that set the very air ablaze. Though Delilah refused to resort to dirty tactics, Abbadon had not. He ruthlessly set winged angels aflame—causing them to plummet to their defeat.

Finally, it was the last round of the heavenly war games. The winners would be elevated to the squad of most renown. She, being the squad's Strategist, would be promoted to Chief Strategist of Heaven. All angels were in assembly. Cheers erupted every time a sword raised in triumph. Only one problem prevented her from winning this contest. The team she respected most was the trio meters across from her and her team. Delilah was finally up against her lovely rival, Anura.

Xandus and Ikrlez gave Anura a very balanced team. Delilah hated that she was unable to recruit Ikrlez. Next to Abbadon, he was the most powerful angel left in the competition. Ikrlez intimidated most angels with his relaxed swagger and effortless ferocity. His uncanny speed and sinewy strength was shocking.

Xandus was an unknown. He displayed much awkwardness in the challenges. Anura and Ikrlez carried him in most fights as he seemed nervous or clumsy. Delilah wouldn't disregard the blue-skinned angel, but she had him with the least priority.

Their plan would be as usual. She hated to be routine, but why complicate things? No one could stop them, so the pressure was on

Anura's team. Abbadon would take Ikrlez, strongest versus strongest. Delilah felt apprehensive as she and Anura would square off. If Kromrom could hold off until either she or Ikrlez defeated their foe, they would help him defeat Xandus. It's worked this far, just one last round.

Something was off though. She couldn't underestimate any of her competitor's members, and Xandus was probably better prepared than he let on. She watched Anura go from angry and stressed to relaxed and confident, all in the matter of moments. She didn't appear to be talking. Delilah told her team to be prepared for any surprises. The evenly matched teams faced each other, matching up with the predicted nemesis.

Abbadon flexed as he twirled his magma sword. It looked heavier than a mountain, but he swung it around like a hollow branch. His face softened as his gaze fell upon Delilah. "You were chattier in our previous bouts," he said.

The pressure she was under was greater than the depths of space. She was compulsive when it came to practice and preparation. It took weeks for everyone to get paired with their mates. Lucifer told the contestants that they would have a month to prepare. Instead, he gave them a day.

She looked up to meet his eyes. She smiled, waving off his concern. "Just ready to get this started."

The Demigod turned fully toward her. "I'd rather you tell me an untruth than a lie." He cupped his hand around one ear. "You hear that?"

"I don't hear anything."

"Exactly. Action moves air; air generates sound. The more movement, the greater the sound. Movement creates sound. Sound means life. Life is love." The Demigod blushed. Then he bounced his sword off his shoulder. "You've prepped us to the best of your ability. We will win. The spoils of victory will be ours. Songs will be sung throughout the ages. Angels will cheer your name. Let's make some noise."

His beautiful smile became sinister. She was thankful they were on the same team. She would hate for him to chop off her arms with that dastardly smile while he did it. Her team nodded to one another with extreme confidence.

They signaled that they were ready. The officiator was none other than Lucifer himself. His bejeweled body reflected the high sun, causing him to sparkle. It was hard for her to keep her eyes off the decorated Master-Commander. The other team also signaled their readiness.

The Master-Commander raised his hand; the heavenly host was silenced. All waited in anticipation of the coming fray. The wind whistled throughout. Wispy clouds passed through and around the host. The warriors held their battle stances with great discipline—not even blinking. Those beautiful blazing sun stones that Ikrlez used for eyes seared Delilah's sweat to her skin. Even Xandus's eyes were callous.

Moments turned into minutes, yet none moved a muscle. The sky darkened. She lost track of time. Lucifer wasn't only testing their physical prowess or strategic implementation, but also their mental fortitude. A droplet of sweat broke from her forehead and ran down the side. Yet her team kept their poise. The sun moved, and the stars and moon shone visibly. Still, the host remained silent as baby breath.

The last light was captured on Lucifer's gem-studded skin. With the speed of a jet stream, his hand sliced the air. He barely moved his mouth, but a thunderous sound shattered the silence. "Attack!"

Everything happened so fast. Delilah was ashamed as she was ill prepared for Team Anura's assault. This was the most frenzied attack she'd ever seen. All the participants flashed toward one another. Anura's team flew toward their assigned targets. Then in an instant, Xandus and Ikrlez neglected their attackers and joined Anura to engage her.

A collective shout spread through the host. Shocked gasps and cheers roared for the surprising move. Anura, already tapping on her bracer, jammed her comm device. Cheater. Delilah's frenzied movements tapped on her bracer in an attempt to reestablish communications. Now that their leader and link were severed, her attackers were at an advantage. She barely had time to draw her luminescent blade before Anura's team converged upon her. She was desperate to throw up a defense. Her left hand tossed the vigor-infused frags of an emerald. She used more vigor to control the vines that the frags became.

They were shredded before Ikrlez as he led the way after blocking an attack from Abbadon. However, the Demigod was too slow to realize she was the focus of their assault. The still-smiling Abbadon chased after Ikrlez while Kromrom hovered in shock. Ikrlez, the silver-haired angel, was magnificent. Simultaneously, he fended off attacks from the flaming great sword as well as pressed his attack on Delilah.

In moments, Team Anura defeated Delilah—her wings were gashed, causing her to plummet. She was appalled as Anura smiled when she stabbed her through the gut. Anura kept her sword in her, riding her down. Ribbons of red blood marked her descent. She screamed in absolute excruciating pain. Never had she seen so much of her own blood or felt so much pain at one time. Her innards were shredded, and she was weak from the vicious attack. Then she started to lose consciousness.

Anura grabbed her luminescent sword by the hilt and heaved. "Spoils of war, pupil," she taunted.

Delilah held on to her sword with a viselike grip and had the presence of mind to hold Anura's weapon within her so she couldn't rejoin her team right away.

She realized two things as she fell from the sky. One was that she had a new respect for the cunning of Xandus. His unorthodox plan beat her. Delilah also knew she would never live down the embarrassment of this failure. Abbadon held her to a higher standard. Now he'd question her tactics and decisions. She would never recover from the humiliation—never. She was conscious long enough to see Anura rejoin her team. She was saved by angels sent to catch the losers.

Delilah taps her chin as her thoughts return to her present circumstances. She still tries to figure out what's different about this version of Abbadon. In particular, his physical features stood out. He had virtual wings instead of the reptilian version she fought against in her war room, which was refreshed continuously. She continues to analyze her enemy. His demeanor is different. Not aggressive at all. Hardly even arrogant. He splashes his smile enough though, but even that is not in the mocking way she was accustomed to. Her mind continues to clear, and her ability to process information is much faster. Dissecting information and categorizing it like a computer. Then she comes to the conclusion. "You're not Abbadon."

"I never claimed to be."

"Then who are you?"

"Let's just say, a friend of a friend," he answers, splashing that mocking smile.

"A blood spawn. I may not know how, but I definitely know who."

"Anura," Evnore warns weakly.

Delilah nods.

"You can't do anything about the past. You can only live this moment. Don't let him imprison your mind," Evnore replies.

"The blood of his blood defiled me," Delilah replies. "He's close enough."

"You are in the midst of a hurricane, yet you are worried about a bruised eye."

"Now is our chance," she whispers.

"Now is not the time. Naomi needs our help. 'Two are better than one. For if one should fall, the other will lift up his fellow.'"

She's right; she's always right. Delilah lowers her head in shame. How could she forget that she left Naomi alone? Guilt washes over her as she has failed her again. A sure sign of weakness and not the characteristics of a leader. Naomi could be taken to the Crypt of the Conquered. She will not be able to hold off such a high-ranking demon alone for long. She can't allow that to happen. They have to leave fast. If they leave too abruptly, this Abbadon spawn could belay them.

"'But woe to him that is alone when he falleth, for he hath not another to help him,'" Delilah continues.

"'And if one prevails against him, two shall withstand him, and a threefold cord is not quickly broken,'" Evnore finishes. She takes a step closer to the blood spawn and growls. The sound reverberates the ground.

Delilah halts her with a motion of her hand. Despite Evnore's ability to reason, she has seen her protective instincts surface. She can be as aggressive as a cornered wolverine.

The blood spawn stands as he rolls her *enode* between his fingers. "I don't fear you, dog," he addresses to Evnore.

"Of course. You're too stupid to be scared," Delilah responds.

The blood spawn furrows his head in anger.

"I'll ask again. What are you called, Spawn?"

The blood spawn smiles that mocking grin again. "I am Cyrus, my lovely Delilah."

"I would have my *enode* back."

He shakes his head while wagging his finger. "Finish this later?" he says innocently.

"You have my word," she promises through clenched teeth. Then she taps her *kameraad* and backs away.

"This could be yours now. I just want us to talk. We have so much in common, you and I. We're both leaders, our memory, our power. So many similarities."

"You've attained quite a bit of knowledge in such a short time, Spawn."

Cyrus bows as he smiles. Her *enode* hovers in front of him. "Verily, verily, I can't take all the credit, for I have you to thank."

"I have come to an understanding. Defeating you won't give me victory over Abbadon. I realize that now. You are a vessel of vengeance. A sword can be used to kill a man or to clear a path. That is all you are…a tool. Justice will be mine, Spawn. But not through you."

The angels both back away. Cyrus waves at the departing angels as they sprint to Naomi.

***

Once the angels leave, Nil drops his camouflage and walks up to Cyrus. "Why he no attack?"

"You said it yourself. My options were to capture, kill, or persuade. I'm going to try and persuade her to our side," Cyrus explains.

"He think her am will?"

"A spider can catch more flies with its web than it can with its legs," Cyrus recites.

"Who am told he that? Ikrlez?"

Cyrus smiles and chins to Delilah's *enode*. Then a thought comes to him. He runs a quick analysis of Nil's fighting power. He's just class A. The blue devil can't question his authority.

"Oh, and from here on out, don't rebuke me again. Otherwise, you will be reprimanded."

Nil and Cyrus stare each other down. Then Nil folds his arms. "Yes, sir."

***

Sinxin snickers. So very hard for her to just dispatch an enemy. Maybe it isn't all her. Maybe it is Prexel's influence on her mind. She can't remember how she felt about enemies after the Fall and before she devoured Prexel's persona through her fetish. All she knows now is she has a torturous compulsion. The Eye-blotter is helplessly pinned to the ground by Mazck's shadow claws. Her teeth clench in anger as the angel breathes heavily. She steps closer.

"Back off, fly eye!"

Oh, how shall we kill her? Dear Sinxin, dear Sinxin? Prexel sings within her mind.

"Silence!" she yells aloud. Prexel laughs softly in the background of her mind. As much as she wants to eliminate this threat, she wants to teach the angel a lesson on not to challenge her authority. She'll make an example of the infamous heroin. She'll make her beg. "Eye-blotter. May I call you Eye-blotter?" she asks sarcastically. She tilts her head listening for a response.

"It's your tongue—while it's connected to your throat," Naomi answers boldly.

Demons hoot and holler at her bravery, in mock awe.

"It's funny you should say fly eye. Did you know that flies can't eat solid foods? Well, not as a solid," Sinxin explains.

"I'm not interested in your rise from vomit, maggot."

Now she's just downright disrespectful. Sinxin must be careful. She doesn't want to lose any of her notoriety in this verbal exchange. She was sure Naomi would be begging for mercy by now. Cyrus's change is nearly complete. He is more powerful than his human form. Sinxin almost didn't recognize him. He might even be strong enough to take on Delilah and her pet lioness.

"Admirable bravery, Eye-blotter. Let us see if this will make you howl!"

Sinxin's neck stretches away from her body. She weaves a heavy dose of vigor within her acid. She allows it to drip from her mouth, like drool. Naomi tries to squirm back, but is still held down by Mazck. Smoke wisps up from the large droplets of anything it touches.

Yes. Yes! Flay her flesh from her bones! Suck the marrow within them! Prexel whispers.

***

Naomi refuses to give the demon the satisfaction of yelling in pain or showing fear. The acid burns through skin, muscle, and tendons. The pain. So intense. She begins to lose consciousness. Her mind becomes red with agony and rage. Sinxin moves closer to Naomi's head. A large glob of acid death gathers around her mouth, bouncing gently on its salavic thread. The thread snaps, and the globule descends. Naomi stares at Mazck. How could he? She hates him.

A loud crash thunders through the wall. Sinxin and her demons look behind to see what the source is. Delilah riding on top of Evnore. The Strategist flings a sun stone in their direction. The gem fragments join together in a single thread of sunlight. A thick laser beam of sunlight disintegrates the acid, dissolving anything in its path, including a three-inch hole in Mazck's shoulder.

***

The protective Evnore roars her warning at those gathered in Kromrom's smithy. She becomes exceedingly angry upon seeing the dire condition that her Oather is in. "Careful, demon! You tap generously into your supply of vigor. Continue if you are Mist bound! I would hate for us not to finish our dance," she warns.

"You tread precariously close yourself! Whatever you are!" Sinxin answers.

"Whatever I am?" Evnore questions. Has she looked at herself in a mirror lately? A heterogeneous of insect and human parts. Focus. Sinxin is right. If she wants to outlast this battle, Evnore must consume less of her vigor. Empowering Naomi and Delilah drains a low but steady amount of her power. Thankfully, she consumes less power in her various lioness forms as well as when she dwells in her helm.

She has always been the most protective of their squadron. Her decision to stay with Delilah ripped her heart apart. Their Strategist is second-in-command of their squad, so she understood that she must be defended at all times. She is bonded with Naomi, however. They share their thoughts and ideals without ceasing.

She's been angry before at Naomi. Many times, but she's always consistent. Naomi only thinks of the mission and never of herself. She will always adhere to the objectives first and protecting Delilah or Aurum. It was most obvious here. Evnore could have taken the five extra seconds to gather Naomi; then they both could have assisted Delilah as she ran off. After sharing so many memories and thoughts with Naomi, she knew why Naomi insisted on staying with Sinxin. Had they all stayed together, then Sinxin would have gave chase. Then they would have been surrounded by powerful foes. Naomi has the greatest prestige and notoriety of their whole squadron. Even greater than Xandus, so no one is going to give up an opportunity to take her down.

Then she notices Mazck is here. With her anger clouding her senses, she hadn't noticed he had Naomi pinned down. He hurt her. Calm down. Evnore's sharp vision falls upon her mangled legs. She roars. No more, no more. She must protect. All cover their ears from her empowered boom. She enlarges her size. Understanding begins to fade, and instinct takes over.

"Evnore!" Delilah pleads.

Too late for that. Evnore is enraged. Betrayed by Mazck. She knew their uneasy alliance was a dumb idea. It's her own fault for not speaking up. That will stop from here on out. No longer will she stay quiet. She slashes and chomps through the mass of demons. Black blood splatters against the walls and her fur. The demon bodies crash against the ceiling, and their bones crack with concussive force. She continues to slash her way toward Naomi.

Naomi spins away while he is distracted and breaks free. She snaps up on pure adrenaline and sheer willpower. She grabs a sword and swings it in a vicious diagonal strike and partially severs Mazck's neck and shoulder. Now betrayal creases his skeletal face.

Naomi screams and collapses in pain. Her muscles and tendons severed. Fire and acid inhibit spiritual beings' ability to heal. She tries to pull herself to safety.

Delilah's eyes widen in shock too as she sees Naomi crumple to the ground. "Stay focused, Evnore," she says calmly.

In response, Evnore stays enlarged, retains the anger, but pushes it away from her mind and toward her limbs. She reaches the fly-eyed demon and goes on the offensive. She uses controlled bursts of speed to keep Sinxin on the defensive.

However, the demon goes on the offensive by whipping the remainder of Mist around as if it were a corkscrew. Evnore becomes intangible. The Mist passes through her, though now Evnore can't attack either. She can only occupy this demon's attacks and wait for an opening.

***

Delilah dives to Naomi, just as Sinxin spits a fireball into her hand. As it enlarges, she tosses it into the air and backhands it at the angels. Delilah smacks a tigereye gem to the ground. An earthen wall erupts and absorbs the blast of the fireball.

"Go! Now!" Naomi yells. "Finish the mission!"

Delilah points at Naomi's legs and breastplate. "This is what happened last time we left you. I'm not making that mistake again!"

Kromrom's structure begins to crumble from the strains of battle. Evnore ducks her head and swoops underneath her *kameraads*. In a practiced and instinctual motion, they grab the nape of her neck as she carries them away. As long as they are in contact with Evnore, her power of intangibility transfers to them as well. All three are able to phase through buildings as they make haste to safety.

Delilah looks back to see Sinxin sidestepping the falling debris as if she were dancing. Once clear, she grabs her belt and flings it in the air. A snake sprouts wings with a hiss and flies after the angels. Another joins the winged snake in pursuit, but on the ground. An elk demon, standing at almost two meters, uses his enormous antlers to burst through the collapsing walls and charge after the angels.

"Those horns. That's the elk demon, Rakgron," Naomi says.

Once through, he uses the empowered sounds of the elk to pierce their eardrums. The shrieks make Evnore stumble. Naomi seems more susceptible to the cacophony of sounds. She screams in pain.

Delilah must do something, or this demon will catch them. "Eyes in the sky!"

Evnore is fast. They blaze the trail in moments. The snake flies higher. Rakgron must crash through each building to keep pace. He is extraordinarily strong. The elk demon reforms his horns to the shape of ram horns. Instead of losing speed, he actually gains speed. He digs up compacted earth to spring his legs ahead, using long strides. More shrieks. He uses his ear-shattering shrills as a weapon and to let his demon horde know in which direction they are traveling.

"Hold on to Evnore!" Delilah says.

Naomi nods and is able to wrap her arms around Evnore's neck. Delilah's practice time with Evnore in her feline forms, pays off. With Evnore at full speed, she is able to lie on her back and keep her balance. She uses her thighs to latch on when the lioness makes any sudden maneuvers. While passing through one of the shacks, Delilah cracks a bloodstone into two pieces. She uses the sharp edges to gash her skin. Beads of blood seep out. Blood and vigor are absorbed into the bloodstones.

She flings them to the ground, and they become exact copies of Delilah. Before the copies separate, she tosses each a vigor-augmented gem. Both catch the precious stones, and the copies run into two different directions.

She hopes the snake takes the bait. Sinxin was hardly damaged throughout that whole attack. They expended much energy from Delilah's disorganization, her temper, and abandonment.

The flying snake spins and follows one of the copies. The copy cracks the gem and flings it at the snake. The pearl fragments turn into an acid cloud and partially melts the snake.

The other copy uses a jade. Rakgron is slowed down by the brambles and vines that rise from the ground.

Evnore continues running full speed. She runs as fast or faster than most flying creatures. She must be empowering her speed to increase that rate. Not that she can't fly, but raising her altitude would obviously make it easier to be seen from the air and the ground. For now, they must flee.

CHAPTER 19

NO REST FOR THE WEARY

Delilah had to loop her arm underneath the leather straps that secured Naomi's armor. The Eye-blotter was too weak to hold on for herself. Evnore runs as if her tail is on fire, and at this rate, she'll never stop. The various landscapes blur in motion as the angelic trio zoom to safety. Delilah wonders if she has a destination in mind or if she's just running to a random area. She yells at Evnore to stop, but the words are lost in the whipping of branches and leaves.

The lioness heads full speed to leap a chasm. From the corner of her eye, Delilah glimpses a storm cloud in the distance as it heads toward the trio. The whistling wind and the acidic air dominates her senses. As it draws closer, it collects dust and rocks as it becomes larger and darker. She tightens her hold on to Evnore with one hand and clings to Naomi with the other. The lioness still can't hear. Without an arm to spare, she can't link them to her comm channel. She has no way of making her stop. "It's too far to jump! We're not going to make it!"

Her words are lost in the wind. They reach the cliff's edge, and Evnore's leaps with perfect form. Her hind legs coil like a spring and stretch out, cutting the wind like an air foil. Below them, stalagmites protrude from the chasm, waiting to impale them. A bubbling river of lava cuts a winding path through the chasm like an anaconda.

Halfway across, Evnore's body goes limp as she faints from exhaustion. Without sourcing her body with a constant supply of vigor, her body shifts into her humanoid form. The angels begin to separate in the air.

"No!" Delilah yells.

She flash imbues an emerald with vigor and cracks it. The frags turn into a hastily created rope made of vines, which she uses to wrap around the unconscious angels waist. She stretches her wings and pops them open, slowing their momentum like a parachute. She flaps as hard as she can, stretching her free hand toward the cliff. With one hand, she grabs the edge and hangs on and attempts to pull them all topside. Centimeter by centimeter. She strains her muscles, flapping her wings frantically to create an upwind. Not enough. Her grip is strong. She can snap diamonds like peanut shells, but when she grabbed the cliff's edge, her fingers were too close together. Her grip won't falter, but the ledge will crumble. Now she drops the few centimeters she worked so hard to achieve until her arm is fully outstretched. "I can't."

The whirlwind reaches them. The sand and debris obscure her vision. The violent wind buffets and knocks her head forward onto the rocky cliff, causing her to lose her grip. The angels get sucked into the whirlwind. As quick as it was formed, it ceases. Dizzy and disoriented, she can't figure which way is up. The sand and debris sting her eyes. The landscape warps as she fights to remain conscious as they all fall. Sliding down the slope until it is too steep to slow their descent. In mere moments, the angels will be impaled on the natural spikes.

The Eye-blotter slows her descent by digging her bloodied hand into the cliff, while wrapping the vines around her other arm, and Delilah's waist. She soars above as she strains against the weight of her *kameraads*. Her wings beat strong as she drags her *kameraads* through the air and over the cliff. She looks down at Delilah in disappointment. "As a man thinketh, so is he."

The fog of unconsciousness darkens Delilah's vision.

In her mind, voices fight for clarity. Globes of light were in her field of vision. Those light globes solidified into Xandus as did his voice. She reached for his hand. He pulled her through the cloud he lounged upon. As the Strategist for Chrysos Squadron, she spent long periods of time with each member. This was to keep up with any new powers or abilities a team member developed. It enabled her to keep abreast of their power level and to establish new battle plans to incorporate. To lead, she must know what each member's capabilities were. At least, that's what she told Xandus. Of course, that was part of the reason.

The earth's hemisphere brightened from the sun's reflection. Lower cloud formations passed underneath.

"No time, long see, Xandus. Let's get to it. Tell me what you've discovered," she replied.

"I've been experimenting with my lightning travel. I believe I can take a passenger with me when I turn into a bolt. I call it One with the Bolt."

"Corny," she whispers jokingly. "How do you know?" she asked.

Xandus displayed a rainbow-colored rose.

"Aw, you shouldn't have," she said, beaming.

He cleared his throat. "Uh, I didn't. I mean, not exactly."

"Awkward." Furious at herself for letting her stupid guards down for even a moment. She should've known he wasn't committing himself to her. Stupid.

"No! I meant I chose the rainbow rose because I knew you like rainbows."

"And flowers."

"Right, and flowers. Let me explain. If I turn myself into a negative charge and whatever I'm touching into a positive charge—"

Delilah finished the thought, "You should be able to build up enough static electricity to transform you and a guest into lightning!"

"Exactly! So I was experimenting with weeds first. Once I perfected that, I went to one of your favorite rainbows."

He handed her the rose. She took the rose and took a whiff of the beautiful colors. It smelled of jelly-flavored cupcakes, her favorite. She placed the rose in her hair. She glided to Xandus and gazed into his eyes. He grabbed her hand, pulling her to him. She put her hand on his chest and leaned against him. She turned his face toward her. A strong breeze brushed against the two as they hovered in each other's arms.

Delilah dropped her eyes and cleared her throat. "So what do I have to do?"

"Be forewarned. I haven't done this yet with a breathing creature," he explained.

She scoffed. "I like the description you gave me. 'A breathing creature.' Next time you'll call me a knock-kneed moose!"

He laughed. "No! You know what I meant!"

She pouted and pushed him away and inclined her head like an offended princess.

"If you don't forgive me, I'm taking that rose back!"

"Don't you dare!"

"Whoa. Calm down," he said jokingly.

He invited her to step next to him. She glided next to Xandus. "Now what?"

"Um. We have to get closer."

"Mmhmm," Delilah said suspiciously.

"I'm new at transferring something your size. Don't say it! You know what I mean."

She smiled and stepped in closer. He put his arm around her waist. He was cold. They both faded from view, as their metaphysical bodies quickly transformed into scribbles of light. The rays bounced within the boundaries of their bodies. She could feel his vigor mix with hers as it spread throughout her body all the way to her extremities. Their bodies, senses, and even their thoughts began to merge. She could see what he saw and hear what he heard.

Xandus established a clear line of sight to his target destination. His pupils enlarged, allowing lightning to enhance his vision. Far-off distances now seemed as near as an outstretched arm. Immediately, sparks popped from their skin. Black negatrons floated around their bodies, and his temperature dropped drastically.

Delilah expressed her concern. "You're freezing! Are you okay?"

"N-n-never better," he responded, teeth chattering.

Her body turned into hot positive energy. Red positrons floated on, around, and through her body. The two began to merge.

"Don't be—" he started.

"Frightened. I'm not—" she continued.

"Scared," Xandus finished.

Once merged, "Xanlilah" threw the lightning sword at the base of a rainbow. As the lightning became a bolt, he grabbed the shaft end and merged with the bolt as it left the cloud. Star lines passed them by as if they were going through a warp. There's not much leeway to alter their aeronautics, but his aim was true. They sped through gaseous clouds, past sky mansions, and over angelic squadrons. The rainbow was now in sight. Still hundreds of kilometers away.

"How do we—" Delilah started.

"Stop? Just apply the—"

"Brakes?" she asked.

Xandus decreased their speed by severing his supply of vigor to his lightning. They both separated as their positron and negatron forms instantly divided, and they became their normal selves. They flew through the rainbow and were millimeters from touchdown. Xandus wrapped Delilah in his arms and skidded to a stop, but they had built up too much momentum. He tripped, and they both tumbled for meters. He lost his grip on her, and she was flung away.

Once Xandus stopped, he staggered to his knees, searching for her. Frightened creatures flew and scurried away from the commotion. He reached for a trail of dust that began to settle and crawled toward it. "Delilah! DELILAH!"

From his vantage point, he could see an arm and leg on the other side of a large rock. When he crawled to the rock, he cradled her head in his lap. "Wake up! Please be okay!" he begged.

Her body melted rapidly in his arms.

"No! What?" he said.

Delilah sneaked up behind him. "That was awesome!" she yelled and grabbed his shoulders from behind.

"Whoa!" he yelled. He jumped into the air and tripped over the rock her body was just near.

Delilah stood over him, pointing and laughing. "Aww, did I scare the big, *stwong* angel?" she said in a baby voice. She used a snowflake obsidian and made an ice clone of herself. Though the clone was made of snow, it was able to cushion her crash. Her body was still blazing hot from the positrons, which was why it melted. Xandus broke off a small piece of his lightning blade and rolled it into the puddle.

He activated it, shocking Delilah. She screamed and fell into a bloom of rainbow flowers. Xandus laughed, then after a few seconds, he sat up. She wasn't moving.

He crawled over to her again. No ice clone this time. Xandus grabbed her hand, but she started to laugh. He sighed and began to laugh along with her. He collapsed next to her in obvious relief. "Stop scaring me like that."

"You started it," she responded. "Might I make a suggestion? You need to work on your brakes."

"I should have warned you. That first step is a dozy! Besides, I know nothing scares you. You're fearless."

"There is one thing that scares me," she responded.

He leaned on his elbow and looked at her. "What?"

"Never mind." She laid back, chewing the petal of a turquoise flower.

Xandus dropped the subject and leaned back with her. The tops of their heads touched as he chewed his lightning like straw. He pointed out the different nebulae by name. Even the radiance of the rainbow wasn't enough to wash out the wonders of space.

"Do you get your gems from rainbows?"

"Mmhmm. Some of them. They produce most of the rare types of gems that I use. Like the snowflake obsidian," she answered.

"They look like bite-sized candies."

"Silly," she said, giggling. "I have to harvest them. That's why I use my gems sparingly. Some of them take decades to cultivate. The rarest ones take centuries."

"Really?"

She nodded and flopped back. Butterflies of all shapes and colors floated above them. A marshmallow cloud passed over them. Xandus pulled a chunk off and placed half of it in Delilah's mouth. She chewed it slowly. They looked at the glorious sky in silence. Galaxies spun above them. Constellations frozen in their eternal battles. She was quiet for so long that he glanced at her as she stared blankly to the sky.

He knocked on her forehead. "Anyone there?" Xandus asked.

"Anyone there? Delilah? Naomi! Come in!" Aurum's voice blasts through their comm link's emergency channel. Delilah sits up high enough to lean on her elbow. She rubs her temples, then looks around. They are in some kind of deserted cave. Shaking her head, she checks on her *kameraads*. Naomi's in bad shape, and Evnore is exhausted. She expended much vigor in their escape from Sinxin.

"Delilah! Come in, over!" Aurum commands.

With the stroke of her finger, she activates the comm link alongside her jaw. "Delilah here."

"You haven't answered my pings! Status," Aurum demands.

"We're all together. We're following a lead. Let me get back to you."

"Delilah, wait—"

She cuts off the transmission. No need in worrying him any more than necessary. Truthfully, she doesn't want him to think that she's incapable of leading this splinter, or to pull her from this assignment. She wants to see the capture of the bug-eyed demon through not just for her *enode* either, but for Xandus and Benjamin too, so she tells herself. She must not neglect the small matter of the blood spawn.

She crawls over to Naomi. Her breath comes out slow and ragged. Delilah uses another aquamarine to wash away the dried blood on her body. Unfortunately, it doesn't work on acid burns. Not much blood, but the acid continues to advance. Acid and fire – two forces that impede or negate their regenerative abilities. She makes Naomi as comfortable as possible. Now to check on Evnore. Her wounds have healed; she just needs some rest.

She walks to the mouth of the cave while stretching her back and arms. Then she checks their surroundings. Sand dunes all around. Looking to the sky, she doesn't recognize the points of reference. She checks the locator on her bracer. She remembers that she disconnected the locator. She sighs and keeps the connection severed. When Evnore wakes, she'll have to figure out where they are. She wants herself and Evnore to be as close to full strength as possible. They'll have to look over Naomi.

Sorrow washes over her. It's all her fault. Breaking rank to chase the fake Abbadon. Idiotic. Now they're in this predicament because of her. All the training and discipline blown away in an instant. Failing the mission, the cause of Naomi's injury, and not causing any damage to any of their foes. She taps her other Word of Power that's emblazoned into her breastplate. "Yeah. Brilliant," she mumbles.

In over two millennia, none of them has ever been this hurt before. Naturally, the fly-eyed demon would specialize in a power that cancels out their ability to heal. They took their successes for granted. Not a good leadership quality, especially since Delilah chooses to be a support unit. Besides, they all heal so fast—they can afford to be aggressive, but she wasn't aggressive; she was reckless.

Naomi dragged them to safety. Power wise, the weakest of the squad was the one that carried all of them to safety. Unbelievable. Then again, not really. Physically, the weakest angels of the squad, regarding their power level, are the toughest mentally. That would be Naomi and Valorian. If she were choosing sides, she'd pick them over Abbadon and Ikrlez, with no hesitation.

She moves back to check on Evnore, shaking her gently. Evnore stirs; then she pushes Delilah back, shifting into her lion form. She growls in a threatening manner, analyzing her surroundings.

"Easy, easy. We're fine," Delilah says.

Evnore pads over to Naomi and nudges her with her snout. Not very long ago, she was angry at her partner. Concern is all over her animalistic features now.

"She's still unconscious."

"No, I'm not," Naomi answers, straining.

Delilah rushes over and hugs Naomi. "Are you okay?"

Naomi grimaces in pain. "Peaches. My legs are burning a tinch."

Evnore looks at Delilah.

"There's nothing I can do. I already tried an aquamarine on her."

Evnore cocks her head to the side, in confusion.

"I'll heal up. It's only a scratch," Naomi answers.

"Not from acid," Delilah explains.

Naomi sits up to her elbows with the angel's assistance and shivers. Shivers? They both look at each other in confusion.

"Evnore, is it my imagination, or is it cold here?" Delilah questions.

She drops her head in agreement. That shouldn't be possible. Angels are invulnerable to extremes of temperature. This is a supernatural cold. It cuts to the bone like a shade blade.

Evnore shifts into her humanoid form and walks to the cave mouth. "The Dunes of Faudinroar," Evnore answers.

"Right. Who's Faudinroar? The four-headed leopard?" Naomi questions.

"Yes, we are in his domain now," Evnore explains. "The beast called Faudinroar was the same creature in the biblical Book of Daniel. Scholars debate of its relevance and historical significance. The fact of the matter was Faudinroar is the literal manifestation of the prophet's dream."

"In other words," Naomi continues, "the creature didn't exist until Daniel dreamt of it. Because of that fact, its powers are unknown. The beast is unknowable, and the unknown concerns me. We need to leave this place."

"So that explains it. Faudinroar saturates the very land with its vigor. For him to be able to do that, he must be extremely powerful and have an extremely large pool of vigor. It's using this power to sap our strength," Delilah says. "We need to move fast!" she adds.

Once more, Naomi tries to test the strength of her legs. Her fellow angels assist, but she falls again—unable to even sit up. Delilah checks her inventory of gems. Maybe she missed something. The aquamarine won't help her. The acid is immune to the water properties of that gem. Tourmaline has some healing aspects. Neutralizing poison and other toxins in the body, but again, no use against acid. "I'm sorry, Naomi. I'm so sorry," she apologizes sadly.

Then there's—Suddenly, she interrupts her previous thoughts with a new thought. The gem that God gave her. Was this gem given to her because He knew that she would lose herself? He was preparing her for that possibility. She grabs at her neck, but the silvery threaded necklace is—"Gone!" she yells.

"What is?" Naomi asks.

"The angelite! God gave it to me after you both left me at Torix's store," she answers. "He said, 'Crumble wounds that stem from rash decisions. Soothe words that inflame with crystals of life.'"

"So you can't remember if you had coffee, tea, or milk, but you can recite verbatim what the Lord said once? Very suspicious," Naomi chides.

"My short-term memory is better. This is serious, Naomi."

Naomi points to her decaying skin. "Sorry, boss. Didn't realize," she responds, dripping with sarcasm.

Evnore's tired body shrinks to the size of a small cat. Panting, she pads to the cave mouth. Tongue wagging, head drooping. She sniffs the air and sneezes. "Give me my assignment, Delilah."

"No, Evnore! You can't go by yourself. We have to stick together. You've never been on a solo mission in the Archfiend before!" Delilah says.

"I'm open to suggestions," she offers.

Their other options are nonexistent right now. Besides knowing many regions of the Archfiend Zone, Evnore is their best tracker. Also, whatever her smaller size can't avoid, her intangibility will. The trick is to not be seen so that she won't lead danger back. She can follow their scent back to Kromrom's forge and make it back to them. After all this time, she has never trekked out in the Archfiend on her own. Then again, there was never a reason to until now.

Removing a star garnet from her armor, Delilah crushes the gem into powder and rubs the substance on both her and Evnore's brows. She cocks her head in confusion but asks no questions. She raises her tiny head up. This time when she sniffs, she doesn't sneeze. The night life of the dunes rises as howls and growls fill the air. The sky darkens and converges in the direction Evnore must travel. She pads off, raising her head with each step. In seconds, she bounds off without looking back as she crosses over the next set of dunes and out of sight.

CHAPTER 20

A TREACHEROUS SOJOURN

Evnore left the relative safety of the cave far behind. She still is unable to generate heat even while running. Her strength, sapped in this cold sector. Can it really be a demon's vigor, or does her fear attribute or even assist in her own frigid condition? Fear, an emotion and sensation she hasn't felt in thousands of years. She almost doesn't recognize the feeling. Her body is releasing pheromones into this hostile environment. The Archfiend has many minions who would be able to track her by the biological chemicals. Her sweat smells horrible. Correction, her fear smells horrible.

She is alone in a powerful demonic province. To complete her mission, she must overcome insurmountable odds with no backup. The inability to recede into her mask nullifies the element of surprise she has. She gazes at the stars for a few moments in an effort to discern the direction she must trek. Storm clouds obscure the fiery sky, making it difficult for her to find her points of reference.

As much as she enjoys watching the sky, she can't afford to keep her eyes skyward for long. Hazards are just a step away if she's not careful. Pitfalls, quicksand, salamander demons, or any variety of perils could hinder her. She will do her best to avoid any confrontation.

She thinks back and continues to be amazed at Naomi's strength. The fact that she was able to carry both of her *kameraads* all this way as weak and mutilated as she was had Evnore's utmost respect.

Guilt washes over her as she thinks about her harsh words to Naomi during their battle at Wrath Reign Courtyard. Trust that is broken is a bond best forgotten. Naomi was right; she's always right. Self-preservation and selfishness had Evnore thinking about her existence in the void—or lack of an existence—instead of completing the mission. Instead, she chose to flood her *kameraad* with guilt. Finding this gem Delilah spoke of should heal Naomi. It's the least she can do, and even that won't rid her of her shame. Hopefully, Delilah's theory about the aspects of the gem is correct.

She arrives at the edge of the desert, and still there are no dangers. That's a good sign. Evnore enhances her senses with only a trickle of vigor for two reasons. One, so that she can conserve her power. Two, the more vigor she expends, the easier tracker demons can detect and sense her. Her feline forms use much less power to transform and sustain than other creature forms.

Ahead, foliage overtakes the desert. Weeds and vines, brambles and trees. Soon, she is in the midst of a forest? Here, an unmapped region? How could this be? This territory could be contested with battling demons who are fighting over the land. As a mapper, her duty is to observe and report any undiscovered region and find out who the new occupant is. Not mapping an uncharted region is like leaving a stranded boat adrift as she sails past. If any angel comes into this region unaware, they can be trapped, ambushed, or lost within.

She decides to take mental notes about the region. She checks the placement of stars and adds a possible border from the boundaries of the known sectors this area is surrounded by. Less than ten foot pads later, she is in the thick of the forest. Wildwoods is more accurate. The dense canopy of trees obscures her view of the sky. As much as Evnore enjoys walking on the earth, she hates the inability to see the sky. She hardly flies as she prefers to empower her *kameraads* instead.

The branches, thickets, and vines crowd in every direction. She enters deeper into the wildwoods with caution. It's freezing in here. She is shivering like a spring leaf clinging to a winter branch. Every time a paw touches the ground, she must lift it back up to keep from freezing to the ground. Tongue wagging, tail dragging, she perseveres. Not an icicle of frost is visible, but she feels as if she's under an avalanche.

She continues to avoid any confrontations or creatures, but observes the danger only moments before she approaches. The green glowing skulls of fox fires roam and patrol the forest. They use line of sight for detecting enemy activity, so she must stay from in front of them.

There are many hiding places here, not only for her, but for enemy stalkers as well. She must check every nook. Every moving vine oozes of danger. The darkness is tangible, like ink hardening on skin. Her senses are on overload. Everything makes a slight enough movement to perceive itself as a threat. A leaf shakes with no breeze. A vine moves as if it were a snake. The ground itself trembles as if she is atop a sinkhole. She must continuously check her rear for threats. Growls and howls assault her with every step. Finally, a voice interrupts the sounds of the wildwoods.

"I pray for my prey. The Great Huntsman will seek and destroy you!" the voice says.

The Great Huntsman? More important, the host is aware of her presence. Now she needs to piece together the identity of her host. She can name the region as discoverer. The name of the sector's host should be included in the name so that future travelers will know who and what to expect when entering this territory. Many of the high-ranking demons already have their own terrains. Is this a demon who is recently promoted, or a demon that is expanding their existing territory?

She's slipping. This unnatural cold dulls her senses. No, it's not that. Not ever being on her own in the Archfiend has dulled her survivor instincts. If she were out on her own more, she would naturally rely on her senses. She attempts to filter the scents here. For sensory specialists, the list also includes demon's essence. The coppery scent of blood mixes with the mildew of the woods and decaying flesh. It shouldn't be hard to filter out. Better yet, she uses the very power that saps her strength to identify the region's lord. She shifts the scents away mentally, if they don't match her internal catalogue of olfactory demonic tags. After several minutes of trial and error, she discovers who the dominant scent belongs to. Udokas.

"Flee, weakling! The chase is more satisfying than the kill!" the voice of who Evnore assumes is Udokas yells.

Evnore recalls little of the Fallen angel. She has the name of this region though. The Wildwoods of Udokas. Just from the province he created, she can tell he is an elemental demon. He exudes his power into the land as vigor, creating plant life. Thorns stick into her coat, causing irritating pain. Brambles bar her way, or he leading her into the way he wants her to go?

Sinxin's flying serpent flies overhead. Evnore dives under the large leaves of a larger tree, and freezes in place as the serpent circles the area. The leaves opens and closes as if snoring. Evnore positions herself right under the widest part of the leaf, hoping it provides enough cover. She dares not even breathe. She drops her vigor to the trickle minimum. Maybe this creature has poor eyesight like most snakes, but she won't take that chance. She hopes that the competing scents mask her own. The serpent flies away. Evnore breathes a sigh of relief.

Looking at her coat, she observes dozens of thorns in her side. She yawns. Then she becomes angry at herself. These thorns could have venom in them. This would never have happened to her in her "youth." As soon as she stops to remove them, branches and vines aggressively stretch to entangle her. The wildwoods won't allow her even a small respite.

She yawns again as she continues on and searches the ground for secure footing. Then she looks to the side. A small haystack? She moves toward the mound expecting danger, sniffing all around. Yawning again, she moves closer. Her curiosity supersedes her caution. The haystack actually smells clean—like freshly cut grass. As soon as her paw touches the haystack, she feels warmth. She yawns again as she curls up into a ball on top. As soon as she lays her head down, her eyes slowly close. Even the sinister eyes atop the creeping vines are of no importance.

Evnore's eyes pop open. She rises and squints through the darkness. Where is she? Looking up, she still can't see any points of reference. The trees crowd her view of the sky. She lost her direction and dare not climb. The flying serpent may spot her, among other things.

Then her bare skin burns all over. She panics. Who did this to her? How is she naked? She attempts to lunge forward. Some kind of nest made of thorns. They slither toward her, snakelike. Incapable of flying or running. She can't change forms and unable to even move. Struck with fear, she visibly shakes. She tries to roar to gather her courage, but she hacks instead. The thorns continue to surround her, cover her, then tighten around her, ripping into her body making deep gashes. The thorns tighten around her every time she tries to breathe, like a boa constrictor.

"You are weak!" Udokas says. "Slip into eternity!"

Evnore's weakened condition wins out. She can't breathe and is in a full panic. She begins to lose consciousness. Everything closes in on her. Even the treetops seem just above her head. The sounds of the wildwoods become louder. Eerie sounds from otherworldly creatures become more threatening.

"Die, that I may consume you."

Tired, so tired. Why resist? Only a matter of time. She can sleep now. It has been over nine millennia since she's had any real rest. Everyone always depend on her. She's tired. Let them fend for themselves. Her vision is blurry. Her eyes begin to close; her eyelids are heavier than gravity.

"Be at ease, *kameraad*."

Evnore feels her fur smoothing out as if someone rubs her fur. Her coat is back. Her eyes open to slits. She tries to focus on the fuzzy image before her.

The ever resourceful Delilah. No, it must be a dream. Delilah is a bloodred color with six lines of vigor intersecting near her heart. This form brushes away the thorns from off Evnore's sides and lifts her head. The thorns crumble once they are removed. She sits up on her haunches. Delilah. What a beautiful sight for sore eyes, even if it's a dream.

"Wake up, *kameraad*. You are in danger."

Evnore cocks her head to the side. She is safe right now. How can there be danger? She must be dreaming. She checks the area around her. Just grass as far as the eye can see.

"You are still asleep. Naomi and I need you. You must awaken."

Head heavier than a cinder block. Now a crushing weight pressing down on her chest. Her breath escapes her as she gasps for air.

Delilah pulls out her sword and plunges her weapon at Evnore's head. "Wake! NOW!"

Evnore's eyes pop open. The star garnet apparition of Delilah disappears once she awakens. Udokas stands above her now. Scratch that, he stands on her. Bark for skin and vines for veins. Thorns for teeth and dead branches for hair. Tree stumps for feet and roots for toes. His near giant-sized frame wields an exquisite spear. Her sharp eyes begin to take in details a lot faster now. Kromrom the Shaper's mark on his weapon. His stump crushes her into the hard ground. The ground cracks underneath the extra weight, but now spikes rise under her from the ground. The elemental demon raises his spear and plummets it toward her head.

***

The contact with Evnore was severed. Was Delilah able to warn her in time? Was she attacked or poisoned? A worried look drains the blood from her face. Naomi stirs awake at hearing Delilah speaking harshly. Then she looks at her leg. The zombie flesh spreads halfway up her thigh now as it continues to cause her skin to decay.

Naomi grimaces in pain as she grabs Delilah's hand. She grits her teeth so hard her gums bleed. She tries to sit up, but each move creates new pangs of pain. She tries to speak, but Delilah shushes her. They both listen. The sands shift, and the earth rumbles.

***

The power of intangibility saves Evnore from her head being crushed. She stares at Udokas's eyes. Dead embers of hate stare back. He quickly raises the spear again. This time he twists the haft causing green energy to crackle along the spear head. Then he plunges the spear again. While still intangible, Evnore rolls through Udokas's body and out of the way. The spear shatters the ground.

"Run! Coward!"

She shifts into her lioness form for speed and dashes away. Not even five strides later, Udokas takes over the form of a nearby tree. A branch changes into his crackling spear and nearly impales her again. How did he get in front of her already? Should she calculate the distance that she travels or the time between attacks? She turns back in a tight spin and slashes at his leg. Her claws are as ineffective as beaver's teeth on petrified wood. Her claws may be ineffective, but there is a weapon that is effective.

"The guppy can never defeat the shrike."

Changing direction again, she sprints away. Instincts tell her to leap, and she does. Had she not, the spear would have gutted her. He's in front of her again. He takes over the form of another tree. She realizes that Udokas was aware of her presence ever since she stepped paw on foliage. He isn't a part of the wildwoods; the wildwoods are a part of him.

It isn't the distance and the other versions of him are not clones, she realizes. It takes him two seconds to transmit his body to another location. Her speed is running in a straight line. However, the speed of a straight line no longer gives her an advantage. She must take a page from Delilah and act at the quickness of strategy. Evnore bounces off trees randomly. Trying to become as unpredictable as possible. She navigates her way toward a copse of trees in a tight formation.

Udokas becomes more aggressive. With one arm, he shoots out vines to capture Evnore. With the other arm, they become thick branches that are pointed at the ends. Her avenues of escape are closing fast. She must end this even faster.

"I hunger!"

Evnore waits for him to strike before bouncing off the side of two trees. Once he attacks, she bounces off a third tree, streaking directly for the disappearing Udokas. His new form reactively lashes out.

And obliterates himself.

He howls as he shatters like lightning striking a tree. His spear spirals wildly, then lances itself into the ground in front of Evnore with a loud thud. Energy explodes from within Udokas. His body changes into husk as it withers away. The wildwoods rapidly decay, almost as if he needs the woods to expedite his healing.

"I claim this spear as a trophy. Come if you think you can take it from me," she declares.

The mark of Kromrom from before the Fall is on the spear. That means, the spear was created before he became a demon. Therefore, it is an uncorrupted weapon. She still needs to bless and cleanse the spear. Naomi will love this.

Evnore grabs the spear in her mouth and attaches it to her side as if magnetized. It shrinks to her size automatically. She pats the husk of Udokas with her paw, scattering the ashes to the wind. He'll be back, without a doubt. He'll eventually regenerate back to full strength, but he won't bother her. He better not. With two winks of rest and a newfound confidence from defeating the Prince of Decay, she can continue her sojourn in safety. Now for the hard part.

CHAPTER 21

REGROUP

Sinxin's ire hushes all but the mightiest of her subordinates as dozens of demons gather around Kromrom's shop. Some demons call her the Atrocious One, but only behind her back. She searches the dark skies waiting for her winged serpent, Kalvara, to bring her news. On the ground, several eye vermin do the dirty work of scurrying through the rubble. They seek clues of any kind the angels may left behind. Her preference would be to reverse engineer an angelic gizmo to take to Anura. She needs anything to soften the blow of another failed attempt at capturing the angels, especially when they were in the Archfiend. Once word goes out to the impatient general, it'll be her head on a guillotine.

She ponders if she evaluated her enemies accurately. Did she overestimate them? They weren't much of a factor in battle. She can't discount their ability though. If that were the case, she should have captured them. Then again, the fight was cut short with the appearance of the blood spawn. His arrival did splinter the angel's group. So factoring the angel's fighting prowess can be hard to determine.

She scopes the rubble in the middle of a wasteland. Even though there are many small structures here, most are decrepit. The wind picks up the sand and covers everything in a layer of crud. Some of her subordinates cover their mouths with cloth. Imps huddle in a nearby corner gnawing on the blackened bones of some creature.

Sweet memories. Thousands of years ago, Sinxin was charged with assisting stranded humans. It was her duty to seek out suffering humans that were lost in the wilderness, desert or seas and give them aid. Her squad was small and efficient. Though she was their herald, she didn't feel empowered by her rank. It was the humans that glorified her. She would shimmer or even materialize in front of these pitiful constructs of clay, in a glorious vision of power. She smiles to herself at the memory of reforming her visage to that of mermaids, majestic stags, and created temporary oases. She lost those abilities after the Fall.

In the times when humans worshipped many gods, they often gave thanks to whichever entity they believed had given them aid. Sinxin gave the humans very little doubt, however. When she wasn't showing off her shape-shifting skill, she would flaunt her own image. There was no need to use vigor to enhance her beauty, for she was a sight to behold. Her eyes were sparkled like glitter. Her hair flowed behind her, as if the wind was combing her hair. Her skin was as soft as cloud-stuff. Unlike most female angels, she kept her skirt high above her knees.

Yet, obtaining disciples wasn't her most significant discovery. A secret was revealed to her. Possibly the very key that separated angels from God. From her subject's devotion, her pool of vigor had increased. Did God need humans to worship Him in order to have an unlimited supply of vigor? Was that why He hoarded praise for Himself; to keep angels inferior and unable to usurp His authority?

She took her theory to Anura, who in turn, was credited for taking it to Lucifer. Sinxin was furious. Instead of her receiving the status and notoriety that she so rightly deserved, it all went to the fiendish Anura. She was always a step ahead. She dismissed Sinxin's concept as pure heresy. It wasn't very long until Anura was in Lucifer's good graces and company all the time.

She wanted to ingest Anura like her fetish devoured Prexel. One day. Maybe one day.

A few of her vermin crawl up her leg, making their trek to her shoulder. She rubs one of her spies at the rear of the eyeball. It chitters in response. On the ground, her eye vermin and imps continue to sift through the rubble. Two of her critters fight over a new discovery. Something sparkles, even through the dust and the remaining Mist. The eye vermin tug and smack each other with their pincers. A third vermin joins the fray. The other two stop short. The newest creature easily snatches away the gem. One tries to fight for it while the other scurries to Sinxin.

The vermin chitters something to Sinxin. She holds her finger up to her subordinates and looks down with interest. Every demon in her line of sight shuts up. She drops down into a crouch and motions to a rather large demon. He grabs some debris with one hand and tosses it to the side. This gives Sinxin a better line of sight of the commotion. A gorgeous gem twinkles like a newborn star. It doesn't emanate negative energy like a fetish. In fact, it's almost soothing. Very curious.

Sinxin smiles as she opens her hand for the vermin to give her the gem. The little bugger refuses. She looks up to the demon, and he stomps down on the vermin. Still there. The other devils laugh until Sinxin silences them with a slight backward glance. The demon steps on the vermin again. When he raises his foot, the creature lies on its side next to the gem. He squints at the fallen bug.

"Don't just look at it! Give me the gem!"

He steps on the bug again for good measure. Then he slowly reaches for the gem. The other vermin race toward it, but the devil swats them away.

She drills her gaze into his eyes. "No! Eye vermin are more useful than the whole lot of you! Tread carefully!"

The demon reaches for the gem. His fingers are too stubby. He scoots closer and tries again. The eye vermin that had the gem transforms into a female lion. As she enlarges, she severs the demon's head with her claws. Sinxin falls back in surprise as the feline tries to pounce on top of her, but she flips out of the way. The cat bounces off the side of a wall and dashes out the building. A spear attached to her side crackles with green energy and impales any demon it touches—even while the lioness is intangible. Purple energy blasts chase after the angel but shatters against debris.

"Fools! After her!"

***

Delilah looks on helpless. It seems as if the symptoms of Naomi's acid burn is similar to snake venom. She has difficulty breathing, is sweating, and has nausea. Danger. A flash of adrenaline and wrath finds a home in her heart. Her sword changes to the color of blood. Not good. Somewhere in her mind, she knows that's not good.

She slashes horizontally behind her. She turns to face her adversary. Cyrus materializes right behind her. He moves just out of her reach. He's cornered, but he's all smiles. How did he sneak in here? And how did he get behind her? He could have beheaded her if he wanted.

"Temper, temper. I'm usually a hit with the ladies."

Delilah takes an offensive stance in front of the spawn and tries to calm herself down. "Why are you here?" she says through clenched teeth.

"I'm here for you. Maybe we can work something out."

"Don't let him manipulate you. He can access all types of information about you now. He knows exactly what to say and where you'll be, but don't let him control you," Naomi warns.

"Wherever you are, there I'll be," he promises, splashing his beautiful, horrible smile. Cyrus blows her a kiss before he fades from view. The last thing she sees is her *enode*.

***

Evnore runs much slower now. She expended much more energy than needed. She doesn't have her *kameraads* to rely on. Going through the southern part of Satan's Spine, she arrives at the lava-filled chasm. Much lighter without the weight of her partners, at least. She runs right to the edge and decides to leap instead of fly, using her momentum.

Her pursuers fly over the chasm. Unfortunate that the peace she feels as the acidic wind whistles in her ears is short-lived. She grunts when she lands, with enough force to crush the ledge. She digs into the other side on hard earth and bounds forward. Behind her, a few demons leap across instead of flying, crashing into earthen spikes of Satan's Spine. This is an all-or-nothing objective. This gem must be their salvation. They'll need Naomi's prowess, knowledge, and battle skills to place the odds in their favor.

She reaches the outskirts of the Wildwoods of Udokas and continues on through with no further incident. Long strides and adrenaline-fueled muscles help her to keep her four-second lead. She gains more ground as her enemies can't fly through the dead brambles and thickets overhead.

Bursting through the other side of the wildwoods, she races across the dunes. Seconds later, open air for the demons. They take flight and gain ground. Evnore pushes more air through her lungs. She must make it to her *kameraads* before the enemy can catch up to her. She must give them enough time for the angelite to take effect. The demons continue to gain ground. Sinxin must be putting the fear of Lucifer into them to pursue her so adamantly. Some of the demons that took to the air are throwing spears at her now. Bastages. Her energy level runs dangerously low. She dares not stay intangible. She zigzags more, which slows her down and will take her longer to arrive at her destination.

Almost dizzy with exhaustion, she can identify the cave where her partners dwell. That isn't a cave. It looks more like the mouth of a giant snake. She hadn't realized that when she left. Another lesson learned about her not being as aware of her surroundings as she should. She should be ashamed of herself.

***

Delilah rises quickly to the mouth of the cave. Grunts and howls are heard from outside their sanctuary. The loud noise, not unlike a stampede of bulls. Obviously, not bulls, but not Faudinroar either. Above the distant tree line, she can see dozens of demons chasing Evnore. "Crap and crud!"

A slew of demons are in hot pursuit after Evnore. Now they are compromised. She rushes to her impaired *kameraad*. "Naomi! Wake up! Evnore's in danger!"

Naomi's eyes pop open, alert. Delilah stands in front of the cave mouth and positions her arms across her breastplate—ready to toss gems and give her fellow angels cover.

When Evnore views Delilah, she surges forward with a fresh burst of adrenaline. Her spine coils and springs her ahead, pushing her forward faster. She spins and tail whips an object toward her. Then she turns to face the horde of demons, growling—cutting off the demon's path to Delilah and Naomi.

Even in this sunless sky, Delilah can see the object. It sparkles like a firefly. It streaks toward her like a fireball. The move sends the gem hundreds of meters to cover the distance to her. She flies up to catch the gem like a winged outfielder. She checks the object and sighs with relief. The angelite. So beautiful she hates to destroy it, but it must be sacrificed. Then again, she wouldn't have to destroy the angelite, if she hadn't lost her temper. No regrets now. Evnore sacrificed the lead she had on the demons to fling her the precious gem. Delilah's attention split between Evnore's dilemma and caring for Naomi. She can only look on as the demons tackle and pummel Evnore into the ground.

Evnore buys them some time after all. She allowed herself to become caught, so they would have time to activate the gem. Delilah hopes it will work. They must hurry to help her. She rushes to Naomi, fills the angelite with vigor, and crushes the gem. She sprinkles the frags over the decaying skin. The frags resembles glitter as it shimmers and adheres to her remaining skin. It fills in the gaps of her skin, like a mesh net, layering her body with new epidermis. The frags connect muscles, tendons, and veins. Acid is purged as new blood flows through Naomi.

The acid oozes from her body like purple sweat, creating a large-sized puddle beneath her. In moments, she can stand on her own as she tests her revived limbs. No scars and no damage. Responsive to her flexing and bending. Naomi looks good as new and just in time.

***

Demons part when Sinxin and Mazck arrive. The demons that bashed the shapeshifter stop to apprehend her. They separate themselves, eager to brag on which caused the most pain. They look down and see another demon that was bludgeoned. They look to one another, but only see their fellows among them. A shoving match ensues as they are confused to where their prey escaped to.

"She's among us! She's a shapeshifter!" Sinxin warns.

Each demon gives room. Looking one another up and down. Sinxin spins around looking each of her mercenaries in the eye. Above her is her winged serpent Kalvara, and Sinxin holds out her arm to give her a perch, but the serpent flies on. "Kalvara! To me!"

The serpent ignores her summons and continues to fly on toward the unnamed. Then the unnamed holds out her arm as Sinxin just did, and the serpent lands there, wrapping her body around her forearm. Then she understands. The shapeshifter.

***

Evnore slithers off Delilah's arm and drops to the sand—taking on her lioness shape—and roars.

Naomi joins them as she puts her arms around Evnore. "Thank you, Oather. You saved me."

"I am sorry for my harsh words, Naomi," Evnore replies.

"We are all sorry. We've been under enough pressure to create a pearl. There is nothing to forgive," Delilah says.

Evnore twists her head to the side to detach her trophy spear from her side. Naomi's eyes widen in awe. She takes the spear in both hands.

"A gift," Evnore offers.

"Kromrom's mark. This can only be the spear of Quiloth! It was the only spear he ever crafted. It's been lost for ages! I can't wait for you to tell me how you came across this lovely!" Naomi exclaims with glee.

The regal lioness nods her head. Naomi twirls the spear over her head and behind her back as if it were a baton.

"Time for you to test out that spear," Delilah states.

"Shall we get back to work?" Naomi asks.

"It's what we get paid for."

"Wait! You get paid?"

Delilah smiles and gives her a nudge. Naomi's confidence comforts, assures, and motivates her. The Strategist looks across the dunes at her enemies. A scowl replaces her smile.

Naomi pats her bag of eyeballs. "By all means. I think it's high time to expand my collection."

Evnore growls in anticipation. The threefold bond is back together again and stronger than ever. Delilah hovers above her *kameraads*. Her authoritative posture pulls the demon's attention away from their bug-eyed leader. A hush quiets the rowdy demons as they raise their optic orbs to her.

She raises her voice effortlessly in a commanding voice. "This will be your only warning. We are Chrysos Squadron. You are outmaneuvered, underpowered, and outnumbered. Anyone who interferes with our investigation will be held without bond! The Angel of Death is on standby and will drag—you—to Hell. You were warned."

Demons laugh and snicker. Sinxin and Mazck step to the front of the demon horde.

"Did she say we were outnumbered? Who are you, unnamed? A pea pod to be crushed? Be gone that we may address the real threat!" Mazck yells.

Sinxin places a hand on Mazck's shoulder. He steps back. "Duly noted."

CHAPTER 22

THAT HE SHALL REAPETH

Anura can hardly keep herself calm. The first real break in eons on Delilah's *enode*. Croaking eagerly, she forgets to swallow from her excitement. For millennia, she tried to decipher the *enode* enigma with no success. It was her pet project to gain control of it so she may corrupt the angel. Oh, the folly she could cause with her sinister mind inside of an angelic body. The problem was she addressed the challenge incorrectly. Since Anura dwelled just above Hell for thousands of years, she can only think of inciting pain and turmoil.

This *enode* retains some part of Delilah's brain and/or consciousness. So what she needs to figure out is its desire. If she knew which region of her brain the *enode* was taken from, she could narrow down the options. In other words, what would be her reward stimulus? Such a stimulus could be one of a trillion different things. Anura is still overjoyed about the progress she made. It would take time, but what is time to an eternal? She must figure what object from the Virtuous Culture would yield control of the *enode*.

How exciting. Her dreams will come true. Now she and Xandus can be together again. She would be able to enter Heaven and not be discovered. She could pervade Heaven subtly and corrupt it from within. So many schemes she could hatch if she can figure out what Delilah loves. She must expend much more resources to learn more about her former pupil. She will be able to eliminate erroneous guesses once she is intimate about the angel.

There was a time when Anura and Delilah discussed their views together. They ranged from differing to similar. They shared opinions on how the army was to be organized and dispersed. They were in agreement as to Michael the Archangel's use of the phalanx was inefficient. She believed she knew Delilah; she was sorely mistaken. She was wrong to think Delilah would join Lucifer's Separatists. Even worse was that she was unaware of Delilah's affections for her love, Xandus. How could the whore betray her so? There was no way Xandus could want her skinny bones over her voluptuous body.

Drool streams down the corners of her mouth and down her jerkin. It pools beneath her as she samples different organisms she obtained from the Virtuous Culture. sSylk had some specimen in stock. Cloud particles, flower petals, condensed sunshine. A froth of frustration emerges. Eventually, she must collect samples of each type of flower to rule them out of the sample. She tries them in different quantities and combines them. Nothing. Frustration tries to dampen her mood, but there was too much progress to regress into depression now.

Smoother than an oil slick, sSylk withdraws from the shadows. Anura maintains her composure, but she will never figure out how he can slink into her fortress. She will set a trap for the slick bastard one day soon. "What do you have for me, sSylk?" she asks without turning around.

sSylk moves to her side and shows Anura the inside of his cloak. He procures many vials strapped within. She claps with glee and takes the samples, placing them in a vial rack.

"Yes! These will do nicely. Why are you still here? There is much more you must confiscate!"

He smiles like a wolf going back to his kill. Stepping back, he blends into the darkness. His fanged silkworm symbol is last to disappear. His voice lingers a bit longer. "Xandus's *charge* still lives."

Anura croaks angrily. She raises her hand—about to crush her experiments when the giant-sized image of Lucifer emerges before her. The foundation of her Nexus Nodule shakes. Dust descends from the ceiling in streams. Tiles crack under the image's weight. She gasps and kneels to the ground. "Master!"

The image of Lucifer stoops down to caress Anura on her cheek. She cringes at his touch. She can only wish it is Xandus's instead. Anura plays the roll. She's a survivor—and intends on surviving for eons to come.

"Anura the Conniver. There has been a change of plans…"

Anura smiles knowingly. She would never say that Lucifer was predictable, but there are some plans and desires that weigh on his mind like a dragon lies on gold. To keep her in the Master-Commander's good graces, she must always have the foresight to advance Lucifer's plans during these times. He is generous, but impatient. This is how Anura rose through the ranks of God and then the Separatists. The ability to convey action before thought remains infinitely more efficient. "Master, I anticipated your desires. I set into motion your intention."

Lucifer flexes his storm-cloud wings as he rises. Anura shelters the vials with her body so that the wind won't knock over her experiments. Satan raises his chin, glaring down on her. His tail swishes back and forth, knocking over her lamps and tapestry. "Your master is well pleased."

***

"Demons," Delilah says. "Too stupid to be scared."

"I think now would be a good time to give them a reason to be afraid," Naomi agrees.

She gazes at both of her *kameraads*. Both are willing to do anything for her and accomplish any goal set before them to complete their objective. Their energy and ire are as intense as a firestorm. She absently taps the Word of Power on her breastplate: fearless. Naomi and Evnore are more deserving of it. There were many times they've protected her from herself or had to carry her throughout the mission—literally.

Delilah expands her wings in all their radiance. She won't let her remnant down now. She'll earn her *kameraads'* respect today. She'll feel worthy of her Words of Power. Despite the odds, her faults, and missteps, she remains proud and confident. She couldn't be more honored being here with angelic companions. They will fight and die for her. They would lay their very souls down for her. Nothing less will do. The love she feels right now makes her brim with delight. Demons know her not, but they will learn today.

How can she think of love and not think of Xandus. She wishes he were here now. His body a blanket. His soul, irreplaceable. In the last three decades, they had less time to spend with each other than in times before. His absence makes her heart fonder of him, day by day.

She misses the times they would meet in secret and talk for hours. They would gaze at the stars that were just out of arm's reach. A myriad of colors washed over his blue skin in Heaven. His eyes bright with joy and happiness. Unfortunately, her recollections are blurred at the end of her older memories. She remains most frustrated with the inability to recall her most precious memories.

Once she recovers her *enode* from the fiend, Sinxin, their relationship status should change. Time to get sharp and focused. This devil is not of the common variety. Delilah surveys the battlefield. The open plains work in the demon's favor. They will be able to surround them on all sides and above. Beneath as well, if the angels take flight. There are only two options: flee again or end this quickly by taking out Sinxin.

The fly-eyed demon is the key, the demon's spine. After any momentum that the angel's built, Sinxin was unflappable. If they can defeat her, the horde will flee like frightened roaches. Delilah makes the decision to attack, but how? She is very powerful and doesn't just use her strength and speed like a male devil would. That makes her much more dangerous and unpredictable. Sinxin uses fireballs and wields purple energy, yet she isn't using that now. She wants to make an example out of them. Get in close. Feel her hands around Delilah's throat. That means she's mad, angry, and upset. She's making this personal. Her mistake. A lesson Delilah had to relearn.

This enemy has been a thorn in Delilah's side for this whole mission. Her primary objective is to apprehend the murderer and bring her to justice. No demon wants to be locked up in Hell. Swift justice and a lengthy trial awaits these vile devils. Chrysos's success at protecting humans was uncontested. Somewhere down the ages, their squad's reputation had faltered. This would never have happened a few centuries ago. Then again, during that time, the squad did more patrolling than guarding. First responder patrols always obtain more prestige.

Delilah turns her back to her foes and addresses her *kameraads* in a low confident tone. "Sinxin and Mazck underestimated us. We will expose their weakness, and they will be defeated. Our element of surprise has vanished, and they will be more cautious. Evnore is no longer our pocket assassin, and they have seen me use my gems."

"What is our move?" Evnore asks.

Delilah must reassure them that they will succeed. Any doubt in her plans or hesitation in her voice could spell their failure. Not an option. Tapping on her bracer, she instantly assigns everyone a Greek letter call sign—including friendlies. Every being on the battlefield was assigned an insignia over their heads that only the angels can see. Alpha, kappa, omega represents Delilah, Naomi, and Evnore, respectively. With a resigned sigh, she rubs her three fingers together. Might as well give Time his show. "I have a plan. We're going to hold our ground here. We'll not waste energy meeting them halfway. Besides, some are faster than others. The quicker we dispatch the leaders in front, the better. Naomi, you will take point, just to the side of me."

"Point, huh? About time," Naomi says with a sinister grin.

"You will attack the call sign on my mark," Delilah continues. "Do not hesitate. I need you to follow my exact orders. Evnore, you're on guard position. Anything that gets past Naomi, take it down."

Both nod grimly. A sharp breeze picks up as dust devils swirl past. Sinxin must be up to something. She stands silent in front of a mass of devils, staring directly at her.

***

Sinxin grunts to herself. Prexel's irritating voice taunts her to no end. *Hold back. Let the Hideons weaken our foes*, Prexel advises. *That will make them use their resources and allow you to see more of their tactics.*

Quiet, fool! You know nothing! They're weak. You would have me pull back that they can escape! I won't be filing that report to Lucifer! You must think me an idiot!

A soft chuckle retreats into her mind again. Hiding in the shadows of her consciousness. What if he's right? The bastard Prexel wants her to doubt her plans. She underestimated their power. She doesn't have any more silver skin to shield her now. Her newly crafted sword remains untested. She didn't get the chance to learn all its benefits. Angelic whores. "Concentrate all attacks on the unnamed!" she commands.

***

Delilah can hear the fly-eyed demon from here. She just ordered her demons to attack only her. That strategy worked against her millennia ago.

She was partnered with Abbadon and Kromrom in the war games. Anura's team, consisting of Ikrlez and Xandus, converged on her all at once. She never had a chance. The team fell apart when she was defeated. That can't happen again. She can't fail again. Back then, it was only three. Now she's against hundreds.

Sinxin the she devil leads the charge. A funnel of her Hideons run, fly, and charge behind her. None is faster than Sinxin as she moves at the speed of fear. Evnore and Naomi step in front of Delilah and brace for impact. A cloud of dust rises behind the demons from the ground along with a thunderous roar. Even from this distance, the gnashing of teeth and the hate in their eyes is overbearing. Wrath emanates from the evil horde like locusts on corn.

The she devil must be overdosing her body with vigor. She crosses the field in seconds, and in one more second, she'll be in the midst of them.

"Kappa, heart strike! Call sign: Alpha!"

"What?" Naomi yells in confusion.

"Do it, noow!"

Naomi torques her body and aims Quiloth behind her—millimeters from Delilah's heart—at the same time that Sinxin slides into
a horizontal backslash.

"Time!" Delilah shouts.

Time can be an asset or a foe. Time always wants to bargain—to
gamble. Delilah promised to keep her word to the bastage, Time. It
was the only way to persuade him to free her. She refused to be a
prisoner in Time. All around Delilah, everything stops. The sands of
Time swirl at the mention of his name. She reflects on the bargain
she struck with the powerful entity all those years ago.

"You have my attention," Time responded as he leaned forward
from his sands that cut off her escape.

"For one year, I'll notify you of any actionable conflicts that I'm
a part of."

"One year? Infinity of all actionable conflicts."

"Infinity? Ten millennia. And I get to call you as a participant."

"Deal."

Time arrives when called. As everything around Delilah halts,
the fabric of Time flows around his body like a fitted cloak. Space is
contained within it—dwarf stars and constellations merge with his
continuum. His smile unnerves Delilah. She hates to bargain with
Time. He's such a bastage.

"Beautiful and capable Delilah," Time begins, "how can I help
you? Customer service is my specialty."

"I need more time, Time," she answers.

"Oh, hoo! Time is friend to no one! This precarious predicament you're in shall pass. Unless—"

Delilah interrupts, "I've changed my mind. I will deal with this
demon in another way. I won't negotiate with Time anymore."

The fabric flows around him. Moments pulse as Time stands
still. The fabric brightens and tightens as Moments slide along a
nexus within. His clockwork eyes spin in thought.

"You're stalling for Time. However, I will generously spare you
one full second."

Delilah sighs. "It will do. I count the seconds until our agreement ends. Our 'partnership' allows us both to benefit."

"Yes. How Time does fly. Not everyone dreads their partnership with me…"

"There are others? Who…else?"

"Isn't that right…Sinxin?" Time says mockingly.

Delilah spins around, where Sinxin stands with her arms folded along the nexus of Time's fabric. The gold clocks refracted in her compound eyes. She confidently walks next to Delilah and faces her.

It is just as she suspected. When she watched the footage of Benjamin's death, she noticed the demon's uncanny speed, which she realized was granted to the demon by Time. She wanted to avoid a confrontation with Xandus and exploited their agreement. Delilah's eyes stray to her *enode*. Time's head swivels from one nemesis to the other. A slow rumble of laughter rises in crescendo.

Sinxin walks a circuit around Delilah. "You proved to be a worthy adversary," she begins. "I thought it would be months before you would figure out I was the one to execute the protected *charge*. We had to adjust our plans radically."

Delilah scoffs at her enemy, frowning as she half turns her head toward her. "I'd rather fail than to receive a compliment from a demon."

"Are you so afraid to join us? You know your end. That is why you're here, no? If your negotiation fails, you will be defeated. Like Crackle Blade's *charge*," Sinxin brags.

Delilah must think. She won't have long in the space-time continuum. Sinxin did a good job of distracting her. She thought to stall for more time to think of a plan, but that's no longer an option. She turns to face her adversary—the she devil. "I will accept my fate. I hope you are prepared to accept yours."

"As lieutenant to Lordess Anura and Lord Ikrlez, I'd like to redeem a half second through this alliance," Sinxin says.

"Ikrlez?"

A knowing smile stretches across Sinxin's grotesque features. The Father of Time rubs his chin in wonder. Calculating the possibilities, maybe? He nods his agreement, and it is settled. The fabric recedes—pulling from under the combatants like a magician's tablecloth.

"No, please don't negotiate with her!" Delilah yells. "Time, wait!"

"Time waits for no one—unless you're tipping!"

Time and Sinxin both laugh as Time fades from view and the Archfiend Zone rematerializes.

This will be her only chance to defeat Sinxin, for she's a formidable foe. Without help, she was able to cancel out the angel's attacks. Normally, Delilah only takes calculated risks. She'd take as much time as possible to coordinate a plan of attack, from gathering as much intel as possible. She doesn't have that luxury now. Sinxin left her no choice.

Delilah's mind races as she does her best to calculate the distance and speed of Sinxin's attack. If the angels are surrounded by the demon horde, they'll succumb, for sure. She must take a page out of Aurum's strategy and risk it all. If they're to beat this fly-eyed demon, she will have to put all her silver on one number.

A ghostly blur, only Delilah and assumedly Sinxin are aware of resets the region to Sinxin's half second. The pressure of this tense moment swells within her chest. Time is reset and moves along—for Sinxin. Instead of battling the demon by alternating their surplus seconds, Delilah allows her time to calculate first.

The entire attack will happen in half of a second and will last for a fraction of that second. The microseconds tick of systematically as Delilah can only watch the demon rush her with a strobe-light effect. Sinxin is approximately eight meters from her—already moving into her backswing. The demon moves so swiftly and fluidly Delilah wonders if she miscalculated. She won't be able to recover or carry out any plan if Sinxin severs her head.

Delilah is unable to move a muscle. She can't even look to either side of the demon. She's thankful that she has her eyes open at the reset of Sinxin's attack. The torment of not knowing exactly where the demon is as the microseconds tick off would be horrifying.

Sinxin's half second puts her horizontal backslash at about ten millimeters from separating her head from her neck. Once the demon's calculations are over, Delilah is able to move only the digits that has her matrix overlay over them. Her two fingers and thumb manipulate the time stream as she uses her full second. Her digits glow as she moves time back by point one thousandths of a second at a time. Once Sinxin backs into the perfect spot in front of Delilah, she releases the time stream.

Sinxin's compound eyes reflect Delilah's grin a hundred times. Then just as Sinxin's arm goes through its backslash, Naomi pierces Sinxin with Quiloth through the back. The she devil's arm reflexively follows through with her strike. Delilah grunts as she flips her sword around to execute a hard block on Sinxin's attack. The move sends the demon's sword flying. As Quiloth punctures all the way through the demon's chest, the fetish is knocked from its gaudy clasp. The other jewels fastened on the fetish along with her *enode* pop free. Delilah catches her precious gem in the palm of her hand. "Having a power and knowing how to use it is entirely two different things, demon."

"In other words, you just got played, beach!" Naomi yells.

Naomi kicks the demon off her spear. Sinxin flops on her back in obvious pain, working her mouth wordlessly. Black blood squirts through as her corrupt heart continues to pump. Naomi puts the spear over her heart and impales her again. The demon grabs at the spear's haft in a futile attempt to pull the weapon away. She pulls up slightly then drops her hands and body. Blood splatter ejects from her mouth. The compound eyes crackle away, like ash—drained of her life force. Naomi snatches the spear out and snaps the black blood off her spear.

The Hideon horde freezes in fright. Right before their eyes, their leader is defeated. The horde presses against themselves to stop their advance. Overlords snap their whips to make their foot sol-diers charge—but they are safely in the rear. Large carrion birds circle above the battlefield.

The angels three advance aggressively toward the demons, with Naomi returning to her position at point. She twirls Quiloth with a sinister grin.

Mazck steps to the front. "What are you waiting for? Attack!" he yells.

A few demons gain courage, push pass, and charge toward their enemies.

"Eye-blotter! Maintain formation!" Delilah commands.

CHAPTER 23

STRATAGEM

Naomi never felt better in her life. With the healing and restoring properties of the angelite gem, she was refreshed as if she's rested for a year. Her newly acquired spear pulses in her hand with untapped potential. Her weapon emanates with power as if she possessed dominion over a collapsing star in her hand. These low-class soldiers will help her adjust to its weight and balance. When she twirls it, the spear is lighter than a baton, though she feels as if she could crack the earth.

She belongs in the trenches of battle—alive. The ebb and flow of combat. Her skills are the valley of the shadow of death to the ill culture. The dumbest demons roar at her in a charge. She twirls destruction in a spinning circle of annihilation. Three step up, only to be hewn down. With Quiloth in her hand, she is unstoppable; the spear is an extension of her will. She cuts a path through the demons, and her *kameraads* secure the flanks. With only a thought to extend her weapon's reach, it does so through multiple demons. The Quiloth spear slices through these lesser demons, like a laser through paper. As she withdraws the weapon, it narrows its size just enough to slide through the hole it just created. It breaks bone as if it were twigs; it severs heads as if they were atop a scarecrow.

The monstrous size of Evnore is enough to make most demons avoid her flank. The few that challenge the lioness are welcomed with savage swipes of her claws, fear-instilling roars, and gnashing of her fangs into their putrid flesh.

On the opposite flank, Delilah incredibly has the same dilemma as Evnore. The demons credited her for subduing Sinxin. Few demons brave her side. They would rather take their chances with the infamous Eye-blotter.

A fist of demons streams toward the trio. The fist chants with the audacity of a cackle of hyenas. They establish a blockade to halt the angel's advance. Its arrival steels the cowardly demon's nerves. Banners from the emissary of greed flap in the howling wind. Large drums reverberate from behind along with the deep notes of ram's horns. Once in position, they stomp in place, slam their shields, and grunt with impressive discipline.

At a different time in her life, Naomi may have been intimidated at the demon's show of strength, but she is the Eye-blotter, from Team Chrysos. She is an angel of the Lord under the Heraldry of Aurum. She is accompanied by the most brilliant Strategist in Heaven. And she ain't scared.

The demons split into two groups. Half going around Naomi to Delilah and the other half going around Naomi and to Evnore. When they do, the gem-studded angel takes a short leap toward the flanking monsters, torques her body in a tight circle, and spins her sword in a perfect horizontal arc in front of her. The blur of the slash extends from Prism ten meters. The colors become solid, cleaving her enemies. Body parts are lopped off as the weapon attack extends to and through them. In the same sinuous move, another iridescent slash extends above angle—severing more than half of the flying Hideons.

As Naomi spins in her spear kata, she catches a glimpse of Delilah. In that split second, she watches her move around the battlefield like a tactician. Naomi makes eye contact with Evnore. Moving as one, Naomi and Evnore pivot-shifts into flanking positions under Delilah's low-to-high diagonal slice. She moves the triangle in the direction Delilah is facing.

With Delilah at point, she radiates wave upon wave of multicolored energy from Prism. Each buffet slices through the concentrated enemy. She runs behind the energy attack. Her flanking angels keep pace and keep the precise amount of spacing needed to maintain the tight formation. The few foes who are unscathed, flee from battle. After this display of destructive force, none approaches her again. In a matter of seconds, the angels attack the now-fleeing Hideons until Delilah holds up her fist. Her *kameraads* discontinue the chase.

Mazck moves in front of the rest of the resisters. He enlarges his shadow. Naomi's heart quickens. Anger swells up inside her; at the same time, her soul soars at the sight of him.

More correctly, the sight of his angelic self, Gjestice. In a split second, her mind disperses the shadow, deflates the fluff, and reskins his skeletal face. His handsome features reappear. Majestic wings resurface, and his eyes that are spinning nebulae fight through his shroud. This version of Mazck wishes only to hold Naomi in his arms forever. To cause no hurt nor harm. This version of Mazck died over thirty millennia ago.

The greater shadow demon's arms lengthen and circle around the angels—attempting to attack the flanks. Any demon that impedes his path to the angels are sliced clean through with his vicious claws. Once his claws approach Naomi, she easily deflects his attacks. Evnore chomps on his other arm. Between the two angels, he withdraws his shadow.

Mazck tries to fade into ash. Naomi becomes a blur of speed and movement. She steps into his defensive circle and strikes his center with Quiloth. She juices the weapon with her vigor. The weapon crackles with green energy. She plunges the spear into his body, causing him to materialize uncontrollably. Quiloth punctures his stomach as she pins him to the ground. A weak gasp escapes his lips. Sad eyes stare up at Naomi as the light in his eyes dim.

Her battle rage fades as Naomi realizes she just felled her former partner. Her beloved. "No! You were supposed to—" Naomi starts. "You could have—"

Delilah steps up alongside Evnore until the area clears of attacking demons. Naomi wipes blood and smudge from off her face with her forearm. She keeps Quiloth in Mazck's belly and kneels down. A trickle of red blood escapes his lips as he smiles weakly.

Rakgron, the stag demon, looks back at the trio. "Clever girl—Stratagem."

Delilah and Evnore cover Naomi's flank. They turn away from the Fallen and let her have a moment of privacy. She lifts Mazck's limp hand to her mouth and kisses it. As she holds it, the solidity of his shadow wanes. His whole arm, for that matter, is less dense. In these last seconds, he seems less evil. Less insane. More angelic.

"Leave me. Don't waste your tears for me," Mazck says.

"Why did you attack? You could have fled. Why did you—"

Naomi glances at her *kameraads* and stops her line of questioning. Delilah turns her head away—sheathing Prism. Evnore takes on her *lionoid* form. Now the carrion birds become bold with hunger as they descend on the battlefield. That will help delay their regeneration.

"I'm sorry, Naomi. You had to do what needed to be done, but we must serve these warrants. Especially Sinxin. She'll be the first to heal."

Naomi nods as she rises to her feet. Frowning, she spits at the unconscious body of Mazck. His body flattens like a deflated balloon. "Go handle her. I'm fine. I should be the one to serve him," she says with determination.

***

Delilah makes an about-face. She and Evnore leave Naomi so that they can serve Sinxin her death warrant. She frowns when she realizes that Evnore is staring at her. "What?"

Evnore looks on to her with a proud smile. "Another work of art, Strategist Delilah," she answers. "You even have the respect of the vile. 'Stratagem,' they will call you now. You have earned your rank today as in all other days. May honor and prestige follow you."

"Quiet, you. Stop teasing."

Evnore stops and looks at her with loving admiration. "Honor and prestige, Strategist."

A subtle smile sneaks onto Delilah's lips. She is always good at her job. They have always gotten through tough spots before, but this is their greatest challenge to date, and this is only the beginning. The pair comes to where Sinxin fell. Even now, Delilah can visibly see the wounds healing.

She scrolls through her bracer and pulls out her *aether* chains. The fluorescent metal materializes into shackles to bind Sinxin's wrists and feet. She scrolls to the document's section on her bracer and checks for death warrants. "Ah, here we are, Sinxin. Didn't mean to keep you waiting," she apologizes lightly.

She slaps the demon on the cheek, then brushes the crud from her hand onto her thigh. The demon with the compound eyes stirs. Her eyes are less dull now. She heals just enough to be aware of Delilah's actions. The reading of her rights. "Sinxin," she begins, "I, Delilah—Strategist of Chrysos Squadron—serve you with a death warrant. You have been issued said warrant for the crimes of conspiring against Heaven, abhorrent crimes against humanity, and the murder of Benjamin Hale: a protected *charge* that was not notified among the ill culture as Fated. You will be held in Hell and bound there until you are judged. Do you understand these rights?"

Sinxin grunts something unintelligible.

"I'll take that as a yes."

Swiping to the side of her bracer, she prints a physical copy of the death warrant. It floats to Sinxin's head and wraps around it. Naomi walks over to join her *kameraads*. From here, none of Sinxin's demon horde is visible. The demons won't ambush them, but are curious. They are probably over a dune taking notes from a safe distance, possibly, to report the defeat of their leader. The red moon hangs low but seems a little brighter than before. Delilah smiles fondly at Naomi. "You both did excellent out there. That spear suits you."

She looks about her surroundings. *Why is Naomi still smiling?* She observes no movement around her. In fact, nothing moves.

Time. He swirls around Delilah. His arm turns into the sands of Time as they encircle her in a blur. Gold clocks tick loudly as if they are angry. The space-time continuum spreads from his back and into a 3-D barrier around them. Time wags a sand-created finger at the angel. "You used me."

"How could I?" she responds.

"Clever girl. Clever, clever girl. How did you know she would come? How did you know that you would have enough time from the reset to manipulate Time? Answer me!" he demands.

"How could I calculate fractions of a second in fractions of a second?" she queries innocently.

Time backs away. He gives her "space" by enlarging the space-time box. The sands connect back to his arm—no longer encircling Delilah.

"I've watched you for eons. If you would enlighten me, I will consider our arrangement fulfilled. As a bonus, I will add two full seconds to any future requests, starting tomorrow. Guaranteed," Time negotiates.

She taps her chin in thought. She can accomplish much in two seconds.

"Deal," she agrees. "I figured that she used your services before when she assassinated Xandus's *charge*. She had no imagination or control when using the time allotted, so I knew she was relatively new to the power. She only knew to clump the reset time together, like it was an NBA shot clock. There was no finesse in her use of your Time."

"Clever girl. Clever, clever girl."

"Oh, please," she admonishes with a frown, "I'm almost as old as you, Time. Girl? Indeed. Just keep in mind you assisted a demon in the assassination of a protected human. I'm sure you'll have to answer to the Son about that. An audit may be in order."

With no further words, Time releases his hold. The clocks fade, and the space-time continuum recedes.

"Keep your line open, Time. I may call on you again."

The last to wane is the fabric. She reaches for the unraveled strand of thread and pulls. The rest of the fabric winks out of existence, but the thread in Delilah's hand stays. She places it on her bracer, where it becomes digitalized. Then time is restored. When real time becomes current, to no surprise, Delilah's *kameraads* were unaware.

"Don't forget to bless and cleanse Quiloth," Evnore reminds the Eye-blotter. "Let's leave here. Like now! Death will be here soon."

Evnore turns her head to the sky. Delilah and Naomi notice her concern and turn their heads to the skies as well. In front of the red moon, a large carrion bird glides down. No, too big for a bird. A devil. The vultures and crows on the battlefield take flight noisily. A loud cheer is heard from the Hideons. This devil's features are obscured by its own shadow. It glides down with the control of a hawk. It—he folds his arms in defiance, hovering over the largest dune. The lioness growls.

"Who's there? Announce thyself!" Naomi demands.

Though he touches down with control, the dune shakes and rumbles as if over an earthquake. The shadowed figure descends from the tallest dune with the grace of an emperor. The wind whips up around the area suddenly. His chin held high like a king. Booming laughter emits from him. Loud and boisterous. He runs his hands through his hair. The roar from the horde gets louder—yet they yield plenty of room. Who is this? Then she grunts with anger. "What is it, Blood Spawn?" Delilah requests. A desperate gasp escapes Delilah's lips when she truly recognizes the devil. "No!"

A broad smile stretches across the face of this nefarious demon. He appears larger, darker. Her *enode* is embedded on his forearm. Delilah rubs her scaly arms subconsciously. She begins to feel light-headed.

Naomi looks at her partner, confused. "The spawn? Beat it kid, ya bother me."

Evnore gasps. "He's not the spawn."

Waves of nausea bombard the Strategist. Her knees buckle. He steps closer. The dark clouds pass by the red moon. The dunes glow with night-light. Now they can see his smile.

"What?" Naomi asks, confused.

His wide smile.

"He's…the real Abbadon," Delilah answers.

His beautiful, ugly smile.

CHAPTER 24

THE MIND'S EYE

Delilah can't believe the real Abbadon towers before her. Her mind reels with fear and horror from his sudden appearance. Lucifer's army received their most decorated officer. His arrival will inspire devils from the Archfiend, both allied and estranged. The ability to extract the confined will rally all demons under one massive banner. Abbadon boosts the damned's morale and demoralizes the Virtuous Culture, all at the same time.

They were partners for centuries before the heavenly rebellion. They worked together seamlessly on his Alpha Strike squad. Delilah believed there was much good in her Herald. He was a Champion of angels and humans alike. She wished she were able to talk him out of his dissention, but it was to no avail. He was the most stubborn being she had ever met.

The real conundrum is how can anyone escape Hell? Impossible and has never been done. He must have escaped only recently. She just encountered Cyrus. Abbadon's first order of business is to confront her. She can only imagine how his power has grown over the time he has been imprisoned.

The Threshold of the Damned will have increased his strength a thousandfold. Hell siphons the souls of enslaved and leeches their essence as vigor and other abilities to the Fallen. The rankers in the upper echelon receive proportionately more.

Her mind races almost as fast as her heart bangs against her rib cage. She can barely concentrate. She sparred against her greatest ally and foe, because somehow she knew this moment would come. In the safety of her war room in Heaven, she wished, begged, and even prayed for this confrontation.

God answers prayer.

Now that the time is nigh, she wishes this is just another one of her nightmares. For millennia, she's never been able to defeat her demon.

Abbadon the Demigod takes his time. He splashes his smile—relishing every bit of confusion and fear that he instills in his angelic adversaries. He spreads his arms wide—like a gladiator playing to his audience's cheers. Actually, he is playing to an audience's cheers. The distant demon horde, indeed, goes wild. Stale sweat glistens his powerful biceps. Those mighty limbs of his could lift the weight of a skyscraper. A red aura of uncontained power emanates from his body, crying to be released. "No see, long time. Weren't you expecting me?" Abbadon says with a toothy grin. "'Coz rumors had it you were."

"Im-impossible. He's in Hell," Naomi utters.

"I got out on good behavior," he answers, laughing.

His sinister smile holds Delilah still, like the gaze of a cobra. She suppresses her fear just below her eyes. She'll not give him the satisfaction that she's afraid. She wonders if Evnore can smell her fear. If she can, they're all doomed.

"No need to fear me, Delilah. Your friends maybe, but you?" Abbadon snorts. "Maybe you should fear me too."

Naomi drops her spear and shakes her head in denial. Evnore breathes heavily and takes a step back and then another. Delilah slides her foot behind her but stands her ground, her arms to her side. The monster steps closer. Evnore and Naomi take another step back. Maybe they're already doomed.

"Do you know how long I've waited for this? Wanting what is out of reach for thousands of years? Now having you by my side is a dream realized! I watched you—even from the pit of Hell. Maybe it was God's way of tormenting me with my deepest desire. In any case, I observed you become stronger and more beautiful by the day. All for me. My delicate, priceless doll."

"How, Abbadon? How did you get out of Hell?" Delilah demands. Then she realizes the only other person in existence who was responsible for his escape. "Anura!"

He takes another step closer. He reaches out and caresses Delilah's chin. He clicks his tongue and eyes her up and down seductively. "Yes, my love. Details, details. Suffice it to say, Anura the Conniver was able to transfer my consciousness to my blood spawn. He seems a quick study. I'm sure he'll grow fond of his new title: king of Hell."

No, not again. Please not again. His touch pricks her like brambles. As he rubs her cheek, her skin becomes sandpaper rough. Her mind recoils, just like before.

"Finer than fox fur," he continues.

"Finer than fox fur" echoes hauntingly in her mind. Abbadon surely savors the fear that must be wafting from off her skin, like spoiled meat.

He stands there confident and full of arrogance, just like he did thousands of years ago. Delilah has no idea how long it was from when Abbadon approached her to the assault on Heaven. If she were to guess, she was unconscious for days, maybe even weeks. With all the activity in Heaven with the rapid rebellion recruitment, she was overlooked. Abbadon probably lied and said she was on a sabbatical or on a solo mission. She can't recall why they met on top of a rainbow in Heaven. She does recall that the Demigod believed he was giving her a compliment with his undesired pickup line, before the honorable became a distorted shadow of his former self. She wished that was the extent of his unsolicited advances.

"You know what I always say. Indulge thyself!" Lucifer smiled as he faded from view.

She fought to remain conscious, but the injury that Lucifer caused just from the pop of his finger to her forehead cracked her skull. The shoddy *aegis* defense she put up angered Lucifer more than anything. She was punished for her defiance. The Father of Lies scrambled her brain and ripped pieces out of it. It took weeks for her to recover. When she compared Lucifer's atrocities to Abbadon's, she realized that the Soul Severer was kind.

Abbadon unfastened his armor. It hovered in place as he smiled. Her body was freezing, and her mind was melting. She had to fight, but was unable to. Her extremities were numb, and her body refused to respond to her commands. She couldn't fathom the defamation of her body by this monster. She would forever be tainted—not tainted, rotten. She would never have the chance to save herself for the one she loved. Who would want her after this? *Fight, weakling.* His grip was tighter than Death's fist.

"My love, you are as affectionate as a cactus. Relax, or this will hurt you more than it will hurt me. I'll make sure of it," Abbadon said.

As he caressed her, Delilah's skin became scaly. His very touch was toxic. Her armor crumbled away. Every place he kissed her became boils. Her breathing was panicked. All she saw were his bright white teeth. Saliva dripped generously from his mouth—causing acid burns to her neck and chest. Her skin burnt from pain.

"Your body disagrees with your lips, my love."

Abbadon rubbed the small of her back. She wanted her voice to echo her pain, but her voice was gone. She hated herself for her body reacted naturally to his physical touch; and the miniscule thought of pleasure as he used his fingernail to rip away her underarmor. He held her tight against his bare body. Anyone, please help. She was helpless and hopeless. Weak and spineless. Couldn't she had fought him better than she did? At all? She mumbled something continuously.

Abbadon leaned in closer to hear. "What are you saying, my love?"

"Whoreson," Delilah whispered. She mustered enough strength to spit in his face.

Abbadon's grin was full of acidic venom when he brought his elbow down on her shoulder. A loud crack sounded. She groaned in extreme agony.

Horrific thoughts of self-loathing entered her brain in fractions of a second. Finally, the darkness consumed her. She tried to fight the darkness. Those teeth, those bleached white teeth. She tried to focus on them. She couldn't pass out now. She'd never know what he did to her. Not knowing was worse than the actual act. Her imagination would haunt her forever. She'd always believe every part of her was desecrated. She couldn't allow this to happen to her. *Please fight. No.*

She blacked out.

A wry smile slides across Abbadon's face, and his eyes brighten. "I'm impressed you remember that much," he states.

His menacing voice brings Delilah's mind racing back to her current dilemma. *What?*

"We'll create new memories," Abbadon promises.

"I can't resist you, but together we can," Delilah responds.

"Together, huh?"

Abbadon pulls Delilah toward himself by the neck. She tries to resist by putting her hands on his chest and pushing back.

Evnore roars, shaking the ground. Her roar deepens as she shifts into her most aggressive form—the *czekja*. Her body lengthens and thickens. Long bone spikes start at her forehead and down the center of her back. Fangs longer than a sabretooth tiger protrude from her massive maw. Different shades of red spread across her body like a furry inferno.

Her ears pin back to the sides of her head as she lunges for Abbadon. She rams him with her head spike and impales the Demigod in the gut. The puncture almost completely heals by the time she withdraws. She snaps her head forward and bites his forearm, crushing it with over two thousand PSI. Abbadon releases Delilah and clenches his teeth. He lifts his arm up, with Evnore still attached to it. His knuckles crack as he balls up his fist. With one well-aimed punch, his fist crashes into the side of her head, sending her flying through two dunes.

"Evnore!" Delilah screams.

Delilah spins around toward Naomi and draws two circles on her own forehead. Naomi's eyes widen; then she nods as she grabs her spear and leaps toward Abbadon. The demon stomps on the ground, causing it to rise up to meet Naomi. It knocks her up and behind him. She crashes to the ground and rolls. The impact knocking her out.

He lets his arm hang to the side. The bones shift, crack, and reform. He flexes his hand into a fist. Shortly, his arm regenerates.

His power is incredible. To her knowledge, Abbadon is the only being able to heal *during* a battle. He laughs again. Those teeth and his smile. He steps closer. "Now that we're alone. All these eons, every second, you were always on my thoughts. We can start over. Take over Heaven, even Lucifer. You'd be my eternal queen. Your two friends can be your handmaidens. I'll give you the very stars, Delilah."

"What's the point of gaining the whole world only to lose your soul?" she pleads.

"What's a soul if you can't gain the whole world?"

He steps close and begins touching her again. Her skin crawls from his caress—pulling away from her skeleton. Goosebumps form all along her back and neck. "No, don't," she begs.

The former commander becomes increasingly angry. Grabbing her roughly by the arms. He stares into her eyes with fresh rage. "Stay with me, or I'll strip your skin and make gloves of them," he threatens. "I will destroy your soul. I will crush your body. I will devour your mind! Either way, I win. Your choice. Make your decision."

Like a madman, he calms down. Seemingly, unaware of his sudden outburst. He takes her hand. Those eyes. That smile. An eternity passes in that fraction of a second. Is there anything she can do?

He said he would devour her mind. She won't allow that to happen. She empties her mind by pushing away fear, anxiety, pain, and wrath. She places it in a safe place. *Cage my mind and protect it.* It is the only thing out of reach. She sets up an internal shelter of her mind's eye—her *aegis*. She constructs barriers to contain her sanity, but realizes it's too small. She expands the shelter by resetting the walls. She looks up at the sky from within her *aegis*. It will need a roof. She doesn't even want the stale air of the Archfiend to invade it. A roof hinges up and over, slamming down on her self-containment with a loud clang.

No longer is she in Lucifer's domain, not her mind anyway. The burnt sky of the Archfiend is transformed. No longer full of storm clouds, smoke, ash, and ire. It changes to an azure blue. Rainbows all intersect with one another. Birds flitter about—out across the horizon. Fly, be free. Horses gallop across a field of lavender. The Strategist seats herself against a great oak, wrapping her arms around her legs. She is safe now. No tears, no feeling, no pain. Nothing exists outside her center. In her sanctuary, she is free.

***

Abbadon smiles. After thousands of years, he's free. After thousands of years, he will have what's coming to him. He'll regain his former status next to Lucifer, but most importantly, he'll have Delilah. Everything is in this instant for him. His desires, his love, his purpose, and his goal. She goes limp in his strong arms. He cradles her against her body. Pulls her in close. He rubs his head against her's and kisses her neck. He almost expects her to fight her, but no. She relents. Her indomitable will is broken, like a wild mustang. His to command. What can't he conquer? If he can bend her will to his, everything else will fall before him.

He searches for her Words of Power on her armor. Unimportant what she was. Important is what she will be. What he'll make her. He discovers the clasp for one Word of Power. He laughs to himself audibly. How ironic. Once found, he removes her leather mantle that contains the word "honor." Her nape is long and seductive. Her jugular pulses quickly as he touches it. Abbadon lays her down to the hard earth. This will be their bed.

Though unaware of the physical corruption he causes to her. If he were mindful, he would notice her cracked skin and how her veins turn blue as if it lacked oxygen. Her hair falls away in clumps.

The Demigod searches her mind. Ah, there remains one more place of resistance. His *aegis* enshrouds her imitation sky with shadow. It tries to cloud the rainbows, disperse the clouds, scare the horses. It encroaches her shelter and looms over her sanctuary. The shadow spreads like an eclipse—dripping along the sides like runny paint. Chaos invades her solace, but a star rises and passes through the shadow. It pierces beyond the chaos and through the darkness. He reads her thoughts. *Better to be blinded by the sun than to see in darkness.*

***

Delilah stares directly at the star as it brightens and draws near. It warms her and soothes her various aches and pains. Even better, it soothes her soul. Now the star is within her shelter. In her mind, she can finally feel at peace. Butterflies swirl around her as if caught up in a whirlwind. She smiles at the colorful insects. The star pushes—no, melts the shadow away.

The massive umbra becomes a man-shaped entity. Abbadon has always had minimum control over his *aegis*. His thoughts and emotions become open to her. He's curious at the life within these walls. Walls that he can't break. He becomes frustrated at his inability to seep deceptively through her barrier. He wants in. Delilah can feel it. He wants every fiber of her being. He wants her mind, body, and soul. She can sense his desire. He pounds dense shadowed fists against the shelter. Not even a crack. Now the shadow is just as obsessed with her mental as her physical. She can entertain him for ten eternities here. He would never give up or leave.

Within her shelter, a drizzle of rain begins. The invigorating droplets tap on her skin. It mentally cleanses her. The refreshing rain washes away the crud from the Archfiend. The clouds thicken, but the rainbows disappear. The rain turns into a monsoon, and her shelter is full of fog that even Abbadon's enhanced eyes would be unable to penetrate.

"I am the rain," Delilah's physical self says.

"Yes, my beloved. Yes, you are the rain," he agrees. The terrible smile fumbles for her next Word of Power. These are harder for him to detect. *He no longer knows.*

What don't I know? In reality, his body moves lethargically. He is enthralled. Shouts sound in the distance. He continues to fumble and search Delilah's armor to dismantle and remove the other pieces. He becomes restless until her arms wrap around his neck. He smiles almost to tears of joy. His body relaxes. She rubs his hair and neck.

A peephole burrows through the fog. His shadow self creates an eye located at the center of his forehead to see through. Her hair becomes damp from the rain.

The shadow stares at Delilah as she pulls at her clothes—clinging to her body. She shakes her head free of the rain. Dainty feet playfully kick water in his direction from a pool. The shadow smiles. She removes her leggings, but the fog rises and thickens. The shadow angrily presses his eyes toward the glass structure. She pulls off her blouse; but only her head, neck, and shoulders are visible. She half turns toward the shadow and blows a kiss at him.

Delilah continues to half turn to the right, then the left—blowing kisses all the while. The shadow continues to press his head against the shelter to see. Now Delilah seems to be getting closer and closer.

The eye of the shadow is closer because his optic nerves stretches forth through the sanctuary. She beckons toward the eye. Smiling all the while. Slowly, it comes toward her. She carefully reaches toward him.

Naomi lands hard on Abbadon's physical back. He seems to be unaware of her presence. She drops a miniaturized Quiloth into Delilah's outstretched hand; she somersaults over Abbadon and inhales deeply. The Demigod's eye leaps out of its orbital socket—stretching toward her. He growls as he grabs his physical optic nerve and yanks it back, but not before Naomi severs the cranial nerve. The eye rolls down her sword and into her velvet pouch. Abbadon roars in excruciating pain.

At the same time, Delilah's uses her *aegis* to shape her hand into a sword, and severs the shadow's eye with her hand. His physical self tries to rear back, but thick vines are anchored deep into the barren ground around them. *Got your mind's eye!*

His shadowed self yells in pain simultaneously with his physical self.

"I am the lightning!" Delilah's physical self yells as she slams the miniaturized Quiloth into Abbadon's ear—and expands it. The Demigod is shocked. His mouth wide open. Wide enough for her to see the spear bridge through the inside. The haft bridging the entrance and exit of her attack.

The vines wither when she brings her knees to her chest and kicks the monster off her. She rises to her feet with the assistance of Naomi, both breathing heavily. Delilah braces herself by placing her hand on Naomi's shoulder. They both limp to Abbadon's body.

One eye socket wide in fright and horror. The other has an optic nerve that dangles out of it like a dying millipede. His body still goes through convulsions from the sudden attack.

"Evnore!" Delilah yells.

The partners sprint to the dune that Evnore was thrown into. The carrion birds descend back to the battlefield, cawing. She was thrown so hard that she shifted back into her true form. Each angel grabs one of her arms and carefully pulls her out. Delilah pats her cheek. Evnore's eyes flutter open. She looks around; then her eyes open wide as she struggles to get to her feet.

"It's okay, sister. We won. Delilah defeated Abbadon."

Evnore's eyes widen in awe and joy.

"We all defeated him, Oathers," Delilah corrects.

Evnore smiles at them both. She swishes her tongue around in her mouth. She opens her mouth to show her *kameraads* a beautiful azure-colored gem.

"My *enode*!" Delilah exclaims happily as Evnore almost swallows the gem from the hug.

"Gross! I'd wipe that off first if I were you, Delilah!" Naomi advises with a wide grin. "Two down, five to go." She puts her arms around both of them. They all embrace for a quarter of a minute. Her hand brushes against Delilah's arm; then she leans away to look at her exposed arm. "Delilah! Your skin!"

"What?"

The Strategist looks herself over and gasps. She observes her hands and arms. She touches her face. Her smile brightens the horizon. Her scars and scales have vanished. The two hug each other with joy.

The Hideon horde retreat to safer ground, giving the heroines plenty of room in the wake of yet another angelic victory. Evnore lifts her head up first. Hearing the stampede of demonic footsteps and clinking of armors retreat. They all rise from the dune. The wind picks up before settling.

Eye vermin skitter to and from, keeping a safe distance from the angels. Observe and report, they will do. As a matter of fact, everything seems to just watch them. Curious. Even the Mist maintains its distance. Now that is interesting. Let them fear the angels of the Lord for once. They take an angry walk back to the body of Abbadon.

"Don't worry. This will hurt you more than it'll hurt me. I promise you," Delilah whispers.

She twists the haft of Quiloth to reduce it to the desired thickness. She yanks the spear out of the devil's head. Black blood pools beneath his head. She snaps the blood off the spear—and onto the still body of the Fallen angel. She cleans the spear with her ever-clean chiburi cloth and hands the weapon over to Naomi. Evnore hands Delilah her leather mantle, her honor.

"Don't leave home without it," Naomi jests. She kneels over Abbadon. "Didn't you know?" she taunts, tapping his head with the spear. "Girls are smarter than boys."

"I'll put the *aether* chains on him," Evnore offers.

Delilah shakes her head.

"What are you doing?" Evnore asks. "Are you going to defeat him again?"

Incredibly, as soon as Delilah removes the spear, Abbadon begins healing, fast. His withered skin begins to stretch across his skull. His dark blood staunches as his wounds close. His dull hair brightens.

Delilah lies on the ground centimeters from her former commander. She moves some of the hair that was plastered onto his face with his black blood. She almost pities him, almost. Abbadon encouraged her when she suffered from self-doubt. He stood by her when she was loathing in self-pity after her shameful loss to Anura in the war games. She thought he was a true friend and a brilliant commander. Someone she could admire.

His remaining eye brightens vibrantly. The pupil swirls to life. Once the eye fully regenerates, it suddenly fixates on Delilah.

"Delilah," Naomi says.

She turns to the speaker with a stare that could blast stone. Naomi clamps shut her mouth.

"Now that you're awake, I need some information from you. I need to know what Lucifer and his cabal are up to. What's his next move?"

She receives raspy breath and a hoarse laugh as her response. He manages to blow a kiss. Defiant to the end, or maybe stalling for time.

"Delilah!" Evnore yells. "Serve him. Now."

She rises to her feet. The red moon sinks lower into the horizon of the Archfiend—darkening the charred sky. She cycles through her bracer to the appropriate document's page to read Abbadon his rights. His body continues to heal. He stirs—yet still unable to lift himself. "Abbadon the Demigod, for the charges of conspiracy to overthrow Heaven, for the charge of fleeing legal custody without authority and attempted rape, you are hereby confined to Hell as a resident to be judged by the chief warden. Any last words?"

The Demigod smiles. His beautiful smile. It's genuine this time. No malice, no intimidation, no rage. All respect. His voice is clear and low. Delilah must draw near to hear him. "You're making noise now, Delilah."

The newly christened named angel, Stratagem, takes a long look at her former Herald. Pity softens her eyes. There was good in this demon, eons ago. A twinge of regret makes her hesitate. Of course, this all could be a trick for Abbadon to heal up and mount a counterstrike. She rubs his cheek just the same. The Demigod closes his eye. He seems to be at ease. At rest.

Not for long.

Swipe. A paper-like copy of Abbadon's death warrant rises above the bracer. *Flutter.* It floats and lands on top of his head. It wraps around his skull like a death shroud. His optic nerve snaps back into his skull. He attempts to rise, but is still unable.

The Hideons know what that means; they all leave the area. Demons, eye vermin, even the carrion go swiftly out of sight.

"Let's go. Death will be here," Naomi says.

"You both go. I'm staying," she replies.

Evnore grabs her elbow. "Don't be foolish! You have nothing else to prove. Let's go!"

"I'm seeing this through," Delilah insists as she pulls free of Evnore's hold and folds her arms.

"Not a good idea!" Naomi yells. "Death believes everyone was usurpers to God! Death knows we all thought about joining Lucifer! We have to go!"

"Not all of us did," she says. "And Death knows it."

Fifteen meters before the angels, the ground breaks open. Claws are visible, pushing earth away through the opening. A raspy moan escapes a tongueless mouth. The sound instills fear into the bravest of souls.

The Angel of Death.

CHAPTER 25

A CONVERSATION WITH DEATH

Naomi isn't sure if she hears laughter or yelling. It is both and neither. More accurately, it's Death's wail. The ear-shattering sound reverberates throughout her body – rattling her bones—shaking her to the core. They are pushed back as if a mighty gust assaulted them.

Delilah circles a foot behind her as if to brace herself. Naomi manages to keep upright by anchoring Quiloth into the ground. Evnore keeps low and drops to her knees. The defeated souls of the battlefield all yell along with Death. Their screams join into one ominous cacophony. Naomi can feel something within her rising to the top of her soul. She is nauseous and light-headed, feeling almost like an outer-body experience. The screams become louder. She realizes the screams are louder because she yells too. No, her soul does. Even Delilah can't resist. All eyes are on the all-powerful being.

Death wears a hooded cloak over a bleached skull and carries a scythe that shines like a polished skull. Featherless wings seem to stretch across the horizon. The black weathered robe covering the skeletal form flaps rapidly, despite the lack of wind. Purple pinpricks of intense light blaze within the eye sockets. Nothing moves. Not wind, nor sound.

There are billions of mysteries unknown to man, and there are trillions of mysteries in Heaven alone. One of the most glaring enigmas is of the great entity before them. Who is Death? The Angel of Necrosis wasn't created like Eternity or Time. Death was promoted. Angels asked Michael the Archangel, but not only did he refuse to answer; he heatedly ordered the entire host never to inquire again. Thousands of years ago, a census was done under the auspices of cataloguing the Fallen. In actuality, it was a concerted effort to try and figure out the identity of Death. The investigation is still open.

The red moon respectfully sinks beneath the horizon. Naomi's heart beats faster. She sweats. She reduces Quiloth and attaches it to her back—showing her palms and lowering her head. From the corner of her eye, Evnore does the same.

She gazes toward Delilah and almost shouts at her. What does she think she's doing? She stands tall with her head held high, saluting. She can't believe her eyes. She takes a deep breath to still her rapidly beating heart, to no avail. No other time has the Eye-blotter been more proud of her *kameraad*. Her leader and Oather. No other time has she been more afraid of her.

Death stretches a skeletal hand toward Abbadon. The angels now hear two sounds: his black heart beating out his chest and his soul scream. Less a scream and more like a cowardly shriek. With no outward effort from Death, the soul separates from its host.

The soul of Abbadon bleeds a sickly yellow-and-black ichor. Barbed wire threads inside and out. Any facial features are indistinguishable—merged together in a barely discernable mass, like a thick ooze. The smell of Abbadon's fear is toxic and nauseating. It smells like skunk feces. Large eyes suddenly bulge out of his soul.

Edging her eyes high enough to gaze at Death, Naomi subconsciously admires the weapon of choice. Legendary in both Shadow Domain and the Virtuous Culture. The weapon was named Ego Gorger. The scythe's black blade was created from soul steel—actual souls melted into living ingots like a metal. The edge shines, even with no light source in the area. The haft looks to be made from the onyxweald trees from the Copse of Corpses.

With the speed of a striking scorpion, Death impales the wretched soul with Ego Gorger. The body and soul both scream. Death drags the dark soul back with the scythe. The soul claws at the earth, leaving black streaks of blood.

Even with Death dragging his soul, the eyes all fixate on Delilah, lusting after her even now. His soul reaches out for its host, grabbing for any skeletal part it can grasp.

"You cannot escape Death. I have so much to show you, usurper," Death explains. "What shall be your pain criterion? Your escape changes everything. I have a special punishment for you! Any last words, tyrant?" With a slight gesture, Death allows his vocal cords to mend.

Then his throat and tongue. Enough to allow the creation of sound. Abbadon works his mouth like a man who hadn't water to drink. "Please. Take my life as payment. Spare my soul. Don't send me back!"

"Your life is worthless. However, your soul is priceless. Why would I yield such a treasure? Shush now, child. Have you ever had an itch that you couldn't reach? Yes? A cyst that wouldn't stop bleeding? Yes? A pain that wouldn't fade or a wound that wouldn't heal? How does it feel, usurper? To be touched so?" Death's voice echoes across the dunes as if spoken in a metal can. Hollow and cold…and cruel. *"Eshun'lar, devilae."*

"It's you! No! No! I'm sorry! Please!"

Death laughs with a hoarse cackle. It shrieks with treble and booms with bass. The ill soul screams. Death's finger becomes not unlike a needle, and it appears to emit some type of threading. The Angel of Necrosis sews the soul of the demon's mouth shut. Taking time to stitch section by section of Abbadon's mouth.

"Delilah, let's go!" Naomi whispers.

The outer layer above Abbadon's unholy soul's core peels away like skin on bone. Grotesque sores grow and burst. The soul quivers in pain as it shrivels. Tears sever the blotched soul.

"Your soul is more sensitive than others, usurper. I can anticipate every shiver. Every tremble! Your flesh is unable, and your spirit is weak!" Death lifts the soul up by its neck with one skeletal finger.

It continues to scream in soundless horror. The spirit gasps for air, like a gutted fish. Death squeezes the neck—making the eyes bulge out of its sockets.

Death seems angry. Angrier. Teeth chatter with ire. The soul erupts into flame. Death devours the soul—chewing slowly like a socialite sampling caviar. Teeth mashing and breaking the soul into bits. Salavic acid pours over his soul like an anaconda eating a rat. His soul collapses through multiple explosions as if it were being pulled into a black hole. Naomi looks away. She's seen enough. Yet, she must bear witness. Her eyes are drawn to the magnificent display of strength over weakness. She almost thinks his punishment is too much…almost.

Death's black robe flaps open to reveal Abbadon's soul being ingested. The dark spirit constricts to make its slow trek inside the torso. Death's entire abdomen is comprised of a large maw. It continuously grinds the souls within to make room for as many as needed—like a trash compactor. It congeals with other souls that are stored there. Death's ribs turn within itself to pierce and immobilize the immortal spirits.

Death turns toward the angels, with an intimidating glance. Naomi and Evnore fly back. Delilah holds up her hand. Death stops in curiosity.

Delilah steps closer. Her partners both protest, but she ignores them. She speaks to the soul's skull with cracked teeth that belong to Abbadon. No longer beautiful and white. Now they're just horrible. "You won't be in your cell alone for long. The Father of Lies will also be judged. I'll let your roommate, Lucifer, know he's next!"

Death bends down to peer into Delilah's eyes. Her steely stare burns right back. Tattered robes absorb light like a void.

"Thank you for answering my summons so quickly, Angel of Death," Delilah offers formally.

"You don't fear Death?"

Delilah shakes her head. "No, I highly respect you as one of the most powerful entities in all creation."

Death continues to regard Delilah with interest. The screams of souls are muted within Death's torso. Then the unstoppable immortal straightens up—towering above the dunes. The skeletal angel nods at the Strategist.

"Impressive. You remind me of someone…" Death mentions in a blank voice. "You are fearless. Honor and prestige, Strategist. You are favored among females. I will take good care of the one called Abbadon. The scenic route maybe?"

"Yes, Master Death. I'd like that," she responds.

Stretching to full height, arms extend out. Weaker souls are siphoned into frayed sleeves. They stream into a froth of stinking goo. Each soul with rusty nails, broken glass, soot, and spikes that desecrate their own souls. A myriad of colors that represent desecrated souls. Yellow, gray, black, and red—all twist into one another.

Death nods, gathering the souls farther away, and drills another hole into the ground. The screams of the imprisoned are heard long seconds after they are gone. Naomi collapses in a nervous heap. Evnore struggles to her feet. Delilah turns to Naomi and assists her. She gives her a look of compassion.

Delilah shakes her head. "Could we have done more?"

"What are you talking about?" Evnore asks.

She gestures at the husks of the Fallen. "Them. They were once our brethren, our *kameraads*. So many lost their way, and here we are, fighting them. An eternal battle against those we loved."

Naomi softens her thoughts of her brethren at Delilah's words. She's right as always. She should be less angry at demons, for she was almost one herself. Maybe that was what she was most angry about. Not about so many of angels rebelled against God but they didn't have the heart to change their minds, like Mazck. If only he had, they could be together now.

Evnore lowers her head as well. "It was their choice. Lucifer's twisted tongue is sweeter than buttered honey." She looks the Strategist in the eye. "It's not your fault nor any of ours. Satan is a designed flaw. And like all flaws—"

"They must be corrected," Delilah finishes. "I'm extremely sorry, about Mazck."

Evnore nods in agreement. She puts her arm around Naomi's shoulder and squeezes it. Naomi shrugs Evnore's arm from off her shoulder. She glares at the blackened skies and flies away. Her Oathers look to each other in sadness—then head toward the skies in tow.

***

Under the cover of darkness, nothing stirs. When the threat vanishes, there is movement. Life. Sinxin's decayed body shifts in the dust. Roaches and millipedes flee from the disturbance. Eye vermin chitter among themselves as they circle around their master. Her arm rises. Rises from her makeshift grave. Then her torso. The vermin chitter in excitement. Then they scream.

Sinxin's body is thrown back on itself. It crashes in a heap of ash and bone fragments. The compound eyes flake away in the brisk breeze. What rises is not Sinxin. Not the eye vermin's master.

The previously trapped soul of Prexel now has a physical form. The Anubis demon now claims freedom from the leader of the Hideons. As he rises, he grasps Sinxin's fetish. The jackal-headed demon steadies himself, getting his knee under him to support his frail weight. Bones creak from nonuse. He inhales acidic air, and exhales ash and dust. Wonderful. Seeing for the first time with his own eyes in how long? Ten? Twenty millennia? Tasting the foul stench of death and corruption. He yelps in laughter—more like a hyena than a jackal.

He stretches his arms and arcs his back. His ancient bones creak as he walks of his own accord. He breathes with his nostrils. His lungs. Life is good. A trio of eye vermin skitter to Prexel. They drag something that gives off a faint silvery glow—even in this darkened sky.

"Ah! Yes. Yes! I almost forgot about the sword Izum'vlema!" he yells.

He holds the sword to the sky. Once, he was worshipped. One of his prominent roles was as a god who ushered souls into the afterlife. He chuckles to himself in irony. He is Sinxin's afterlife. Yes. He was once worshipped, and it will be so again. Eye vermin chitter and cling to their new master. He shakes his head in mock sadness for his mental captor. For thousands of years, he was pushed to the back of her mind. Hushed from existence. The time is right now. Perfect, in fact.

He lifts his foot—and smashes the skull of his former warden. Malnourished for millennia, Prexel must now feed and accumulate power. There are bodies here that weren't served with warrants. Inciters only, more than likely, but weaklings. Not much better than an imp. They wouldn't serve much more than a nipple on a bull, ingesting those wimps. Prexel sniffs. Whirls around and sniffs again. Though he struggles, he climbs a dune and straightens up as best he can in his weakened condition. A broad smile stretches across his canine head. He yelps his hyena laugh as it echoes across the dunes. "Tonight, I dine on a god!"

What causes Prexel's eyes to dance and his mouth to salivate? The stalking form of Faudinroar—a giant-sized leopard with four heads, turns in his direction. What causes him to cackle uncontrollably, is the hollow voice of Sinxin yelling, and pounding on the inside of his skull to be let free. Her pleas are music to his pointed ears.

CHAPTER 26

THE MOST PRECIOUS MEMORY

The Oathers three enter Delilah's war room. She can't help the overwhelming feeling of accomplishment for the completion of her ultimate objective. She flies to Abbadon's virtual image and motions with her hand. His electronic card slides out from among the other demonic listings. Across his image is a set of words that makes her extremely proud: "Recaptured by Strategist Delilah, also known as Stratagem, to the Shadow Domain."

Now on all battle images pertaining to their mission in the Archfiend, her name will appear as a mission complete. It will be her name that is on Sinxin's capture as well. This arrest will go down in infamy. A slight smile spreads across her face. It was not her goal to seek prestige from either the realm of darkness or the Virtuous Culture. However, this accomplishment will help her attain the rank of Chief Strategist of Heaven. All the Strategists will see her accomplishment. Sure, she didn't defeat her enemies alone, but she gets credit as mission leader, nonetheless.

This was a decisive blow to Lucifer's goals. His favorite son and second-in-command recaptured after all the resources he used to clone him as a blood spawn. Hopefully, it will push back whatever schedule they were on.

The capture of the demon Sinxin won't go unnoticed either. She had a disciplined army of followers, and she was a worthy foe.

Her sphere of influence was greater than she thought. Naomi's theory is that Sinxin had sieged Bloodroot and was the current castle lord. If so, the demon's defeat is just as instrumental as Abbadon's. It will also create turmoil in the Archfiend as a new devil will attempt to claim the prime parcel of land. Lucifer will be a bit perturbed at her for defeating his minions so handedly. She may become the prime focus of his next attacks. *Come at me, whoreson.*

Another wave of her hand, and the roof of her war room becomes transparent. It seems like forever when Chrysos had a day off. Maybe they can afford to take a day off now. They covered for other squads for centuries; they shouldn't mind covering for them in return. She has a spectacular view of the heavenly skies. Beautiful far-off nebulae dot the vast horizon.

"Well," Naomi says to Evnore, "let's get out of here."

Evnore nods, and they both turn toward the exit.

"Hey! Don't go. Please?" Delilah asks.

Naomi whispers loudly, "She said 'please'?"

Naomi and Evnore eyeball each other, then back to Delilah with wide smiles. The three gather around. Delilah detaches one of her *enodes* from her socketed breastplate. She cups it like a baby bird and breathes on it. The gem sparkles with wonderful life. She places it between her fingers. Her digits seek out the weak points of the gem; then she cracks the encasement, freeing her *enode*. The spark within glows bright. She balances it on her fingertip and places it on her forehead. It melts on her skin, like dew upon sunrise.

Blue synapses connect to severed nerves. Some of the missing puzzle pieces within her mind are restored. For such a little thing, this *enode* holds much information. She can recollect minor occurrences such as when she dropped a stack of her scrolls in a waterfall to when she thought about cutting her hair. A mass of her thoughts, dreams, and other aspirations are restored as connections are remade.

A sharp gasp escapes from Delilah's lips as she falls backward. Naomi reaches out, but too slow in her reaction. Their fingers touch, but she won't make it. Evnore does. She shifts into her lioness form and dives under Delilah, cushioning her fall with her own body. She curls up around Delilah, making herself a pillow. Naomi kneels down and makes sure she is fine.

Delilah can't help herself now. Tears of relief, accomplishment, and joy overwhelm her. She closes her eyes, pressing out more tears. She smiles, then laughs at the major flood of memories. "My most precious memory. I remember it now! God, I remember…"

It was like an outer-body experience as Delilah recalls from the Ancient of Days. God stood atop the largest rainbow ever created. Every color imaginable was seen. Pinks, every shade of blue, even browns were within this bow. It was as wide as a skyscraper was tall. It was as beautiful as a butterfly landing on a sleeping kitten's nose. God looks up into the cosmos as He regarded the sun and stars orbit. Life in a vacuum. Somewhere out there, over the rainbow.

Delilah was on the underside of the same rainbow, looking down on earth. Her full attention was on an ark in the midst of a world-covering flood. Storms crashed against the ark—almost to tipping. It dipped well below sea level and rose dangerously above the height of the tidal waves. She flew through the top of the bow and approached God. She kneeled with her head lowered. "Master, may I sit?"

"You are always welcome to sit with me, Delilah. You are my favorite after all," God responded.

"You say that to everyone, Lord," she said as she smiled.

"Am I lying?" God asked as he turned his head to face her.

"No, you're quite right." She moved toward the edge of the bow and sat. She placed her head on one of her knees and let her other leg swing back and forth in reflection. She admired God's handiwork. From here, she could see distant galaxies. Stars split, and black holes are swallowing light. "Lord, what are you to do about earth? It's one of your greatest creations."

"Everything created is my greatest phenomenon. Earth is just as important as a quasar or gravity or this rainbow. All has its place."

"But none of those entities breathes," Delilah retorted. "There is a human family that needs you. He obeyed when you said to build. He endured humiliation when you told him it would rain so much that it would flood the earth. How alone they must feel as the last humans. Sadness from all the friends and families that they lost. When the sun rises, it will be forty days."

"Yes. Forty days," God said absently.

"How long must they endure?"

The Lord turned His head back to the sky. He took a deep breath and exhaled—changing the trajectory of a group of asteroids headed to earth. The rocky onslaught whizzed past the two watchers from their vantage point on the rainbow. Delilah reflected as the huge rocks continued to spin safely away.

"They will endure as long as I endured mankind's wickedness. I won't continue to tolerate disobedience. Not from angels. Not from demons and certainly not from humans!"

"But they will die," she continued. "Surely, you didn't bring them this far only to drown. Did you not promise that you would save him and his family? Would you go back on your word?"

God pondered the streaking asteroids and turned his attention back to Delilah. She lowered her head in embarrassment.

"Why do you care, precious Delilah? Humans do nothing but make your job harder. They are stiff-necked and care not for their fellow man. You yourself never took much of an interest in them before. Why now?"

Delilah lowered her other leg and swung both of them over the rainbow, mixing some of the colors together with her hand, and beams as they separated into their individual colors again. "I care about what you create," she answered. "I care about what others think of you. I care about your name. Humanity is lost without you, and I aim to do my best to right whatever is wrong in the world."

God rubbed His chin. His eyes were suns…literally. She turned her head from His intense gaze. She could feel the heat, wondering if she pushed God too far.

"Demons accumulated much power," God explained. "It has taken them dozens of millennia to do so, but accumulated they have. They were organized and aggressive. They carry out assignments as angels do. And this was their objective."

A flash of lightning startled Delilah. The bolt split all around God and His Strategist. Each thick bolt showed humans committing atrocities. Pillaging, raids, and murder. And not just murders—but the combination of murders.

The images within the bolts of lightning slowed when it displayed the array of bloodshed. Murder suicides, murder rapes, murder by torture. The rapes, public orgies on the steps of temples, idolism worship, lying, cheating.

Horrible acts on helpless creatures. Videos slowed once again when showing the variety of ways humans mistreated helpless animals. One bolt showed a malnourished cow barely able to move. Its neck strained against the rope that was leashed around it. While pulled along a road, another person behind the cow struck its back multiple times. The ribs showed through. A mass of flies bit its ears and nose. It collapsed in a heap while its masters continued to beat it.

"The purpose of the great flood was to not only cleanse humanity," God explained, "but to disperse the demonic foothold they had on earth and on humanity. The flood not only affected the material realm but the spiritual realm too. More so, in fact."

Delilah nodded. "That's how we got our furlough."

Another bolt showed a puppy that suffered from mange—trapped in an alley with children throwing rocks at it. The list continued on. The Moments flashed quickly in front of her eyes. God's eyes flared in anger, yet His eyes welled up with tears of sadness. Almost as if the flood itself were directly related to his disappointment in mankind.

Filtering out the humans, God showed the demons through the *veil*. Thick as a swarm of locusts. Demons possessed humans like a fitted suit. They incited riots and sat on the shoulders of their "host" with no angel to challenge their persuasions.

"The envious demons wanted humans to Fall like them," said the Lord. "They succeeded. The fall of humanity is a thousand times worse than the Fall of Lucifer and his flock. All of these incidents happened in one day. These images are from the day before the flood," God explained. "The peak of wickedness. The best at their worst and the worst at their best. My people suffered and were the instruments of suffering. Free will. I gave them the freedom of choice, and corruption and cruelty is what they choose. Heinous acts that humans commit without a second thought. No conscious or remorse. My people! Yet they murmur and curse their God! Using my name in vain! The hate! The scorn! They're better off dead!"

The images wouldn't stop. Humanity at its worst. War. The reasons varied from kingdom to kingdom. They would war over water, land, resources, even love. Thousands lie dead or dying in the screen of one storm bolt. Ash from razed castles thickened the air and mingled with smoke. Crows pecked at the eyes of the dead. Wild dogs gnawed at their bones. Killing. The slit throats, beheadings, torture. So much torture. Men held down other men and castrated boys. They pulled off fingers, gouged eyes, snipped tongues.

Delilah wept for the victims, and even wept for the offenders. She wept for those afflicted with racism, prejudice, sexism, genocide as evil doers thrived. She continued to weep. Poverty. The videos of people who starved and others who died of thirst. Skin draped over bones—naked in the heat with bloated stomachs. The rich spat on the beggars as they rode past.

So much horror—the angelic beauty can't take it anymore. "Stop!" she cried.

The bolt that she pointed at showed a man that was stabbed in the heart. The image frozen just as the blade entered his chest. The attacker's yell frozen along with the act. People all around the men witnessed while others bet on sides. Others passed on by ignoring the act altogether. Even still, another man reached into the victim's pocket to steal his coppers.

"Do you still love humans?"

"Of course, I do," God says through contained anger. "I'm saving them from themselves."

Delilah gestured and took control of the image. With her affinity for Heaven tech, she zoomed in on the dead victim. "Had I been there, I could have saved him, Lord."

Now God reversed the image feed, showing how the stabbing victim had robbed the attacker earlier in the day. He struck the other man about the head.

God froze the attack there. "Today's victim, yesterday's assailant."

"If I were there that day, I could have helped him, Lord."

"Humanity is lost, sweet one. They forsake my statutes and laws. The people have not a pulse. They are rotten to the core."

Emphasizing the point, He filtered the humans and showed their black souls. Wrinkled, gray, bland, cracked, bruised, and rusted souls. Each person's soul was dead or dying. He time lapsed the sin-sick souls, showing how it affected their flesh. He showed Delilah how the souls seeped death into the flesh of humans. The blood of the souls turned the body into acrid hosts. Squeezing every good thing about that person out, like water out of a sponge. Most souls became bloated, like a corpse fished out of a pond. Sores burst open and affected the humans' personas. It gave them bitter, rebellious, and vengeful dispositions.

The worst their personalities became, the more it affected their soul. It was a never-ending cycle. Their bodies decayed faster, dried up quicker, and died sooner. Disease and pestilence was attracted to the blackened souls like flies to fecal matter. Leprosy, plagues, gangrene, and all other sorts of fatal ailments seized the body and brought on despair. Then the despair infected the caregivers as the sickness spread.

Delilah was wrought with grief. "I have never seen the righteous forsaken, Lord. What must I do? This was all before our Master-Commander put in place the jailing system. Now is our chance to start anew! Humans could be given a fresh start! If you don't give them another chance, Lucifer wins! I'm not willing to accept that! Let us do what we were created to do! Let us do our job!"

God turned His head sharply and glared at Delilah. His beard of chained lightning sparked with His ire. His hair, also streaked of a lightning storm, flashing madly. She realized only then that she shouted at God and pointed. She pulled her hand back and grabbed it against her breast. She was frightened, but just underneath, she didn't regret her outburst.

God shook His head at His favorite Strategist. "It's only one of you, Delilah. You can't be everywhere."

"I speak for Chrysos Squad. If there ever be an incident that needs to be addressed, you can always, always count on us. We'll forego our days off, training, anything that must be done to save humanity. I swear it."

Anger was no longer in God's eyes. It was replaced by reluctance. His hands behind His back as He looked over the edge of the rainbow. Giant waves smashed against the ark below. From this distance, they were so small and helpless.

She stood to her feet and saluted. "If Lucifer wants to go to war with God, let's go to war!"

His beard transformed into a stream of firestorms. Hot cylindrical tornados that curled around God's fingers while He rubbed His beard.

"If you will not save them from themselves, would you save them for me?" she pleaded. "Your favorite?"

God smiled, then laughed. On earth, His smile swept aside the black storm clouds. The ferocious wind and flashes of lightning subsided. The torrential rain stopped. The gleam in His eye became sunlight that penetrated the clouds and gave the humans hope. The waves ceased as the ark settled. The oceans receded. The unknown depths were filled. Mountain caps became visible again. She saw a dove fly out of the ark. Hope was freed.

"I admire you, Delilah," God admitted. "I admire your strength and initiative—and how they're both tempered with mercy. Because of your love, you pleaded for humanity," God declared. "Your unselfishness will be rewarded. Your favorite phenomenon, the rainbow, will now be shared for all to see. No longer saved for Heaven. My covenant with earth will be sealed with the bow. Because of you."

Then God spoke to the rainbow, "Go. Show Noah peace. Show him hope. Show him my promise."

Delilah had to cover her eyes. The rainbow glowed bright enough to outshine the sun. She flapped her wings to stay afloat as the rainbow twisted toward the earth. Delilah began wiping new tears. The sour tears were replaced by joyful ones. God placed His arm around her as they beheld the solar system spin. As God walked away, he offered one final statement to the beautiful angel. "Be prepared for a heavy workload."

"Bring it."

Delilah's eyes refocus. Naomi smiles as she holds her hand. She realizes that the stars moved significantly. The sun sits higher over the horizon. Much time had passed. Yet her sisters stayed with her.

"Now for the other one?" Naomi asks.

Tapping her chin, Delilah thinks about it. Then shakes her head. Instead, she starts to replay the cherished memory.

It is in the Ancient of Days. God stands atop the largest rainbow ever made. Every color imaginable is seen. Pinks, every shade of blue...

Naomi looks at her bracer. She sighs, then reaches down, and takes Delilah's hand—helping her to her feet. "Duty awaits, Oather."

Evnore growls. She shifts into her humanoid form. Looking at her TAC bracer, she speaks in a deep correcting voice. "Her title is Strategist, Oather."

Naomi nods. "Apologies."

"I don't like the sound of this, Strategist," Evnore points out after checking the summons on her TAC bracer.

Delilah feels the fool. In her anticipation of seeing her name over Abbadon's image made her completely forget about the rest of Chrysos. How could she be so selfish. They spent many minutes here when they could have been of assistance to the others. "I agree. We'd better leave. This sounds deadly important."

CHAPTER 27

THE CROWN OF VANITY

Anura has a million issues she must deal with. Her list doubled with the defeat of Lucifer's overlords. More responsibility will transfer to her, though it gives her job security. She must weigh her options on how she should proceed. Where should she concentrate her efforts? News of Delilah's victory spread through the Archfiend, like Lucifer's wings over the scorched sky. Anura was surprised. Her former initiate won some decisive battles.

Sinxin was a good pupil, but only a shadow of her greatest pupil. Sure, she had the will, determination, and physical attributes at her disposal; but that's only part of what she needed. There was nothing wrong with wanting to be at the forefront of battles to inspire troops and intimidate the enemy, but there's a time and place. Sinxin had tried hard to overcome the prejudice of her ugly features, and ultimately it was the cause of her downfall. She wanted her name to be attached to Delilah's capture so badly that she neglected to use the tools at her disposal. She had a full horde, a new weapon, eye vermin, and gadgets that Anura lent out to her. Yet, she charged ahead and made a fool of herself, the pathetic ugling.

Abbadon was a massive waste of resources. For thousands of years, she tried to set up his coming, but the first thing he did was to attack Delilah, the fool. However, she knew that was exactly what he would do. In fact, she counted on it. If he could conquer or defeat the harlot, Xandus could focus his affections toward Anura. This puts Delilah in a completely different category of angels. Last she checked, the angel only had a B ranking. How in Hell did she defeat an S-ranked demon? It's akin to an adolescent defeating an Olympian in anything.

Anura realizes how the angel was able to win. Abbadon had the advantage of physical strength, size, and speed. He was superior in hand-to-hand combat, weaponry, and all forms of melee combat. What he had a shortcoming in was Delilah's strength. Her *aegis*. Somehow, she was able to work her way into his mind and possibly stun or delay him until she was ready to unleash her ambush. Whatever she did worked. Anura will take note. It was one of the reasons she didn't use her *aegis* in the heavenly war games all those eons ago. Her *aegis* was considered among the best, but Delilah may have a slight advantage.

And so the game begins—a true challenge. The Conniver versus Stratagem. It had a nice ring to it. She will not underestimate her foe. She will enslave Xandus's lover whore or eradicate her. It won't matter much to her. How could Xandus choose Delilah over her? So much to do.

She rises from her throne and walks to a mirror—taking measured steps as she contemplates the future. The glow of the red moon reflects brilliantly off her towers. She frowns in confusion. She could have sworn that the moon had sunk beneath the horizon.

According to the reports, Stratagem wasn't the only one with her name mentioned with victory. Although Anura accomplished a mission or two, her victory will go unrecognized. Already, Delilah overshadows her.

She continues to take her leisurely walk to her favorite mirror. Her worker goblins stare at her with their mouths open. When she meets their gaze, they bow and run away in the opposite direction. She's done all she can do with Delilah's *enode* for now. She needs more materials to experiment with. She'll figure it out. She always does.

Another thought comes to her. With the defeat of Abbadon and Sinxin, the whore recovered two of her *enodes*. She is gaining in power and confidence, not to mention whatever intel or stratics were contained within. She will be aggressive to keep the angel off guard. That means taking the battle to any of Chrysos's *charges* as well.

This time she is so deep in thought she had not noticed the mercenary sSylk leaned against a nearby pole. He suddenly straightens, with his eyes wide as he gapes at her. She covers up her shock, appearing as if she knew he were there all along. sSylk touches his own face and drops his fingers to the base of his neck. She reaches the mirror. Looking at her reflection, she twirls her hair around a finger and releases it. "What is it, sSylk?" the Conniver asks. "What do you have for me?"

His mouth is still wide open. She turns her head toward him, flashing him with a look of annoyance, but he continues to stare.

"If you offer no information, I suggest you find some or leave. It's simple."

"Your face!" he says in confusion. "What did you do? How?"

She whirls back to the mirror and looks again. Is it the moles? No, her skin looks fine. In fact, the moles have disappeared. Something in her hair? Is he playing some game? She wouldn't be surprised. He's the smartest, dumb demon she's ever known. He's as mature as a tadpole. "What do you mean, fool? I see nothing wrong with my face!"

The demon doesn't respond. He simply stares. Making Anura uncomfortable. Why is he looking at her face? Her neck and shoulders? She ignores the foolish devil now. She looks back into the mirror. She straightens her clothes. For some reason, it doesn't fit her like it should. Falling all off her shoulders. Maybe that was what the fool was looking at. Her exposed shoulder, flirting bastard. Like he's never seen a naked body before. Let him watch. A mechanized eye vermin enters as she steps closer to the mirror. Finally, she'll be able to examine all the video feeds it accumulated over the past few days. She gazes into the mirror, admiring her reflection.

For the first time since the Fall, her reflection is no longer a lie. Anura the Conniver is no longer a toad demon. She is not an ugly amphibian hybrid. Not a slick-skinned creature of the swamp. She's a beautiful sight to behold. She straightens her head accessory.

A reddish gold crown. The Crown of Vanity.

***

In the bowels of Hell, Cyrus walks against Hellheat. No matter what direction he turns, the ravenous wind cuts and digs into his skin. Its appetite for flesh never abates. Hellheat lives, like a beating heart. If he looks hard enough, he can almost see its form. Angular shapes stretch to slice off bits of his skin—barely giving his body enough time to regenerate. At times it is intense enough to dig into enough skin and muscle to expose bone. In the places where his skin is thinnest, like his face and hands, his bones are blackened there. An agonizing cycle of extreme pain. The sensitivity of his healing skin is magnified as more Hellheat flays at the new skin, for eternity.

He squints as much as he can to limit the damage to his eyes. Incredible that his eyes are more resistant than other parts of his body. The weighted spiked balls are heavy. The hooks that dig into his flesh interlock with bone. He can sense them move with each step, and each flap of his wings. He cracks his teeth from clenching his jaws tight. A feeble attempt to push back the agony. The balls must literally weigh a ton each. His will and pride keeps him moving. He's not even sure if he could walk again if he stops. Moving seems to be the only option and relief.

Now Cyrus is king of Hell. He laughs madly. He wishes he had the chance to pass on the power that Nil and Lucifer promised him. This was not what he had in mind. Walking amidst a never-ending dungeon of torture and terror. He thought it would be different. Switching his consciousness with Abbadon was his worst decision ever, though he's sure he didn't have much of a choice. They'd force the dragon demon to immobilize him and take his body. This way, at least he holds a position of power. The position of power. He's not like the damned souls sinking in the oceans of Hell.

He laughs again. A glance in one of the direction of a soul—and enormous pit fiends begins lashing a whimpering soul with a flaming whip. The pit fiends are terrifying, or would be, if they weren't under his command. They are giant devils with tusks that protrude from their lower jaws. Blood-red skin that match their bloodshot eyes. Hooved feet and the wings of a giant bat. His eye of analyzation still works. The whips are one of the few items that can flay the "skin" of souls, but who cares? He doesn't care about how the fiends are jailed demons that got promoted in Hell. So what about that the temperature here exceeds thousands of degrees. He wants to get out of here.

Panic rises. His breath comes in short gasps—giving the Hellheat another way in. Searing his lungs and burning its way out. Another affliction he will have to get used to. He coughs, spewing out black blood. The spiked balls roll backward in an attempt to pull him down. So he must force himself to stand—still seized with the hacking spell.

Cyrus receives an alert that a strong entity was jailed here. He can sense whenever a new soul arrives. He ignores most as they are only low-life humans. A few powerful demons, probably defeated by angels. He could care less, but this—this one is familiar. He summons up some strength and flaps his wings. Gravity, Hellheat, and the spiked balls are his enemy now, but he must subdue them. He possesses no control over flight. Corded muscles contract, then explode with power. He lunges forward and up—rising over the fiery lake.

Snakes and giant insects chase and capture souls underneath him. Everything here, designed to cut and sever anything it comes in contact with. Lava falls, stream down, pouring fresh hate-filled firewater on the occupants.

The presence gets stronger in this direction. He can almost pick out the screams of the new arrival. Cyrus had already grown accustomed to the wailing of dark souls…but this—this is different.

Opening his wings wide to glide to his landing, he drops down and slides to a stop on the precipice. Almost proud of himself for making a good entrance, he straightens himself to gaze upon his new slave. He takes one long look in disbelief and erupts in laughter. "The great Abbadon!" Cyrus yells. "The Lost Son! The Inciter! The Demigod! The first occupant of Hell is back in Hell—and under my command!"

Minutes go by as he continues to bark and howl at Abbadon, pointing. His bellows echo throughout Hell, but no need to rush his mocking comments—he has an eternity. Nearby pit fiends look up, then away from Cyrus. He drowns out even the moans of the suffering souls. What a pitiful sight for sore eyes. Abbadon's arms are chained over his head. He burns under his own personal lava fall, melting his skin and muscles. He regenerates with only enough skin to keep his skeleton from complete exposure. "How long have you been gone, Abbadon? An hour? Two? You are Lucifer's finest?!"

Cyrus laughs hysterically. Madness surely taking over him. There remains no hope. Despair fills his heart. Left here with incompetents. The losers. He doesn't feel the weight of the spiked balls digging into his flesh and sinking into the ground. His mind pulls away as if it's trying to go in separate ways.

"If we both bleed, maybe we can create another spawn in half the time! Sounds like a plan?" Cyrus says, laughing. "How could Lucifer choose you over me? I was too slow to learn? I pawed at my mouse? But you! You were beaten! I had a chance! You had none!"

Worms flop out of Abbadon's empty eye socket. He struggles to lift his head. A smile creeps across his dissolving face. Even though Abbadon is chained and defeated, his relentless power exudes from within him like Mist in the Archfiend. His intimidating gaze makes Cyrus shiver where he stands.

"I left something behind."

***

Within Naomi's velvet pouch, Abbadon's eye trembles and shakes. The eye stem flails about and digs into a neighboring eye. Then the eye stem does the same to another and another. Until all the eye stems are networked together. All the pupils shift and move around rapidly. Then all the eyes fixate straight ahead.

CHAPTER 28

THE CONSEQUENCES
OF SUCCESS

Delilah and her Oathers race to the other exit of her war room. Many angels salute and nod to Delilah. Words spread of her success. She smiles to herself. Many even cheer, though far too many wear a solemn face. That's what worries her. What happened while they were away? More than likely, the assault on humanity has many angels disheartened. She neglected to check those feeds as well. "Crap and crud."

Xandus sits with his head between his legs in deep sorrow. Iulas's face is pressed against his forearm, leaning against the door. The orphaned bunny sits atop Iulas's shoulders, sleeping. The she-wolf rests her head in Xandus's lap while he absently rubs her head. The wolf must be a small comfort to him. Now she must find out why. "What happened? Speak up, Xandus!"

The wolf and bunny jump and spring to Naomi. She crouches down to accept their embrace, but continues to look at her male *kameraads*. Iulas doesn't acknowledge their presence at all. He just stands frozen against the wall. Xandus rises to his feet. Anguish and sorrow in his eyes. She can tell he wants to reach for her and hold her. He needs to be comforted, but he retains his composure. He lowers his head in obvious shame. She stands before the blue-skinned

Champion and waits for an answer. Evnore and Naomi flanking her. The she wolf pads back around Xandus, leaning against his legs. Delilah looks around. "The whole squad was supposed to meet here. Where's Aurum and Valorian?"

Now Xandus surely drops his gaze as well as his head. Shoulders sag, and his wings droop. He's shaking—though Delilah isn't sure whether from rage or sadness. Even the she-wolf whimpers.

"I—we. This was all my fault," he admits, choked up.

"What is?"

God appears in their midst. The squadron turns in His direction and looks up at his tall frame. The female angels drop instantly on bended knee. The male angels, in their obvious depression, are much slower. Iulas is not even facing God, but instead, turns away from Him in shame. God beckons them to rise. The females do, but the males refuse. "I must report dire news, Strategist. Your squad leader, Aurum, is with the Light."

A collective gasp escapes the lady angels' mouths. Evnore completely crumples to her knees. She mumbles something undecipherable over and over again. Naomi covers her mouth with her hands in shock. Delilah turns her body away from everyone while holding her hands over her heart. She tries to mentally push her erratic heart back within her rib cage. It beats so fast she becomes dizzy and nauseous. Everyone is speechless. She affirms that Xandus and Iulas know the circumstances with their Herald. They do not receive the news as shocking. Their shame only deepens.

To be with the Light means Aurum not only exhausted his allotted amount of vigor, but exceeded it. Doing so allowed him access to more power than he could normally wield. Power enough to defeat whatever danger that threatened his squad. His "death" increases the squad's collective power threshold. In essence, he redistributed his vigor amongst the team. A thousand questions float through her mind. A tinge of anger mingles with her sense of loss. Was any of this Xandus's fault? If so, would she ever be able to forgive him? Even better, will he be able to forgive himself? "What happened, Lord?" she demands. Amazed that she can even speak.

"It is unimportant as to the why right now," God responds. "I must regretfully add, Valorian was captured. He has been taken to the Crypt of the Conquered."

The lady angels moan loudly. Even thick-skinned Naomi leans in a kneeling position against the wall. The men never get to their feet. Delilah can hardly stand, but she's the only one to do so. How did they lose two squad mates? They must have been through a multitude of trials and tribulations.

"We must act fast!" Delilah orders. She claps her hands to get everyone's attention and spins around in a tight circle to meet everyone's eyes with a fierce gaze. "He'll be tortured beyond recognition. Everyone, on your feet! Tortured until he curses God's name!" Everyone stands to their feet at Delilah's raised voice. "We can't allow that to happen. To your feet! Do it noow!"

With an upraised hand, God halts everyone's hastened movements.

"Psychologically, Valorian is the strongest of us all," Xandus reminds the team. Some of the Champion's confidence returns. "He'll give us enough time. I know he will."

"Agreed. I know you all feel terrible about the dire update, but do not blame yourselves or your teammates. My Will be done. For now, the next order of business is to promote the next Herald. I will do this internally from the members now in attendance. This decision does not come lightly as all the members of Team Chrysos are easily able to command not only this unit but any unit. Line up!"

Everyone kneels next to one another. It's unbelievable that the mood can become more serious than the fall of their team members, but it has. God paces back and forth gazing into each of Chrysos's member's eyes. She stifles a chuckle as even wolf and bunny join their ranks.

God stops in front of the lovely creatures. "Not yet, precious ones." He pats them both on their heads, but the wolf actually seems to understand. She whimpers as if she had a chance. She gulps hard as Evnore is first among angels in line.

"Evnore, you are one of the most loyal and wisest angels in Heaven. You are most qualified to run this team. However, you will be best served as advisor to the new Herald of this team."

"Thy will be done, Lord," Evnore answers.

The thought never occurred to her of the lioness as leader. However, seeing her in action these last few cycles changed her opinion. As always, Evnore was crafty and able to adjust to any situation. She's not outspoken, but neither was Aurum. Evnore would make an awesome leader.

God steps over to Iulas, who was next in line, but he shakes his head in a vehement display. "Iulas, I accept your open refusal for promotion. You shall continue to assist your new Herald with insight, intel, and imagination."

"My existence is to serve," Iulas replies.

This is the most serious she's ever seen Iulas. Even fighting against all odds versus demons, he can always come up with the funniest and most absurd comments. His confidence always helped her realize that she may take the mission too seriously. God was right; she can envision Iulas as a confident leader as well.

Naomi lowers her head when God steps in front of her. He stoops down and locks gazes with her, flashing a sparkling smile at her. "Resourceful Naomi. You are the backbone of this unit. You enforce the Herald's orders and always stay conformed to the mission objectives. You are steadfast and one of the most reliable angels in all of Heaven. I dare not remove the spine of such a squad by changing its complexion. You will continue to serve the new Herald as the core of this unit."

"Sir, yes, sir!"

Delilah almost cries at the beautiful speech He gave to Naomi. She also feels saddened. It's almost as if she is overqualified for Strategist. Even with such flowing words, she might feel as if she were demoted.

God stands before Xandus silently. Is he the new Herald? He wields the heart of Heaven as one of the most successful Champions ever. Then she spies the bracer overlay she created for him. It took her over a decade to finally finish it. She had to put together enough minutes in between missions to do so. She had hoped it would motivate Xandus to be more connected to the squad. The hardest part was to be able to find allies to be summoned by the overlay. She hopes he likes it. She is so proud of him; she can hardly contain her smile.

God does something she didn't expect. She removes Xandus's bolt of lightning from his hair. *Oh, no! He's being demoted.* She is still proud of him though. He takes it like a champ. He doesn't contest nor scream in outrage. He lowers his head and accepts his new rank.

"Xandus. You made a great many steps toward the role of Herald. You overcame your mistakes and have a renewed passion for humans. You made the hard call, but it was the right call. Your *charge*, Katherine, would not be alive if not for you. It is no wonder I chose you to be one of the few Champions of Heaven. You've earned the rank and renown."

Wow.

God plucks a bolt of lightning from his beard, combines them both, and presents Xandus with his new gift. The angel's reaction is pure joy. He extends his palms up to receive the superb weapon. Is he shaking?

"You are hereby given the promotion of Z rank, Champion Xandus. May your ability to protect spread among all beings on earth as it is in Heaven. May those that love you continue to be loyal and support you in your quest for justice and redemption. May every angel in Heaven and every demon in the Archfiend acknowledge your reverence."

"I humbly accept this wonderful token of your trust in me, oh Lord! I pray I will never stain your name!"

Delilah gasps. *That means...*

The Lord takes one last step to the last member of Chrysos. Her heart pounds like she is beating the bongos.

God offers her a hand. "Rise, Herald."

She blushes as she takes His hand. She glances at Xandus who is all smiles. What a wonderful smile.

"Strategist Herald Delilah, I am most proud of you. All obstacles set before you were destroyed under your leadership and guidance. Your determination and brilliance was displayed for every demon to see. You overcame wrath and humiliation to complete your mission. You used excellent judgment to outthink and outsmart your foes. You stood fearless in the face of chaos and mayhem. And now, they shall fear you! They will know you as Stratagem. All will cower before your might! May you honor your team as did Aurum for thousands of millennia."

Aurum. She wishes she knew what happened to him. She hopes God will not forbid them from sharing information of his demise. He was a great mentor to her. She learned a lot about leadership from the golden angel who she will never forget. He obtained final rest now. She wonders how Evnore will cope.

"At your convenience, you may appoint a Strategist or Anchor as your second-in-command. Think this through. Be ye not hasty. There are other objectives, and you must debrief and share information. Your TAC bracer has been updated and upgraded. You also have the option of changing your squad's name."

"We will always be Team Chrysos, Lord!" she says with determination.

God squeezes Delilah's shoulder in congratulations, then fades from view. The newly appointed Herald cycles through her updated TAC bracer. The first folder she comes upon is encrypted. How is there an encrypted file on her bracer? She can barely contain her shock. It is a file sent posthumously from Aurum. Why is it still locked? She must look into this file later, but it seems terribly important. She moves the file to the side and skims through the male angel's mission objectives and accomplishments.

With a mixture of sorrow and joy, her Oathers can only offer a slight smile of congratulations for the promoted Herald. This time it will be different. It won't be like before. She is more sure of herself—and of her abilities. A memory was fuzzy before, now as crisp as a winter morn. Must be the benefit of the recovery of her *enode*.

She remembers that God was prepping her for Chief Strategist. Despite her failure at the war games, it was rumored that she still could be promoted to the most prestigious position. Though it was hard to believe that she could be more qualified than Anura. A precious memory—and a fatal one.

She curls her arms out in front of herself and brings her arms closer together. In response, the team gathers around her. "Congratulations on defeating Ikrlez, Xandus. I know how much he meant to you, so my condolences as well."

Xandus nods.

"Did you ask him where the Crypt of the Conquered was?"

"I did. He refused to help. Laughing as he lay there broken."

Delilah taps her chin. Something's not right. She knew Ikrlez. They were almost teammates in the war games. It was well-documented that Xandus never defeated Ikrlez in battle. Now that he did, wouldn't he reward him somehow? Even as a filthy demon, he had some honor, or what he called honor. "What exactly did he say?"

The Champion scratches his head in thought. "When I asked Ikrlez where they were holding Valorian, his exact words were 'You wish, Xandus. You wish.'"

"This is important, Xandus. Think. Are you absolutely sure of what he said?"

The Champion paces back and forth for a few seconds. "You vish," Xandus corrects.

Evnore's ears pop up at attention. She turns toward her team—astonishment in her eyes. "Uuvish," she utters.

"Uuvish?" Delilah asks. "Territory or a demon?"

"Both! If I recall, it's a demonic entity the size of an island. Like a turtle, it can pick itself up and move about."

"No wonder no one has been able to figure out its location. It's never in the same place twice!" Delilah ponders. "Iulas?"

The transparent angel floats back, meeting her gaze. She only just now notices his innards are filled with gray clouds and rain. He nods and faces the exit. He half turns his head around to add, "I'll find it."

"All right. Give me time to analyze all the current problems and crisis to prioritize them." Then to Xandus, she says, "Meet me at our last location, Champion."

He nods and leaves the war room. She brings up her TAC bracer and looks for a previously submitted report. It's not there. She double-checks, but doesn't find it. She glances at Naomi, who answers her unasked question with a wink. Delilah mouths her a thank you. The rest of the team disperses. Wolf and bunny bounding off behind Naomi. Her mind drifts off as Xandus calls after Naomi, toting an exquisite sword. Could that be Ikrlez's blade Contra? Interesting.

Once the team leaves—once her team leaves—she likes the sound of that, Delilah taps and swipes her TAC bracer. She plays a video on cue. She rewinds the video and zooms in. It was when she and Evnore left Naomi to allow her to read her former partner, Mazck, his rights. Even though the two angels turned away, the visual stayed focused on Naomi.

Just as she thought. Naomi knelt on her knees and allowed Mazck to heal. She is unable to make out what Naomi whispered to him. He was able to dissolve in his disturbing way and escape custody. Delilah is sorely disappointed. What does he have on her, or worst, could she be a mole? She must take into consideration that the demonic bastage could be using her to acquire information.

She stares at the video intensely. Pinch zooms in on Mazck and freezes it. Something is wrong. More accurately, something unusual. Mazck had his chance to retaliate if he wanted. Maybe because of his feelings for her or because she rescued him, he had a sense of obligation toward her. Most demons are backstabbing bastages that won't hesitate at the slightest chance for violence. She shrugs the thought away. She's reading too much into it. He's a demon. Simple as that. Him not being served with a warrant might mean she can take advantage of this information in the future. He will have another role to play—she's sure of it. Delilah will capitalize on it—no doubt. She encrypts the video and files it away accordingly.

Despite the horrifying news of Aurum and Valorian, she can't help but believe that today is a good day. She hopes better things are on the horizon. Their Herald's sacrifice will not be in vain, and he will be avenged. Valorian will be rescued in time. The beginnings of a plan already formulating. She whisks through the grand hallways, past the walls of constellations, and out of the city of God.

Many messenger angels wave at her as she flies overhead. She flutters her wings over the many gorgeous landscapes of Heaven. She never tires of the lush greens of grass and fields of colorful wild flowers that are sprinkled throughout. Rolling hills rise and fall gently. She flies close enough to touch the tall blades of grass.

She looks up to the sky. The cosmos, planets, and all other heavenly bodies are so much closer than they appear on earth. The unobstructed view of the upper atmosphere, appear close enough for her to throw rocks at, it seems. This will be the only respite they will get for a while. Better enjoy the few minutes while they can.

Xandus overlooks a stream on top of the waterfalls. He senses her approach and lowers his eyes. He extends a hand to assist her to the ground. He notices her skin immediately. Then realizes her arms are exposed as well. "Delilah! Your skin!"

"Juices and berries," she replies with a light laugh.

Rubbing her skin with his thumb, he looks at Delilah with an intensity she has never seen before. His eyes flare with passion. He sits on the edge of the cliff, turning his gaze toward the stream underneath. She joins him and intertwines her fingers with his. "Calm down, Xandus. What is it?"

"I'm sorry," Xandus begins. "I made many mistakes during this mission. I let my temper make decisions that harmed the squad."

Delilah taps his knee. "I think I have an idea of how you feel. By the way, the fly-eyed demon, Sinxin? We defeated her."

She is shocked to see Xandus cry. He had the weight of a moon on his back. Whatever experience he had during his mission changed him—probably forever – just like her objectives did. She is at a loss for words. He buries his head into her shoulder as she wraps him in her arms, like a frightened child. She rubs his back and neck in hopes of consoling him. After a few seconds, he roughly rubs the tears away. The new Herald looks down, allowing the gentle sounds of the brook to relax her mind and body.

"Do you know the last thing that I said to Aurum?"

Xandus shakes his head.

"He was trying to establish contact with us. Something I always do. Because the mission wasn't going well, I didn't want to worry him." She shakes her head. "No. My pride was hurt. We were getting our arses handed to us. I didn't want him to think we couldn't handle our assignment. So I said, 'We're all together. Let me get back with you.' Then I severed communications."

Now the enormity and shame of her actions overwhelm her. What she believed were small, harmless decisions in retrospect will haunt her for the rest of her existence.

He puts his arm around her and squeezes. "I'm sorry."

"He could have been calling me for help. As a matter of fact, after checking the logs, I saw Iulas did request assistance. I just cut him off like he was an annoying child."

"Yeah. Nothing we couldn't handle."

She rests her head on his shoulder and sobs softly. A flock of swans fly over the couple. They both look at the birds. The freedom of avians. The sky, full of crayons of all different colors. She turns her gaze toward the sun. Even though the lack of atmospheric noise allows the sun to shine brighter, Delilah barely needs to squint. The sun's radiance warms her face, body, heart, and soul. It reigns over the sky like a king, yet mercifully erodes her worries like a warm bath. She takes it as a sign of Aurum's forgiveness. She won't be any good to anyone if she can't get over herself. She wipes her eyes and straightens up. Xandus lets his arm drop away. "I wanted to share this with you."

He tilts his head with concern. Delilah detaches her second *enode* from her breastplate. He still looks uncertain until he realizes what she holds before him.

"Delilah! Your *enode*! That's wonderful!"

He squeezes her so hard she gasps for air. He releases her and apologizes. She tosses the gem to him, and he catches it in his palm.

"Want to try and open it?" she teases.

He tosses it back. "I don't want to embarrass you. Maybe you should."

Catching the gem, she finds the pressure points instinctively. Once she does, she cracks open the gem and releases the spark of her memory trapped within. It floats like a firefly and enters into her forehead. Xandus looks on in amazement and joy with a smile that could melt polar caps. Her eyes roll back into her head, and her eyelids flutter. Xandus places his hand on her back for support, looking on with concern. Then she laughs. He exhales with relief. She starts to blush. "I always wondered if you kissed me when you showed me your 'travel by lightning.' Now I know," she says mischievously.

"That memory was in there?"

She nods. "The complete memory, yes. I remember now." She rises to her feet. "Well, we better get to work. We have a lot to plan and discuss."

Xandus extends his hand to Delilah after getting to his feet. "I want to share something with you too. Something straight from the heart." Xandus inches closer.

He smells so fresh. Like a new day. Her heart flip-flops in her chest.

"Even with the spinning of time, the unstable anonymity of unknowing is inconsistent with the certainty of adulation. For to know is to never have to try. A certain risk is well worth its reward. If the treasure is but a glance. If the treasure is only a smile. If the treasure is your heart."

Tears well up in Delilah's eyes. He is gorgeous. Not a great poet, but the sentiment is plain. He melts her heart like ice in the summer.

"Delilah, I give you my soul and my sword. My lightning is yours to embrace and wield. The roar of my thunder is my heart when I'm with you. The bolt of my eyes brightens the night when I think of you. The wind of my arms yearns to caress you. Today, tomorrow, and forever more."

Okay, maybe he is a poet. She feels his passion for her. There is no other place she would rather be. More correctly, she would be content in the vacuum of space as long as they are together. "Xandus, my heart and soul are yours. From the depths of the earth's core and the pressures within, my diamond was forged. You have extracted what I thought would be forever lost. May volcanoes come, and magma spill over. For together, we are unalterable and unbreakable. May our strength be fortified. May our embrace be eternal."

He caresses Delilah's head and presses his lips to hers.

"I've waited for you for thousands of years," she whispers as she pulls her head back.

"Something I should have done four millennia ago."

"I would have waited four millennia more," she responds.

"I couldn't."

He traces her eyebrow with one hand. Then drops down to her eyes, her cheek, then her lips. She parts them slightly, then wraps her arms around his neck. Her lips melt onto his. He is stronger than she ever realized. His embrace was like an anaconda's. She locks onto his eyes as they continue to embrace. Their kiss brightened the night—with the rising of the sun as their background.

ABOUT THE AUTHOR

R. L. Cox is a police veteran of twenty-seven years, who has recently retired. His passion is to absorb the stories of both police and victims of crime into entertaining and educational reading.

His storytelling nature was nourished as a youth when he became dungeon master from *Advanced Dungeons and Dragons* game. Here, he became a fan of the fantasy worlds as well as a fan of mystery books, including his first read novel by Agatha Christie.

R. L. Cox is an avid fan of anime, movies of all genres, comics, and would consider himself a gamer. He looks forward to retirement to indulge in his favorite hobbies even more.

His other novel, *The Xandus Chronicles: Veil of the Vile Ones*, is also available for purchase as it was part of his vision for both novels to have a simultaneous release.

Please visit my website and subscribe at sunchrysos.com for updates on future novels and more!

CPSIA information can be obtained
at www.ICGtesting.com
Printed in the USA
BVHW081025230919
559147BV00002B/184/P